THE SECRET DAUGHTER OF VENICE

JULIET GREENWOOD

Ebook ISBN: 978-1-80508-333-7
Paperback ISBN: 978-1-80508-335-1

Cover design: Eileen Carey
Cover images: iStock, Shutterstock

Published by Storm Publishing.
For further information, visit:
www.stormpublishing.co

ALSO BY JULIET GREENWOOD

The Shakespeare Sisters
The Last Train from Paris

The Girl with the Silver Clasp
The Ferryman's Daughter
The White Camelia
We That are Left
Eden's Garden

To my cousin, Lisa Thistleton, with love
(and happy memories of eccentric family holidays in dodgy
vehicles!)

PART 1

ONE

VENICE

August 1939

On the Rialto Bridge a wind stirred. It set the paintings and prints outside the little gallery flapping, as they waited for the few tourists still defying the rumours of war, and eager to take home a memento of Venice and its timeless allure. Some portrayed Renaissance palaces lit by rays of sun, along with delicately arched bridges over the shadows of narrower canals. Others showed an open door at the water's edge, revealing a courtyard hung with washing, or balconies on higher floors over-flowing with greenery so precious in the floating city.

The woman in the blue silk coat barely registered the disturbance to the fragile peace of the summer's afternoon. She stood on the bridge, gazing down to the waterbus, the *vaporetto*, chugging its customary way along the Grand Canal, past the fading palazzos, towards the dome of the Basilica di Santa Maria della Salute and out into the wide expanse of the bay. Her dark hair, with just the first touch of white at the temples, was covered by a long chiffon scarf of deep magenta, crossed under her neck, its ends thrown carelessly over each shoulder, tugging gently in the breeze.

'Can I help you, signora?' A young woman in loose-fitting slacks, topped by a brightly patterned yellow blouse, emerged from the gallery to straighten the pictures. 'Did you decide which one you'd like?' she asked, speaking Italian with fluency, but with a distinctly American twang.

The woman in the blue coat turned, as if waking from a dream. 'Not yet,' she replied in the same language, in a cultured accent that was neither here nor there. 'You've so many different versions of Venice, I'd like to consider a little longer.'

'That's okay,' replied the young woman. 'Just come inside and let me know when you are ready.'

Sofia Armstrong turned back to gaze over the Grand Canal, and tried to imagine planes overhead or bombs falling on these historic buildings. It was unthinkable that the war could be allowed to disturb the timeless calm of this place.

A gondola slid from beneath the arches of the Rialto, the gondolier wielding his single oar in an unhurried rhythm, his passengers sitting close together on the crimson seat, watching the faded Renaissance splendour pass by. The slender craft sailed onwards towards the sea, buffeted by the wake of the vaporetto, followed by a barge laden high with building materials. A small motor launch swerved recklessly in between, almost skimming the gondola's sides, setting it rocking wildly. The young man at the wheel exchanged pithy insults with the gondolier, who steadied his charge before turning to vanish into the network of waterways leading off the Grand Canal.

Sofia sighed. This was the Venice of her childhood. The duck-egg blue of a cloudless sky reflected in the waters of the Grand Canal, lending a faintly mournful air to the buildings, their bases lapped by the wash rising higher with the passing of each vessel. Back then, the rush of lives, lived between watery thoroughfares resounding with laughter and fury, had stirred her blood. The sight of water taxis heading towards the lagoon had fed her girlish determination to explore the world beyond.

She pulled her coat closer around her. The light was now moving towards evening, gaining the magical luminosity she had since sought in vain elsewhere, bathing the city in slithers of golden reflection that danced across its crumbling facades. Her heart was breaking with the old grief, as vivid now as the last time she had stood here, over twenty years before. How long ago that youth seemed; an innocent time before the world was torn apart by the war to end all wars. Then, consumed with the agony of loss, she could never have imagined she would one day return to the Rialto, changed inwardly even more profoundly than she had outwardly, and with another war gathering.

Now, her return ticket to New York was booked. Every instinct told her to get out of Europe while she still could, with tanks already rolling across great swathes of landscape, crushing the lives in their way with a cruel inevitability, as Hitler and Mussolini pursued their vainglorious dreams.

But first, there was one thing she had to do. One answer she had to find. The question that had, in the midst of all her riches and success, eaten away at her, leaving her hollow inside.

She took a last look at the little painting that had caught her eye. Not the grand views that enchanted visitors, but an intimate scene of a woman washing clothes at the side of a waterway, in front of a great wall overhung with purple bougainvillea, while children played around. That was the vision of Venice she wished to take back with her as a reminder of the everyday lives lived between the remains of its historic past, and the perils of an uncertain future. The rest remained as vivid in her memory as the day she had first left. Decision made, she strode inside to make her purchase.

·   ·   ·

A short while later, painting rolled up and wrapped in her shoulder bag, Sofia paused at the entrance to a particularly neglected-looking palazzo a few minutes' walk from the Rialto. Instinctively, her fists curled tightly at either side. But she was here. If she had learnt one thing since she had left all those years ago, it was the art of stubbornness, of never giving up. Unladylike it might be, but it had saved her from a life of grinding misery. She grasped the pull of the ornamental iron bell, sending its ring resounding around the building.

A head appeared from an upstairs casement.

'She's gone,' shouted a woman's voice in Italian, echoing around the brickwork. 'And I don't care who you are, I don't take messages.'

'But you will let me in,' replied Sofia.

'*Dio mio,*' came the reply, and for a moment the woman stared down at her. 'Dear lord.' She recovered herself. 'I have my orders.'

'But not for me.'

'Of course not, she never expected... we never dreamed...' the woman's voice cracked. 'You should go, signorina. Signora,' she corrected herself hastily. 'Get out of here while you still can.'

'Not before you let me in. Come on, Magdalena, or do you want this conversation shouted for half of Venice to gossip about?'

'You wouldn't dare—' From the rest of the sentence left hanging in the air, it was clear Magdalena had no doubts her visitor was perfectly capable of making good her threat. 'All right, all right. But you don't tell on me, d'you hear me? She'll have me thrown into the Palazzo delle Prigioni.'

'Me too,' replied Sofia dryly.

Magdalena snorted. The window closed, followed a few minutes later by the sound of bolts being drawn. 'You'd better come on in.'

Sofia followed Magdalena into the cool, shadowy interior, heading upwards on wide staircases to a large room overlooking the Grand Canal. 'She really has gone,' she remarked at the emptiness, the lack of furniture.

'Saw the writing on the wall, the moment that brute Mussolini decided to throw in his lot with Hitler,' replied Magdalena, darkly. 'Making pacts with the fascists when it was just *il Duce* was one thing, but the contessa is no fool. She knows this can only end one way, even if half of Europe submits to the Nazis. She took the first liner to America, before any hostilities could start.'

'America?'

'She has friends in some city called Seattle. Don't ask me where.'

'Ah,' said Sofia, relieved. Seattle was at least several days' journey from New York. All the same, just the thought of being on the same continent... 'But she left you here.'

'She needed someone to look after the palazzo,' said Magdalena grimly. 'And her personal maid and her cook could not be spared. Naturally.'

'The contessa's comfort must come before everything,' sighed Sofia. 'But if there is a war...'

'I'm expendable.'

Sofia's sympathy vanished. 'So much for doing her dirty work. Did you really think she'd be grateful?'

'Do you think it would have changed anything if I'd refused?' retorted Magdalena. 'One single thing? Apart from me being left to prostitute myself in the gutter, that is. Is that what you want?'

'No,' said Sofia, slowly. 'I was the one who should have fought harder to keep the thing I loved most from being ripped away from me.' The torment of endless regret – the despair that had accompanied her for half her life – shot through her. 'I was the only one who could have prevented it. It has haunted me ever since.'

There was a moment's silence. 'I'll make tea,' muttered Magdalena, at last. 'Or there's a whole cellar of the finest wines, if you prefer.'

'Keep those for bribery,' said Sofia. 'You might need them.'

'Oh, my lord.' Magdalena turned deathly pale. 'I was near here in the last war. I remember the hunger, the massacres, what they did to the women. I can't bear the thought of that happening again.'

Despite herself, Sofia felt a pang of sympathy for this woman, with whom she shared so much history. 'Then come with me.'

'And leave Venice? My aunt brought me here when we had nothing, when we were the last of our village, of all our family, to survive. Imagine that. Every single one gone, from the oldest to the youngest, war showed no mercy. Venice took me in and was good to me. I can't abandon her now. But you should go. Go now, before the borders close. There's nothing here for you.'

The evening light was softening into a purple haze over the Grand Canal as Sofia returned to the Rialto for a final glimpse of the city before heading to the train station. Within days, she would arrive at the port of Marseille, ready for her departure from Europe – this time, she promised herself, never to return.

'*There is nothing here for you.*' Magdalena's words echoed in her ears, as they had done down the decades since she had first fled the city of her birth.

But there is, she replied in English, under her breath. *Oh, there is. The most precious thing of all. And whatever it takes, I will find her. Dead, or alive, I will find her.*

TWO

ARDEN HOUSE

October 1941

Autumn had come to Arden House.

Kate Arden paused in digging the last of the potatoes and gazed over the vegetable field lying between the spiralling chimneys of the crumbling Tudor mansion and its nearby village of Brierley-in-Arden. The sun had faded to a pale glow as the afternoon turned towards dusk, and a low-lying mist stretching towards Stratford-upon-Avon, just visible in the distance, had begun to creep between the trees and the hedgerows.

She glanced up as, high above, a lone plane rumbled its way in the direction of Birmingham, some thirty miles away. With its approach, the clatter of spades and forks in the field fell silent, and the villagers paused in bringing in the precious harvest. As one, they gazed up at the dark shape appearing too briefly between streaks of clouds to determine whether it was friend or foe.

Kate could feel the collective holding of breath. The night sky was all too often filled with the rumble of bombers heading to devastate Birmingham, and the industrial centres of the

Midlands so vital for the war effort. Even this far out, deep in the relative peace of rural Warwickshire, no one was entirely safe. She shuddered, remembering rumours of a woman killed in a village the other side of Stratford when a returning bomber had discarded the last of its load into the dark, not caring what might lie below. In any case, what was safety when you had loved ones fighting at the front, or working in the great cities Hitler's Luftwaffe was so determined to destroy? And everyone was well aware that the Blitz was just a softening up for the real invasion, when all they had ever known could be swept violently away.

'Looks like a training flight to me,' remarked the elderly man in the next row, leaning heavily on his spade as his followed the general gaze. 'Heading for Elmdon Airport, I'll be bound. Nothing to worry about, nothing at all.'

Kate let out her breath slowly, too proud to betray that she had been frozen to the spot. Her companions instantly returned to their digging with a renewed vigour – the energy of those eager to banish the crowding in of unwelcome thoughts. These days, that was the only way you kept sane; not to think of the possibilities, or beyond the next day, the next hour, even.

She bent to shake the damp, leaf-scented earth from her clump of pale tubers, before placing them in the half-filled bucket at her side. This year, and especially with the addition of the Land Girls to supplement their efforts, the harvest had been more successful. Now, there would be carefully stored squashes alongside the familiar root vegetables to eke out the rationing for both those still living in the big house and the village, along with the scattered little hamlets for miles around.

As she reached for the final potatoes, a break in the cloud allowed the sun to send a swathe of pale gold over the heaped earth. At the side of the very last one – a tiny, deformed specimen, scarcely worth bothering with – something gleamed. Kate abandoned her spade and crouched down, eagerly brushing away the surrounding mud with as much delicacy as her frozen fingers could manage, revealing a thin curve of pale blue-green.

'Another Roman coin, is it?' asked Diana de Warren as she stepped over the rotting leaves to peer at the emerging object. The Land Girl pushed her rebellious curls back into the confines of her yellow silk headscarf.

'I don't think so,' replied Kate. 'Looks like it could be glass.'

'Glass?' Diana's aristocratic tones betrayed her disappointment.

'Even more precious than gold,' explained Kate. 'If it's Roman, that is. Glass is so fragile hardly any of it survives.'

'Yes, I suppose that must be so,' sighed Diana, sounding wistful. 'My aunt brought me back a glass necklace the last time she went to Venice. Before the war, of course. Proper Murano glass, all white and decorated with roses and gold. She told Papa it had been especially made for me and was worth a fortune. I was absolutely terrified I was going to break one of the beads.' Her blue eyes filled with tears. 'It was supposed to be for my wedding day, you see. Mama insisted I had roses woven into my veil. That's why we waited so long, so it would be all perfect for when Rupert next came back on leave. I don't suppose it will ever be finished now.'

'I'm so sorry...'

'It's all right.' Diana blew her nose on a monogramed, although none-too-clean, handkerchief. 'I'm not the only one to lose a fiancé in this horrible war, and at least I've an occupation to keep me going and my mind off things. My cousin Eleanor took to her bed when her husband was killed and hasn't left her room since.' She focussed her attention determinedly on the emerging green slither. 'That looks like a handle.'

'I think you're right.' Kate felt as gently as possible around the object, trying to determine where glass ended and earth began. The villagers of Brierley-in-Arden were accustomed to ancient coins and brooches appearing in regular intervals in the fields, along with arrows and flint tools that hinted at even earlier occupants of the countryside around Stratford-upon-Avon. But there had been nothing nearly as complete as this glass vessel.

'I wish Jamie was here,' she said. 'He'd know how to get it out without damaging it. My brother,' she explained to Diana's quizzical look. 'He's always been passionate about archaeology. He started the excavation of the Roman villa, over there, near the walled garden.'

'Well, you can't leave it,' said Diana. 'It'll only get broken anyhow. Someone's bound to step on it, or the tractor go over it, so you might as well try.'

Kate carefully eased the earth away. It seemed to take forever, then suddenly the object came free, almost falling into her hands. The vessel was small and rotund, with the curve of a handle at one side. From what she could see inside the mud, the blue-green of the glass had a milky, slightly grainy appearance. Kate's belly twisted at the deep excitement of holding a little container that hadn't seen the light of day for hundreds, maybe thousands, of years. The last eyes to see this had looked out onto a landscape that was both familiar and utterly strange.

The artist in her admired the craftsmanship of the work, too. Her own medium had always been paint and pencil, with a few experimental forays into charcoal, but she often fantasised about experimenting with other art forms. A familiar frustration went through her: if only she could set herself up independently somehow, and support herself through her art. She felt trapped at Arden, as if her life had not yet begun.

She had tried so hard in the years before the war to make her escape. With the help of Miss Parsons, the village schoolmistress, and Miss Smith, who taught evening classes in the village hall, Kate had overcome her doubts and applied to the world-famous Slade School of Art. Women studied there, she had learnt to her astonishment, and many had even gone on to make a living from their work. She had devoured with growing excitement the illustrations of Kate Greenaway, the delicate atmospheric portraits of Gwen John, and the brilliant modernism of Winifred Knights, who had even won a scholarship to study at the prestigious British School at Rome.

It was possible. All her life, Kate had been told that her only way of leaving Arden House would be as a wife to the first man who asked her, to take responsibility for a similar household most likely only a short car journey away. She had seen other young women become absorbed into providing a comfortable home, being a gracious hostess to her husband's friends and business acquaintances, and with a growing crowd of children at her feet. A life in the background, serving others; the fate, it seemed, of all womankind. The very thought sent a panic through her.

Was it so selfish to want more? Was it so unnatural to crave her days and nights to be filled instead with striving to be the best she could be? Just as the creator of the Roman glass had spent a lifetime perfecting the heating of sand into a flow of translucent material, ready to be manipulated into objects of exquisite beauty.

The twist inside her hardened into a tight knot. There was something familiar about the glass vessel, one that stirred a memory just outside her grasp. What was it? A glow? A colour? She held on with all her might to the elusive sensation, feeling the earth beneath her feet begin to turn from solid to sand. This was the other part of her. The Kate Arden whose true parentage was unknown, and who, while she had been embraced as part of the family in the big house, had never quite been accepted as an Arden, and didn't belong. She had always been an outsider. Her black hair and olive skin were a permanent reminder to the gossips of the village of her rumoured Italian heritage; evidence that the lord of the manor, who should spend every last ounce of his blood in protecting them, had brought an enemy – a subject of Mussolini no less – into their midst. No doubt ready to triumph over them if the fascist war machine ever reached this far.

'It's rather pretty,' sighed Diana. 'Can it really be Roman?'

'I'm not sure.' Suddenly, Kate wished it was hidden away, back deep in the earth never to be found. Since the beginning of the war, the newspapers and the newsreels at the cinema in Stratford had shown pictures of a world that had become increasingly terrifying in its cruelty and destruction. The last thing she needed was her fragile sense of belonging to the only place she remembered calling home being so profoundly shaken. But, once found, such a precious thing could not be unfound. She removed the scarf from her neck with her free hand and wrapped it carefully around the delicate glass. 'But I know someone who might be able to tell us.'

She placed the little bundle at a safe distance, where she could keep an eye on it, and continued digging, while Diana returned to her own harvest.

Bucket full, Kate was carrying it to the wagon attached to a tractor, all ready to make the journey to the barns for storage, when she spotted the slight figure of her stepmother, Alma Arden, struggling along the path from Arden House. Unlike the utility coats of the harvesters, cut to use as little material as possible, Alma's mink swung luxuriously around her ankles, with only its moth-eaten shabbiness betraying that its original owner was a grand Victorian Arden lady, and that it had been liberated from the vast attics of the Tudor mansion rather than the dubious machinations of the black market. Kate could see that the worn soles of Alma's equally elderly boots were sending her off balance with every step, compounded by the bulging knapsack on her back and the basket laden with vegetables on her arm.

'Mama!' Kate abandoned her bucket and stumbled through the cloying red earth of the field. She caught her stepmother just in time as her boots slithered from under her, threatening to send her headlong into the mud. 'Mama, you should have waited. I promised I'd help you once we'd finished here.'

'Nonsense, my dear.' Alma steadied herself with an anxious smile. 'You are doing enough as it is. I didn't like to bother you, especially as the rain is bound to return soon. I'm sure I'm capable of carrying a few vegetables to the Women's Institute.'

Kate eyed her with exasperation. Papa's second wife was a small, nervy woman, some twenty years younger than her over-bearing husband who, despite all her attempts, she could never quite please. Not, admitted Kate to herself with a wince of sympathy, that any of the family could manage that Herculean task. Papa, as the patriarch of the Arden family and lord of equally ancient Arden house, demanded total obedience from each and every one of them. No wonder her brothers had both taken the opportunity of heading out to the fighting in France to escape. Her three sisters had also, each in their differing ways, done the same. Poor Alma – who their father had always insisted they call 'Mama' – had been left to pick up the pieces.

'You don't think I'd overlook an excuse to come to the village do you, Mama,' Kate said, taking the heavy basket on one arm, and steadying her stepmother onto firmer ground. 'Papa won't let me anywhere near Brierley unless I'm chaperoned. I'm not going to give up the chance.'

'Well, if you are sure, my dear.' Alma squinted at her with her pale eyes.

They both knew that Kate, as the most headstrong of Alma's stepchildren (which was saying something), was expert at disappearing from the confines of the house, sketchbook and pencils hidden beneath her coat. Kate could spend hours drawing the remains of the Roman villa half uncovered on the field, the glimpse of church spire, along with the winding roads and fields held within their hedgerows, reaching all the way to Stratford-upon-Avon.

'Besides, I need a change of scene,' said Kate, kissing her. 'My back is killing me with all this digging. So, you see you have to let me come with you. It will be monstrously cruel otherwise.'

'Very well, my dear. If you put it like that—'

'Which I do,' reiterated Kate firmly, ignoring the muffled chuckling from the older members of the village, who were all too aware that the Arden children had run rings around their stepmother from the moment she had arrived. 'Besides, there's something I want to show Miss Parsons. I'm hoping she might want to put it in her museum, with all the other things that have been turned up by the digging.'

'Of course.' Alma beamed, seemingly reassured that Kate was not motivated by a desire to meet unsuitable young men who might be lurking around the village green.

Miss Parsons, despite being a life-long spinster, was known to have been a close friend of the first Mrs Arden, and had retained an unusual familiarity with the Arden family, with a particular protectiveness towards the four daughters of the house. Besides, she was rumoured to have once been engaged to a duke, who had been tragically lost in the First World War, and was therefore eminently respectable.

Kate squelched back to retrieve the Roman glass still safely bundled in her scarf.

'Don't worry, I'll bring these,' called Diana as she picked up Kate's bucket in one hand, balancing the weight of her own full container in the other. 'I hope it is Roman. That glass thing, I mean.'

'Thanks. I'll let you know.'

With much coughing and stamping of feet to remove the heavy earth, the rest of the villagers picked up their own buckets and followed Diana to where another of the Land Girls was already starting up the recalcitrant motor of the tractor.

Several of the older women, flat wicker baskets over their arms, moved towards the nearest hedgerow in search of rose hips and the dark fruit of wild plums, along with any hazelnuts not already commandeered by the local squirrel population. With the Women's Institute in the village having recently taken charge of a canning machine, enthusiasm had redoubled to preserve as much as possible against the shortages of the coming winter.

As Kate accompanied her stepmother across the rest of the field, now cultivated up to the surrounding hedges, a dark-haired young man pushed his way through the kissing gate leading to the village.

'Edmund!' called Kate, waving frantically as he almost immediately struck off on one of the traditional paths leading up to the farms located beyond the tree-covered rise known locally as the burial mound.

'Darling, we'll be late,' muttered Alma, increasing her pace as their former gardener came to a halt, waiting for them to catch up with him.

'It'll only take a minute – I just want to ask him something.'

'But he's no longer in your papa's employment, my dear.'

'I'm not asking him about fruit trees or training roses,' retorted Kate.

Alma's wariness appeared to have worn off on Edmund, who stood with stiff dignity at their approach. 'Mrs Arden, Miss Kate,' he muttered.

'Good afternoon, Mr Ford. I hope your father's health is improving,' said Alma, straightening her shoulders and pointedly becoming the Lady of the Manor.

'Much better, thank you, Mrs Arden,' he replied with equal formality.

Kate ignored them. 'Edmund, you won't believe what I found when I was lifting the potatoes just now.'

'Oh?' He was doing his best to appear disinterested, but she knew that gleam. She had seen it so many times in her brother Jamie's eyes when he had begun to uncover the outline of the Roman villa in the vegetable field before the war, and even more so when he and Edmund had uncovered the first hint of a mosaic floor with its tiny tiles formed into dolphins and spiny fish with fierce jaws, as if ready to consume anything that came their way.

'It looks like a glass cup or container. It has to be Roman. And it's complete.' She unwound her scarf, ignoring Alma's tut of disapproval at her lack of care for her clothing. 'Look, there's not even a chip, and the handle is still in place.'

Edmund's expression softened as he gazed down at the little object. 'That's exquisite. It looks as if it was made yesterday.'

'It must be high status, something glass like that, don't you think?' she said eagerly. 'It must belong to the villa. I remember Jamie saying that something precious like this might even have come from Rome itself.'

'Could be.' He had forgotten Alma and preserving the social niceties, and become the enthusiastic young man who had shared her brother's excitement as they uncovered the lost world beneath the earth. As he inspected the ancient glass, she could see in him the village schoolboy who had won a scholarship and dreamt of studying archaeology at university, until the reality of poverty and social expectations had killed his dream, leaving him grasping at his passion in his few spare moments. Kate's heart went out to him. She might not have to fill her days with backbreaking tasks to keep a roof over her head, but with Papa's adamant refusal to allow her to take up her place at the Slade School of Art, she understood all about thwarted ambition.

'Jamie will be envious,' he added. 'He was always hoping we'd find something like that.'

'I'm taking it to Miss Parsons, she'll know how to clean it up and keep it safe in her museum,' said Kate. 'Jamie can see it when he comes back.'

She glanced up at Edmund. *If he comes back.* She saw the thought reflected in Edmund's eyes, along with something else. Fear?

There was a bitter taste in her mouth. She could not bear the thought of never seeing Jamie again. Her brother had been such a large part of her existence, she couldn't imagine life without him, any more than without Will, their elder brother, who drove the rest of the Arden siblings to distraction with his assertion of his superior position in the household as the heir, simply through an accident of birth. And now, like so many of the young men who had formed her world, Edmund, too, was heading off towards a battlefield and the sights and suffering she could not even begin to imagine.

'Darling...' Alma was growing impatient. 'Darling, we are so late already, we really must get on.'

'Yes, of course,' said Kate, wrapping the scarf back around the precious glass. 'I'm sure Miss Parsons will be pleased to let you see it before you leave, Edmund.'

'Thank you, Miss Kate,' he replied, recollecting himself and becoming formal once more. 'I'll make sure I do.' With a brief nod at them both, he resumed his journey along the path skirting the burial mound. Kate watched him disappear into the trees, as she had once watched her brothers fading into shadows in the softening light, knowing she might never see them again. In the autumn mistiness it felt, more than ever, as if the world was ending.

THREE

As they crossed the fields and drew close to the village, Alma came to a halt.

'Darling, you do know I want the very best for you, and for you to be happy, just as your papa does, too, but that young man—'

Having expected the usual lecture on her refusal to wear the recently discovered silk brocade coat to church last Sunday, despite it having belonged to an Arden ancestor presented at court during the time of King George and Queen Mary, Kate blinked. 'Young man?'

Alma turned pink round the ears, two bright spots of red appearing on her cheeks. 'Darling, I'm sure young Edmund Ford is very pleasant, and he's quite undeniably good looking – even I can see that – and it's nice that he's shown interest in that Roman mosaic in the meadows you and Jamie were working on before the war, but you really... ah, mustn't...' Alma trailed off into embarrassment. 'Your father,' she added feebly, her answer to all things she couldn't deal with.

Kate eyed her with irritation. 'Mama, just because I like

Edmund and we have interests in common, doesn't mean I'm going to fall in love with him. And he certainly isn't about to fall in love with me. He's far too ambitious.'

'Ambitious?' A look of alarm crossed Alma's fragile features.

'Far too ambitious to marry me, I mean.'

Alma bristled. 'My dear—'

'Mama, Edmund's determined to make his way in the world, he's told me that himself. He isn't the kind to saddle himself with a wife, and especially not one without a fortune of her own.' With her stepmother looking unconvinced, annoyance overcame her. 'Not to mention being illegitimate,' she added, before she could stop herself.

'Darling!' Alma was mortified.

'Well, it's true,' retorted Kate. 'Everyone calls me "that Italian girl". I don't even know if Papa is my real father, or who my mother was, and no one will tell me.'

'Your father loves you, just as he loves your brothers and sisters,' protested Alma, eyes filling with tears. 'As do we all.'

'I know you do.' Kate hugged her awkwardly, torn between guilt at her stepmother's distress and damaging her precious find. 'I'm sorry, Mama. Ignore me. That was thoughtless. I know you love me, just as I love you, and I always will. It's just that sometimes...'

She came to a halt, not sure what she meant, or that she could ever explain the tumult inside her. 'You don't think I'm unnatural, do you?'

'Unnatural?' Poor Alma was turning pink again.

'For not wanting to fall in love with Edmund. For having absolutely no desire to marry Henry Luscombe, despite all his riches and his connections with important people. I might not be Henry's first choice, but he's obviously determined to marry one of Papa's daughters. I can't imagine why, when he's got half of London high society to choose from, but he seems to have settled on us for some reason, and he doesn't seem particularly fussy about which one.'

'My dear,' faltered Alma at this bleak, but undeniably accurate, summing up of the most handsome and sought after young man of their acquaintance. 'I'm sure he, ah...'

Kate sighed. 'I suppose he *is* my best chance of attracting a suitor. I know you and Papa would rather I forgot about painting and drawing and found a husband.'

'Darling, a husband who loves you will take care to ensure you are happy, I'm sure he wouldn't object to your little...' At the look on Kate's face, Alma stumbled to a halt.

'Hobby.' Kate frowned at her. 'That's what you were going to say, isn't it? That's what Papa thinks, what everybody thinks. It's all right as long as my painting's a frivolous occupation, like embroidery or playing cards, just to stop me from getting restless. Nothing serious. Not a passion that fills my whole being and that I can't live without. Well, I'd much prefer to be an old maid if it means I can still paint and draw as much as I like.'

Alma cleared her throat. 'My dear, you'll feel different when you are married.'

'Jane Austen never married. She wrote *Pride and Prejudice* instead. Do you think she'd have been happier if she'd given all that skill, that power in her own creativity, and not even for love but for a roof over her head and a comfortable income?'

'A wife has so many duties and compensations,' muttered Alma. 'That is her fulfilment.'

'Is it yours?' The moment the words were out of her mouth, Kate would have given anything to take them back again. The hurt, the despair and the anguish that flashed unguarded across her stepmother's face sent its own answer like an arrow straight to Kate's heart. It was impossible to live in the Arden household and not see that Alma had no life of her own. It was only as she had grown into her own adulthood that Kate had begun to observe that Alma was the shadow, the unacknowledged presence in the background who kept the household running on too few staff, frequently taking on the work of the missing maids herself. It was no secret that Papa had married his second wife not for love, but rather to keep his unruly children in order, his household running smoothly and to defer unquestioningly to his authority.

The rest of Alma's duties Kate would rather not think about. She had managed to glean some basic information from her elder sisters, and since then couldn't help noticing Alma's quiet removal to her bedroom each night, slinking away in painful self-effacement, as if doing her best to avoid notice, let alone encourage Papa to leave his own bed to join her. From what Kate could see, there was precious little fulfilment, physical or emotional, in her stepmother's squashed existence.

'I'm sure it is for most,' Kate conceded hastily, as Alma struggled for words. 'I'm just not sure it is for me. And you really needn't worry about Edmund. Didn't you hear he's joined up? He'll be leaving for France before long. He's made it quite clear he won't want to come back to Brierley-in-Arden once the war is over, so we might never see him again.'

'Oh. I see,' said Alma. 'His poor mother,' she added, under her breath. They stood for several minutes in silence, Edmund himself forgotten, or at least subsumed into a wider, all-too-familiar fear.

'I wish...' Alma began, as they set off again in the direction of the village. 'Oh, my dear, I know there is nothing that can be done about the boys, they were so determined to protect us, but I hate the thought of Rosalind and Cordelia out there in the Blitz in London and Birmingham. I'd do anything to bring your sisters home.'

'I don't think anyone of us is truly safe,' Kate replied gently.

'But at least we could protect them from the bombs and the

destruction.' Alma brushed her hand against twigs of beech spilling over the adjacent hedge, setting the dry remains of leaves swirling around them as they passed. 'I know they don't tell us half of what is going on in the papers. One of the labourers from Habbort's Farm was saying in the Post Office only last week how he'd visited his sister in Birmingham to try and persuade her to move in with him, but she won't leave their grandmother or her mother-in-law.'

Alma came to a halt once more, a sheen of tears gleaming in her eyes. 'The things he was describing, and especially the children... Well, they don't bear thinking about, my dear.' She fished her handkerchief from her coat pocket and blew her nose. 'I've talked to your father about allowing Rosalind back home from London, but he's adamant he won't, not unless she agrees to marry Henry Luscombe.'

'Which she won't,' said Kate, with a shudder of sympathy.

'But at least he has agreed that Cordelia should come back from Birmingham,' Alma continued. 'I know she wanted to do her bit for the war effort, but who knows how long this vile bombing will go on? I can't bear to think of her living there amongst all that suffering. At least if she's back here, we'll be under one roof. I feel I can face anything if we are together.'

'But what if she prefers to stay and work in Birmingham?'

'She can't do. And we can persuade her – I will persuade her.' Alma straightened her shoulders determinedly. 'I shall go to Birmingham myself.'

Kate stared at her in astonishment. 'But what will Papa say?'

'He won't stop me.' An unexpectedly stubborn look came over Alma's face. 'He won't dare. Miss Parsons is due to visit that charity in Birmingham she runs, the one that looks after orphaned children who have no family left to take them in, poor things. I've told him I shall go with her.'

'Oh,' said Kate. So Alma had noticed that the middle-aged

schoolmistress was the only woman to whom Papa demon-
strated any kind of deference. Knowing Papa, it might have
been that rumour of her being a duchess and a fine lady by now,
if cruel fate hadn't intervened. Although Kate had a feeling that
it was more than that. Something to do with her friendship with
his first wife. Papa always kept his own secrets tight within his
chest and, even after all these years of living under the same
roof, Kate found it impossible to tell what he was really feeling
beneath all his noise and bluster. But Miss Parsons had known
him longer than any of them, and from the time when he had
been a young man with a young wife and children, torn from
the life he had made for himself to take over responsibility for
the Arden Estate on the death of his elder brother. The time
before Kate had arrived as a small child, she realised with a
sudden tingling in her belly. If there were any secrets Papa
wished never to be uncovered, the village schoolmistress would
be the one to know.

Birmingham was only a short journey away by train, but
Alma was needed here, at Arden. Papa might not recognise it,
but her stepmother had become the linchpin that kept the
house and village together. If she was hurt, or incapacitated, or
heaven forbid, killed, the whole carefully run operation that
provided scarce food, heat and clothing might fall apart. Papa
would never have the patience to deal with the intricate details,
let alone spend hours tactfully soothing the pride of the various
factions, from the WI to the Home Guard, to avoid any possible
conflicts of interest.

Birmingham. Excitement shot through Kate, along with a
shiver of terror. If she could get Miss Parsons to agree, she could
surely persuade Alma to let her go to Birmingham in her stead.
She suspected her sister's letters were careful not to reveal to
any of them the horror of what she went through on a nightly
basis, but Kate had sensed her determination, her will to carry
on in the face of the worst sights and the most terrible of

dangers to help those being bombed. Every instinct told her that Cordelia would never come back to the relative safety of home, when there was so much to be done, and when returning would mean not being permitted to earn an income of her own, and being subject to Papa's tempers and the ingratiating oiliness of Henry Luscombe.

Kate gazed back towards the faded grandeur of her home just visible between the trees. In the time of Shakespeare, Arden House had been the finest Tudor mansion this side of Stratford-upon-Avon. Now, its rows of mullion windows, some cracked, others boarded up as beyond repair, stood empty and forlorn beneath the sloping roofs and winding chimneypots in tiles as red as the earth of the surrounding fields.

She felt an old restlessness stirring. It was all very well digging for victory, but she wanted more. She wanted to feel she was really doing something. Making a difference. Using her skills and her wits, just as men and women were doing all over England, and even more so in the horrors of occupied Europe.

From her conversations with the Land Girls, she knew most had not volunteered to work in the mud and cold of a farmyard to simply help feed the country, but also to escape their families' expectations. They were an unlikely mix, the maids from Coventry with their broad Black Country accents, almost unintelligible to the society daughters with their clipped vowels who, in another life, would have been ordering them to fetch and carry and barely seen them as human at all.

Kate's sisters had, like her brothers, escaped their father's iron ordering of their existence, and headed out into the larger world, as perilous as it was in a time of war. But at least they were living, taking life by the horns while they could, when at any minute Nazi tanks could roll over the horizon, and all of them could be dead, or suffering the slow death of the enslaved. If only she could get away from the stifling atmosphere of the family home!

Apart from assisting with the growing of vegetables in the fields, her only outlet consisted of the afternoons she spent helping at the village school, encouraging the children to paint and draw with the limited materials they could still find. She enjoyed using her skills to help the village children forget the roar of planes going overhead and the adults' constant worrying over the limited food available on the ration, and fears for the fathers, brothers and sons fighting in lands far away.

She had felt hopelessly ill-equipped when Miss Parsons had first suggested she work with the children evacuated from Birmingham and the surrounding cities – she knew nothing about children. But she had quickly found that it took little more than a piece of charcoal and the back of a sheet of discarded wallpaper for even the smallest and most anxious to become absorbed. She loved seeing them lost in their own worlds, their tight little faces relaxing. Even those who had been pulled out of the rubble of their bombed houses, who had seen horrors she didn't dare imagine, lost their haunted look. It gave her a sense of purpose, using her skills to alleviate the suffering of the most vulnerable, and so making her own contribution to the war effort. It also, she confessed to herself, helped to alleviate her frustration at not being able to pursue her painting, at least until this war was over.

Of course! Kate could have kicked herself. Why hadn't she seen it before? Miss Parsons had always been the key to her freedom. She thought back to the moment the schoolmistress had handed Kate and her sisters a volume of Shakespeare each, saying that the books had been left for them by the first Mrs Arden when she was on her deathbed. She had said that each volume contained a message especially for its recipient. Kate had scoured hers – a volume of sonnets – and found nothing. She had long ago pushed the book out of sight at the back of her wardrobe, certain that Miss Parsons had given it to her just out of kindness, so that she wouldn't feel left out amongst her legitimate sisters, whose books were genuine gifts.

She adjusted the previous bundle containing the antique glass, positioning it more securely in the basket amongst the parsnips and cabbages and the knobbly ends of turnips. If Miss Parsons really was the key to her past, as well as her escape to her own future, now was the time to find out.

FOUR

Pushing through the kissing gate that led to the village, Kate and Alma made their way to the central green of Brierley-in-Arden, whose pond, despite the temptation brought on by rationing, was still stocked with fat mallards and a few darting moorhens. The door to the village hall was open, and Kate could hear the busy chatter of female voices coming from inside. She breathed in the aroma of stew and freshly-baked bread wafting from the doorway. A large ginger tom cat guarded the entrance with an expectant glance, between washing his whiskers with the air of one for whom canned salmon was not entirely a distant memory.

'You are utterly shameless, Montague.' Alma gave the well-fed head an indulgent stroke as she passed. 'I'm sure you've never heard of rationing.' Montague purred loudly, until, with no offerings appearing, he returned to preening his particularly fine set of whiskers.

Inside, the village hall was filled with noise and heat, and the sound of a hundred or so conversations, as women of all ages worked at long lines of trestle tables, preparing vegetables and fruit to be preserved by the efficient canning operation taking part at the far end. Kate deposited her offerings of vegetables on the nearest table, where members of the WI were busily preparing everything that they could get their hands on to add to the soup bubbling away on the range, ready to be distributed later that day to families without the means to cook a hot meal themselves. The women began helping Alma to remove the carrots and onions from her rucksack, along with mountains of spinach and kale, and a large handful of parsley from the greenhouses in the walled garden.

Kate grasped her little bundle. Any minute now, she would be directed to chopping up turnips, or preparing the baskets of apples and pears for the attentions of the canning machine. Squashing any guilt at abandoning their efforts, she slipped unnoticed between the busy women, and through a side door into the little museum housed at one side of the hall.

After the rush and noise of the village hall, the museum was an oasis of stillness and quiet. Kate breathed in deep. She had always loved this space, filled to overflowing with glass cases containing the bits and pieces found over the years beneath the ground of Brierley-in-Arden. They might be small and insubstantial compared to the wonders of the pyramids, but they were reminders of lives that continued through the great battles of history, the machinations of kings and queens. Kate had spent hours here poring over a needle made of bone, or the fragment of a pot, the scoring of fire still visible. To her these objects gave reassuring continuity in a world that was falling apart; a hope, maybe, of survival, and that quiet lives could always be rich and fulfilled, out of sight of those who considered themselves lords and masters.

Shafts of afternoon sunlight crept through the window, illuminating the curtains of dust in the air, along with the worldly remains of all those centuries of men and women who had lived their lives amongst this English landscape and died to become the very fabric of the earth.

'Miss Parsons?' Kate called into the stillness.

There was a rustling at the far end, and Miss Parsons emerged, her dark hair caught into a bun behind her head, a touch of grey at her temples. She moved briskly in a loose-fitting dress and long cardigan that seemed to come from another era, a style uniquely her own. '*Bluestocking*', some of the older men called her, as a sign the schoolmistress couldn't really be considered a proper woman at all – no doubt because she had acquired a university education and, more to the point, hadn't being afraid to use it.

'Kate, my dear, it's good to see you.' Miss Parsons's sharp eyes fell on the bundle in Kate's hands. 'You have something for me?'

'It's glass,' said Kate. 'A vessel of some kind. It was in the field next to the Roman villa. From the look of it, I'm pretty sure it's Roman.'

'Even better.' Miss Parsons watched intently as Kate unwrapped her parcel. 'Well, I never. My, my. Yes, from the fragments we've found there before I'd say that's Roman. How extraordinary that it should survive so complete.' A touch of mischief appeared in her expression. 'Really, we should offer it to the British Museum in London, or one in Birmingham, but given how things are, it will be much safer here.'

'I thought you might be able to clean it up... I wouldn't know where to start, and if we wait until Jamie's back on leave, I'm afraid the earth on it will have hardened and it will be impossible.'

'I'll do my best,' said Miss Parsons, with an unmistakeable gleam of anticipation in her eyes. 'What a miracle that it should remain intact for so long. I'm afraid we are at a point where we need some miracles...'

She disappeared for a moment, returning with a damp cloth, which she used to gently wipe away the dirt from one bulbous side. 'Such a delicate colour. I'm always amazed, with every piece we find, just how sophisticated our ancestors were in manipulating materials like glass – and with what must have been the simplest of tools, not to mention the accuracy of the heat required.'

Kate peered at the cleaned patch of blue-green, now illuminated in the dust-filled glow from the window. That strange feeling of familiarity was back. A memory of some kind, remaining just outside her grasp.

She took a deep breath. 'Diana de Warren said it reminded her of glass beads her aunt brought back from Venice.'

'Did she now.' There was a faint edge to Miss Parson's tone that told Kate she was on the right track.

Emboldened, she pressed on. '"Murano glass", she called it, as if it was a special kind.'

'The island of Murano is what she must be referring to,' said Miss Parsons. 'It's a short ride by boat from Venice, in the lagoon. The craftsmen there have specialised in glasswork for centuries.'

'As far back as Roman times?'

'So I was told. And that it was glassmakers escaping from barbarians who first took their art to the safety of the lagoon. It's been famous ever since for its quality.'

Kate gazed down at the glass. Her stomach twisted. The sense of a memory stirred was even stronger this time. 'So this could have come from Venice.'

'Possibly,' conceded Miss Parsons, 'although we're unlikely to ever know for sure. But if that villa Jamie is uncovering really is from a hugely wealthy Roman family, they would most probably have had goods shipped in from all over the Roman Empire. So it's not beyond the bounds of possibility that this could have originated somewhere in Italy, and that could have been Venice... The workshops on Murano are like nothing else I've ever seen.'

Kate looked at her with interest. 'So you've been there.'

'A long time ago,' replied Miss Parsons, wistfully. 'It was when I was a very young woman, not much older than you are now – before the last war, when the world was a very different place. Venice is such an extraordinary city, like nowhere else on earth. It's such an unlikely existence, palaces and churches built on water, with thoroughfares for boats rather than vehicles, and curved bridges wherever you look... I suppose that's where my passion for history began: I wanted to know everything about it.'

She was silent for a moment, lost in thought. 'I should have gone back. It was where I was to have had my honeymoon. I so believed Venice would be a part of my life forever. But all that was taken in a moment, in the trenches of a battlefield far away. And now it's all happening again.'

'I'm so sorry,' exclaimed Kate. 'I didn't mean to distress you.'

'My grief is here, in my heart, my dear, whether I speak about it or not,' Miss Parsons replied quietly. 'Nothing will ever bring my Phillip back. At least now, after all these years, I can think of him with love and fondness rather than simply pain. I've come to see that it's how you live your life in each moment that counts, not how long your body might remain on this earth. Without love and purpose, life is merely existing. I, for one, could never see the point to that.'

Her words struck Kate like a blow of recognition, taking the breath from her lungs. 'Neither can I,' she said, fervently.

Miss Parsons gazed down at the glass vessel, then up at Kate. 'But, for all that, I could never bring myself to go back to Venice. And now that Mussolini is bent on turning all of Italy into some kind of satellite of Hitler's grandiose schemes, I doubt I ever will.' She turned back to the little vase. 'I like the idea that this once took the journey from La Serenissima all the way to an outpost of Rome near Stratford-upon-Avon.'

Kate had intended to be subtle, to work round to the subject bit by bit, but now it burst out of her. 'I know Mama wants to go with you to Birmingham to get the orphan children from your charity away from the bombing, but let me come with you instead. I can talk to Cordelia and try to persuade her to come home. I'm sure she'll listen to me just as much as Mama.'

'You mean, not at all,' returned Miss Parsons dryly.

'That doesn't mean I can't try.'

Miss Parsons frowned. 'I promised Celia, your Papa's first wife, that I would look after her children, and especially her girls. I've no desire to put any of you in harm's way.'

'But I'm not one of her girls,' said Kate. 'You know that. I told you when you gave me and Rosalind and Cordelia the volumes of Shakespeare that Celia Arden left to us that I remember my mother, my real mother, and that she had nothing to do with Arden House.'

'Celia swore to take care of you, and love you, as if you were her own,' replied Miss Parsons. 'And so, yes, you are one of her girls, and I promised her from the bottom of my heart that no harm would ever come to you.'

Kate glanced down at the glass in the schoolmistress's hands. 'But there was nothing there,' she said. 'In the book of Shakespeare's sonnets you gave me,' she added to Miss Parson's enquiring glance. 'You told us Celia Arden had left each of her girls an illustrated volume of Shakespeare, and that we would each find a message hidden inside. Rosalind and Cordelia won't say what they found, but I'm sure it must have been something. There's nothing in mine.'

Miss Parsons frowned and looked at Kate quizzically. 'Are you sure? Messages, especially secret ones, can sometimes be placed where you least expect them. And sometimes you can look and look in the right place, and still not find them until your mind is ready to see. Why don't you look again?'

Kate's frustration bubbled to the surface. 'Do you know what the message is?'

'No, my dear. Celia told me there was a message there for each of you. She would not have lied, especially not about you.'

'Why not?' demanded Kate.

'That, my dear, I can't tell you. If you truly wish to know about your past, and why you are here, you must ask your papa. He is the only one who can say.'

'He'll probably throw me out,' said Kate gloomily. 'Or insist I marry the odious Henry Luscombe, who I'm sure only wants me so he can look respectable and not have to give up his mistresses. Oh, I know there's more than one,' she added to Miss Parson's raised brows. 'And I've heard that he beats the living daylights out of them, just for fun. Can you imagine what he'd do to a wife to keep her quiet? But Papa is determined one of us will marry him, so he won't listen. He keeps on telling Alma the stories are just gossip from people who are jealous of Henry's wealth and that he's going to be a duke one day, and that we are just being silly girls who are frightened of men. Well, he hasn't had to escape from Henry's hands trying to get up under his skirt at dinner parties.'

'Darling!'

'It's all right. He didn't get very far. I kicked him. Hard. And I made sure I never sat next to him again. And if he thinks he can bully me into marrying him, he's got another thing coming.'

'Good for you.' But the concern in Miss Parsons's eyes lingered. 'Perhaps, under the circumstances, it might be as well...' She cleared her throat. 'I'll talk to your mama, see if I can persuade her to let you go to Birmingham with me instead. But on one condition.'

'Oh?' said Kate warily.

'That you don't try to stay there.'

'I wouldn't...'

'Yes you would. Darling, I know you too well. Your sisters have found ways of escaping your father's demands, not to mention the dubious charms of Mr Luscombe. I'm sure given half a chance you'll do the same.'

'But if I manage to get away, I can't return here,' exclaimed Kate. 'If it isn't Henry Luscombe, it will be someone like him. And besides...' She breathed in deep, feeling panic rising inside her. 'I can't stay here. My brothers and sisters are doing something for the war effort. I don't want to be the one stuck here. I've loved helping you with the evacuees, but I want to do more.'

'But not in Birmingham,' said Miss Parsons firmly. 'Or in London. Your father has two daughters facing death from Hitler's bombs, as well as both his sons. I can help you, but only if you promise me that you won't insist on joining them by putting yourself in such danger. There are other ways you can help with the war effort, my dear. It doesn't have to be on the front line.'

Kate eyed her. There was a stubborn expression on Miss Parsons's face that she recognised. Kate had no money of her own. The shoes on her feet, the clothes on her back all belonged to Papa. Apart from packing a rucksack and finding a way to retrieve her ration book from the locked safe in Papa's study, Miss Parsons was her only means of escape; maybe the only possibility she would ever have of living her own life. Whatever the compromise, she was going to seize the day now, this minute. What had she to lose? Like all those around her, she was all too well aware that there might be no tomorrow.

'All right, I promise,' she said. 'I promise I won't try to stay in London or Birmingham, or any other English city that might be bombed.'

'Then I'll do what I can, my dear.'

'Thank you,' said Kate, kissing her, and hastening out to join Alma and the WI before Miss Parsons could notice that she hadn't specified France. Or indeed Italy, come to that.

First things first, muttered Kate under her breath.

It was only later that she remembered the strange expression passing over the schoolmistress's face. Something like a decision made. An irrevocable decision, from which – for good or for ill – there would be no going back. Not for any of them.

'Ah, there you are, darling,' said her stepmother as Kate reached the WI's canning operation in the middle of the church hall, surrounded by the knitting of socks and balaclavas. 'You remember Mr Vernon, don't you, from Hillside Manor? We used to meet when we attended recitals in Stratford before the war.'

'Yes, of course,' said Kate, smiling with terse politeness at the lanky young man in brown corduroy trousers and a matching Fair Isle jumper standing awkwardly at Alma's side. For as long as she could remember, Eugene Vernon had been in the same rowing club in Stratford-upon-Avon as her elder brother, Will. Not that Eugene had ever so much as exchanged a word with her, apart from the occasional mumbled greeting, preferring instead the company of much prettier, fair-haired girls with peaches-and-cream complexions and not too many opinions of their own.

'Eugene's kindly come to assist us today,' said Alma, brightly. 'I thought the two of you might like to—' She met Kate's eyes and drifted into silence, a deep flush rising from her throat. 'I'll leave you to it.'

'Mama!' hissed Kate, at this unsubtle hint. Surely, she told herself in exasperation, not even Alma could think of throwing her at Eugene? It was no secret that his mother, who was a force to be reckoned with, was insisting that Eugene find himself a wife and provide her with at least one grandson before any danger of him being called up. Eugene, it seemed, could no longer afford to be fussy. But before Kate could protest, Alma had hurried off in the direction of the WI ladies, with the air of a task fulfilled.

'I was hoping I'd meet you here,' said Eugene, sounding

stilted and embarrassed. His pale eyes slid towards the imposing figure of his mother, who was supervising the canning activities with a forceful hand. 'You ladies are all doing such good things for the war effort.'

'Like everyone,' said Kate, her hackles instinctively rising at his patronising tone.

Mr Vernon, it appeared, considered the remainder of the female sex as considerably lesser to himself. She'd heard he'd recently taken over his late father's role of manager of a bank in Stratford-upon-Avon. Where no one, she thought darkly, would dare question his authority. She gave a quick glance at his face. It was thinner than she remembered, with the pallor of a man who spends his time indoors, his light brown hair no longer burnished to golden as he pulled oars on the river, or his skin reddened, like Will's, when too exposed to summer sun. Impatience shot through her; did Alma really know her so little?

'I'm sure it is most appreciated.' Eugene took hold of the nearest box. 'If you fill the others, I'll place them in the van.'

Kate bit back her retort that she'd been loading boxes far heavier since the war began, and turned away to hide her expression. If Mr Vernon thought achieving womanhood had turned her into a wilting flower, he was mistaken.

Within minutes, she wanted nothing more than to escape her less than enthusiastic suitor. His conversation was stiff and clumsy. He offered her detailed descriptions of the failures of his underlings at the bank, his elevation to the local council, and the annoyance of not being able to use his new Rover, bought just before the rationing of petrol came in. It clearly had not occurred to him – or his mother had forgotten to instruct him – that to win a girl's heart he might have to show some interest.

Not that men did, in Kate's experience, other than eyes returning to her neckline and the occasional thigh brushing against hers at the dinner table. Clearly under the impression that Italian girls, even ones raised in good English households, were driven by uncontrollable passions and generally possessed of dubious morals. But Eugene could have at least made a little effort. It wouldn't change the outcome, but it might have made her more inclined to be kind, and willing to remain on civilized terms. As it was, her brain began to quickly seize up with boredom. The thought of spending her life as the silent shadow to his opinions, however well-equipped his house, was not in the least appealing.

'It seems the tide of the war might be turning at last,' she said in desperation, anything to direct the conversation into a more equal exchange. Voicing strong opinions was, she had also discovered, the surest way to dampen a would-be seducer's ardour. 'Now that Hitler has chosen to attack Russia as well.'

'I doubt it,' he said shortly, attention returning to the boxes.

She tried again. 'I've been wishing I could do more for the war effort. I feel so useless.'

'You are a comfort to your parents,' he replied stiffly.

Well, that was at least an attempt at a human emotion. She warmed to him slightly. 'But it sometimes feels so desperate, I would like to do something more practical.'

'You are protected,' he said. He put down the final box and moved a little closer, a sentimental expression overtaking his face. 'I would like to protect you, if you would allow me.'

That was it. Hadn't he listened to her at all? Or taken the hint that her murmured responses to his conversation were those of common courtesy, nothing more. 'I don't need protecting,' she retorted. 'I just need to be able to breathe.'

He frowned at her. 'Of course you can breathe.' He snatched clumsily at her hand. 'I'd prevent any man who dares to stop you.'

'I'm sure you would,' replied Kate. 'I just don't think you'd like me very much if you got to know me.'

He smiled. 'I'm a good teacher.'

She pulled her hand away. 'So you are proposing to teach me how I'm supposed to be?'

'There's no need to be offended, dear Kate.' His smile did not waver. 'All I meant was that I am a patient man, and I can help you to bloom, to become the charming woman I feel certain you are underneath. I have a house in Stratford, near to Mama, and you will be within easy distance of your family. I've a salary that is more than enough to support a wife. And Mama has offered us the use of her cottage in the Lakes for our honeymoon...'

He had already organised the honeymoon? Or rather his mother, who clearly ran the Vernon household with the same fell hand that Papa attempted to direct Arden House. Talk about jumping from the frying pan into the fire...

'And what have I got to offer you in return?' she demanded.

'Yourself,' he replied, gallantly. 'Your charming, beautiful self. What more could a man want?'

To her shame, temptation stirred. Not with the supposed hot blood of her Italian heritage and Mr Vernon's physical charms, but the cool calculation of realising she was rapidly running out of options. Supposing Papa didn't permit her to go to Birmingham with Miss Parsons, leaving her trapped in Arden House? She could do worse. She could see Eugene was a pampered son, easily controlled by his mother. A man who wasn't particularly bright, or passionate, who had been promoted to positions of importance due to his connections rather than any real merit. One too indolent, and too accustomed to having his life organised for him, to even bother his head about his own honeymoon.

If his mother could control him, why shouldn't she? She was easily cleverer than Eugene, and she didn't care what anyone thought of her, especially when in a temper. A seductive vision shot before her eyes of an elegant modern home, built in the art deco style, with a glass-fronted room overlooking the Avon.

Servants at her beck and call. A garden filled with lavender and roses. Holidays in Switzerland. And a husband who would leave all arrangements to her and who would easily give way to anything that threatened to make his life uncomfortable...

Papa wouldn't be able to tell her what to do. Absorbed into the Vernons' impeccable respectability, no one would dare cast aspersions about her birth. She'd even have all the anxious mamas and eager-to-be settled young ladies within twenty miles of Brierley-in-Arden green with envy at her triumph.

Eugene was smiling at her, in his bland way. Out of nowhere, she felt sorry for him. Perhaps the fact that he was prepared to agree to a wife who wasn't like the rest of the young women in his circle was an unconscious wish to break at least a little free. Maybe somewhere beneath the pallor of his skin he longed for excitement, passion, the things that he would never find in himself.

'You must know I'm not an Arden,' she said quickly, before she could change her mind and give in to temptation. 'Not really. And that it's the talk of the village, and in Stratford, too.'

His ears turned a faint shade of pink. 'I'm sure everyone respects Mr Arden for taking responsibility for the mistakes of his youth ...'

Fury went through her. 'Mistakes?' He was avoiding her eyes, and appeared to miss the dangerous growl in her voice.

'He has clearly acknowledged you, and brought you up as his own. That's good enough for me. We need say no more about it.'

Unbelievable! Kate just about held onto her temper. 'And my mother?'

'My dear Kate, I'm sure you don't need to concern yourself...'

'But I have to presume she's Italian. One of the enemy. Maybe even a supporter of Mussolini.' She couldn't resist mentally prodding him, trying to get some kind of reaction.

Something that was real underneath that controlled surface; the man she would find if she ever tied her fate to his.

'Of course not. And anyhow, once we are married, what does it matter? You have been raised as a good English girl; it will soon be forgotten. Our children need never know.'

The blood rushed an unstoppable tide to her head. 'Even if their Italian family came looking for them?'

'My dear girl!' This time he went pale with indignation. 'Do you think I would allow such a thing? I promise I will make it my life's mission to protect you.'

Not bloody likely, retorted Kate silently, who had, despite Papa expressly forbidding it, snuck in to see the village's amateur production of Mr Shaw's *Pygmalion*, complete with Eliza Doolittle's shockingly vulgar outburst.

'Thank you, but I'm afraid I'm not able to accept your kind offer,' she added aloud, pulling her hand away and setting off to find Alma as fast as her boots would take her.

FIVE

The mist had cleared by the time Kate and Alma made their way back over the fields towards Arden House.

A full moon lit the well-worn path, past the meadows with their rows of vegetable beds. Damp hung in the night air, droplets glistening in the hedgerows as the two skirted the half-excavated remains of the Roman villa awaiting Jamie's return from the fighting, the mosaic protected by a tarpaulin weighted down with stones.

Given the events of the afternoon, Kate was grateful that her stepmother was in little mood for conversation. Alma might suspect that Kate's avoidance of any mention of Eugene signalled that his attentions had not been a success. And they could both guess that Mrs Vernon would no doubt have already taken full advantage of the telephone to complain to Papa about her rudeness. Having seen a glimmer of escape earlier, Kate couldn't help feeling more hemmed in than ever. She wouldn't put it beyond Papa to punish her by refusing her any possibility of escaping his control.

'I'd better let Lucy know we're back and help to get dinner ready,' said Alma, turning up the lamp in the hallway once the door was safely closed against any escaping chinks of light. 'You'd better go and change, my dear. You know how your Papa feels about you wearing trousers.'

Rebellion stirred in Kate, as it always did when reminded that Papa dictated every last detail of their existence. 'With all this digging I'm doing, he's going to have to get used to it at some point.'

'He will. I'm sure of it. Just give him time.' Alma gazed at her pleadingly, pale face even more strained than usual.

'Don't worry,' said Kate, taking pity on her. 'I'll change before he sees me.'

As Alma made her way to the kitchens, Kate headed up the wide mahogany stairs to her bedroom. Around her, the time-worn fabric of the house lay still and silent. More than ever, she missed the rush and bustle from before the war, with her brothers always up to some plan or other and Rosalind and Cordelia laughing in the drawing room with their stepmother. Even when the Arden siblings had been quiet, the house had resounded with loud instructions and Cook banging pans in the kitchen, while the wooden panelling had echoed with maids scurrying here and there with buckets and pails.

Now they were all gone. For all its strains, Arden House had been a community in itself. She envied the village, despite its obvious poverty; families clustered together under thatched roofs, enjoying each other's company, each member old enough to work pooling their resources to survive.

After changing into a plain woollen dress, she returned to help Alma. As she reached the bottom of the stairway, she could see from the light stealing from under the library door that her father was in his usual place by the fire, no doubt grumbling at the need for blackout curtains that prevented the view of the stars. The flame of rebellion was still inside her, along with the stirring of memories brought about by the glass vessel. Papa might try and rule the household with an iron fist, but she still wanted answers. For all he resisted, he was going to have to acknowledge her difference from the rest of the family, and her past. It was the only way she was ever going to feel she truly had a family here at Arden House.

'Papa?' Her knock was answered by an indeterminate grunt, which she took as permission to enter.

Leo Arden was sitting in his favourite armchair, his white hair illuminated by the glow of the fire and the small lamp set next to him. The Ardens might have fallen from their aristocratic heritage, but even the most profligate had not disposed of the forests on its edges, leaving a store of logs for Papa's fire. Lucy, the family's erstwhile undermaid, who had recently returned to take over the role of cook following the death of her husband during the evacuation at Dunkirk, was constantly cursing the coal rationing that made controlling the elderly range in the kitchens more difficult. Leo Arden, however, always insisted on a good store of wood in his room, ignoring the icy drafts creeping into the rest of the house.

He did not look up from his book, nor motion her to join him. Kate gritted her teeth. The warmth from the fire tempted her, but she had no wish to approach any nearer. Papa's temper was, at best, volatile, and had grown worse since Will, his heir, had headed off for France, soon joined by Jamie. His eldest daughter was safely married. Rosalind, the second, had been banished for following her own heart, rather than obeying his command to marry the wealth and aristocratic connections of Henry Luscombe. Even Cordelia, the baby of the family, was now working in a factory on the edges of Birmingham. Kate knew he was struggling to adapt to the reality of the family's circumstances and was still grumpily trying to cling onto the past.

'Did Lucy get those rabbits?' he demanded.

'I'm not sure, Papa. I'll ask her.'

'Gloster's son, Charlie, the one with the bad eyesight, was

supposed to bring them this afternoon.' He sniffed. 'He's not much of a gardener, so I hope he's a good rabbiter. He'd be better off breeding the things.'

'I thought the idea was to keep them away from the kitchen garden?'

Her comment was ignored. 'I always said having those Land Girls just meant more mouths for us to feed.'

'They work very hard, Papa. With the gardeners all gone, and so many of the farmhands, I don't know what we'd have done without them.'

'The farmhands didn't need to go,' he grumbled. 'Reserved occupation.'

Kate compressed her lips to prevent the words from spilling out. She'd heard more than one woman in the village, waiting patiently in line outside the village grocer's shop while Mrs Ackrite and her minions behind the counter wrestled with the intricacies of ration books, bemoan the sons and brothers who had volunteered to fight, despite agricultural workers being exempt. The War Office had learnt that one from the First World War, when men had rushed off to volunteer, leaving crops to rot in the fields and no one to tend the animals, bringing the spectre of defeat through sheer starvation.

The truth was, there were still plenty of young men from Brierley-in-Arden who had not waited to be conscripted, but, like their fathers and uncles before them, had seized the opportunity to escape a life of backbreaking toil. Anything was better than working amongst sodden fields in all seasons, for wages so meagre they could barely pay the rent on the most tumbledown of cottages, let alone feed their families.

She winced. It was no good telling Papa, who was pretending he didn't, in his heart, know this. It was too close a reminder that her brothers had also taken this escape, not from extreme poverty and no future, but from the iron rule of their father. Will, as the future lord of Arden, might be planning to return, but she felt certain Jamie had no intention of ever coming back.

That was the thing about Arden House. You conformed to Papa's wishes, to what he wanted you to be, or you escaped, before his rages – which could be terrifying – forced you into submission.

'We are all doing what we can for the war effort,' she murmured.

'Where's your mama?' he demanded abruptly.

'She's helping Lucy. Dinner will be ready soon.'

'Your mama's place is not in the kitchens,' he remarked, the dignity of every Arden whose feet had formed the worn dips in the flagstones over the centuries on his shoulders. 'She should be here.'

'Poor Lucy can't be expected to do everything,' she returned. 'I do what I can, and the Land Girls do their best, but they've enough to do, and we can hardly leave them to starve.'

He looked up, eyes meeting hers. 'I hear young Vernon spoke to you this afternoon.'

Kate's heart sank. So Eugene's mother had telephoned. 'Yes, Papa.'

'I understand you didn't accept him.'

'No, Papa.'

'Good for you.'

Kate stifled her involuntary gasp. This was the last reaction she had expected. 'But I thought you'd approve. Of Eugene, I mean. Or any man who wanted to take me off your hands,' she added under her breath.

She became aware of him watching her closely, with an expression she couldn't quite read. It was the kind of look that came over him when it was about to lose his temper, which usually meant he knew perfectly well he was in the wrong. Then the look was gone, leaving her wondering if it had been a figment of her imagination.

'What on earth gives you that idea?' he demanded.

'I—' She came to a halt. 'I don't know, I'd always assumed...'

'Vernon is a prize idiot,' he snorted. 'My dear, you are worth far more than such a dolt. Besides, his mother is an unsufferable woman.' He turned back to his book. 'And I gather Miss Parsons is suggesting you go with her to Birmingham.'

Miss Parsons had clearly been as good as her word in tackling him, and had struck while the iron was hot. Thank goodness Papa had finally agreed the necessity of a telephone. 'Just to help bring out children who've been orphaned by the bombing, to get them to safety,' she replied. 'Miss Parsons makes the journey every few weeks, she has done since the bombing began. She knows what she's doing. I'll be perfectly safe.'

'Hmm.'

She softened her tone. 'And I can meet Cordelia while I'm there, and persuade her to come home.'

'She won't,' he said, but not quite as decisively as usual. Was it her imagination, or was there a wistfulness in his voice? He did love them all, she was sure of it. He just had no means of expressing it, and that need he had to always feel in control of them was wearing beyond belief.

At least he was still looking down at the same lines, and hadn't turned the page, giving her hope that he was giving her his full attention and was mulling over the proposal.

'But surely it's worth a try? Mama worries about her so much. I'm sure she'd love to have Cordelia home.'

'That is true my dear.' He beamed at her, expression softening. 'Home is where we should all be, especially at a time like this.' He cleared his throat. 'It's good to have you here.'

It wasn't often she caught Papa in such a mellow mood. She wanted so much to bask in his approval, and reach below the bluster to whatever lay beneath. But it also felt like now or never, and she couldn't just let the subject of her past lie hidden forever.

Kate took a deep breath, bracing herself. 'You once promised you'd tell me about my mother. My real mother,' she added. 'And why I was brought from Italy as a little girl.'

'Italy?' He looked up from his book. 'Who told you it was Italy?'

'I—' For a minute she was thrown. All those whispers about *the Italian girl*... maybe they had just been rumours. 'I remember—' But did she? Those elusive memories that crept in at times, were they more than dreams? She steadied her doubts. They were not dreams. 'You told me.'

'Nonsense.' He looked about to fly into one of his rages, which, she had learnt over the years, was also a sure-fire way of deflecting any questioning of his actions.

Well, she wasn't about to be put off, temper or no temper. 'But you did, Papa. I remember it clearly. I asked you once, when I was little, where I came from, and you said I was born beneath the ash clouds of Vesuvius. I didn't understand at the time, but then I remembered when Jamie was reading about the excavation of Pompeii. I remembered what you said. Pompeii is in Italy.'

'I'm not having the Ardens associated with a brute like Mussolini,' he growled.

'I'm nothing to do with Mussolini! I'm sure most Italians aren't either. He's a tyrant. They probably hate him, like I bet plenty of Germans hate Hitler.'

It was no good; she tried to search his face for some sign that the softness of a minute ago still existed, but his expression had closed in on itself, shutting her out.

'You will go and help your mama.'

Kate frowned. 'I am helping her,' she exclaimed, infuriated at this attempt to deflect her attention. 'I'm helping her in the vegetable fields and with the WI, and I help her and Lucy as much as I can. But I can't help wanting to know more about my past and feeling I need to know what my future holds. The

Slade in London told me my drawings looked as if I had been taught by a professional artist, not just the teacher at the library. That's why they accepted me before the war. They said I was too good to pass over. And that's why they are happy to keep my place open until all this is over.'

'Don't be ridiculous.' He stood up, book tumbling in a heap at his feet. 'I won't allow it. I will not have you disgracing the family.'

'Disgracing?' She stared at him. She had never seen him so angry. Not his towering rage that was more than half bluster, cowering anyone who defied him by force of will. This was a cold, hard fury that seemed to shake him to the very core. For once, she was silenced.

His eyes narrowed. 'Who on earth could have given you such wild ideas?'

'They are not wild ideas. It will also give me a way of learning practical skills, like design and illustration, things that could mean I could make my own living and not have to depend on someone like Eugene—' Too late, she stopped. *Or you*, went the silent message between them.

'Your place is here,' he said, turning away, shutting down the conversation, clearly never to be revived again.

Kate stared at the blankness of his back silhouetted against the fire. Immoveable. As if she didn't matter. As if her voice did not exist. Wounded to the core, she fled before tears overcame her.

SIX

Reaching her own room, Kate curled herself tight on the window seat. Outside, the last of the light was beginning to fade from the landscape. A faint hint of woodsmoke hung in the air, drifting up from the remains of cooking fires in Brierley-in-Arden, safe in its hollow, while the breathy hoot of owls echoed across the surrounding undulation of woods and fields.

Before the war, there had always been the distant glow of light from the lamps and candles as night fell, but now the village was muffled in blackout darkness. Crouching, like all the villages throughout England and far beyond, waiting for the deep drone of bombers overhead.

Kate had painted the scene so often in her sketchbook in daylight hours that she could still see it in her mind's eye. The walls of the kitchen garden, with its neat rows of vegetables and the tall wigwams of twigs and canes supporting the ramblings of peas and beans between espaliered trees of peach and apple. The fields beyond, once more turned into the growing of cabbages and potatoes, just as they had been during the last war. The war to end all wars, which had left so many fathers and uncles, sons and brothers as no more than names on the memorial next to the duck pond on Brierley's village green.

The house felt emptier than ever. Hollowed out without the creak of footsteps in its vastness, the distant murmur of voices emanating from the bedrooms as her sisters dreamed of their futures, or her brothers discussed some plan or other to take off in the Austin to walk in the Lakes, free from Papa's eagle eye. She even missed Will, who as the son and heir, could not be contradicted. During his last return on leave from France, he had been particularly loud in joining the condemnation of Mussolini, for whom he had particular scorn. At least Hitler and Spain's Franco were proper soldiers, he had declared, not a fat vulgar little man like *il Duce*.

Closing the blackout curtains, she lit her candle, and turned her attention to the flyleaf of the leatherbound book of Shakespeare's sonnets balanced on her knees. *For Katerina*. Not Kate, not Katherine. Her real name. She rolled the word around her mouth as she traced the swirl of the writing, spidery, faint, as if the writer barely had the strength to hold the pen. *Katerina*.

The page wavered in front of her. That was her first memory of Arden House. A bewildered little girl with salt spray in her hair, abruptly torn from everything she knew, shivering in the silk dress made for the heat of a Mediterranean summer, her skin absorbing the penetrating damp of the booklined room. And the strange man who had brought her here, standing tall and severe, and so very old in a child's eyes, instructing her to call him 'Papa'. She was to speak only English, he'd told her, and be Katerina, the inconveniently foreign child no longer.

'You are Kate,' Leo Arden had said, with the severity of a schoolmaster instilling discipline in a class. 'Kate Arden. You have no other name. It does not exist. It never existed. And you will look a damn fool if you try to say otherwise. You don't want those who love you to be ashamed of you, do you?'

His blue eyes had sharpened at her silence, as the child's instinct for survival had fought the rebellion within her soul. She had seen something flicker in their depths. Love? Guilt? Or, she had begun to wonder as she grew older, if it had been simply distaste. Regret, even. That first evening he had abruptly turned away towards the children, all older and bigger than her, crowding at the door, curious, but waiting for permission to step inside.

'Say hello to your brothers and sisters,' he had said, propelling her towards them.

Katerina.

On the window seat, Kate felt the silence of the house creep around her. Could there really be a message left for her in amongst the lines of verse, interspersed by the fantastical illustrations? She shivered, remembering the deep cold that had settled in her bones in her first terrified days at Arden House; and the feeling of absence – absence of familiar heat, of earth brittle with lack of moisture and yet rich with the scent of lemons and olive groves, rosemary and wild thyme. The absence, most of all, of love.

The window rattled as a breeze tore at the leaves turning towards their autumn brittleness and sent the rafters protesting in sympathy. Kate held the volume tighter, as the wind became the creaking of rigging in her mind, the frantic flapping of a sail, the crash of waves again the hull of the boat taking her into the unknown. Then she was back there, in the terrace under the vines, her ears filled with childish screams – her screams – as she was dragged away, helpless, from the strong arms that loved her.

She shut her eyes, remembering the warmth lingering in the evening air, the reckless bump and rattle of a horse-drawn vehicle on rocky tracks, taking her from everything she had ever known. Of being lifted down in a harbour beneath great towering cliffs etched against the stars. The shouts of sailors, the

swinging of lanterns amongst rigging, and the night-time intensity of salt and fish clinging to her clothes and hair.

She had been taken onto the sway of a boat, that had immediately set off into the vastness of the oceans, as if to ferry her to
the furthest reaches of the universe. The boat was of shiny
polished wood, with a tiny cabin where a woman had looked
after her. A woman, clothed from head to toe in black, her coat
scratchy to the touch and smelling of damp and mothballs, who
barely spoke to her. Sometimes, Kate had been allowed on deck,
beneath the creak of pale sails. At first the sea had been the
calm blue of the Mediterranean, but later the winds had
arrived, sending huge green-grey waves roaring towards them,
shooting spray high into the air. She didn't remember feeling ill,
despite the woman in the black coat being as sick as a dog for
most of the days and nights they rode the storm.

Kate clutched the book tighter against her as the wind
outside sent tendrils of the nearest beech tree tapping against
her windowpanes. A new memory came rushing back, one she
had never quite grasped before, only snatches in her dreams.

One morning she had escaped the closeness of the cabin,
filled with the fear of being sucked down into the depths, with
whales and sharks, and entwining tentacles of the legendary
giant squid. Out in the salt air and the uncertain light of dawn,
the crashing of the night had gone, leaving the water around her
grey, almost flat in the stillness and the calm. She had been
caught in wonder, grief and terror eased, as over the horizon the
sun began to rise, a pale orb creeping through ribbons of cloud.
A streak of lightening crossed the glow and the clouds parted
into an uncertain blue.

'What are you doing here?' She had been jolted out of her
reverie as a strange man – Papa – grasped her arm so tight it
hurt. He had shouted a name. A name that brought the woman
running. 'What the hell do you think you were doing? She
could have drowned.'

That had been the last she had seen of the sea until they had arrived in London. She'd been kept confined to the cabin and had been only allowed out on deck when they were travelling between the banks of the Thames, to watch the progress to the docks, where a large black car had been waiting to take them to Arden House. She didn't remember the woman after that. It must have been just her and Papa, heading through the rawness of an English night, towards the unknown.

For Katerina.

With a new determination, she searched once more through the illustrated pages of the sonnets. It was a waste of time; there was no message. As she closed the book, she paused. The numbering didn't make sense. There was no Sonnet 18. She had been so absorbed in scanning the illustrations for clues she had not noticed the thickness where Sonnet 18 should be.

Closer inspection showed that the pages were stuck together at one edge. Gently, she prised them open.

> *Shall I compare thee to a summer's day?*
> *Thou art more lovely and more temperate...*

Her breath stopped. Not at the declaration of love, but rather the illustration taking up the entirety of the opposite page, showing a covered terrace, wound around with grapes, and the figure of a woman at the far end, long hair in a single plait down her back, looking out to the sun streaming over the sea, the curve of a bay and the sharp-sided silhouette of a mountain in the distance. She knew that view. Hadn't she just relived the cool of the stone tiles beneath her feet that formed her earliest memories? Along with the brilliance of sunbeams creeping between the vine leaves, illuminating the crimson juice captured within the jet-black skin of the grapes.

She could smell the salt coming in from the sun-warmed sea, hear the crash of waves on the rocks below. And the heat.

Kate traced the figure with her fingers, the face unseen. An impossible ache set up inside. She was surrounded by warmth and the rich, lemony smell of verbena. Out of nowhere, grief racked her body; the memory of grief and loss of love.

She closed the volume and placed it on the window seat. Blowing out the candle, she pulled back the blackout curtains to let in the starlight. Moving quietly, she opened the window slightly to breathe the cool of the night air. The scene conjured up by the illustration had felt so vivid, she almost expected to smell the sea and hear the dry song of cicadas rising up from below. Instead, there came the mossy dampness of an autumn evening in the Warwickshire countryside. An owl called. She watched a fox slink across the lawn, followed by the waddling snuffle of a party of hedgehogs, fattening up on the plentiful earthworms and slugs in the flowerbeds before their winter hibernation. Bats swooped and dived for insects against the white of stars.

Slowly, the tears came. Her soul might ache for the lost world of her early childhood, but this was also her home. For as long as she could remember, she had rolled down the steep slopes, amongst the richness of summer meadows. She had run between the thatched cottages of Brierley-in-Arden on her way back from Miss Smith's drawing lessons in the lending library. This was where her memories had been made. And yet—

In the darkness, she ran one hand over the carved leather of the volume of sonnets. Somewhere here lay the secrets of her past, and the reason Leo Arden brought her from the warmth of grape vines and olives to the frigid winter of Arden House. She shut her eyes tight, trying with every last fibre of her body to remember.

Her breathing calmed. She could feel arms around her, the warmth of breath on her cheeks; strong, slender fingers on hers, guiding the uncertain scratch of a pencil.

'That's good. *Va bene*. There, you see: if you hold it like so, *come questo.* Then the world is your oyster. And don't ask me to translate that into *italiano.'*

That had to be a real memory; a woman's voice teaching her to draw, when she had been a small child, barely able to walk, before she had known there was a world outside the terrace and its overhanging grapes. It was real. This was the source of her own passion. It was there every time she picked up a pencil, utterly absorbed in the attempt to capture the scene in front of her or held in her memory. And, as the Slade had so unwittingly informed her, of her skill. Someone who had taken the time and care to encourage her to become the artist she now so longed to be. Her real mother, the shadowy figure she remembered, the body that had made her.

She clutched the volume closer, hard against her, to ease the grief, and as her fingers closed around the edges she felt something she had not noticed before when she had searched the carved leather of the outside cover. Something within the finer leather of the inner cover. Hastily, Kate closed the window and then the curtains as tight as they would go. Taking her torch, she directed the beam, until she made out a slight gap in the stitching, that had a look of having been mended. With the aid of a small pair of nail scissors, she carefully prised it open. There was definitely something tucked inside there. She pulled out a small piece of folded up thick paper, the kind that came from her own sketchbooks.

She prised carefully at the folds, the paper stiff and brittle with age, smoothing until the torchlight revealed a pencil sketch of a great waterway, lined on either side by tall buildings, stretching towards the rounded dome of a cathedral.

Venice.

Kate gasped out loud. The beam of her torch traced the elegant gondola and the larger, squatter form of a waterbus. She had seen enough photographs and paintings to recognise that this was a view of the Grand Canal, looking towards the great bend leading out in the direction of the bay. It was clearly from a height, gazing down. She peered closer. From the angle, it looked as if it had been sketched from one of the buildings on one side of the Canal; maybe even one of the palazzos that lined its banks.

There was something more. A smaller paper, blackened as if from fire and lacey at the edges. Again, it was in pencil, but this time, a portrait of a middle-aged woman in a close-fitting gown, standing tall and straight, one hand resting on the arm of a chair. Heavy jewels hung around her neck and in the intricate styling of her hair. But amongst all her finery, it was the face that was arresting. Narrow and hawkish, with eyes that seemed to bore out of the paper and into the observer's very soul. Not that the lady was impressed. She clearly held any observer – perhaps even the artist – in the utmost contempt. Unbending. A woman who would not be crossed and would never allow herself to be wrong.

Kate dropped the paper as if stung, repelled by the bitterness captured in the woman's gaze. Was it her imagination, or was there something familiar in those features?

There was a scrawl of writing on the lower edge. She picked the paper up again, peering closely. 'La Contessa.' A countess. A member of the aristocracy; no wonder there was power in those eyes, as well as coldness.

That was it! That was where she had seen the face before. Not a memory of her lost childhood, but Cordelia's volume of Shakespeare's Tragedies. Cordelia was as secretive about her gift as all the sisters, but Kate had once found it open on Cordelia's bed when she'd been sent to summon her sister down to the formality of the dining room. Cordelia, who sometimes seemed to spend her life in a dream, had been lost in contemplating the illustration of Lady Macbeth, oblivious to dinner bell.

'Isn't she terrifying?' she had said, as Kate practically had to drag her away, conscious of Papa growing impatient below. Yet Cordelia had remained gazing at the picture, as if spellbound. 'I love the way all the people in the illustrations are so individual, as if they've been taken from life. This is the one that feels the most real. I can't imagine anyone could make up someone like that, do you? She feels as if she could walk out of the page. Mind you, I'm not sure I'd like to meet her.'

Forgetting the disapproval waiting in the dining hall, Kate had gazed down at the drawing of a woman, flowing medieval gown swirling around her, as if caught in the mountain storms of the battlements around her, fierce determination on her face. *Yet do I fear thy nature; It is too full o' th' milk of human kindness,* read the caption.

This was the same woman. It had to be. The features were too striking for it to be a coincidence, despite the ornate chaise longue on which one hand rested, which looked no more to do with medieval Scotland than the glimpse of an intricate glass chandelier above her head. The sleek elegance of a tight-fitting ballgown had never seen a mountain storm, let alone the diamonds arranged around her neck and set as a tiara amongst the elaborate pinning of her hair.

Cordelia had been right. This was no medieval harridan urging her husband on to commit murder to fulfil their ambitions to become king and queen, but a grand society lady, confident in her power, in her ability to order the world to her own satisfaction, and who must always be obeyed.

Kate shivered slightly under the icy implacability of the stare. She couldn't imagine such a woman having anything to do with her. And yet, if the volume of sonnets had really been intended for her, there must be some connection, somewhere. She hastily folded the papers to return to their hiding place.

As she opened up the gap in the leather again, a hint of white inside caught her eye. She had almost missed it, an even smaller piece of paper which looked as if it had been torn care-

lessly from a sketchbook. Unfolding it, she saw that it was a
picture in pencil, with dabs of colour, as if it had been a sketch.
Turquoise blue to represent the sea; the deeper blue of a sky;
and the shadows cast by tall pillars as the afternoon faded into
the soft warmth of evening, broken by the chirrup of cicadas.
Kate felt her stomach clench. In front of her lay the terrace she
had seen so often in her dreams, bunches of grapes peeping
between the vine leaves and the mountain rising up in the
distance.

She smoothed out her finds, laying them next to each other
on the bed. Her artist's eye told her that they were all by the
same hand. There was a similarity in the strokes of the pencil,
the sharpness of the detail. She turned back to the picture of the
woman on the terrace illustrating Sonnet 18. It had to be the
same artist. The small sketch from inside the cover looked as if it
could have been a preparatory drawing for the illustration. This
wasn't Venice, but every instinct told her it had to be somewhere in Italy. Her eyes rested on the mountain with its distinctive outline. A familiar, vaguely ominous shape…

It had to be! Taking her torch, she raced along the darkened
corridor in her bare feet to her brothers' rooms. Jamie's, like
Will's, had been preserved meticulously just as they had left
them, ready for any unexpected return on leave, or the longed-
for ending of hostilities.

She knew his bookshelf like the back of her hand. She
barely had to search in the light of the torch for the well-
thumbed volume on the discoveries at Pompeii, pulling it out
from its place on the shelves between a description of Howard
Carter's discovery of the tomb of Tutankhamun in Egypt and
theories on the origins of Stonehenge. As she stuffed it safely
under her arm, the door of the library opened, followed by
heavy steps making their way upwards.

Kate hastily switched off the torch, waiting with baited
breath until her father closed the door to his bedroom. She

dared not stir an inch until she could hear him moving around inside, changing for dinner. Then she sped back to her own room, closing the door behind her as quietly as possible. She stood rigid in the darkness until she was certain she had not been heard. Nothing. With a sigh of relief, she crawled into bed, pulling the blankets and quilts over her to prevent any glow from the torch escaping from under her door. The last thing she needed was another confrontation with Papa, or questions as to why she was sulking in her room rather than helping Alma and Lucy with the evening meal. She searched through the illustrated pages, seeking the view of the volcano whose eruption had doomed the Roman settlement of Pompeii to its centuries of entombment.

She seized on the black and white photograph she remembered, peering between ruined columns, towards the volcano behind. She was right: the drawing had to be of Vesuvius. Jamie had allowed her to pore over the pages on rainy days; the images had stuck in her mind as she had eagerly sought memories of the half-forgotten country of her childhood.

There had been another view of the volcano in the book, she remembered, from further away, along the coast towards Sorrento. Finally, she found it. Laying the drawing next to the photograph, it was unmistakeable. That was Vesuvius in the background and from a similar angle. The building containing the terrace had to be near enough to Sorrento to share a similar view. She felt a thrill of excitement at piecing the puzzle together. It had not been a dream, remembered from seeing the *The Last Days of Pompeii* in the picture house in Stratford-upon-Avon. It had been real.

All that night, Kate could not get warm. Her sleep was fitful, shot through with dreams interspersed with moments that could have been memories, as wild as the mountain winds that stirred

Lady Macbeth's finery, mingled with the Brierley Players' production in the village hall that had terrified her as a child, with its circling witches and the blood-streaked ghost of a murdered man, for all she could clearly make out the features of Tommy Aiken, the village blacksmith's son, whose Banquo had been talk of the village ever since.

There had never been another attempt at putting on the Scottish play, with none daring to follow the performance of Julia Fields, the baker's wife, whose mild manner when serving customers had been found to hide a steely and terrifyingly believable ruthlessness as the ambitious Lady Macbeth.

In Kate's dreams, the world stilled. No longer a castle, but the painted backdrop of the village hall. She could hear the hush, even from the smallest of babies in the audience, at the sleepwalking scene and the sight of Lady Macbeth, hair wild, pausing in washing her hands over and over, in vain.

Kate shot upright, suddenly awake. She pulled back the blackout curtains, allowing in the first hint of light, along with the trill of the dawn chorus, then clambered back under the covers. Even as a child she had felt the despair of the woman on the stage, whose conscience had been stirred, who had finally understood what she had done, and been driven mad by the understanding.

The final image of her dream returned. Lady Macbeth, not as played by Mrs Fields, but as she appeared in the drawing in Cordelia's volume of Shakespeare's plays. The last illustration was of Lady Macbeth, wandering the castle, face sent into deep shadows by the candle in her hands. It was the same hawkish features of the woman in the sketch, but the power overtaken by a haunted expression. Fear? Regret? Or maybe a terrible anger. Kate tried to recall the illustration in Cordelia's book. It had disturbed her at the time, she remembered, along with the accompanying quotation from the play: *'Will these hands ne'er be clean?'*

Miss Parsons was right; the volume of sonnets left to her by the first Mrs Arden had contained a message, after all. She reached for the pictures hidden so carefully. Miss Parsons had also said the book had come with Kate when Papa had brought her to Arden House. In that case, the pictures could have been placed there by her mother. Her real mother. A message across time, and the wide reach of the oceans. Surely a token of unbroken love, however they had been torn apart, and of hope that they could one day find each other again.

Kate could feel again the warmth of the arms around her as a child, the voice flowing seamlessly between English and Italian, encouraging the pencil in her hand to move freely. The love that had once held her, which had given her the gift of capturing the world in paint that had become the centre of her own being. The gift she was more determined than ever would never be destroyed by the pomposity of Eugene Vernon, or the cruelty of Henry Luscombe. The gift from her lost mother who, Kate was more certain than ever before, would never have relinquished her willingly. Her mother who, if she was still alive, was out there somewhere, amidst the uncertainties of war, grieving, her only hope lying in the scraps of hidden paper sent across the sea, in the hope that they might one day be discovered.

I'll find you, Kate whispered to the drawings in her hands. *Alive or dead, I'll find you. I'll get to Venice, if it's the last thing I do, and I'll find that villa near Vesuvius, and at last I'll know who I really am.*

SEVEN

VENICE

October 1941

In Venice, Sofia admitted to herself, ruefully, the time for choices was most definitely over. As the mists and damp winds of autumn began to make their way towards winter, it was clear the war was not about to end any time soon.

'You can't continue to stay here,' announced Magdalena one morning, returning from the market with the few scraggy vegetables still to be found. 'I told you to go while you could.'

Sofia hid her irritation at this abrupt dismissal. 'I didn't expect to stay at the palazzo permanently, I told you I'd find somewhere.'

'I mean now. Today. At the market I heard that the colonel, a friend of the contessa, or at least someone who might be useful to her, is being stationed in Venice and the contessa has given him use of the palazzo. If she hears you've been here, that I let you inside, let alone stay...'

So that was what this was about. She'd no wish to cause Magdalena any trouble. 'Don't worry, he won't find me here.'

A look of relief, mixed with pain, crossed Magdalena's face.

'There are still hotels looking for business now the tourists are gone. I can tell you the good ones.'

Sofia shook her head. She had not planned to stay. She had brought money with her, but not enough to afford a hotel, and who knew when she could access her bank account in America. She had jewellery she could sell, but no one knew how long this would last. She needed to preserve what she had, and find a way of supplementing her small store to make it last as long as she could.

The contessa had controlled her once by ensuring she was left destitute. Then, she had been too young to know how to fight back, apart from to flee. She silently thanked those years of hardship, back when she had first arrived in America, that had taught her to keep her wits about her, and seize opportunities as they came. There was a place she could go and stay. It had crossed her mind before, but it was linked too closely to the past. Once, if the contessa had given her the chance, and grief had not blurred her vision of the future, it might have been her salvation. Her way of making things right. But now she no longer had time for pride, or resentment, or even regret. It was a place that offered her the possibility of obscurity, the nearest thing to safety in a world falling apart, in a war coming ever closer.

Sofia squared her shoulders. She was going to survive, whatever the conflict might throw at them. Even in Venice, stories had reached them of the devastation wreaked on Europe, and the bombing of the great English cities like London and Liverpool. Who knew what might happen in Venice. Now that Mussolini had joined forces with Nazi Germany, the fact that Hitler was prepared to destroy the great historic buildings of London might mean the British and their allies could one day be prepared to destroy Venice in turn. In a city crowded together between waterways, that would surely mean doom for them all.

As Magdalena disappeared to store her precious purchases, Sofia retrieved the ornate iron key from her purse. It had been the only reminder of her old life left by the time she had made her way to America. Too small and worthless to be sold, it had been a chance object that had remained in her bag until she had come across it again years later. So many times, she had nearly thrown it away. She had only brought it with her to Venice on a whim, certain she would never use it, never even go near the place with so many painful memories of the time before love and hope died.

She'd had some vague idea of tossing the key from the Rialto Bridge into the water below; a symbolic ending of her youthful dreams of becoming a world-renowned artist, her paintings to take their place alongside those of Englishwoman Laura Knight and American Mary Cassatt. But now, in the emptying of Venice of the artists who had once flocked to its artistic vibrancy and exquisite dance of light, this memory from her past had become a lifeline.

Of course, the lock could easily have been changed over the course of the past twenty years, or the place requisitioned by the army. But the old warehouse was in the back alleyways of Venice, amongst the narrow canals making their way between buildings too high for the sun to penetrate, apart from the brief centre of the day. She could hope it had remained empty, awaiting the return of the women artists who had once made their home in its simple surroundings, and shared her dream of defying convention and making a name for themselves.

Mind made up, Sofia slipped out into the mist of the day.

It took twists and turns, and several missteps as her memory failed her, but finally she made her way over a small arched bridge to an abandoned-looking building that had the appearance of an old warehouse. She stood in front of the door, hesitating, the breath tight in her chest. But this time fear and shame were not about to stand in her way. She knocked. There was no answer.

She took out the key and inserted it in the lock. It hesitated, then creaked and turned. Slowly, experimentally, she pushed the door open. Inside smelt of damp, of the canals, the mossiness of unopened windows. They were the ordinary smells of a building that had been shut up for months. She stepped inside.

Still wary, Sofia made her way through the hallway, and up the narrow flight of stairs to a rectangular room with windows on either side. Long trestle tables stood in the centre, as if waiting for activity to be resumed at any moment. A tailor's dummy stood at one end, sending eerie shadows against the wall. On the cupboards lining the walls, small clay animals had been left, along with piles of drawings in different hands, and a variety of styles, some traditional, some more experimentally modern, and almost all unfinished.

At the far end, a few framed paintings had been stacked hastily against the wall. She recognised them from the little gallery on the Rialto, long since boarded up and abandoned. She hoped that the young women she had seen doing their best to tempt the visitors to buy the artworks, in those last weeks before Europe was plunged into war, had made it safely out of Venice. She could not bear to think of the enthusiasm, the energy and the sheer determination that had brought them here being snuffed out, as if it meant nothing at all.

When she had last been here, as a young woman ambitious to make painting her life, the studio had been a bustle of creativity. This room had rung to the eager conversation of other young women escaping the expectations of their families. Those long, hot, seemingly endless summers before the Great War had been a time when women had even fewer choices than they did now. The Studio Theodora had been one of the few places where women lacking the necessary moral and financial support from their families could practise their art, giving them a chance to learn from each other and build reputations that might enable them to make an independent living.

If only, breathed Sofia, into the musty air.

But she had no time for regrets. Not now. There was only the present, with violence and destruction waiting round the corner, to arrive at any moment. Satisfying herself that there was no sign of anyone using the studio, Sofia locked the door behind her, returning to the palazzo to collect her few belongings and safely vanish before the colonel could arrive.

Now, all she had to do was find a way to support herself and survive.

In the end, she went to the hotels that Magdalena had mentioned were still open, but not to look for lodgings. She had heard that there was work to be found there, cleaning, and so she swallowed her pride, securing employment cleaning one of the few hotels still in business.

'You won't last,' remarked Magdalena, as they met beneath the Campanile di San Marco after the successful interview. 'A fine lady like you, scrubbing what men leave behind in their latrines. I'll give you a week.'

'Don't be so sure,' retorted Sofia. 'How do you think I made a living when I first landed in America? When the contessa told you I sold my body, as I'm sure she did, she was quite right. Just not in the way she meant.' It gave her a brief jolt of satisfaction to see the scandal on Magdalena's face at the talk of such things, replaced briefly by something that looked like shame. 'I bet she told you Mr Armstrong was one of my "clients" I managed to fool into making an honest woman of me. And you believed her.'

'No, of course not,' muttered Magdalena, turning scarlet. 'As if I'd think such a thing.'

'But you did believe her.'

'How else does a woman become rich?' Magdalena retorted. 'D'you think if I had the figure and the nice manners, I wouldn't have been tempted to do the same? And lied to the priest in confession and damned my soul to hell.'

That shocked her. That traditional, God-fearing Magdalena – the severe figure who had kept the contessa's discipline for as long as she could remember – could have thought such thoughts. 'You're not going to hell, Magdalena. Not for wanting to survive.'

'And what makes you think I'm not going there anyhow,' returned the maid. They turned to walk slowly through St Mark's Square, towards the wide walkway running along the waterfront leading to the Bridge of Sighs. 'Maybe it would have been better if I'd died, that day the soldiers came to our village.'

'Don't ever think that,' exclaimed Sofia as they stopped at the edges of the walkway to gaze over the lapping waters of the lagoon, these days the only sight of the outside world possible. She suddenly wanted to make at least one thing right. She didn't care what Magdalena thought of her, but all the same...

'And I didn't seduce Mr Armstrong. I became his secretary. He was a successful businessman; we worked long hours together. We were both lonely. It was a natural progression.'

How cold that sounded, how lacking in passion. And yet there had been passion, of a kind. True, she had not been in love with Walter when he proposed to her, any more than he with her. They had both been lost souls in the vast loneliness of New York, who simply found each other. Like her, Walter had been grieving the loss of the one true love of his life. He had never said much, nor pressed her to confide in him, but his grief had led him to understand hers. Yes, it had been marriage of convenience. He gave her security; she gave him companionship and a comfortable home. And yet.

'And yet I loved him,' she added aloud, warmth going

through her at the memory of those years. Even before his illness had begun to show, Walter had been a man to seize the day, enjoying every minute of his allotted time with a gusto that had rubbed off on her.

Her smile died. He would have helped her, if only she had told him. She knew he'd always sensed there was something she was keeping closed into herself, a regret, a torment she could not bear to speak about.

She'd nearly told him, that perfect summer's day when they had been visiting Paris, following his determination to see as much of the world as he could. Italy had been his big ambition for their next European tour the following year and she'd felt she couldn't let him take her to the land of her birth without some explanation. But that day they had visited the Eiffel Tower he had stumbled, nearly fallen, laughing it off with his customary good humour, neither of them knowing the rapid physical decline it foretold. But in the end, the holiday had been cut short. They had never made it to Venice. Next time, he had reassured her. Next time, they would spend a whole week in Venice, before visiting the artistic beauties of Florence and Rome. But by the end of the year, he had been confined to a wheelchair, never to visit his beloved Europe again.

Even those years, those final, painful years when she had been losing a little of him each day, had been strangely happy. The more the big burly man she had first known shrunk to a fragile creature of barely more than skin and bones, the more his zest for life had intensified. He'd love to simply sit in the sunshine in Central Park, watching the families enjoying the changing of the seasons. Stripped of everything that had made him the man he was in the world, he became more human. Just a man, facing existence, and the ending of existence, with kindness, gentleness, and an increasing empathy for the suffering of others.

He would have understood. She knew now that, of all the

people in all the world, Walter would have understood and helped her make the past right. But by then it was too late. It had become about making his last years as joyous and comfortable as they could be. She'd had no right to burden him.

That task, she had sworn inwardly, was for her alone. She was the one who had once succumbed to the cruel choice she had been given, who had been overcome by the seeming hopelessness of her position. Who had not questioned the information she'd been given. She had never once forgiven her youthful self, who had gone against a mother's every instinct without a fight to the death. Now, it was time for her older and wiser self to make things right, if it was in any way possible. If it was not already too late. That was the promise she had made to herself the night Walter died. Her way of facing the future in the absence of his love. A promise that had sent her to Italy, and to Venice, blind to the war, yet again, about to take hold of Europe.

'Well, we're both fools now,' said Magdalena.

'Rubbish,' returned Sofia. 'You'll cook and clean for your colonel, and I'll clean for the guests at the hotel. And we'll both survive.'

'If it doesn't get worse,' replied Magdalena, darkly, turning her eyes towards the tower of the church of San Giorgio Maggiore, rising up through the mist lingering over the bay. 'Who knows what will happen now America has joined the Allies. I'll tell you one thing for free, whoever wins, *il Duce* won't be the next Roman Emperor, that's for sure. And heaven help all of us who are caught in the middle. They won't even notice where the bodies fall. We are nothing, merely dust, as far as him and Hitler are concerned. We might as well be beneath the volcano as the ash falls. There'll be nothing of us left by the time this ends. You mark my words.'

EIGHT

ARDEN HOUSE

October 1941

Kate worked impatiently in the fields all day, itching for the school bell to ring, when Miss Parsons would be free to assist the WI in the village hall and attend to her beloved museum.

Finally, as the clanging of the handbell in the school yard rang through the afternoon, Kate headed off into the village. To her relief, Alma had chosen to remain at Arden house, deep in sorting out which sheets and blankets could be mended, along with how many could be spared for Miss Parson's charity for orphaned children. So long as she returned home while still daylight, and she could have still been working in the fields, no one should be any the wiser.

As Kate reached the village hall, she stepped over Montague, who was dozing contentedly in the last of the afternoon sunshine, and made her way inside. She found Miss Parsons sitting at her little workbench in the museum, contemplating the glass vessel in the beams of light streaming in through the window.

'It's beautiful,' Kate exclaimed, momentarily distracted by

seeing the object again.

'Oh, hello, my dear. Isn't it just. I've never seen anything so exquisite. I was hoping you'd come and see it. It took a while, but it's cleaned up beautifully and still in one piece, thank goodness. It is most definitely glass, and of the highest quality. You should be very proud of rescuing it from the earth, my dear. Strange to think how long it must have lain there, and nobody knew, and how easily it might have been destroyed.'

'I'm glad I found it.' Kate moved closer. With the memories of the night still surrounding her, the soft glow of the glass held her mesmerised. She was back in the heat of her childhood, and being lifted into a deep hole, with tendrils of light spilling around her. Down into shadow after the brilliance of the day's sunshine. Excited, full of wonder, but unafraid; safe in the warm arms that held her.

'Isn't it beautiful?' The voice whispering in her ear was a woman's, filled with admiration and a touch of wistfulness. As her eyes adjusted, she saw a wall, painted with figures on a dark red background, between the stylised green of olive trees, a scene of fields in the background. 'Look, darling; they've only just discovered this one. It looks like a grand house. They think it might have belonged to an independent woman, making her own way, able to do just as she pleased.'

A man's guffaw erupted from a distance, sounding hollow in the cavernous space. 'And I bet we know how she achieved that.'

The woman gave an exasperated sigh, ruffling Kate's hair with its warmth. 'What kind of thing is that to say in front of a child? That there is only one way for a woman to live?'

'Don't listen to them,' came another man's voice, gentle and reassuring, so close Kate felt the warmth of his breath on her hair. 'Only fools think like that.'

The woman's arms tightened around Kate. 'But I suspect the contessa would agree.'

The conversation continued, echoing around her in the hollow in the ground where the long-lost dwelling lay hidden. She could feel the earth closing in on them. The arms remained, protecting her, holding her tight.

The memory dissipated and Kate frowned as she tried to work out what it meant. Was that why she had always felt an affinity with the Roman villa found on the Arden estate? Those had been some of her happiest times, sketching the walls and the mosaic and the fragments of pots, along with rusted nails and the occasional bead. Was that why she had always felt so at home there?

'Kate?' She looked up to see Miss Parsons eyeing her closely.

She shook herself back to the present. 'I'm sorry, what did you say?'

'Nothing of importance, my dear. You looked as if you had seen a ghost.'

'Did I?' Kate tore her eyes from the glass. 'Maybe in a way I did. I'm not sure. I'm remembering so many things, things I never knew I'd forgotten.'

'What kind of things?' Miss Parsons was sharp.

'Papa bringing me in a boat to London, and then to Arden House.'

Miss Parsons was watching her closer than ever. 'Anything else?'

Kate returned her gaze and decided to be truthful. 'The time before. Mainly a terrace by the sea.' She sensed rather than heard Miss Parsons' intake of breath. 'Just little pieces, but they are coming back, more of them each time, and stronger. And now I know they were real, not just dreams. You were right about the Shakespeare...' She drew out the papers from her shoulder bag. 'I found this in the lining.'

'Ah,' said Miss Parsons, peering down at the drawing of the terrace.

'You knew it was there?'

'I wondered.'

'Was it my mother who put it there? My *real* mother.'

There was a moment's silence. Kate made out a struggle on the schoolmistress' face.

'Celia Arden gave me those volumes of Shakespeare when she first fell ill and knew she might not survive,' said Miss Parsons at last. 'She told me she had found the book of sonnets concealed in the base of the little suitcase you brought with you. Such a strange thing to send with a child.' She frowned. 'Or maybe not so strange, given the circumstances.'

'So it must have been my mother who put it there!' Joy knocked the breath out of her, accompanied with a relaxing deep inside. A knot of grief that had gripped Kate all her life, tinged with guilt that something she had done had caused her mother to throw her away, began to ease. She fought down an overwhelming urge to burst into tears.

'It could well have been.' Miss Parsons pressed her hand gently. 'Celia told me that it was the book of sonnets that gave her the idea of putting her own messages for your sisters.' She cleared her throat. 'I don't know if she knew these were hidden for you to find, or she simply guessed. She loved your papa dearly, but he never was the easiest of men, or the most under-standing. Even then, he never allowed anyone to go against his wishes, not even Celia. Especially anything he believed might threaten the future of Arden,' she added thoughtfully. 'That included you and your sisters being encouraged to live your own lives, rather than marrying the richest man available.'

'Like Henry Luscombe,' said Kate, with a shudder.

'Quite,' replied Miss Parsons, a wry expression passing over her face. 'Sadly, I doubt it has entered your papa's mind to ques-tion whether the misery of a daughter's life with a man like Luscombe might be too high a price to pay to restore Arden House to its former glory. Not that Leo Arden would ever be

intentionally cruel,' she added hastily. 'Just very good at
convincing himself that what he wants is for the best, while
being conveniently blind to the well-being of others.'

'Ouch,' said Kate, who had never thought of Papa this way,
but, once stated aloud, made perfect sense. *If I'm to have any
life at all, I have to escape.* The recognition went through her,
more powerfully than before. She gazed down at the drawing.
'My mother must have put this there so that one day I could
find her. She wanted us to be together again. There has to be a
way I can know where she is now.'

'I hope so.' Miss Parsons turned to carefully place the
precious Roman vase in a case that looked as if it had been
made from one of the cold frames from the garden, and had
been cleared to give Kate's find pride of place. 'But, given the
way things are, you are going to have to prepare yourself for the
worst, my dear.'

'You must know something!' Kate bit her lip at the look on
the schoolmistress's face. Italy was the enemy, the ally of Hitler.
Who could know what was happening there, and who might
survive.

Miss Parsons sighed. 'I wish I could tell you more. I'm afraid
at the time, I was too wrapped up in my own grief at the loss of
my fiancé, to take the interest I should have done. Love is utterly
selfish. Shakespeare's sonnets are right. It's just you and the
beloved, and that's all there is, if you are truly in love. I saw
afterwards I should have taken more notice of what was
happening. Maybe I could have done something, though
heavens knows what. I can never forgive myself.' She fell silent,
lost in thought.

'Did you meet my mother?' The words tumbled out of her.
'Did she come to England too? What was she like?'

Miss Parsons turned to scrutinise her. 'Dear Kate. You are
so young, and know so little of the world. Are you sure you want
to go on this journey?'

'Of course. I have to know. It wasn't just this picture I found hidden.' She brought out the other two images. 'There's this.' She smoothed out the view of the Grand Canal on the surface next to the terrace view.

'Why, that's Venice,' said Miss Parsons, frowning. 'I can't think why that would be there. What a strange thing to do.'

For a moment Kate hesitated, then she placed the portrait of the contessa between the two. 'And this.'

'Oh my lord.' Miss Parsons sat down hard. 'I had no idea. Oh, my dear, why didn't I think? Why on earth did I give you that wretched book?'

'You know her?'

'I know who she is.' Miss Parsons held the portrait at arm's length, as if alarmed to have it any closer. 'The contessa is your grandmother.'

'My *what*?' Kate stared at her. She'd never had a grand-mother. Papa's mother had died long before she was born, and she had never met Alma's mother, who had died not long after Alma came into their lives.

'She was said to have been a famous beauty in her day. And ambitious. The story was that she was born poor, to an English mother and an Italian father. An outsider. I was told her father abandoned the family while she was still a baby, leaving mother and daughter to survive on the streets of Naples. I've worked with a charity out there, looking after such unfortunates. Believe me, it's an environment not many could survive. But your grandmother's looks and her charm enabled her to marry into the Italian aristocracy. That must be the view from their palazzo.'

'So that's where I was born? In Venice?'

There was a moment's silence. 'No,' said Miss Parsons at last. 'No, my dear. One thing I can tell you is that you have never been in Venice. You've never seen your grandmother, and she has never set her eyes on you.' She took her hand. 'Don't take that to heart, my dear. Her survival, as it often is, was won at a terrible price. Not a lot of the milk of human kindness there, I'm afraid.'

'Lady Macbeth.'

Miss Parsons cleared her throat. 'Ah. You made the connection.'

'I saw the illustration in Cordelia's book.'

'Yes, of course. You always were the noticing kind, and you have an artist's eye. It was only natural you would see the likeness.' Miss Parsons frowned at her. 'You've pursued your passion, for all the obstacles that have been placed in your way.'

'By Papa mostly,' sighed Kate.

'Well, a lot of men aren't very sophisticated, emotionally speaking,' said Miss Parsons drily. 'I'm afraid your father falls into that category, much of the time. The trick is, if you come across one who has natural aptitude in that department, or has had it drilled into him by a determined mother, make sure you don't let him go.'

'Miss Parsons!' The schoolmistress was known for her forthright opinions, but Kate had never heard her say anything quite so outrageously against everything Kate had been taught about love and marriage.

'It's perfectly true. The rest, I'm afraid, are likely to lead a woman to a lonelier life than living with your own company. At least that way you never have to endure being treated as if your deepest experiences are merely domestic fluff, and that women never have anything serious to say.'

'Papa doesn't believe women can be serious, or follow a profession. He's determined that I should stay at Arden House, and never find out my past. I'm sure that's why he wouldn't let me take up my place at the Slade and go to study in London before the war. Sometimes, I'm not sure he even likes me. He just doesn't want to let me go.'

'I feel certain he loves you in his way, my dear,' Miss

Parsons replied gently. 'But he has no right preventing you from following your own path, even if he believes it is to protect you.' She concentrated on arranging the Roman vase so it caught the light from the window, revealing its colour to perfection. 'Are you serious about wanting to leave Arden?'

'Yes,' said Kate firmly. 'I know I can't study in London, and I'm not sure I could bear to while the war is on. It feels so self-indulgent with so much suffering taking place around us all the time. I want to do something useful. And to live my own life while I've still got the chance.'

'Hmm.' Miss Parsons was silent for a few minutes, deep in thought. 'Very well. You leave it with me.' She patted Kate's hand gently. 'Wait here a moment.' Miss Parsons disappeared into the back of the museum, returning with a small wooden box, dark with age. The top was faded with much polishing, but still revealed an inlaid border of stylised leaves, surrounding the figure of a tufted-headed grebe, which rested delicately on the merest hint of water.

'I think I had better give you this in case Mr Arden proves stubborn and forbids me to speak to you again. Celia told me you were wearing it under your clothing when you arrived. She made me promise to hide it, and especially to make sure your papa never set eyes on it. It's the only time I ever heard her express any regret...' Miss Parsons cleared her throat. 'Yes, well. Hindsight is a truly wonderful thing.'

Kate's heart beat too fast to question her. There was a tiny metal catch at one side of the box. With a bit of fiddling, she managed to release it, opening up the lid to a lined velvet inside, containing a small oval surrounded in a small scrap of raw silk. Gingerly, she lifted and unwrapped the object until it was free, revealing a pendant attached to a necklace made of the finest silver.

'It's beautiful,' she whispered, awed.

'Celia said that it was the only link your mother had with

Venice. I've been unsure whether to give it to you, until now.
Celia sounded so certain that if it was ever found it would be
destroyed, and it would be quite impossible to hide such a thing
completely in Arden House. So while you are still there make
sure you never let it out of your sight, or you might lose it
forever. Remember, this is for you alone.'

Kate nodded, holding up the translucent oval of blues and
greens that appeared to flow within the glass. There was a
strange tingling in her belly. She didn't remember ever seeing
the pendant before, and yet there was the same sensation
flowing through her that she had felt when she had first seen the
handle of the little Roman vessel emerging from the earth.

She turned to Miss Parsons. 'Is it—?'

'Murano glass? Yes, my dear, I believe it is. I don't know
how you came to be wearing it when you arrived in Arden, or
why. All I know is that it is yours, and one day it may open a
door for you to find your past.'

Kate held the pendant in her hands, feeling its smooth solid-
ity, seeing the passion of fire held within. Her mother's hands
had touched this. Perhaps they had been the last to surround it
with her living warmth, as she fastened it around the neck of
the small daughter she was to lose, maybe knowing it was
forever. Kate could feel the love, and the agony of loss, held
within her own grasp.

Why did you let me go?

'Thank you,' said Kate, tears welling up in her eyes. 'I
thought I had nothing from my mother.'

'She was always there with you,' replied Miss Parsons,
kissing her. 'I'm sure of it. Every hour of every day, for all of
your life. Believe me. She may not have been able to prevent
you from being taken away, but as long as she breathes, I am
certain she will never abandon you. She will always be there,
somewhere, waiting to be found.'

NINE

Miss Parsons was as good as her word, arriving at Arden House late the following afternoon.

Kate hesitated at the top of the mahogany staircase, trying to catch the words in the library. As voices were raised, she crept down as close to the closed door of the library as she dared.

'At least this way you have a choice of where she goes,' said Miss Parsons. 'You know she will be looked after and kept safe. If conscription of women comes in, which it is bound to before long, Kate could be sent anywhere. Do you want her working in a munitions factory, where she will most certainly be a target for German bombers?'

'Alma needs her.' Papa sounded even more stubborn than usual. 'Besides, the young are marrying like there's no tomorrow. She could easily have a husband and with a child on the way within months. That would release her from any forced service in a factory or an auxiliary service. She will stay here.'

Kate gritted her teeth. This was hopeless.

'Is this what Celia would have wanted?' Miss Parson's voice was sharp.

'That's got nothing to do with it.'

'Of course it has. She accepted your choice because she loved you and wanted what was best for the children.'

'I will not be told...' Papa's voice was dangerous, all set for flying into one of his rages. Kate braced herself. This was when even the bravest of the household usually fled. But there was no opening of the door, no footsteps high tailing it away from danger. Miss Parsons was standing her ground.

'You can shut your ears all you wish, Leo,' she said, 'but that won't shut out the truth. Don't you think that one day they're bound to find out? If they find you've tried to hide such a thing, you will lose them.' There was a moment's pause. 'All of them.'

Kate held her breath for an almighty storm. Instead, there was just the crackling of the logs in the grate. In the hallway below, the sunset was reflected on the flagstones, showing up ghosts of dust, swirling in the corners.

'I'll think about it,' Papa said at last.

Kate paused from turning to retreat back upstairs. She had never heard her father sound so unsure of himself. More than that, defeated; his customary bluster gone. This was another Papa, another Leo Arden. And another Miss Parsons, who addressed him as if they were equals, rather than he the lord of the manor and she the village schoolmistress.

Kate should have been triumphant to find the chink in his armour, but instead she felt an icy line sliver between her shoulder blades. Miss Parsons was talking about all of the Arden children, not just her. What on earth could Papa have done that could have such dire consequences for the entire Arden family? She instinctively touched the pendant of Murano glass, which she was now wearing around her neck, carefully hidden beneath her blouse and jumper. Was that why she been dragged from her mother's arms? Could that be the secret that might destroy them all?

She might have rebelled against her place in the world, but it had given her a form of security: the world strong enough to be rebelled against. Now it felt fragile, as if it could be torn apart at any minute, to reveal foundations more crumbling than Arden's walls, and more haunted than any strange creaking in the attic as the wind blew in from the east.

'Mark my words,' remarked Miss Parsons, 'you'll regret it if you don't.'

At that, he gave a low chuckle, a sound so surprising Kate jumped, nearly betraying her presence by knocking the suit of armour quietly rusting next to the door.

'You've looked out for my girls over the years. I don't know what they'd have done without you.' His voice softened, sounding even more like a version of himself Kate had never heard before. A younger version, she found herself thinking. The man he had once been, before the unexpected death of his older brother had dragged him from being the second son of less worth, but at the same time free to live his life as he pleased. The time before he had been forced to take over the responsibility of Arden House and its vast – if now diminished – grounds, and the ever-increasing shabbiness of Brierley-in-Arden. 'D'you know, I sometimes wish—'

'No you don't.' Miss Parsons was tart. 'You never were very fond of loudmouthed females with minds of their own.' She sniffed. 'And you clearly haven't considered my feelings on the matter. So there's no good turning sentimental at this late stage.'

Kate choked back a laugh. She'd never heard anyone speak to Papa like that before.

'None of us were children,' Miss Parsons continued. 'We all made our choices over the years. You, me and Celia, God help us. Now we must live with them. But we all agreed, all of us,' she added with emphasis, 'that the children should never be the ones to pay. Whatever it might cost us. Celia once swore she'd hold you to that. Well, I'm holding you to it in her place.'

Kate headed back up the stairs, pausing in the shadows as Miss Parsons emerged. The schoolmistress gazed around at the faded interior for a moment, lit by the stained-glass window halfway up the stairs, with its scenes from Shakespeare's plays, now half covered even in daylight by a blackout curtain too heavy to pull fully back. Kate caught a look of profound sadness crossing the schoolmistress's features. Was it also grief? Her expression was hastily banished as Alma appeared from the direction of the kitchens.

'You are very welcome to join us, Miss Parsons. You mustn't feel you'd be a burden – thanks to the Land Girls we aren't wholly dependent on rationing. We have plenty to share.'

'Thank you, Mrs Arden, but I'd rather get back before the light goes, and the constable is after me for using a flashlight and bringing the Luftwaffe down on our heads.'

'I hope my husband wasn't impatient with you. He is always willing to help the children of the village and evacuees as much as he can.'

'He's been very generous,' replied Miss Parsons.

'Yes, of course.' Alma's voice was thin, with the tremor of a woman who understood perfectly well that the conversation in the library had been about more than a loose tile or the sourcing of old wallpaper for children to draw on, but did not dare confront either her husband, or a woman whose connection to the family went back to the days of the first Mrs Arden. A wife whose memory, Kate saw in a flash, was forever caught in an idealised haze, one that Alma was all too aware she could never compete with.

Love is a strange thing, thought Kate, as she watched her stepmother accompany Miss Parsons to the front door. Love in all its forms and variations, not just the love lost and gained that was described so passionately in the sonnets. Kate was no longer sure she understood the meaning of the word.

· · ·

Later that night, as the dishes were cleared away after the evening meal, which Papa insisted still be taken by the family in the formal drawing room, Kate was surprised to see him beckoning her to abandon the last set of dishes and sit opposite him.

'I promised I'd help Lucy,' she said, unwilling to face a fight.

'You are not a servant.'

'It's all right, my dear, I'll take them,' murmured her stepmother, seizing the offending plates and vanishing.

Kate sat, hiding the nervous twisting of her hands under the table.

'I hear you have a hankering to leave us.'

'To do my bit for the war effort, Papa. I've always enjoyed helping Miss Parsons with the village children. I can't think of anything more important than helping those who have been through such terrible suffering and lost everything.'

'Hmm.' He frowned at her, eyebrows bristling in the light from the single candle on the table. The flame swayed in a breeze going through the rafters, setting shadows dancing in the corners. She held her breath.

He cleared his throat, awkwardly. 'I shall miss you.'

'I'll miss you too,' she said, with an unexpected tightness in her throat. Did this mean she could go? Her heart soared.

'Indeed.' There was a brooding look on his face. It went through her mind that he felt that, once gone, he would never see her again. Perhaps, for all his irritation and impatience, there was some deep link between them, after all.

'Papa—'

But he had already turned his head away, concentrating on the fire. 'Your mama should really not be assisting Lucy quite so much, war or no war. Between that and her interests in the village, she's hardly here at all. This is where she should be, no wandering off all over the place.'

'I'll go and help her,' muttered Kate, escaping before he could protest. As she reached the corridor she breathed in deep, her whole body loosening. She was going to escape! Her life was going to be her own, at last. And perhaps she could use that freedom to follow the clues left to her by her mother and find her, wherever she might really be.

Unable to face anyone for few minutes, as the mix of emotions whirled inside her, Kate stepped outside into the garden, where the evening was darkening, all lights extinguished. The last bus was making its way along the road in the direction of Stratford-upon-Avon, lights lowered. Unexpected sadness went through her. For all she wanted to find her past, this felt like saying goodbye to the only family she had ever known. Whatever happened, if she found the secret of who her mother was, or not, she would be changed by the time she returned.

She missed her siblings with a deep ache, straight to the heart. The silence felt unnervingly vast, spreading out of the landscape of fields and hedges disappearing into the dark. For as long as she could remember, she had wandered these fields, given, like her sisters, a freedom denied to the daughters of the other large houses around. Many of these more ladylike acquaintances were now volunteering, perhaps taking advantage of their distance from the eyes of watchful parents, heading for their own escape from domestic tedium.

'I thought you might be here.' Kate looked up to find Alma watching her, thin shoulders hunched against the wind. 'It seems you are leaving us.'

'Yes.' Fear went through Kate. She was feeling too fragile, her emotions too raw, to wish for a fight. With Papa it was a battle of wills, but with Alma it would be the struggle of conflicting emotions where there was no winner, only loss and hurt left behind. 'You can't stop me.'

'No.' A strange look passed over her stepmother's face. 'Don't worry, my dear, I'm not about to try. I will be sad without you. I'll miss you, as will your father, but I understand. This vile war can't last forever. I hope you find what you are seeking.'

Kate eyed her curiously. She had always seen her step-mother as a shadowy presence, too subject to their father's whims to be an ally. All the children had known her first loyalty was to him. In a flash, Kate saw a bleak reality she had never recognised before. Without Papa, Alma was nothing. She might be trapped in her life; she might, for all Kate knew, hate it and everything about it, and resent the unruly pack of children who had faced her, furious and lost in their grief, rebelling against her presence and all that it represented.

'You don't blame me for leaving?'

Alma sighed. 'How can I? I left home once, when I was young, and a war seemed to offer me an escape and a way of being free from being stifled at home.' She pulled her coat closer about her. 'But I didn't have a passion, like yours for drawing and illustration. I didn't have a skill that might enable me to escape from the drudgery of clerical work. I lost faith in myself.' She winced. 'Returning was the worst thing I ever did.'

There was a moment's silence, then her chin rose. 'I wouldn't want that for you, my dear. I know my family only wanted to protect me, in the best way they knew. But we all have our destinies to fulfil. The thing is to take them, whatever the difficulties, whatever the journeys. Otherwise, all too soon, the opportunities are gone.'

'I'll come back,' said Kate, impulsively. Now she was on the verge of escaping, a deep pull was bringing her back to the only home she had ever truly known, the place that, for all its conflicts, was the secure centre of her existence. She couldn't bear the idea of leaving, with no way back, like Rosalind. That would leave her truly adrift.

'You'll always be welcome, darling,' said Alma. 'This will always be your home.'

Kate hugged her, trying to ignore the startled look in her stepmother's eyes at this unwarranted show of affection.

For all Alma's words, she had a feeling that that her stepmother sensed that this was goodbye. Just as much as Kate knew, with an exhilarating mixture of excitement and terror, that Arden House would never be her home, ever again.

TEN

A few days later, Kate travelled with Miss Parsons to Birmingham, first taking the bus from Brierley to Stratford-upon-Avon, followed by the train.

As they finally arrived at the station in Birmingham, Kate was thrilled to see Cordelia waiting for them on the platform.

'You did it,' exclaimed her sister, hugging her tightly. 'You've escaped!' She smelt of soap and city streets, with the lingering hint of cigarette smoke that these days seemed to pervade everywhere.

'Told you I would,' said Kate affectionately, returning her embrace.

Cordelia turned to the schoolmistress with a smile. 'It's good to see you again Miss Parsons.'

'And you too, my dear,' replied Miss Parsons, kissing Cordelia.

'I'm afraid you'll find there are even more children than we expected at the house. There was an even worse raid a few nights ago, with so many people killed. It's filled to bursting. There are so many tragic stories, poor things, and you can see they relive them all each time they hear the slightest noise – a vehicle outside, a bang of a door – let alone when the raids start. They really need peace and quiet.'

'Then the sooner we can get them away into the country-side the better,' replied Miss Parsons.

Cordelia took one of the bags containing precious vegeta-bles from Arden and swung it easily over her shoulder.

'The car's just outside,' she said, falling into step alongside Kate. 'As soon as I heard you were coming with Miss Parsons, I rearranged my shifts at the factory so I could be the one to meet you.'

'I'm so glad you did,' replied Kate. She had expected to find her sister pale and nervous, but apart from the evidence of a lack of sleep around her eyes, she had a confidence and a poise Kate did not remember. 'You've cut your hair.'

'More practical,' said Cordelia, running her fingers through her fair curls, now shaped into a bob around her face. 'It's so hard to get hold of soap, even though it isn't rationed, thank goodness, and I'm always too tired to think about washing it. Besides, there isn't always water, or electricity, after a particularly bad raid. You never know what's going to happen next.' She smiled at Kate's own dark locks, which she had chopped to below her ears several years ago in a moment of rebellion at only ever being praised for the length of her hair, and had kept it short ever since. 'You had the right idea, after all, you see.'

They emerged into a scene of rubble and broken buildings, causing Kate to stop in her tracks. It was one thing seeing photographs of unknown cities with only the skeletons of build-ings left standing. It was quite another to be faced with the remains of the wallpaper in rooms torn apart, with rubble and glass collapsed onto the road and the pavement, where they were being cleared away as if it was nothing out of the ordinary.

'Is it very terrible?' Kate queried, feeling a sudden sliver of fear. 'I'm sure we don't hear the half of it out in the country, and they only ever say a 'Midlands Town', so we are never sure if it's Birmingham or not.'

'It can be hellish at times,' replied Cordelia. 'Other nights not so much. The worst thing is that you never know. I suppose you get used to it, after a fashion. St Mary's, the old hospital where the orphans are staying, has been lucky so far with just a few incendiaries. We can hear the bombing in the city and see it.' She grimaced. 'I never thought I'd spend the night fire watching on the roof, then pick myself up and go to work in a factory the next morning. Everyone else is in the same boat. At least being busy doesn't give you time to think.'

'I suppose,' said Kate, not entirely convinced she would be brave enough to do the same. She looked around at the men and women passing the station in their utility clothing, everything mended to make it last as long as possible, exhaustion mingled with dogged determination in every step.

She realised that she, like all those living in the countryside, knew nothing of the war taking place on home soil. They had the dread of a stray bomb, along with the ever-present fear of Hitler's parachutes appearing in the sky signalling the start of the invasion and what that might mean for all of them. But none of them had experienced the bombardment of the great cities and the industrial heartland of the Black Country surrounding Birmingham.

Kate shuddered. The haunted look of the evacuee children she'd worked with in Miss Parson's school took on a new meaning, along with their crayon drawings of shattered houses, the bright red covering the fallen bodies, some with limbs severed and lying to one side.

What must it be like to have lived through such destruction, to see all those you loved torn to pieces in front of you? It had been agony enough to be torn from loving arms, but she had been taken to a place where she had been loved and cared for, and given the freedom to wander the countryside (up to a

point), and pursue her childhood passion for painting and drawing. This house was the last refuge for those who had no one
left, and none to care for them. She remembered how terrifying
it had felt as a child, totally dependent on those around her, to
be sent off into the unknown, where anything might happen,
and she had no power to do anything about it. Her heart went
out to the children who had been left with nothing, only the
most haunting of memories.

'We're all surviving together,' explained Cordelia, leading
the way to a battered Ford parked a short way from the station.
'At least most of us are. Some, like the black marketeers, are
making a fortune, but the rest of us are taking care we all have
enough and keeping each other as safe as possible.'

They loaded their bags into the boot, and Miss Parsons took
the passenger seat in the front, while Kate squeezed into the
back with piled up offerings of pillows and blankets destined for
the charity. Cordelia, like all of the sisters, had been taught to
drive by Jamie, but had been the most nervous behind the
wheel. Kate watched in admiration as her sister manoeuvred
expertly between the few cars to be seen on the roads, dodging
ambulances and fire engines, and the mounds of rubble from
last night's raid still partially blocking some streets as it was
hastily cleared away.

Peering through her window, Kate could see the city was
not at all as she remembered from the few times that she had
been permitted to accompany Jamie to lectures held by the
Archaeological Society. The starkness of broken walls and
empty windows of shops and homes sent a chill through her.
Much of what remained was blackened by fire. She dreaded to
think what might have happened to anyone who had not found
their way to shelters in time.

After a while, the signs of destruction lessened as they
headed out into one of the smaller suburbs. Finally, Cordelia
turned into a tree-lined street which appeared almost

completely untouched, and bordered by a small park. She eased the Ford through a gate bearing the name St *Mary's*, stopping in front of a large building that must have once been the pride of the street, but now appeared more than a little shabby.

As Cordelia drew up in front of the main door, it was opened by a dark-haired young woman Kate recognised from lectures at the Birmingham Archaeological Society she'd attended with Jamie before the war. She remembered Gina Sidoli had been fascinated by Jamie's description of the Roman villa he was uncovering at Arden. Their discussions of its possible links to the rest of the forgotten world beneath their feet had been beyond Kate, but she'd caught their enthusiasm.

'Miss Parsons.' Gina exclaimed. 'It's so good to see you again. And bearing gifts as usual, I see.'

'These are from Mrs Arden, Gina, dear,' replied Miss Parsons. 'She knows how much you need fresh produce.'

'Whatever you bring from the countryside always feels like a miracle these days,' replied Gina with a grin.

'You remember Kate,' said Cordelia. 'I think you attended lectures together before the war.'

'Yes of course.' Gina's smile was warm. 'And your beautiful drawings of the mosaic that Jamie was uncovering. They made me feel as if I was really there. Cordelia showed me one of your drawings of the remains of a ship found at Sutton Hoo, from when you visited before the war. I would have given my eyeteeth to go with the rest of the Archaeological Society, but I'm afraid my family didn't approve, even when my cousin Peter offered to act as a chaperone. Very traditional,' she added with a wink. 'The way Jamie described it made me want to see the excavation even more. It seems so sad it's been buried again, even if it is to keep it safe.'

'I'm sure you'll get a chance to see it once the war is over,' said Kate. 'Jamie told us that Mrs Petty was determined the excavation would resume once the men came home.'

'Let's hope so,' Gina replied. There was a moment's silence, thoughts travelling, as they always did, to those fighting to keep them free of invasion, and dread of the news arriving to end all hope that they would ever see them again. You couldn't think of it every moment of every day, or it would drive you mad. But it was there beneath the surface of everything they did.

Gina led the way into the house. The once-grand hallway had been stripped of furnishings, leaving a strangely echoing space that led into the main rooms, which were larger and plainer than those of a private house, a reminder of the building's past as a small private hospital. Kate could hear a man's voice coming from one of the rooms, interspersed with the subdued murmur of children's voices.

'We've turned the ward next to the gardens into a schoolroom, as you suggested Miss Parsons, and Peter is coming each day to give lessons. My cousin, Peter Sidoli,' she explained to Kate. 'I'm not sure how much they are taking in, but that's not really the point.'

'I'm sure the routine and something to occupy their minds will do them good.' Miss Parsons smiled. 'Kate has been working with the children at the school in Brierley-in-Arden, especially the evacuees, encouraging them to draw.'

'I'd love to try it with the children here,' said Kate, eagerly. 'If you think it will help.'

'I'm sure it will do them the world of good,' replied Gina. 'I don't have the skills myself – I feel far too self-conscious. But wherever I've taught, both here and back home in Wales, I've always found children, especially the very young, tend to express their deepest joys and fears best through painting and drawing. It seems to be their natural medium, far more than words.'

'So it is,' replied Kate thoughtfully, aware of Miss Parsons sending a knowing glance in her direction. Drawing had come so naturally to her, she'd never thought about it that way. The rest of her education, like that of her sisters, had been fairly minimal, made up for by devouring the books in Papa's library. But drawing had always been her refuge, the one thing she could hold onto from her past and that elusive memory of the woman – who had surely been her mother – holding her, guiding her, encouraging her.

How had she forgotten that she had felt inexpressibly lost when she had first arrived at Arden House? Until, that is, the little suitcase with her few bits of clothing and her favourite doll had revealed a sketchpad and a set of coloured pencils, carefully tied up with a silk ribbon, tucked inside the neatly folded cardigans and underclothes. If Magdalena had found them, or the book of sonnets, she had not mentioned their presence to Papa.

Magdalena.

'Kate?' She found Cordelia gazing at her with concern at her sharp intake of breath. 'Are you all right?'

'It's nothing,' Kate reassured her. How could she explain the name that she had been searching for suddenly appearing in her mind out of nowhere, another piece of the puzzle that had just fallen into place?

Magdalena.

That had been the name Papa had been calling that day she had escaped from the confines of the little cabin on the yacht taking her to Arden and the freedom of the wild air. *Magdalena.* Not her mother, but someone close; the woman who had accompanied her to England.

So now she had a name. A name with a link to her past. Although how she was to find the woman in the black coat, even if she was still alive, any more than the contessa in her Venetian palazzo, or her mother herself, Kate had no idea. But one day this war must end. If there was a Venice left, she would find a way of travelling there. Miss Parsons managed it, long ago, when women wore trailing skirts and corsets and weren't even allowed to vote. If she survived and the world began to heal again, Kate told herself, there had to be a way.

Mind still whirring, Kate followed the others into the corridor towards the back of the house. As they passed the open door of what had once been the dining room, she caught a glimpse of children sitting round the table, many on cushions to enable them to see over its edge, supervised by a dark-haired young man in a battered corduroy jacket, one arm in a sling. There was an unnatural silence in the room, not even a cough or the dropping of a pencil, as their teacher quietly continued with a story of King Arthur.

At the sound of footsteps, Peter Sidoli looked up, his eyes resting on Kate. For a moment, there was a look of such hostility within their depths that she stopped in her tracks, returning his gaze with a frown. He turned instantly away, resuming his story of Excalibur and the Lady of the Lake. It was such a brief exchange, Kate wondered if she had imagined it. She was certain she had never set eyes on him before in her life. With his arm so heavily bandaged, surely she must have mistaken an expression of pain, not one directed at her in particular? All the same, the sensation remained as she hurried after the others.

They deposited their gifts of vegetables on the table in the centre of the large kitchen, before being provided with cups of tea. As Miss Parsons headed off to join the volunteers sorting out bedding and clothing for the new arrivals, Gina led Kate to a large room at the back of the house, overlooking the large garden.

The room was filled with children quietly playing with dolls and toy trains. The older ones looked up, as if to reassure themselves that the new arrivals posed no harm, before hastily returning to their occupations. Most were around seven or eight, although several looked to be barely walking. They were all dressed warmly in jumpers and coats against the rawness of the unheated room, as precious coal and wood were reserved for when the weather turned icy. Several of the younger children were swathed in cardigans that were clearly too big for them. Kate felt a catch in her throat at the realisation that their own clothing had most probably been damaged beyond repair, or they had been dragged out of homes and shelters in nothing but their night clothes.

For a moment Kate was unnerved by the silence, so unlike the suppressed eagerness of the children she had taught in Brierley. She could see the haunted look in the eyes of those few among them who glanced at her briefly as she passed.

'Miss Arden has come to help you with drawing pictures,' said Gina cheerfully, laying out rolls of wallpaper, placing the unpatterned side upwards, along with pencils and crayons on the table set. 'Who's going to be the first to choose a colour?' No one moved, or even betrayed that they had heard.

'It's all right,' said Kate, quickly. 'Anyone can join me if they want. They don't have to.' She had learnt patience from her time working with the evacuees at Miss Parsons's school, and to have faith that a child's natural curiosity and impulse to draw would bring them of their own accord. Gina looked a little dubious, but was soon distracted by a boy of about five, who was squirming uncomfortably, in need of the latrine.

Kate sat quietly as Gina vanished with the boy. She drew a quick sketch of the garden, followed by the view from her window at Arden House, still so vivid in her memory, until two of the girls playing with a well-loved poodle on wheels whispered to each other and abandoned their toy to stand behind her.

'Is that where you live, Miss?' asked the first girl who appeared around seven, fair plaits running down her back, each tied with a jauntily crimson ribbon.

'Yes, it is,' replied Kate, smiling.

'Posh,' opined the second girl, who was smaller and appeared a few years younger, eyes straying longingly towards the coloured crayons.

'Falling apart,' replied Kate, with a grin. 'You should hear the windows rattle when the wind gets up.' A faint ripple of amusement went through the room. 'You can come and join me, if you like,' she added, casually. 'That's what the crayons are for.' The two glanced at each other, as if for reassurance, before clambering onto the chairs.

'I'm Pamela, Miss,' confided the girl with plaits as she reached for the brightest red crayon in the tin.

'And I'm Elizabeth,' said the second girl, peering solemnly at Kate beneath a dark fringe. 'But you can call me Nell.'

'Pretty names,' Kate said, cutting two pieces from the rolls of wallpaper and placing them in front of the girls, aware from the corner of her eye that the boys playing with the Hornby train set were following their every move while pretending not to. 'There you go.'

'Can I have pink?' asked Nell, uncertainly.

'Yes, of course. It's up to you which one you choose,' said Kate.

'It was her mum's favourite colour,' explained Pamela, in a whisper. 'We're cousins,' she added, confidentially. 'We lived next door to each other. Auntie Pat didn't have an Anderson shelter, so they always came in with us.' Her crayon slashed a bright red line across the page.

'I see,' murmured Kate, feeling suddenly overwhelmed and not sure what to say. The children evacuated to Brierley-in-Arden had mostly escaped before the worst of the bombing began. From the bruises and scratches visible on Pamela's arms as she reached for a second crayon, the girls had escaped from the shelter only days ago. If they were here, that meant the adults with them had not survived, or had been too injured to take responsibility.

'I'm going to draw the garden,' said Pamela. 'Just like you did.'

'That sounds a good idea,' replied Kate. 'It's beautiful, even though the summer flowers have gone.' She turned to Nell, who was hesitating, fat pink crayon in one hand.

'I don't know what to draw, Miss,' she said.

'Anything,' replied Kate.

'But I'm not very good.'

'It doesn't matter. Draw patterns, if you prefer. Or the teddy,' she added, nodding towards the toy placed on the table.

'Can I draw the seaside?'

'Of course you can.'

'I've never seen the sea,' Nell remarked, starting with tentative lines. 'Mum said we could all go to Blackpool one day. She was saving. Only that was before...' Her face scrunched up, fighting back the tears.

Kate's heart went out to her. She might not know much about children, but she did understand being alone, bereft of everything that had been her world.

'I came over the sea when I was a little girl,' Kate said, taking a fresh piece of paper, 'in a boat.' She began sketching a picture story version of a boat, with a curved bow and a sail. Nell watched, intrigued. 'From a place far away.' She smiled down at the face that had relaxed a little, absorbed in the emerging vessel. 'I didn't know anyone, and I can remember being frightened about where I was going. But people were kind to me when I got there.'

'Didn't your mum come with you?' asked Pamela, looking up from her own drawing.

Kate became aware of the group of boys joining them, followed by several more of the girls, each one hanging on her answer with an unnatural intensity. 'No,' she replied quietly.

'Did she die?' asked Nell.

'I'm not sure,' said Kate. Nell was small for her age, but the

brown eyes that looked up at her were solemn with an understanding far beyond her years. A childish face that life had
touched with its sorrows and, like so many of those now settling
around the table, would never quite be that of a child again.

'You mean, she sent you away?' demanded one of the boys.

'I think she had no choice,' said Kate gently. 'I'm sure, if she
could, she would have found a way for me to not be sent away,
or to come with me.'

'Yes, she would,' said Pamela, voice wavering. 'Mum and
Dad and Auntie Pat didn't make it,' she added. It must have
been the first time any of them had voiced it aloud. Kate could
see in the child's face the full dawning of a terrible realisation.
'We're never going to see them again, are we?'

There was a moment's silence. What was there to say? Kate
could feel the tears welling up in the preoccupied faces
around her.

Pamela blew her nose on her handkerchief. 'What's the sea
like, Miss?'

'Beautiful,' replied Kate. She began to sketch the shoreline
of her memory, the cliffs seen through the pillar opening out
into the sweep of the bay with the mountain in the far distance.
She felt the eyes watching her every move, and the tension ease
at the distraction. 'It's deep blue, deeper than the sky even. It's
warm and clear, goes on forever, and fishes dart between the
rocks and nibble at your feet.'

'That sounds very exotic,' said a new voice.

Kate jumped. She had been so absorbed she hadn't seen
Peter Sidoli appearing at the door.

'It's just the sea,' she returned.

'I remember it at home in Wales as cold, with sand blowing
in your face,' he replied, his eyes resting on her face, with the
same expression she had seen before, the one she could not
read. 'And gritty in the sandwiches. I'd have preferred your
beach.'

'It's just my imagination,' she returned. 'It can be anything I like.'

'As you wish.' He turned to Gina, who was now returning with the small boy. 'I'll take the children out into the garden to get some fresh air now it's stopped raining. It'll be dark before long.'

'Good idea,' said Gina. 'You can come back to your drawing,' she added to the beginnings of protest. 'Usually you can't wait to get outside.'

'Will you still be here, Miss?' asked Pamela.

'Yes, I will,' replied Kate. 'I'm staying here tonight.'

'You coming with us to the countryside?' said Nell.

'We're going by train,' added one of the older boys, sounding impressed.

'I hope so,' said Kate. 'And I'm bringing my crayons and my pencils. I wouldn't go anywhere without them. Wherever we go, there's bound to be bits of old wallpaper to use.'

Reassured that the drawing materials were not about to vanish into thin air, the children clambered down from the table to join the others now chattering in the hallway. Minutes later, Kate saw them heading outside onto the lawn.

As Kate reached for her own coat, she found Cordelia beckoning to her. 'They'll be fine out there – Peter and Gina will keep an eye on them. Come on, I haven't seen you for ages, and Miss Parsons is arranging for you all to leave as soon as possible, so we might not get another chance to catch up. I've so much to tell you, and you told me in your letters you had something to show me. Come on, I'm dying for a cup of tea, and I've a place we won't be disturbed.'

ELEVEN

Cordelia filled the teapot in the kitchen, pouring the tea into tin mugs before leading the way up to the highest floors, through a small attic and out onto the flat roof at the back of the old hospital.

'This is where we take it in turns to do fire watching,' she explained. 'It's the tallest building in the area, you can see for miles around. If an incendiary hits the roof, it's my job to put it out before it does any serious damage.'

'Is that often?' asked Kate, who had never thought of Cordelia being quite so exposed to the bombing.

'Only occasionally. The thing is, you never know when. There are firewatchers on buildings all over the city. I'm not sure I'd want to be one of those in the centre, or in the industrial parts that are bombed all the time. That must be terrifying. From what I can see, I'm sure they don't say half of what's going on in the newspapers and the newsreels. So as not to frighten people, I suppose. Bad for morale.'

Kate peered over the parapet towards the rows of roofs of terraced houses, the long strips of gardens where housewives were bringing in the washing. Children played in the streets, as the smell of cooking arose. In the green of the park, she could see mothers pushing perambulators around a small pond, while couples walked slowly, savouring every moment together in the brief calm of an autumn afternoon. It was hard to believe that somewhere beyond the English Channel men and planes were being prepared night after night – now, this minute – to destroy such a peaceful existence.

'Aren't you afraid?'

'Sometimes,' confessed Cordelia. 'The tiring bit is that you know they are trying to hit the factories and the main industrial parts, but there's always a chance they might misread their maps or just not care. So we take it in turns.'

Kate hugged herself. 'I can't imagine being up here, night after night.'

'It doesn't bother me really. Not since the first few times, and then I was mainly scared I would fall asleep. It can get cold, but it has a magnificent view of the stars on clear nights – and gets you away from the others for a bit. It's always such a rush here, and at the factory there's never much time for a bit of peace and quiet to think things over. Gives you a kind of perspective, if you see what I mean.'

'I suppose,' said Kate, still unconvinced.

They settled down on the corner of the flat roof next to the door, sheltered from the wind. Kate could hear the children running around in the garden below, playing tag, much as the children did in the playground at the school in Brierley-in-Arden. Such sounds of normality drifting up through the cooling air felt more precious than ever.

'Papa thinks you've come to persuade me to go home,' said Cordelia.

'What made you think that?'

'He wrote to me.'

Kate stared at her in astonishment. 'Never!'

'A few days ago. Quite out of the blue. Alma's written

before, of course, but he's never tried to contact me, even though he knows where I'm staying and we haven't been bombed out yet, so he can hardly say he doesn't know my address.' She pulled a face. 'I was convinced he was writing to tell me he was coming to fetch me, or sending Alma, which is pretty much the same thing. But he wasn't.'

'Oh?' Kate prompted her, as her sister fell silent,

'It was odd, really. I was sure he was trying to tell me something without actually saying it, if that makes sense.'

'Perfectly,' replied Kate gloomily. 'It's the story of my life. What did he say?'

Cordelia cradled her hands around her mug. 'I think he was instructing me not to listen to you. It was something about you suffering the strain of worrying about the rest of us, and getting funny ideas into your head about your past.'

'Then why doesn't he just tell me the truth?' exclaimed Kate.

'Maybe he feels he can't,' said Cordelia, mildly.

Kate laughed. 'I've missed you, Cory. You always were the peacemaker, seeing everyone's point of view.'

Cordelia squeezed her hand. 'And I've missed you, more than I can say.' They were silent for a moment, and Kate knew that her sister was thinking too of their brothers out in France and their sister in London. 'You might as well know, I've an opportunity to go out and work in France. Oh, not as a spy,' she added hastily at the expression on Kate's face. 'To work with the refugees. One of the volunteers here also works with a charity providing aid out in the French free zone. Something like the Red Cross, only smaller, and specifically for women and children. I've said I'll think it over.'

'But you'll go,' said Kate, catching the look of determination on her sister's face.

'Of course. I wouldn't miss it for the world. Don't you dare tell Alma, or let on to Papa. He'd definitely come and fetch me back to Arden and lock me in my room for the duration.'

'He should be proud of you.'

'Even if he is, that still wouldn't stop him,' sighed Cordelia. 'I do love him, but he can be quite impossible at times, and I'm not marrying some callow youth just so he can make Arden House grand again. I'm certainly not marrying the dreaded Henry Luscombe now Rosalind has escaped his clutches and he's turned his attention to you and me.' She gave a theatrical shudder. 'I mean, can you imagine it?'

Kate tucked her arm inside her sister's. 'I'd rather not, thank you very much.'

Cordelia giggled. 'I know what you mean. Vile little man. I don't know what Papa sees in him – well, apart from his vast fortune of course. I don't want a fortune, I want to do something with my life. Something useful.'

Kate peered at her, trying to make out her sister's expression. 'Isn't here useful?'

'You know what I mean. Something that makes a real difference. There is so much suffering in the world, and especially the women and children. I can't stay safe at home, not even here which is almost safe, and not do anything.' They fell silent, finishing their tea. Then Cordelia shook herself. 'You said in your letter that you'd found something in your volume of sonnets?'

'The nearest thing to my family.' Kate pulled out the drawings.

'That looks like the place you said you used to dream of,' exclaimed Cordelia, seizing the picture of the terrace. 'So it must be to do with your family. Could Miss Parsons tell you anything more?'

Kate shook head. 'I'm sure she knows a lot more than she's letting on. For some reason it seems she feels she can't tell me.'

She held out the portrait. 'Although she did say this was my grandmother.'

'Really? So you have found your family. How exciting.' Cordelia scrutinised the picture. '*La Contessa*. Your grand-mother is a countess? I'm surprised Papa has managed to keep that quiet all these years. So Miss Parsons must know something about your mother.'

'I think, from what she said, she might have met her, a long time ago.'

'But that's wonderful!' Cordelia hugged her. 'Surely she didn't leave it like that, she must have told you more.'

'Not really. She said I needed to find my own way, and that coming here would help me. She didn't say how.'

'So that explains Papa's letter. I bet he's worried what you might tell me.'

Kate nodded. 'That's more or less what Miss Parsons said.'

'Well, then you have to find out.' Cordelia was peering at the drawing of the contessa. 'Oh my goodness. That's who she reminds me of. I thought she was familiar. I can see why you asked me to bring my Shakespeare.' She pulled out the volume from her shoulder bag, flicking through the tragedies until she reached *Macbeth*. The two looked at each other.

'That really is her,' said Kate, with a shiver. 'I didn't imagine it: Lady Macbeth.'

'Whoever drew her, must have hated her to portray her as a murderess,' said Cordelia, thoughtfully, peering closer at the drawing.

'Or perhaps believed she really was one,' put in Kate, unable to suppress the suspicion in the back of her mind. 'Miss Parsons said I'd never been to Venice, but I know that's where the contessa lived.'

'Venice!' Cordelia practically dropped the portrait in aston-ishment, catching it at the last moment, before it sailed over the edge and out into the streets below. 'How totally romantic.

People would give anything to have family in Venice...' She stopped. 'Sorry, that was thoughtless of me.'

Kate swallowed. 'Italy is the enemy, you mean.'

'But you aren't.' Cordelia hugged her, fiercely. 'And just because they are Italian doesn't mean that your family are fascists. You could never be the enemy, dearest Kate.'

There was a moment's silence. Cordelia returned to her inspection of the portrait of the contessa, while Kate gazed up to the haze of industrial smog turning the sky a vivid orange as the sun began to set.

'I'm going to find a way of going there,' she announced.

Cordelia gasped in dismay. 'You can't, not in a war!'

'I don't mean now this minute, Cory,' Kate reassured her. 'But I'll find a way, just as soon as I can. I have to know what happened to my mother. Why she gave me up. And if she's still alive. If she wants to meet me at all, that is.'

'She will,' said Cordelia firmly. 'She's your mother. How could she not?'

Kate sighed in frustration. 'I wish I could remember more, or I had a name to work with, but Miss Parsons won't say.'

'She might not remember... it was a long time ago.'

Kate snorted. 'I'd remember something like that. It's like she's taken a vow of silence, or something.'

'That doesn't sound like Miss Parsons,' said Cordelia, frowning. 'And anyhow, if she didn't want you to find your family, wouldn't she have just said she didn't know anything and not given you the book of sonnets. She could easily have given you something else, and pretended there was never a message for you at all.'

'That's true,' replied Kate. She watched the ebb and flow of a cloud high above, its shape billowing like a sail, tinged with crimson. 'I know I was in a villa by the sea, and that's got to be Vesuvius in the background, so from Papa's map of Italy it's got to be somewhere near Naples. And I'm sure I have a memory of being taken to the archaeological dig at Pompeii. I'm sure that must be why I'm so drawn to the Roman villa at Arden House. It always somehow felt like home, being there when I was helping Jamie. I thought that was because I loved uncovering the finds and drawing the best ones. But now I'm wondering if it wasn't also because it was something familiar, even though I didn't begin to remember it properly until recently.'

'You'll find your family,' said Cordelia. 'I can feel it in my bones. You were always the most determined of all of us. You'll find your past.'

'Our past,' replied Kate, realisation hitting her. 'We were each left a copy of the illustrated Shakespeare. You, me, Rosalind and Bianca. It can't be just coincidence. Even if Papa is not my real father, and I'm nothing to do with the Ardens, there's something that's tying my fate to yours. I'm going to find a way of getting to Venice and Naples as soon as I can.'

A worried expression appeared on Cordelia's face. 'They're on opposite sides of Italy, Kate. Even I know that. They must be hundreds of miles apart.'

'But they are both on the coast,' said Kate, stubbornly. 'Even if they are opposite coasts. I came to England by boat. If I can't get to either of them by train, I can find my way back by sea.'

Cordelia bent over the illustrations of *Macbeth*. 'You're right, you know. About the Shakespeare books. Even if we're not connected by blood, we're still the Shakespeare sisters.'

'I hope so,' agreed Kate, slowly. The scene before her wavered.

'Don't.' Cordelia dropped her mug and held her tight. 'Dearest, darling Kate, don't cry. You'll always be my sister, and I'll always love you, whoever you are. We all will. In fact, you don't have to be anything else. Just our sister. Just one of those headstrong Arden girls, who are determined to find our own way through life, wherever that takes us.' She looked down at the portrait. 'And you're an artist. You've inherited that skill from someone. Not from the contessa, I'd have thought; I can't see her wielding a brush, she looks far too grand.'

'Unless she did, and she used herself as the model for Lady Macbeth. That would mean she'd know for certain what she had done to be chosen to portray a murderess.'

'I wonder.' Cordelia turned the page to the final image of Lady Macbeth. It was just as Kate had remembered it. Lady Macbeth, most definitely still the contessa, but wandering the castle in a long nightdress, like a ghost, lit only by the candle in her hands. The light sent her hawkish features into one of horror.

'That's her tragedy, isn't it,' said Cordelia. 'Lady Macbeth's, I mean. That's what always scared me about the play. At the end, she's not just a cold-blooded murderess; she understands what she has done, and it drives her mad, just like it does Macbeth.' She shuddered. 'I wonder if that's something real about the contessa, or a threat. Like a curse, that this picture is foretelling her future.'

'In that case, she must have done something terrible. Now do you see why I have to find out?'

Cordelia nodded, her eyes resting on the caption for the illustration of the sleepwalking scene, not quite able to tear them away as the contessa, in the guise of Lady Macbeth, attempted to wash the invisible blood from her hands.

'Will these hands ne'er be clean?'

TWELVE

Kate worked for the rest of the day with the volunteers, keeping the children occupied, and preparing everything they would need for the journey to a boarding school in Shropshire that had agreed to take them in. After the children had gone to bed and the volunteer ladies had headed off to their own homes, Kate slipped away to join Cordelia on the roof once more.

It was a clear night, with only the gleam of stars to reveal the great city stretching out around them as far as they could see in all directions.

They didn't have long to wait until the sirens howled through the air, followed by the drone of bombers filling the sky, then the distant thuds as the raid began over the city. Kate watched in a horrified fascination as the explosions lit up the night, followed by the glow of flames.

'You'd better go down and join the others,' said Cordelia. 'I really meant it, we don't often get incendiaries out here, but it's still not safe.'

'I'm not leaving,' said Kate. 'If you can risk your life out here to make sure the building doesn't burn down, then so can I.'

The pounding went on for hours, again and again, into the

night. Kate tried not to think of the families caught beneath explosions that shook the earth even that far away, let alone the fires now spreading through the distant streets. Around her, frost was forming, glistening on the bricks of the building in the pale light of the stars.

'That was a close one,' exclaimed Cordelia, as a flash lit up the park, followed by the glow of orange flames reflected in the pond. 'You'd better get down to the cellar with everyone else—'

The end of her sentence vanished into a rumble reverberating through the night. There was a crash on the roof, followed by another, and flames began to lick around them.

'Use the sand,' yelled Cordelia, grabbing buckets of water and throwing them on the largest flames. Kate ran with the nearest bucket of sand, smothering every ember she could see. As they stamped out the last flickers, the roar of bombers overhead faded into the distance.

'That was too close,' said Cordelia, leaning against the chimney as she caught her breath. 'Are you all right? I shouldn't have let you stay up here.'

'I'm fine,' gasped Kate, equally out of breath.

'At least we put them out before they took hold. It could have burnt the whole place down.' Her voice wavered slightly. 'I thought it would get easier, the more it happened. It never does.'

Kate hugged her sister tight. Her legs were shaking and every part of her felt stiff and bruised. At the same time, her body was alive with exhilaration. She had survived; she hadn't panicked, she hadn't had time to feel afraid. She had acted on instinct and done what needed to be done. After this, she could face anything.

'It'll be light before long,' said Cordelia. 'You go down and get some rest. You've a long journey ahead of you.'

As Kate turned towards the door, an explosion ripped through the air again, knocking them to the floor. Kate instinctively put her arms around her head, ears ringing, waiting for the end. In the eerie silence there came the crackle of fire in the distance, followed by the crash of falling masonry.

'That was just down the street!' cried Cordelia, as they crawled to the edge of the parapet, where an orange light revealed one of the rows of terraced houses glowing in the darkness, their innards lit up by flames. 'Oh my lord, it's Hellebore Row. There are so many families living there.' She jumped to her feet, rushing down through the house. Kate followed hot on her heels.

'It looks as if an unexploded bomb went off. The whole row was damaged,' Miss Parsons said as they reached the ground floor. Kate could hear Gina in the cellar below attempting to sooth the terrified children. 'Peter's gone to see if there's anything he can do.'

Cordelia grabbed a first aid bag and headed out into the street. Kate followed, heart pounding as she raced behind her sister, heading towards the flames.

People from the neighbouring streets were already arriving to help douse the flames until the fire engine arrived. Several others were bringing out mothers and children as the fire spread, threatening to take the whole row.

'The one at the far end got it,' said one of the women, ushering a family with children to where houses in the next street were taking in those made homeless by the fires. 'Marian was terrified this would happen, she insisted they always slept in the cellar. I haven't seen her. She'd have brought those kiddies straight out.'

'I'll tell them,' Kate reassured her. She ran after Peter who was joining men and women pulling rubble away from the collapsed house, almost as efficient one-handed as the others were with two.

'You shouldn't be here,' he snapped, as she arrived. 'This could collapse at any minute.'

There wasn't time to react, so she ignored him. 'One of the women said the family always slept in the cellar,' said Kate breathlessly. 'She hasn't seen them; she thinks they must be still down there.'

'Fire'll get them if the building don't fall,' said the elderly man in front of them.

'Then we'd better be quick,' said Peter, heading towards the front of the rescuers.

Kate joined in the line of men and women, taking stones out of the way, dousing fires that started amongst the rubble. With attention focussed on the flames in the main part of the row, and the danger of the roofs collapsing, there were only a few of them clawing desperately at the rubble. Finally, the fire brigade arrived and were soon directing their hoses, leaving shells of homes standing stark in the mist of early morning, smoke still rising from the ground.

'Got it,' said a man at the front who was working with Peter. 'That's the door to the cellar. Mrs Wilson? Anybody there?' The little group fell silent. 'Looks like the whole thing has gone, no one could have survived that.'

'Wait.' Peter lay down flat on the ground, next to the hole. 'There's someone.'

This time Kate could hear it: the faintest whisper of a cry. Before anyone else could move, Peter edged into the rubble, wriggling awkwardly as near to the hole in the ground as he could. The next minute he completely disappeared. She could hear him talking to someone inside.

'Follow me,' Kate heard him call. 'We'll pull you up.' He emerged a few minutes later, helped out by the men at the front, followed by a girl of about six, covered in white masonry dust and streaked with blood.

'Susie!' One of the women in the crowd dropped her

bucket, folding her arms around the child, enveloping her in the folds of her coat. She looked towards Peter. 'Thank goodness you found her. The others...?'

Peter shook his head. The woman's face collapsed into tears. She fought them back instantly, holding the little girl tight. The girl murmured something, muffled in the folds of the coat.

'I'm sorry,' said the woman, 'I'm sorry, darling, they've all gone. I'll take you home, you can stay with me.'

Kate glanced at Peter, who was struggling to get his bandaged arm back in his sling. He had clearly knocked it while he was manoeuvring through the rubble; she could see him grit his teeth as he attempted to pull the sling back over. She reached out and steadied the cloth, holding it open while he slid his damaged arm back into its support.

'Thanks,' he muttered. 'Damned stupid thing.' He pulled his coat back over him. 'Better get back, the rest of this could go at any minute.'

The woman holding Susie's hand began to urge her away. After a minute she stopped.

'She won't go, she says there's someone still under there.'

Peter crouched down next to Susie. 'I'm sorry, sweetheart, no one else down there survived. I checked. I'm very sorry. Now you go with Mrs Henderson, she'll look after you.' He stood up as shouts erupted from further along the row.

'Oh my lord!' whispered Mrs Henderson. 'There's a parachute bomb lodged next door.'

Kate followed her gaze to where the front of the next-door terrace had collapsed in a cloud of rubble. In the light from the flames, she could see a large cylindrical container perched on the top of the stairs, held in place by a billowing silk parachute, its strings caught on the remains of the walls.

'If that falls, it could go off any minute, and they haven't got Mrs Pagett and her kids out yet.'

'You go with Mrs Henderson,' said Peter, placing his hand

briefly on Susie's head, in an attempt to comfort her when there was no comfort to be had. 'You'll be safe there.' He raced off through the smoke and the dust to where the neighbours were frantically trying to pull the rubble away from the next house. Kate could make out the firemen with their hoses battling to keep the flames erupting at the far end of the row from creeping any closer.

'Come on, dearie,' said Mrs Henderson, taking Susie's hand.

The little girl shook her head. 'Peggy,' she said. 'Not without Peggy.'

'The baby,' Mrs Henderson mouthed at Kate, tears filling her eyes. 'I'm sorry, sweetheart, your brother and sister are gone, too. There's nothing you can do for them now.'

Shouts came in their direction, warning them to move back.

'Come on, you come and sit by the fire with my John and Ruby, and I'll make us all a hot cup of tea.'

'Peggy...' repeated Susie. There was a desperation in her voice that made Kate stop in her tracks and turn back. Susie's eyes met hers, dark and pleading. She abandoned Mrs Henderson, grasping Kate's hand tightly. 'She's there. I heard her.'

'Mr Sidoli checked them all, darling,' said Mrs Henderson gently. 'Every single one. I'm so sorry.'

'Not Peggy.' Susie stood immoveable. Her eyes still pleaded with Kate. 'Please Miss, I know Mum is dead, and Nana, and Bobby, too.' Her voice wavered, but remained clear, explaining firmly like one much older. 'But Mum always put Peggy under Dad's workbench. It's a metal one,' she added quickly. 'Dad got it from a factory in Dudley that was closing down just before the war. She was still there, I heard her.'

'Oh my lord,' whispered Mrs Henderson. 'Jim did have a metal workbench; he had my Donald help him fetch it. Great big heavy thing it was, Jim used to say it was as strong as a battleship.' She called towards the men pulling the rubble frantically away as the parachute holding the bomb flapped

ominously in the heat from the fire, but her voice was lost
beneath the roar of flames and the falling of rubble. The nearest
fireman waved them away with even greater urgency.

'Are you sure you heard her?' said Kate.

Susie nodded. 'I tried to get her. I did. I tried. Then I
couldn't breathe...'

'It's all right, it's not your fault,' Mrs Henderson soothed
her. 'Poor thing.' Her eyes turned instinctively to the flames
reaching towards the wooden banisters holding the parachute of
the unexploded bomb in place.

'Wait here,' said Kate. She pointed her torch at the hole in
the rubble.

'You can't go down there!' Mrs Henderson was horrified. 'If
that thing goes off... And if Susie says she couldn't breathe, how
could a baby survive at all?'

'We can't just leave her.' Kate took a deep breath. All she
could feel were the arms around her that had once held her so
tightly, unwilling to let her go, and of being torn away, into the
terror of the dark. She couldn't bear the thought of another creature, left in the noise and the terror of the world cracking and
breaking apart around her, to take her final breaths alone.

Taking the torch, she crawled through the rubble, inching
her way on her belly through the gap. How Peter had managed
it with his injured arm, she couldn't imagine. Dust caught in her
lungs, along with a faint smell of gas. She found the entrance to
the cellar, into a place where the roof had collapsed under the
weight of masonry. She wriggled through the small space
between bricks and mortar, and a heavy beam that had fallen,
crushing everything beneath.

It was a miracle anyone had survived. She tried to block out
the sights at the corner of her vision, the small hand, mitten on a
string still attached, just visible from under the beam, alongside
the broken remains of what had once been Susie's mother and
grandmother. She could hear shouts from outside, the falling of

plaster. The beam shifted slightly, sending dust into her lungs. It was hopeless. She swung her torch round. There was no sign of a workbench. Susie must have been mistaken, or the shifting of the supports had led to a further collapse.

She was just about to make her way back up when there was a rustle a little further along. A mouse? A rat? She held her breath, trying to locate the sound. It came again, this time the faintest of whimpers.

'I'm here,' she called, as loud as she dared, swinging her torch in the direction of the cries. Suddenly, it caught the sheen of metal. A beam had fallen across the workbench, but it remained supported at one end by bricks and rubble, leaving the smallest of gaps underneath. She crawled as quickly as she could towards the small space, directing her torch beam inside. To her relief, something moved. There was a glint of eyes, immediately followed by a faint cry. 'Sshh, sshh, you're all right. You're safe now,' she whispered, terrified that any loud sound might bring the rest of the roof on their heads.

Placing the torch on the floor, she reached inside, pulling the little bundle of shawls and scarves towards her, and gently eased the tiny body through the small space. There was only just enough room to slide Peggy's head through, followed by her shoulders and her swaddled body. As Kate turned the child round to face her, the eyes watched her silently. Peggy was clearly too cold and terrified to protest any longer against her fate.

Crawling back was agonisingly slow, holding the child as close as she could with one arm, the torch in her hand to show her the way, its beam dancing crazily with every move forward over rubble. The dust was stifling. At least there was the first stirrings of dawn outside. She moved towards the pale glow, the sound of voices and the smell of burning rafters.

She had nearly reached the entrance when the masonry above her gave way with a woosh and a crash. She curled herself around Peggy, trying to protect the little body as much as possible, as rock and bricks crashed into her back, pinning one of her legs. Behind her, she heard the roar as the beam finally shifted, and the cellar collapsed behind her. The rocks around her shook and creaked.

'Get out of there,' came a voice from the entrance. 'Looks like the whole thing's about to go.'

'I can't move,' she called back. In the narrow space, it was impossible to turn round to free her leg. The more she tried to wriggle free, the more she knew she was trapped. Already dust was clogging her lungs, making it hard to breathe.

'I've got Peggy,' shouted Kate, manoeuvring the precious bundle towards the light. Hands wrapped round the child, taking her out.

'You next.' Peter was at the entrance, his good hand reaching out to grasp her. 'Inch forward a bit, and I'll pull you.'

'My foot's stuck,' she replied. 'Something fell on it. It's wedged.'

She caught the look in his eyes. The space was so small, no one could pass. The longer they stayed, the more danger of the bomb going off or the tunnel collapsing completely. She manoeuvred her foot inside her boot. Desperation gave her strength. She stifled a yell as pain went through her foot. She felt the laces go. The boot loosened just a fraction. 'Just pull me,' she called, grasping Peter's hand. She held on, ignoring the agony shooting through her leg. Then her foot was free. With a yelp, she was hauled out into daylight, just as the tunnel collapsed behind her.

'You fool,' shouted Peter. He pulled her to her feet, helping her to hobble over the bricks and broken glass as fast as her bootless foot could manage, until they were at a safe distance from the collapsing ruin.

'Is she all right?' she demanded. 'Peggy, I mean.'

'Mrs Henderson is looking after them both. The baby was

crying by the time they got to her house, which seems like a good sign.'

'Thank goodness. She was so quiet, I thought she mightn't survive with all that dust.'

'She certainly wouldn't have done, if you hadn't gone in after her,' said Peter. 'I'll never forgive myself. I should have asked.'

'You didn't have time. And of course you'd think a baby would be with her mother. And no one could have survived that.'

'All the same...' He grimaced.

They were shooed further out of the way as the bomb disposal men arrived. The fire had been extinguished, but the parachute looked in a more precarious position than ever.

'Kate!' Cordelia broke through the cordon as they reached the relative safety of the next street, hugging her tightly. 'You idiot. You stupid idiot. You brave stupid idiot,' she added, kissing her.

'Don't you dare tell Mama,' said Kate, who was beginning to feel lightheaded.

'You must be joking. Not before the war's over. She'd come and fetch us herself.'

'My boot,' exclaimed Kate, in dismay. 'What on earth am I going to do?' She hadn't enough money on her, let alone enough coupons, to buy another pair of shoes.

'We'll find you some, don't worry,' Cordelia replied. 'There's bound to be someone who's the same size. You'd be amazed at how quickly something like that can be located, especially when the story gets about. You saved that child's life. Come on, you're starting to shiver. I'd better get you back to the house.'

THIRTEEN

They returned to find Miss Parsons doing her best to distract the children from the all-too-familiar tragedy unfolding only streets away.

'Thank goodness you are both safe,' she exclaimed, as Cordelia paused outside the half-open door. From the pale and silent faces looking at her around the table, Kate guessed just how dirty and dishevelled she must be. A quick glance down revealed her skirt torn, white dust clinging to every part of her clothing, and her big toe protruding through a hole in the sock where her left boot should have been. One of the smaller boys began to cry.

'It's all right, Ted,' said Miss Parsons, gently. 'Miss Arden's not hurt, she's just been helping people. It's only dust.'

'I'd better get clean,' Kate muttered, seeing the haunted looks in the eyes of the children.

'Mr Sidoli will be back soon as well,' Cordelia reassured them. 'He just stayed behind to help.'

The two headed upstairs to remove the remainder of the dust and the dirt. Kate had no sooner changed into her spare skirt than there was a knock on the door, followed by Gina appearing with a pair of sturdy walking boots.

'Mrs Partridge from next door has brought these for you. She hopes they fit. News travels fast,' she added to Kate's astonished look.

'I can't deprive her of her boots,' protested Kate.

Gina grinned. 'Mrs Partridge is eighty, if she's a day. She's still fit as a fiddle, but she's quite certain she won't be scaling the Alps as she did as a young woman, and none of her granddaughters have inherited the passion. She assured me she won't be needing them again, and she'd be honoured if you can find a use for them. And don't mind them not being elegant.'

'I love them,' replied Kate. 'They look far more practical than my old ones. I'd rather be sure of foot than elegant any day.'

While Cordelia headed back down to help supervise the children, Gina watched as Kate tried on the boots. They were a little stiff from lack of use, but they fitted and were sturdy.

'Perfect!' Gina beamed. 'I'll tell her, she'll be so pleased.' An excited chattering of children's voices sent Gina hastily to the window. 'Peter's back. Thank goodness. He should never have gone to help. The surgeons warned him not to use that arm until it had fully healed, but he won't be told, and when he sees something like that, he can't help himself. It's probably set it back weeks.'

Kate winced with guilt as they prepared to head downstairs. 'Is that how he was hurt?' Perhaps his surliness wasn't personal after all. If he'd recently had surgery he must be in pain, and possible concerned that he might never be able to use it properly. All the same, she couldn't quite get the look of hostility when he had first set eyes on her out of her mind. She was certain he'd never accompanied Gina to the archaeological lectures, and Jamie had never mentioned meeting him. She would remain wary of him until she could gauge why he seemed to have taken an instant dislike to her.

'Vile fascists,' said Gina, causing Kate to jump. 'Oh, not Mosley's lot. The British Union of Fascists is a pale imitation once you're come across Mussolini's thugs.' She frowned. 'I thought Miss Parsons told you? We don't tend to tell people we were working in Italy before the war, let alone that we have family there. People might get the wrong idea. She said you had Italian connections, so would understand.'

'Did she?' said Kate, warily.

Gina grimaced. 'Our nonna, our grandmother, came from a village on the coast, near Sorrento.'

Kate just about managed to suppress a start. No wonder Peter had recognised her view from the villa.

'She said it was all impossibly poor, even then,' Gina continued. 'That's why they left. Our grandparents I mean. They ran away together when they were very young. Nonna says she was barely more than seventeen and grandfather only a few years older. They had saved enough between them to get a passage to Wales, where Nonna had an uncle who had created a successful business selling ice cream. It sounds very romantic, although I'm sure it must have been terrifying at the time, and they both must have worked all hours to save enough to start their restaurant.'

Kate eyed her. 'So you were in Italy before the war?'

'Miss Parsons has always insisted that the charity looking after orphans here before the war also worked with street children in Europe, mainly Italy for some reason.' She bit her lip. 'I'm afraid it was all my fault. The Archaeological Society held a lecture on the excavation at Pompeii, when they were looking for volunteers.'

'I remember Jamie talking about it,' exclaimed Kate. 'He even tried to persuade Papa to let him go.'

'In a way, he was the lucky one,' replied Gina. 'Oh, I don't mean the work itself, that was the most incredible thing I've ever done. It was a bit unnerving at times, seeing all those lives lost in the eruption, and seeing they were really just like us. But the buildings were so beautiful. It was like finding a lost world. I suppose that's the same with your Roman villa.' She sighed. 'It was what happened afterwards.'

'Afterwards?'

Gina fetched their coats and scarves from the corridor outside. 'Dad would only let me go if Peter went with me as a chaperone,' she said, as she handed Kate her coat. 'Peter isn't really interested in archaeology, but he volunteered for Miss Parsons' charity, working with the street children. He's much more political than me. Very against the fascists, just like our grandfather. The conditions there were so awful for ordinary people, especially the children. The charity works, or at least it did, with the *Croce Rossa Italiana*, the Italian Red Cross. The things we saw...'

She paused tying her scarf securely on her head. 'They nearly killed him, you know. The fascists. That's why we had to leave. They said they had some information about us. It was someone who knew the charity, or had a grudge against it. It was all nonsense, accusing us of being spies for the British, and passing on plans for the port and the industrial centres. The family from the house next door managed to get me and some of the other women away. But the fascists took all the men. They did vile things to them. Worse than you could ever imagine. They broke Peter's arm so badly it's never properly healed. The most recent operation is his best chance of being able to use it again. If not, he could lose it.'

'That's terrible,' exclaimed Kate, horrified.

'He's one of the lucky ones,' said Gina. 'Several of the others were shot. Peter would have been too if someone from the charity hadn't got there in time. I'm sure bribery was involved, but I don't care. They got us out. I swore then I'd never waste one moment of my life again.' She gave a faint smile. 'So perhaps it's as well Jamie didn't manage to make it out and join us, as he was planning. He might never have made it home.'

They headed downstairs in silence. What was there to say? As they reached the main room, Kate couldn't help noticing that Peter was moving more stiffly than before. His arm must be hurting. Yet he had thrown himself into helping the families in the burning building with a determination that had overcome any lack of strength, or any pain he might have suffered.

She remembered the strength in his good arm as it freed her from the tunnel in Mrs Wilson's collapsed home. That kind of single mindedness she had to admire, but it was a little unnerving, all the same. He was clearly a man who would not be easily dissuaded once he had made his mind up. Was that the same for his opinions as well? She watched as he removed his bad arm gingerly from its sling in order to tie the laces of one of the smaller boys, who was scarcely old enough to walk. Peter talked to the boy, his smile gentle as he appeared to reassure the child. Looking at Peter now, he was not the dour-faced man who had eyed her with such palpable hostility when she first arrived. Maybe she had been mistaken, too quick to take his expression personally. He didn't know her. All he knew was that she was Jamie's sister, and Jamie was a gentle soul – not the kind to make enemies.

She must have been mistaken. It must have been merely an expression of pain she had seen. As if sensing being watched, he glanced up. Kate turned hastily away. She followed Gina, who was already heading for the nearest table.

Later that afternoon, as preparations were in full swing for the children to leave for Shropshire the following morning, Kate stepped into the garden for a few minutes to clear her head. She found Miss Parsons sitting on a bench in the last of the sunlight, and was surprised to see she was smoking a cigarette, something Kate had never seen her do before.

'Ah, there you are, my dear. I was hoping I'd catch you,' you said, indicating to Kate to join her. Kate obeyed. The patch of sun was warm and peaceful. She could hear the sounds of conversations and children playing in the streets around. The occasional vehicle passed in the street outside. It all felt so normal, it was hard to think that every one of the families would soon be bracing themselves for another night of bombers rumbling overhead, crouched in the dark, praying they would see the following day.

Miss Parsons finished her cigarette. A look of determination came over her face.

'My dear, I wanted to talk to you. With all these new children, the boarding school in Shropshire doesn't have room for them all.'

'I don't mind staying here,' said Kate quickly. 'And I would be with Cordelia.'

'I know, my dear.' She cleared her throat. 'But the children can't remain. It isn't safe, and they've been through enough. They really need peace and quiet. I have been thinking...' She was silent for a moment. 'I do know of another place that might take them. I telephoned this afternoon, and they've agreed to house all those that can't be accommodated by the boarding school. The only problem they have is that they're not an educational establishment, so they will need teachers to stay with them. I've suggested some of the younger volunteers should take the children to the boarding school. It's only a short train journey and the school has agreed to pick them up in a bus at Ludlow, so there will be teachers waiting for them at the train station. That means you should go with Gina to Cornwall.'

'Cornwall?' Kate eyed her in dismay. Ludlow might be out in the countryside on the borders of Wales, but it was within driving distance of Arden House, even with petrol rationing.

She didn't know much about Cornwall, apart from the fact that it was as far down in the south as you could get, away from everything. Even by train it would take a day to get there. It might be months, years, before she saw her family at Arden House, or was able to meet up with Cordelia again.

'The place is near St Ives,' said Miss Parsons. 'It has been an artist's retreat since before the last war. Most of the artists will be working for the war effort of course, but they are bound to return once this war is over. And there may be some left in St Ives. There will be a life once this is over, my dear. I understand you want to do what you can for the war effort, but don't let your painting and drawing go completely, especially if you want to remain independent and follow your passion. This might be a way. And you are good with the children. You will be a great help to Gina. To be honest, I'm not that keen on insisting young women don't stir without a chaperone, but it does help if there are two of you, so you can look out for each other.'

'Yes,' said Kate, fighting down a sense that she was abandoning Cordelia to face the dangers of living in a city under nightly bombardment on her own, accompanied by excitement that she could be living near the legendary St Ives, famous for its painters. Deep inside an ache took hold of her to have the chance to learn more and perfect her painting, war or no war. Papa might not allow her near the Slade in London, but perhaps she could learn from the artists in St Ives. There might even be drawing classes. Besides, hadn't Cordelia warned her that she might be leaving herself, heading out to France?

'So you'll go?' said Miss Parsons, watching her closely. 'If Gina agrees, that is.'

'Yes, of course,' said Kate, unable to hide her eagerness.

'Good.' Miss Parsons took out second cigarette from her pocket, lighting it with a match that wavered slightly in her hands. 'This takes me back to my youth,' she remarked, drawing in the smoke deep into her lungs. 'We smoked like chimneys in those days, like so many do now. I haven't looked at a cigarette for years.' She smoked in silence for a few minutes. Kate had a sense of her choosing her words carefully. 'You'll suit Tregannon Castle. It's a beautiful place, overlooking the sea. Lovely and peaceful, and only a short walk into St Ives. I stayed there for a while, before the last war. Before the world went mad.' She drew on her cigarette. 'It was famed as a school for artists in those days.'

Curiosity overcame Kate. 'What kind of artists?'

'It was unusual in being set up exclusively for women painters and sculptors,' replied Miss Parsons, avoiding her eyes. Kate's heart began to thump in her chest. Miss Parsons had hinted she'd taken a vow of silence about the past, but there were more ways than one to direct her towards where she might find out more about her mother. 'The kind who were serious about their art, who wanted to make a living from it rather than simply as an accomplishment.' She grimaced. 'Talented and ambitious young women came there from as far away as America. We thought we were going to change the world, as the young do. We never imagined, in those days, that the world might choose to break us.' As if suddenly making up her mind, she stubbed out the remainder of her cigarette and turned to Kate. 'The thing is, my dear...'

In the darkening air, the air raid sirens set up, howling through the dusk. Inside the house, they could hear Gina, along with the volunteers, directing the children down towards the cellar.

'Trust the Luftwaffe to be early,' remarked Miss Parsons, rising to her feet. 'On the other hand, it may be for the better. Some things are best found when you are ready. And some, maybe not at all.' She smiled, a strained, rather mournful smile. 'You take your own journey, my dear. Whatever happens, you will find a way. But it needs to be your way, and no other's. Life can so easily break the unwary. You hold to your own path, wherever it takes you. Promise me that.'

'Yes, of course.' Kate's mind whirled with questions. But Miss Parsons was already brushing herself down, becoming the responsible schoolmistress once more, as she headed to help take the children down to safety before another night of bombing began.

'Hurry up!' She found Peter beckoning impatiently at her from the side door. 'I nearly missed you out there.' He gestured to where the volunteers were swinging heavy wooden shutters in place across the windows, and preparing to do the same with the door. 'We need to get this boarded up before the planes arrive.'

'I'll be there now,' replied Kate, hurrying to join them.

FOURTEEN

That night, the raid wasn't as intense for the streets around the little park. Kate joined Cordelia up on the roof of the hospital for the final time, braced for incendiaries to fall, or explosions to rock the night nearby, but the bombs fell further away. They watched the splash of light in the darkness, the distant crunch of explosions. Kate marvelled at the eerie beauty it lent to the night sky, combined with the knowledge that every plume of firework brilliance signalled death and suffering for those caught within its grasp, along with the destruction of homes and neighbourhoods, and the ending of everything they knew.

'I can't leave you to face this,' Kate said as they stood up to watch flames reaching towards the night sky as a factory or warehouse was hit.

'Yes you can.' Cordelia crouched back down beneath the shelter of the wall. 'It was my choice to find work making uniforms when it was obvious the Black Country with all its industry would be a target. And besides, I meant it when I said I'm planning to leave and work with refugees, wherever that might be, even if I end up in France. Then I would be leaving you here on your own.'

'It still feels like running away...' Kate joined her and pulled a woollen blanket over them both for warmth.

'There are plenty of places that are untouched by the bombing, but people are still working for the war effort,' replied Cordelia, blowing on her hands to get the circulation going again. 'Getting those poor children away from all this is at least creating hope for the future.'

'I suppose,' said Kate, a little doubtfully.

'And besides, a castle in Cornwall, next to St Ives – St Ives, Kate. Even I know that it was a mecca for artists, and it's likely to be again once the war has ended. We can't give in; we have to hope Hitler won't win, and fight for our futures too. Papa will never let you go to London to study, but he can't stop you studying in St Ives.'

Kate sighed. 'I agree. But I can't help feeling it's frivolous and self-indulgent when all this is going on.'

Cordelia guffawed in a most unladylike manner. 'When your painting brings such pleasure to people? And I saw how you managed to encourage the children to paint and draw even in the short time you've been here. And several of the volunteers have said that was the first time they'd seen any of them relaxed, with their minds away from what they had been through. Or at least not bottle it up, but begin to work it out, tell themselves stories to make it make sense.'

'Like I used to do,' said Kate.

'Yes,' said Cordelia. 'You were always drawing. That's the time you seem most at peace, too.'

They were silent for a while as a burst of explosions shot into the air, a little closer, but remaining at a safe distance.

'Cornwall's still a long way away,' said Kate.

'Then write to me, and I'll write to you. As long as the postal system is working, we can at least exchange letters.' In the light from the distant flames, Kate could make out Cordelia's smile. 'After all, *"They who one another keep alive, ne'er parted be*". John Donne might have been talking about lovers, but surely that can be just as true for sisters as well?'

'Agreed,' said Kate, the tight knot inside her loosening a little. 'I'll write as soon as I get there.' Despite the frostiness of the air, a deep warmth enveloped her. The only safety there was in this world was knowing you were loved, she thought. Her heart began to break for her unknown mother, who might still be alive and wishing for news of her daughter, just as she longed to see her.

'Which side of St Ives?' demanded Cordelia, abruptly. 'The castle, I mean.'

'I'm not sure. North, I think Miss Parsons said. In a harbour towards the north Cornish coast.'

'That's all right then,' said Cordelia, sounding relieved.

'Why?'

'Didn't anyone tell you that the Luscombe family have an estate down there?'

Kate's heart sank. The last thing she needed was Henry appearing the next time he was on leave. It was one thing having him pursue her when she had Papa and her brothers as protection. In Cornwall she would be amongst strangers, who might be dazzled by his wealth and connections and assume she should be flattered by such male attention.

'I'd totally forgotten,' she muttered.

Cordelia slipped her arm through hers as they huddled together for warmth. 'Don't let that put you off. From what Henry said it's further inland. He was always boasting about the Luscombe's woodlands being some of the oldest in England. I can just see him as some follower of William the Conqueror, turfing the peasants out of their homes to make way for hunting. At least Henry won't have time to get there when he comes on leave, and the last I heard, the rest of the family had decamped to some grand house they own in Somerset. So hopefully you'll never bump into any of them.'

'I'll make sure I don't,' said Kate. 'They'll only look down their noses at me anyhow.'

'I always knew they had no taste,' replied Cordelia with a smile in her voice.

The next morning, the children were collected together, each with a favourite toy and a rucksack of clothing collected by the volunteers. Kate said a hasty goodbye to Cordelia, who was heading back to the uniform factory to resume her shifts.

As Kate returned to the dining room, where the children were being fed before their journey, she found Peter deep in discussion with Miss Parsons.

'He's determined to come with us to Cornwall, rather than go to Ludlow,' whispered Gina, to Kate's enquiring glance. 'He promised my parents, and his, that he wouldn't let me out of his sight. It seems he's sticking to it.'

Kate listened in with interest.

'You said yourself, there are more than enough teachers at the boarding school,' Peter was saying. 'Either Gina stays with me in Shropshire, or I go with her to Cornwall. My aunt and uncle will never forgive me if anything happens to her.'

'I'm going to Cornwall,' put in Gina. 'Ludlow is far too close to Wales,' she added under her breath. 'I can see me being dragged back over the border at a moment's notice.'

'Then Cornwall it is,' said Peter stubbornly. 'Didn't you say it isn't really set up to be a school, so the more teachers the better? Especially for the boys,' he added, with a faint air of an argument won.

Miss Parsons held a rapid discussion with the remainder of the volunteer ladies. 'Very well,' she said, at last. 'Brenda has offered to go with the children to Ludlow. And it is a long journey to Cornwall,' she added.

Kate glanced at her. She could have sworn there was an

undercurrent of apprehension in the older woman's tone. Which probably meant she thought Kate was going to prove a silly girl after all, and fall hopelessly in love with Peter before they had reached Bristol. Kate sighed. She admired Peter's courage, but at this point she wasn't entirely sure she particularly liked him, plus he hadn't shown signs of liking her, rather the opposite. She wasn't going to fall in love just for the sake of it, and especially when every part of her was alive with the anticipation of spending time close to St Ives and being able to take up her painting again.

I'm probably far too selfish to ever find love, she told herself, sadly.

FIFTEEN

VENICE

October 1941

Sofia hurried through the alleyways, making her way to the hotel near St Mark's Square. In the brief time she'd been working as a cleaner, she had taken care to always be at the hotel on time. Today, she'd no intention of giving Signor Alessi, the rotund manager who fancied himself as another Mussolini, the pleasure of ticking her off like a schoolgirl.

As she reached the square, her steps took her towards an elderly man leaning heavily on a stick, making his laborious way towards the ornamental arches of the Doge's Palace. A group of boys dodged between the arches, brushing carelessly past, knocking him to the ground.

'Idiots!' she yelled after them, catching the man as he hit the floor. The crack of breaking bone went through her. 'Stay still, signor,' she said urgently. 'I'll find a doctor.'

'Signor Bracci!' To her relief a woman walking behind her stopped, dropping her shopping basket to bend down. 'Stay still, signor, stay still.'

'I'll get help,' said Sofia. 'Looks like he's broken his leg – if he moves he could do more damage.'

'Yes, yes of course.' The woman took Signor Bracci's age-mottled hand, soothing him as he muttered under his breath. He attempted to raise himself and fell back immediately with a sharp cry of pain. 'Doctor!' she exclaimed in relief, as a young man with dark hair appeared, having been alerted by someone in the crowd. She waved frantically, sending him hurrying towards them. 'Dr Conti, over here. It's Signor Bracci, it looks bad.'

'It's all right, Signora Giannelli,' he said as he reached them. 'Signora,' he added, nodding briefly to Sofia as he bent over the elderly man.

Sofia stayed as long as she dared, helping the doctor splint the broken leg with two lengths of wood, before Signor Bracci was gently lifted by several willing passers-by, to be taken away for treatment.

She reached the hotel only minutes late, managing to slip past Signor Alessi while he was distracted. As she scrubbed the kitchen floor, she realised she was shaking slightly as reaction to the events of the morning set in. She was glad of the hard physical activity of the day to prevent her mind from straying back to the drama in the square. It was a reminder of how things could change in an instant. But more than that, it had brought back her years of caring for Walter, and the time, long banished from her memory, she had served as a nurse in the last war, when she had been an eager, sheltered girl, idealistically rushing into a horror she could never have imagined. The sights and smells and the sheer shock of being confronted with the torn bodies of young men, some barely more than children, remained with her all day.

· · ·

Sofia finally emerged into the evening light, aching and with barely enough strength left to drag herself home.

'Signora Armstrong?' Her eyes, dazzled by the sun streaming behind him, could not make out the shadow making his way towards her until he arrived at her side.

'Dr Conti.' She nodded politely. 'How's Signor Bracci?'

'As well as can be expected. His leg is badly broken, but it should heal. He's a tough old bird, a proper old soldier, and he has family to look after him while he recovers. In many ways he's lucky. He was also fortunate that you were passing.'

'I was glad to help.' She found the dark eyes scrutinising her. This wasn't a coincidence, him being outside the hotel as she finished her shift. Dark eyes in a pleasant face. She could see the exhaustion that hung about him.

'You've been a nurse.'

That caught her off guard. 'I beg your pardon?'

'You've worked as a nurse. The way you acted, the way you knew exactly what to do. The way you could conceal your distress to sooth him.'

'I nursed my husband while he was dying,' she returned.

'Oh.' The taut lines on his face deepened. Embarrassment overtook him. 'I am so sorry, I beg your pardon, Signora. I should have thought. I'll take no more of your time. Thank you for your help, Signora Armstrong, and I wish you good day.'

It was the embarrassment that settled it. She'd met doctors who were hardened to their patients, some who even enjoyed their position of power, and also those who simply fought for their patients with all their heart and soul, and who could never be inured to their suffering.

'I also volunteered as a nurse in the last war,' she called, as he began to walk away. 'Most probably before you were born.'

He turned. 'Did you now? I'm always in need of nurses.'

'I'm not trained,' she added, determined to be honest. 'At least no more than the basics, and times have changed.'

'But you have the experience. And you are used to working with very little,' he added, a little grimly. He handed her a card, declaring him to be Dr Niccolò Conti. 'I can't offer much, probably no more than the hotel are paying.' He cleared his throat. 'Look, think it over. Believe me, I wouldn't blame you Signora, if you prefer to stay with the hotel. I'm sure you've seen enough suffering to last a lifetime, and things here may well get much worse.'

'Yes,' she said.

'Very well.'

'I mean, yes, I accept,' she added, before she could think long enough to run from the idea and hope never to bump into the doctor again.

'Excellent.' He beamed with unmistakeable relief.

A new lease of energy suddenly went through Sofia. 'I'm also very good at scrubbing floors,' she said wryly.

'Let's hope there isn't too much of that,' he replied in the same tone.

Within days, Sofia began working at the makeshift clinic dealing as best as it could with the cuts and broken bones, the childhood illnesses and the mothers trying to keep their babies alive. The little group of doctors worked hard, reaching patients who had no means of getting to a hospital.

In a strange kind of way, she enjoyed it, for all the pain and heartache. Cleaning had been safe and contained. She could do her work and slip out again, barely needing to speak to anyone apart from take orders or the periodic reprimand – which both she and Signor Alessi knew was unjustified and just a way of ensuring she knew her place – at her lack of perfection.

At the little clinic, she just worked with the doctors and nurses battling on behalf of their patients. It was like entering life again – the life she had known before Walter had become ill. More than that, she acknowledged, with a mixture of sadness and the faintest of optimism, it was a return to the passionately committed young woman she had once been. The woman she had thought was lost. She was still there, the girl who had grabbed life with all its opportunities, who had worked day and night to develop a talent for catching likenesses with her pencil that had dazzled all those who saw them. The young woman who had once been determined to use that talent to break free from the confines of the contessa's expectations.

She was older now. Wiser. With a lifetime of griefs and regrets behind her. But the passion was still there. It struck her with a force she had never felt before as she sat in the little square next to the clinic, listening to the quiet rush of the fountain, watching the life go on around her. Life goes on in war, changed, and yet the same. Washing must be done, the cleaning of houses to keep vermin and bugs away. The preparing of food to keep body and soul together, the mending of roofs and broken shutters with whatever material might be to hand.

Without thinking, Sofia took out from her pocket the small sketchbook and pencil she had found abandoned in the Studio Theodora. Soon, her hand was moving with its old fluency, catching the lines of the fountain and the benches set around the edges of the square.

'Tea.' She started at the sound of Niccolò Conti's voice. She had been so engrossed that she hadn't seen him arrive and place a cup in front of her. 'You look as if you need it.'

'Thank you,' she replied with a smile of gratitude, hastily closing the sketchbook.

'So that's what brought you to Venice,' he remarked, taking the remaining seat. 'You are an artist.'

'Hardly.'

'You could have fooled me.'

She sighed. 'I haven't practised properly in years. Probably since before you first went to school,' she added.

He laughed. 'I don't believe that.' At her expression, he stopped. 'You are serious.' He turned away, cradling his own cup in his hands. 'I can't imagine not working in medicine.' He cleared his throat. 'If you don't mind me saying, when I saw you here so engrossed, it struck me that it's the first time I've really seen you at peace.'

'Drawing always was my way of finding peace,' she replied. 'I had grand plans of being famous once – I was famous,' she added. 'Briefly. Although sometimes I doubted that it was really my skill, rather than being young and well connected. I threw it all away.'

He was still concentrating on his tea. 'For love?'

Sofia hesitated. She had kept her secrets, her deepest loves and regrets, for so long, concealing them even from Walter; her instinct was to lock them away even tighter. But there was something about working together under such impossible circumstances that drew even the most unlikely of companions together in ways that would never happen in the outside world. It was a stripping away of everything, leaving only their shared humanity, and the awareness that life could end at any moment. Besides, she was tired of secrets.

'What else,' she said quietly.

'That's the only thing that nearly made me give up medicine,' he remarked, lost in thought. 'The girl I wished to marry. Well, her parents didn't think a country doctor would be good enough for her; they insisted I should join the family firm and become a businessman. So I could provide for her, so they knew we would have security. Otherwise, they said they would never give permission.'

'But you didn't give up becoming a doctor.'

'No.' His face was still bent over his cup. 'I came so close to throwing all my training and my dreams away. But they sent Maria away to stay with an aunt in Rome. She died of malaria. I never saw her again.'

'I'm sorry.' So that explained his understanding, his kindness, she thought sadly. The confidence and arrogance of youth had been knocked out of him long before war and the endless stream of patients came to test him.

'We were very young,' he muttered. 'That's the irony. Her parents were probably right that we were too young. But I'd still rather have had the chance.'

'I feel the same,' she replied. 'He died,' she added abruptly. The words hung in the air. All this time, she had never spoken them aloud. The grief seared through her, as sharp as it had been some twenty years before. 'In a boating accident.' She grimaced. 'All through the last war, I was terrified for him. I was one of the lucky ones. He survived, he came home to me, so we could live our lives as we'd always planned. In freedom. Away from others' expectations. It felt doubly cruel that he came through all that destruction unscathed to die from a freak wave overturning his yacht on a calm summer's day.'

She met his eyes, reading in them the shared understanding of grief. 'I've never felt so alone as I did then. His family and mine didn't approve, you see. My mother had been set on me marrying someone rich and influential, and his family wouldn't even meet me. And by then I had a child.'

'That must have been hard. My sister lost her husband when her children were small,' he added. 'If our mother hadn't taken her in, I don't know what she would have done.'

'No,' said Sofia. He must have read on her face that this was a subject that went no further, quietly turning the conversation to the latest puzzling case to reach the clinic. Shortly afterwards he left her alone to finish her tea.

Sofia sat for a while, deep in thought. Her hand returned to the pencil and she opened the page. The scene in the little square had shifted, the balance of light and shadows transformed. Her grief and regret were still there, but no longer frozen. No longer holding her in their twin grip.

She looked down at her drawing. She could see its faults and the stiffness of the figures where her lack of practice had prevented her hand from flowing with its old ease. But, with renewed application, that could return. Painting had once been her life. However few materials she had to hand, she could make it so again.

Nursing Walter had left her feeling old. With the smallest flicker of guilt, she felt the years peel away. She wasn't ancient; she was a woman in her prime. No longer bound by uncertainty and a wish to please others. Her future, if this war allowed her, was in her own hands.

'And this time,' she said, setting her pencil to work again, 'I've nothing to lose.'

One day this war must end. Until then, like all those around her, she was living every day as if it were the last, focussing only on the things closest to her heart. A few more minutes, and she would be in the fray of the little clinic, with all its griefs and tragedies, and its brief moments of joy. But for now, she was sitting in the square with the fountain dancing in the light, regaining the passion she had relinquished so long ago. This time, if she lived, she would not give it up again.

SIXTEEN

CORNWALL

October 1941

On the long journey from Birmingham to Cornwall, Kate caught glimpses of countryside flying by, clothed in its autumn brilliance of reds and yellows. A few trees had already been denuded of leaves, their branches stark against the deep blue of the sky. Hedges bordering the fields were turning towards their winter brown. Smoke from bonfires rose, as gardeners cleared the ground before the frost and snow could arrive.

After reaching Bristol, the train slowed, taking its laborious way, station by station, to Exeter and along the coast to their final stop in St Ives. With many now sleeping or occupied with board games, Kate slipped out into the corridor to stretch her legs. She was exhausted from keeping the children amused with 'I Spy' and other entertainment, and reassuring those who had never been more than a few streets from their homes. While the younger were excited at heading out into this unknown landscape, several of the older children were clearly unnerved by the wide open spaces, so very different from the network of roads and buildings that had formed their entire world.

As Kate emerged, pulling the door of the compartment closed behind her, she found Peter smoking by an open window, watching the coastline and the view of the sea.

'Beautiful, isn't it,' he remarked, as she made to pass by.

'Very.' She stopped. The train was running alongside a wide beach, where rollers broke in the deep turquoise sea, blown back into arched froth by the wind, before collapsing onto the shore. Pillars of light appeared from the clouds on the horizon as the sun began to sink towards a golden end to the day. She took in deep breaths of sea air, the taste of salt on her lips bringing back memories.

'The reality?' he remarked, watching her expression.

'Rather than the sea of my imagination, you mean.'

'Yes.'

'I was a small child when I last sailed on the sea,' she replied, irritated by his teacherly tone, as if he viewed her as simply another of his pupils to be instructed. 'But I remember how wild it can be, and how I was terrified and thought we might never reach the shore and I'd be dragged down to the bottom knowing I wouldn't survive, feeling every last bit of breath leave my body. I still can't put my head under water when I'm swimming in the lake at home. You don't really think I'd be telling the children that, do you, when they'd just come from such destruction?'

He at least had the grace to appear disconcerted. 'No. You're right.' He drew on his cigarette, eyes on the far horizon. 'I should have thought.'

She wasn't letting him off that lightly. 'Is that an apology?'

This time he smiled, his face softening from its customary severity. 'I expect it is.'

The train rattled and jolted them as it turned inland, crashing his bad arm against the side, cigarette spiralling to the floor.

'Damn.'

'You all right?' she demanded.

'I'll live,' he muttered, turning his face away to hide his expression. She retrieved the cigarette while he caught his breath. 'Thanks.' He took it from her, lighting it clumsily with his good hand, and drew in the smoke as if his life depended on it.

She didn't like to leave him, when he was so obviously in pain – one that must surely bring up memories he'd no wish to dwell on. She suspected the very least of them must be far worse than those they shared of the family in Hellebore Row crushed beneath the weight of their home, and which she found impossible to erase from her mind. She pretended to gaze out of the window at the fields that had now replaced the rush of waves, until his breathing eased again.

'Thanks,' he said, easing a fresh cigarette out of the breast pocket of his jacket as she turned to leave.

'That's all right.'

'Why did you come over the sea?' he asked.

She frowned at him. 'What a strange question.'

'Indulge me.'

It was a simple answer, and she had nothing to hide. 'Papa came to fetch me.'

'Mr Arden, you mean?'

'Yes.'

'From those warm idyllic waters you described to the children?' His face was back to the severity again, eyes watching her, but this time as she imagined an interrogator would watch his prey. Gina was right; at this moment he looked like the kind of man who could easily turn into a fanatic. Whether that might be for good or ill in his case, she didn't care to think, given that they were destined to spend the next months – maybe years – in close proximity.

'I don't remember,' she lied, returning to the compartment at speed.

. . .

Once they reached the station at St Ives, Kate forgot her weariness and a nagging sense of discomfiture at Peter's questioning. The group sprang into action, reaching for bags and suitcases from the overhead racks and under the seats, and shepherding their now tired and crotchety charges onto the station, where a cold wind swirled around them, bringing in the scent of the sea.

They had no sooner counted heads twice over, and divided the children into manageable groups, when the lumbering of a large vehicle could be heard pulling up, with a loud squeal of brakes. Gina led them outside to where an elderly cream-coloured school bus, the frames of its windows painted a jaunty crimson, was coming to a halt. It had the battered look of one well used to winding its way through the lanes and network of farmsteads and villages along the north Cornwall coast.

'Seems we're just in time,' announced a fair-haired young man, jumping down to greet them. He shook Peter's hand vigorously and gave a mock bow to Kate and Gina. 'Laurence Elliot at your service, ladies. Here to escort you safely through the wilds of the Cornish countryside, keeping wreckers and pirates at bay.' The older boys grinned at this and a few of the girls braved a giggle, while several of the younger looked as if they were about to burst into tears.

'Don't be such an idiot, Lance,' called a young woman clad in bright red dungarees and a matching headscarf, disentangling herself from the driver's seat to join him. 'There's no need to terrify everyone with your nonsense. Don't listen to him. There aren't any wreckers, and I'm not sure pirates ever existed, at least not ones with parrots and wooden legs. I'm Ellen Nancarrow, from Tregannon Castle. Call me Ellen. You'll be relieved to know I'm your driver for today, so you're safe from Lance crashing you through walls on the way back.'

'As if I'd do such a thing,' he protested, grinning.

Kate exchanged glances with Gina. They had both assumed Miss Nancarrow, the owner of Tregannon Castle, would be an elderly lady, with the stately bearing of the late Queen Mary, complete with diamond tiara, and not a breezy young woman, who seemed perfectly at home behind the steering wheel of a cumbersome bus. Kate had a suspicion Ellen Nancarrow would be equally confident at the wheel of a tractor, bumping across the fields, Land Girls following behind.

Ellen came to a halt at the sight of the weary and bedraggled group of children, instantly forgetting her levity. 'Oh my goodness, there are so many of you! It's all right, I'm sure you can all fit into the coach. It's used for the school in the harbour every day, and it's not far to go. It'll be a bit bumpy, and it will take longer because of the dipped headlights, but there's a hot meal waiting for you at the castle, and your beds are all made up. Although some might have to share, just for tonight.'

'We're used to that,' called one of girls from the back of the queue. 'Top to tail at home.'

Ellen took this in her stride. 'Well, I don't think it will be nearly as squashed as that.'

'Is it because of planes?' piped up one of the boys.

'The headlights, you mean?' said Ellen. 'Yes, it is.' A slight frisson went through the group. 'Only a precaution. Tregannon Castle is high up on the cliffs above a harbour, you can see any light for miles. Don't want to give Jerry the slightest excuse to come nosing over here. No one has dared so far.'

Across the rows of small heads, Kate met Gina's eyes. How long since any of them, Gina and Peter included, had enjoyed a calm night's sleep, she wondered, without the dread of instant death? Or, even more terrible, not so instant.

With everyone settled, Lance jumped in behind the last child and pulled the door closed, before taking the seat next to

Kate. Ellen was already seated at the wheel, and within minutes was manoeuvring the heavy vehicle with ease.

'So,' said Lance, as they bumped and roared over potholes between tall hedges on either side, 'you're the one who's not a teacher.'

'I came to help with the children,' returned Kate, bristling slightly at the suggestion that she was the spoilt daughter of a wealthy family, playing at doing good. 'And anything else that needs to be done. I'm not squeamish and I'm quite happy getting my hands dirty.'

'I'm glad to hear it. There's plenty of clearing away of scrubland to be done if you feel up to it.'

'Of course,' said Kate, firmly.

'Well, at least you don't seem as weedy as some of the Land Girls,' he replied. 'They look as if they'll faint after half a day's work; you look as if you might last a bit longer than a few weeks.'

'Take no notice, Lance likes provoking people,' called Ellen above the roar of the engine. 'And especially the female variety.' She concentrated for a few minutes as the bus swung round a double bend. 'He's only a volunteer at the castle himself. And a city boy at heart.'

'But you couldn't do without my expertise with forestry to help clearing the ground,' he retorted. 'There aren't many volunteers to be had.'

'Fair point.' Ellen conceded. 'I'm afraid it's true, the whole Tregannon estate had been left to go to rack and ruin in my aunt's last years.' She concentrated on a particularly tight corner, avoiding the delivery boy coming the other way, racing down the incline with the glee of an empty basket on the front of his bicycle, with not a light to be seen. 'Now it's my responsibility, it's up to me.'

Kate looked out at the landscape as the coach reached the

top of the cliff and made its way along fields dotted every now and again by the shadows of windblown trees, the glint of water caught in the starlight. From the moment she had arrived at Arden House, she had lived amongst swathes of fields divided by lines of hedges and scrubby trees. The only expanse of water was the lake on the Arden Estate, and the only hint of salt water the tidal River Avon, seen at a distance apart from occasional visits to Stratford-Upon-Avon. Despite her exhaustion, she felt the deep thrill of being so close to the sea.

'Can we go swimming, Miss?' demanded one of the boys.

'I'm sure we can,' she replied with a smile.

'I can't swim,' exclaimed his neighbour, sounding alarmed.

'Don't worry, I'll teach you,' replied Lance. 'There's a beach below the castle that's still open. Plenty of the bigger ones are closed off, of course, but there are always one or two that are too small to be, ah—' He came to a halt as Ellen gave a loud cough. 'To be of any interest,' he added, lamely.

Kate suppressed a grin. She couldn't decide whether to be irritated or charmed by Lance's boyish enthusiasm. Ellen, it appeared, had him firmly under control when his ebullience threatened to get out of hand.

'You mean to the Germans,' said the first boy solemnly.

'Only a precaution,' said Lance, in more measured tones this time. 'We're quite safe here, and there are all kinds of anti-tank defences and pill boxes, just in case.'

'The coast is well protected, by both the army and the air force,' added Peter firmly, from his place at the back of the bus. 'No one's going to invade.'

The boys fell silent. Kate smiled at them reassuringly, along with the row of girls just behind them, who were looking pale and wide-eyed, memories of the bombing they had left behind written on their faces. Several of the smaller children seated just behind them burst into tears, to be instantly comforted by Gina.

'Sorry,' said Lance, sounding a little guilty. 'I'm not really used to youngsters. I should have thought.'

'You can say that again,' remarked Ellen, concentrating on the road.

He didn't remain crestfallen for long. 'So, what brought you here, Miss Arden,' he resumed, turning to Kate. 'Apart from helping the teachers. A love of Cornwall?'

'I've never been to Cornwall.'

'Really?' He peered at her intently in the faint light, with a closeness that was slightly unnerving.

'I'm sure I'd have remembered if I had,' she retorted.

'I'm surprised, since you've travelled as far as Suffolk.'

Kate blinked. 'How on earth did you know that?'

He chuckled at her surprise. 'I saw you there. At the archaeological site at Sutton Hoo, the summer before the war. You were sketching the impression of the boat left in the earth. I'm sure you were quite too absorbed to remember me.'

'I'm afraid so,' she replied. He was right, she didn't remember him. Usually she had a painter's memory for faces, however briefly or imperfectly glimpsed, and Lance, she could not help noticing, had the classical, Roman-nosed kind of male beauty any red-blooded woman would be unlikely to forget. It crossed her mind he was playing one of his games, seeking to disconcert her. But then he smiled, and the moment was gone.

'I thought it was you,' he said, returning to his conversation with the boys, half-turned away from her, preventing further conversation, as Ellen inched the coach carefully between two gateposts and up a drive to the pale stone of a building through the trees. Even in the rapidly falling darkness, Kate could see that the castle, perched on the top of the cliffs, had nothing of the Tudor grandeur of Arden House. Instead, it had the look of being hewn out of the rock itself, with a battlement on one side and a round tower punctuated with small arched windows that gave the appearance of something infinitely older.

'Tregannon Castle is medieval,' said Ellen, as her passengers murmured between themselves, peering through the windows at their destination. 'It was built to guard the harbour and the coastline, but there are stories that the original fortress went back much further. The people from the harbour say it is as old as time itself.'

Kate gazed at the round tower and the outline of battlements silhouetted against a sky of stars, with the glint of water beyond, and couldn't help feeling a thrill of excitement. Yesterday, she had been in the midst of imminent death and destruction, today she was about to enter a time-honoured castle, the kind fit for kings and queens. It didn't feel real, apart from the fact that it has also been built for defence, to keep an enemy at bay. She glanced back towards the sea and the long line of coast, with no defences visible. It felt uncomfortably exposed.

But she had no time to think. Within minutes, the coach drew up in front of the building. The front door opened up to reveal a darkened hallway, with figures emerging to help the weary children to descend from the coach and hurry inside. Some, Kate could see, were no more than children themselves. Once the door was shut, the lamps were lit, allowing everyone to blink in the sudden light. The vast, cavernous room could have been a medieval feasting hall, save for the telephone on a stand. Cold rose from the flagstones, giving it the air of a place that could never quite get warm.

The evacuees trudged after Ellen, up large stone stairs to the higher floors. Kate followed with Gina, taking the case from a small girl who looked as if she was about to drop with exhaustion and was beginning to cry. To Kate's relief, the higher floors felt a little warmer, with polished wooden floors covered with rugs. Any previous furniture had been removed, leaving rows of beds in each room.

While Gina and Peter settled their charges, Kate followed

Ellen up a narrow winding staircase to a series of small rooms at the top of the castle.

'There are a few camp beds in the attics, thank goodness,' said Ellen. 'I think there should be enough until we can find some more proper beds for them all. There's an amazing view of the sea up here. These were the old servants' quarters, not that the castle has had more than a cook and a couple of maids for years. No butlers, thank goodness. I thought this would be the best for you and Gina; you'll have peace and quiet away from the rest.'

'It looks perfect,' said Kate, placing her knapsack on the empty bed next to the window. She didn't care if the edges of the curtains were stirred by the breeze. Already she could hear the little panes letting in the sound of the sea and the distant call of seagulls, stirring excitement in her blood. She couldn't wait for morning and the chance to look down on the promised vista of waves and cliffs.

She followed Ellen, who crawled into the attics to retrieve old army beds and mattresses, left over from when the castle had been used as a hospital for soldiers in World War I.

'They're a bit rusty, but they'll do.' Ellen manoeuvred a metal base through the trap door.

'Here, I'll give you a hand.' Kate found Peter arriving to help take the weight with his good arm, and they lifted it to rest on the floorboards. 'I'm afraid we've overrun you.'

'It's nothing we can't deal with,' said Ellen, cheerfully. 'We put these away after the first rush of children at the start of the war found places with families in the village. A couple of us might have to do with a mattress on the floor for tonight, but the WI will find us more beds if we need them, and bedding. People have been wonderfully generous.'

Just as they were in Arden, thought Kate. She wondered how many other little towns and villages were making the same attempts to house those left homeless and friendless by the bombing of the Blitz in the major cities. The children they had accompanied were just a tiny fraction of those displaced and traumatised, with nothing left of their lives but the clothes they stood up in. Pity went through her, along with a sliver of fear. Even here, deep in the rural landscape of Cornwall, they were struggling against impossible odds to keep the children housed and fed, let alone help them deal with their loss and the horrors they had witnessed.

Gina joined them to help Peter and Lance carry the beds into an empty bedroom that wasn't yet crammed. As the final one came down, Kate followed them, carrying the mattresses to fit on top, to the relief of a group of forlorn-looking boys, who were standing by their suitcases clearly under the impression that the floorboards were to be their destiny. Peter soon had them organised, putting together the beds and placing the mattresses, to be covered by sheets and blankets and a some-what patched selection of eiderdowns to go on top against the cold.

A sound of a gong deep below, accompanied by the school-room smell of cabbage and steamed pudding, sent them down towards the castle's dining room, set within a vast vaulted space that must have once served as the great hall.

Kate came to a halt at the doorway, heart clenching at the sight of row upon row of silent children, taking bowls of steaming soup politely, as if afraid they could be taken away just as easily. She saw more than one slipping a piece of bread surreptitiously into a pocket. What you did when the rich, who had plenty, offered such bounty. Hungry faces crouched over the meal, some with none of the roundness of childhood, but already having the careworn look of adults. Several of the girls, Pamela among them, were helping the younger children with the practiced hand of ones who had been expected to cook and clean and childmind since they could walk and had now been left in the position of caregiver.

'That should warm them up,' remarked Lance, arriving behind her. 'Some look as if they can barely stay awake. I didn't realise they were going to be so small.'

'They'll settle,' said Kate. 'Children are good at adapting.'

'Let's hope so.' He was watching them thoughtfully. 'I can't say my own family is easy. Conform or excommunication awaits. But at least they are there.'

'Yes,' said Kate. A pang of unexpected homesickness went through her. Arden House already felt as far away as the moon. In Birmingham, Cordelia might be spending a precious night free from fire watching, but already she, and the houses around the little park, must be crouching beneath the sounds of the Blitz.

'So what constitutes excommunication?' she asked, to distract herself.

'Sorry?'

'In your family, what leads to excommunication?'

'Oh, I see what you mean. Disobedience. Not toeing the party line.' He grinned, returning to the Lance she had seen at the station. 'But then aren't we all? Toeing the party line, one way or another. Trying to live up to expectation.'

'Are we?' It was a mask, she saw, his bonhomie. The mask of what he felt – or been told – he should feel and be. Just like her mask of defiance was often a way to hide her fear of being cast out friendless into the world. *I don't care*, she had told herself since she'd been a tiny, vulnerable stranger in a strange land. *Do what you please, I don't need you, I don't care.*

'If you don't see it, you're fooling yourself,' he retorted, heading off to join Ellen and Gina, who were handing round steamed pudding – no doubt of the carrot and turnip variety, attempting valiantly to recreate the stodgy comfort of the pre-war version.

Kate watched him frowning. That chink of insight into the Lance beneath the teasing and joking had been to someone she could warm to. But the Lance who enjoying provoking, however many feelings might be hurt, made her wonder how far deep the mask might go. At this point, she didn't much care to find out.

SEVENTEEN

Once the evening meal was over, and their charges finally settled for the night, Kate and Gina joined Ellen in taking cups of tea in the conservatory at one side of the castle. The night was clear, with a half-moon reflected in the waters of the bay. It sent an eerie light through the cracked panes, set in a wooden frame that, even in the faint glow, Kate could see was clearly rotting. The leaves of the few remaining ferns and a large palm hung limply, with the forlorn look of having been neglected for years.

'It might be battered, but it's my peaceful place,' said Ellen. 'The garden out there is sheltered, and there's a clear view of the sea. It's lovely out there in summer. One day I'll get it back to the way it used to be. My aunt loved this part of the castle. She always said it was the only bit that felt the same way as when it was an artists' colony. I have a feeling that in her later years, she regretted she hadn't turned it back into a place for painters after all.'

'It's beautiful,' sighed Gina wistfully.

'Miss Parsons told me it used to be well known for the

artists who stayed here,' ventured Kate, who had been itching to ask from the moment they arrived.

'So it was,' said Ellen. 'I remember it from when I was a little girl, in the years before the last war. The house was filled with paintings, hung up on every wall, and there were painters with easels everywhere you went in the grounds, whatever the weather. This part of Cornwall is known for its light, of course. But there was always something very special about the castle. I suppose because it was one of the few places dedicated to women artists.' She sighed. 'But even then, it didn't escape the First World War. It must have felt like it does now: a bit indulgent to carry on creating beautiful things when there's so much that needs to be done for the war effort. Most of the artists volunteered as nurses, or to work in the factories and on the land in the last war too.' She sat for a moment in thought. 'Perhaps it's as well. The links to Venice would have been broken anyhow, now that Italy is on the side of the Nazis.'

'Venice?' Kate kept her voice as casual as she could, thankful that the darkness hid her expression.

'Aunt Theodora always had close ties with a studio for women artists in Venice, right up until she was too old to travel, but she still contributed paintings whenever they had an exhibition. A number of well-known painters were part of the studio, right up to a few years ago. There's a poster upstairs in the office, from the time Vanessa Bell contributed paintings to one of their exhibitions. Aunt Theodora loved her work – she was so proud her own pictures were exhibited alongside such a talented painter, not to mention the sister of Virginia Woolf, of course. You can see Godrevy Lighthouse, the one in *To the Lighthouse,* from the cliffs.'

'So was it the last war that stopped artists coming to the castle?' asked Kate. Her mind was reeling from this sudden connection with Venice. Yet, at the same time, it made sense. Miss Parsons might have had made a promise not to give any information about her mother, but that didn't mean she felt unable to point her in the right direction. Was that why Miss Parsons had been so insistent on Kate accompanying Gina to Tregannon Castle?

'In a way,' Ellen replied. 'There were other things too...' She shook herself. 'Miss Parsons said you're an excellent painter yourself, Kate.'

'She's brilliant,' remarked Gina, before Kate could say a word. 'And such a good teacher; you should see the way she was encouraging the children to draw when we were at St Mary's, and on the train, too.'

'I just gave them the materials,' said Kate, embarrassed.

'You encouraged them, too,' said Gina, 'by not judging what they did, or trying to control it so their work looked like any other painting. You gave them the space to express themselves. You should have seen them, Ellen, they were all so much calmer.'

In the faint light, Kate could just make out Ellen's smile. 'To be honest, it's why I jumped at Miss Parsons's suggestion that a painter should come with you.'

'Did she?' Kate's heart began to race. So Miss Parsons really had done her best to engineer this time at the castle.

Ellen finished her tea. 'She understands we are trying to follow therapeutic models here, even though it's tricky when you're still in the midst of a war and you don't know what might happen next. But I like the idea of encouraging the children to make things. That's what my aunt did with the soldiers convalescing in the last war, especially the ones suffering from shell shock. It seemed occupations that absorbed them, like gardening and painting, helped them. We've started to do that kind of thing with the evacuees who are already here, and I'm certain the painting will help. Really, we could do with a dedicated space where they can be as messy as can be.

'My aunt died just before the war, and since then there's

been so much to do, I haven't really had a chance to explore. There are supposed to be a couple of old barns further down where it's overgrown. We're clearing it to make room to grow more food, so I'm hoping we can make a path down there and maybe use them, if they haven't fallen down.'

'I'll help you,' said Kate. 'When I'm not with the children, that is.'

'Excellent,' said Ellen. 'I like to encourage the children to be outside for at least part of the day, and some of the mothers from the harbour are happy to bring their own to work on the vegetable patches and keep an eye on them. It gives us a bit of freedom to do the things needed in the grounds.'

'I'd like to as well, when I can,' added Gina.

Ellen sighed. 'You know, once this war is over, I'd love to carry out Aunt Theodora's last wish and revive the castle as a place for artists. If the barns are still there, I'm sure they could be converted into studios once they are no longer needed as classrooms. There were so many artists in St Ives before the war; I'm sure they'll come back once it's over.'

Kate could hear a slight edge, mirroring all their fears that peace might come at the price of freedom. Rumours of atrocities being carried out by the Nazis, both on their own people and in every place they conquered, had reached even out-of-the-way Brierley-in-Arden. She felt so close to finding out more about her past, and yet she might never have the chance to follow up any lead she might find at Tregannon Castle. If the Allies lost the war, they might soon be living under enemy occupation, and even if they won, the destruction all over Europe might mean finding anyone impossible. Miss Parsons herself had cautioned Kate that the uncertainties of war could well mean her mother might be lost forever.

There was a moment's silence, until Ellen cleared her throat. 'I'd love the opportunity to rebuild the connection with the studio in Venice. Aunt Theodora was always an internationalist. She believed mutual understanding could be fostered between nations. I've a feeling we are going to need that more than ever once this war is over, and I like the idea of women artists reaching across the divide. It feels a way to build lasting peace. If Venice survives, of course.'

'It has to, surely,' said Gina. 'I've never been, but everyone I know who has says it is the most beautiful place you can imagine, and completely unique. Surely not even a monster like Hitler could destroy such a historic place. Didn't he fancy himself as some kind of artist?'

'St Paul's only just survived the Blitz,' said Kate, despair going through her. 'It feels like anything could happen. I'm sure not even Venice can be completely safe.' It was hard to know what was going on in a place so far away, or how much worse the destruction might get as armies battled for control of Italy. The city in the drawing she had found in her volume of sonnets might already no longer exist.

Kate was glad of the distraction of following Ellen into the garden to breathe in the night air. They headed out through a small gate onto a path overlooking the sea. Kate shivered in the cold, but drank in the sight of the moon bathing the land in silvery light, sending the dew on the grass glistening and the distant cliffs into dark shadows. All was still, not a light to be seen, and no sound to be heard apart from the roar of waves against rocks and the murmur of pebbles dragged to and fro. Kate gazed out over the vastness of the Atlantic Ocean that stretched unheeded to America, and realised how painfully close this jutting piece of land was to the continent where war was raging. She wondered what dangers lurked in the peaceful-looking sea.

Gina must have had the same thought. 'Do you think there really are Nazi submarines out there?' she whispered.

'Probably,' replied Ellen, in an equally low voice. 'The fishermen say the waters are mined to catch them. There were submarines out there in the last war, so there must be at least one or two out there now. The Home Guard keep a watch on the cliffs in case they attempt anything, or if anyone tries to come ashore. The fishermen are brave venturing out there, but we're grateful for the fish. Believe me, there's nothing like a bit of fresh mackerel to liven up the usual potatoes and turnips.'

'I can't wait.' Gina sighed, clearly glad of the change of subject. 'I so miss cheese. The ration's hardly worth it. You can't make a good bit of cheese on toast and trying is torture.'

Kate dropped a little behind as her companions strolled on ahead, deep in the remembered delights of butter and proper ice cream, not to mention enough rashers of bacon as you could eat for Sunday breakfast. All the things they had once taken for granted.

Kate turned to look back towards the dark shape of the castle, silhouetted against the stars. It couldn't be simply a coincidence. In her mind's eye she could clearly see the drawing of Lady Macbeth, and the window opening up onto the Grand Canal in Venice. Women artists, in Cornwall and in Venice. There had to be a connection somewhere. Now it was up to her to find it.

As the three returned to the warmth of Tregannon Castle, a cold wind blew in from the ocean, throwing the hint of spray, cold, in their faces.

For her first months at Tregannon Castle, Kate was too worn out by the end of each day to do anything more than crawl into bed and fall into a dead, dreamless, sleep.

She helped Peter and Gina, and the volunteers from the village looking after the children, getting them into some kind of routine of learning, between tending to the rows of winter vegetables in the garden near to the castle and preparing for the following spring.

On fine afternoons, when the children worked in the gardens, Kate helped Ellen clear the overgrown land leading down to the shore and learnt how to fell trees accurately, so as to know exactly where they would drop. Since the start of the war, she had been used to digging and weeding, but she had never attempted to do such hard physical work. Her back ached, her muscles ached, but her lungs were filled with sea air and it was wonderful to feel herself growing stronger by the day.

That Christmas was as cheerful as they could make it, with a tree festooned with paper ornaments made by the children, along with ornate glass baubles Ellen had found in the attic. Like the evacuees, Kate was used to winters of heavy frost and snow in the landlocked countryside around Birmingham. It felt strange to be in the relative warmth of a winter this far south and so close to the sea.

Like the previous two years, 1942 dawned with little sign of the war ending. But spring brought new life to the castle grounds, along with the need to cultivate as many vegetables as they could, with the future remaining so uncertain.

As spring turned towards summer, and the urgency of planting eased a little, Kate found the itch to start her own drawing again returning. With the return of longer days, the children spent more time playing on the beach below the castle, reached by a series of steep steps cut into the cliffs. Finally, she could sneak a few hours for herself.

Late one afternoon, while Peter supervised the children braving the sea, Kate clambered up onto a small ledge next to the steps leading down to the beach. She drew out her battered old sketchbook and pencil and began sketching the scene. It still gave her a strange feeling watching the ocean. Its vastness and its changes of mood exhilarated her; she never grew tired of watching the light change on water, as she had once watched the gleam of the distant River Avon, back home in Brierley-in-Arden. She could see why artists flocked to St Ives.

From this height, she could just make out the fishermen in the harbour, busy with the mending of boats and nets. Small children, many of them also evacuees from the crammed city streets of London or Birmingham, watched, or raced around in the unaccustomed cleanliness and freedom.

A wave broke on the rocks at the harbour entrance, sending up a half-hearted rush of spray into the still air. Around her, the sun warmed the grass and released the scent of lavender from the castle gardens. The voices of Peter and Gina on the beach, mingled with children's laughter, floated into the distance. Kate felt a kind of peace as she closed her eyes, caught in the bubble of a calm summer evening.

Memories stirred. The old memories, that had hovered around her since childhood, and had crept closer since her discovery of the sketch of the terrace. She could feel the power of a far more intense sun. Her ears were filled with the deep quiet of a distant sea that, so unlike the long lines of rollers on the beach below, barely moved in response to its tidal pull.

She held the vision tight, drinking in the rustle of vines, the sharp sweetness of rough-coated lemons. This time it was more real than ever before, like a tunnel opening up, her senses reaching into the forbidden rooms around her. Voices echoed from deep within the villa. *Villa.* Not a house, not a mansion, not even a castle. The villa. It had a name. She could feel it coming towards her, with the quiet tread of footsteps along the stone walkway.

'*Darling, cara mia...*' A woman's voice, from far away. Imagination? Wishful thinking? The dream of a love that must have been hers once, the ache for a mother's arms she had felt all her life. A love that had been lost. Or had thrown her away. Because she was not good enough? Eyes shut tight, Kate strained her whole body to listen to the elusive voice that was both strange and yet familiar as a heartbeat.

The footsteps were so close, she could feel the warm breath

on her skin. In her mind's eye she searched for the face, shrouded in the darkness beneath the vine. The woman stepped out into the patch of sunlight, the features of her face resolving, growing ever clearer.

'Watch it!'

Kate started. Her eyes shot open as her body began to slide from its hollow, and gathered speed as it reached the grass that led to the jagged rocks beneath. A hand grasped her, pulling her back to safety.

'I'm all right,' she said, freeing herself from Lance, who had a concerned expression on his face.

'Wrong place to doze off; you'd have hit your head on the rock or slipped down that edge. There's nothing between you and the beach, you know.'

'I wasn't asleep.' She scowled at him.

His dark gold hair stirred around his head in curls as the wind blew up from the sea.

'Well, you should be more careful in future.'

'All right, all right. No harm done.' She pulled back away from him. 'Thank you,' she muttered, reaching for her sketchbook as it tumbled away.

Lance caught it at the last minute before it headed over the cliff, and handed it back. He settled on the grass beside her. 'So you really are an artist.' He reached for the paper with its drawing of the beach, which had become detached from the rest, catching it as it drifted towards the edge. 'You're good.'

'There's no need to sound surprised,' she returned.

'Sorry.' For once, he looked slightly abashed. 'I'm afraid I'm surrounded by lady artists, the kind who really should find some other way of displaying their accomplishments.'

'Your sisters?' she asked, curious. Lance had never revealed much about himself. His crisp English accent indicated a public-school education, but he didn't demonstrate the blind

arrogance she had always associated with wealth. A poor rela-
tion, perhaps?

Ellen, she noticed, was careful to keep him at arm's length,
despite being glad of the help he volunteered during his free
hours. It made Kate wonder if Ellen suspected Lance wasn't
above trying to charm his way into becoming master of
Tregannon Castle, along with all its presumed wealth and
status.

The observation made Kate wary of him, too. She was
becoming increasing certain she could detect a hint of Birmingham drawl now and again escaping his carefully cultivated
accent. If he moved in the right circles, he could well have met
one of her brothers before the war, or known their Birmingham
friends. If he was indeed on the lookout for a rich wife, he could
well have recognised the Arden name as belonging to local
landed gentry. Kate sighed. She couldn't help feeling that, even
so far away, she could never quite escape the shadow of Arden
House.

She wasn't going to ask him outright. So all she really knew
about Lance was that, like Peter, he had a reserved occupation.
She'd been told by the Land Girls that he was managing an
estate of extensive forests containing precious stores of timber.
The younger and more impressionable were convinced his
coast-watching duties as a volunteer with the local Home
Guard meant that he was really a dare-devil spy, working for
the War Department, all ready to go into action should the
enemy invade.

Lance, Kate had noted, clearly enjoyed their giggling admiration as he passed. It made her wonder if he'd put around the
rumour himself. He seemed rather too careless to be secretly
equipping underground bunkers to carry out acts of sabotage
behind enemy lines. She felt sure he had been lying about
seeing her at Sutton Hoo. During their brief exchanges when
she worked in the grounds, she had slipped in several remarks

that, without him noticing, had confirmed that he had little interest in archaeology. After she had deliberately started up a conversation with Gina about the finds at Pompeii, he had tended to avoid them both, turning his flirtatious attentions instead onto the Land Girls. If he was a spy, Kate concluded with a grin, he wasn't a very good one.

'My sisters don't have time to play at being lady artists,' he remarked loftily. 'Not like all those frumpy spinsters clogging up St Ives before the war.'

'At least they were trying,' she retorted. 'It's easy to criticise when you're not taking the risk of being made a fool of yourself. Especially as it's assumed women are fools before they start.'

'Ouch.' He coloured. 'That's the kind of thing old Miss Nancarrow used to say.'

'Then I like the sound of her.' She retrieved her pencil from her pocket and resumed working on the sketch. 'I'll ask Ellen to show me her paintings.'

'You're wasted here, you know,' he remarked. 'I mean, clearing brambles and watching those children splash paint around. Why did you come here when you could have stayed at home and practised your art?'

'What makes you think I could have practised my art at home?' she said. 'And more to the point, what makes you think watching the children paint and working with my hands isn't benefitting me, as well as being for the war effort?'

'Is it? When you could be studying Canaletto and Van Gogh? Or a modernist like Picasso.'

'You don't think there's room for both, then.'

He frowned at her. 'Are you comparing children's painting to Canaletto?'

'No, of course not. But I'm learning a lot from them.' Down on the beach, the evacuees were beginning to gather their buckets and spades as the sun slid behind the bank of clouds hovering above the horizon.

'I like their freedom. The way they express things uncon-sciously, and without fear, given the chance. I'm always afraid of what people think, of whether I'm good enough. They don't have those doubts; they simply let their emotions and their imagination flow. I find that rather liberating. And besides, personally speaking, I prefer the pictures Vanessa Bell made of Venice to those of Canaletto. I like her use of colour and the delicacy of her lines.'

He raised an eyebrow. 'Really? Or are you just making a point because she's a female painter?'

'I don't think one is better than the other,' she retorted. 'I don't want to compare them. It's just a preference. A personal thing. Are you sure you aren't thinking Canaletto is the greater because you've been told he is? Particularly as it's men who generally decide these things.'

Instead of taking offence, he laughed. 'A suffragette, too.'

Kate snorted. 'Hardly. Mrs Pankhurst was over twenty years ago.' She scrambled to her feet, placing her sketchbook and pencil in her shoulder bag. 'Although I'd agree there's still a long way to go, and especially where women artists are concerned.'

With that, she headed off down the beach to join the others, collecting towels and returning jam jars of shrimps and crabs to the rockpools. When she looked back up at the cliffs, Lance had gone.

EIGHTEEN

CORNWALL

Summer 1942

As the days continued to lengthen, Kate joined Ellen most evenings to start clearing the tangle of scrub nearest the cliffs. They were joined now and again by Gina, escaping the confines of the schoolroom once the children were in bed. There was no sign of any barns, apart from a pile of stones and slates that looked as if it might have been an outbuilding, but had long been raided by the local population for valuable building materials.

Kate enjoyed watching the impenetrable twists of brambles being defeated. Ellen, who seemed to be able to turn her hand to anything, taught her to fell trees accurately and divide the precious logs with Gina, each of them either side of the two-handed saw.

She felt very far from home, especially with the news about bombing of the cities remaining so vague, let alone what might be happening with the fighting abroad. She received brief letters from Alma, interspersed with more detailed ones from Cordelia, who was still sewing in the uniform factory between helping at St Mary's. She didn't say, but Kate retained a distinct impression that her sister was planning to head off to work with refugees in France as soon as she was able.

Although the London Blitz appeared to be over, Cordelia told her the bombing of Birmingham and the Midlands was still continuing. Cordelia was still fire watching on a regular basis, and St Mary's was already bursting at the seams again with more orphans than it could cope with, leaving Miss Parsons at her wits end trying to find places of safety for them.

Cordelia's most recent letter, hastily devoured before Kate headed off to help Gina with the clearing of the scrubland, told her that Jamie had been wounded. Not badly enough to send him home for a long period of time, but still a painful reminder of the dangers both their brothers were facing. Kate hugged the paper, which had been scrawled over to fill every precious inch, and wished she could reach out and embrace her sister, and Jamie too. Cordelia had seen him briefly on his way to see Papa and Alma in Arden House, and Kate knew her sister well enough to pick up the concern underneath the words of reassurance. Jamie was changed by his experiences in France, was all Cordelia would say. But it was enough for Kate to understand that it was his mental, rather than his physical, well-being that had alarmed her sister.

I hate this war, she whispered, folding away her letter and taking her working gloves from her pocket, glad of the distraction offered by an afternoon of hard physical work. Everyone she knew had someone they loved in the army, or serving as nurses near the front line, as well as family living among the endless pounding of the major cities. They were all living in dread of the letter or telegram that would tell them the worst, not to mention the continued whispers of an invasion force massing on the other side of the English Channel.

. . .

That evening, Kate and Gina were the last to leave the area of scrubland far from the castle they were clearing. With rain sweeping towards them, they hastily completed their sawing of their final tree of the day, an ornamental cherry that must have been planted long before the scrubland took over, and was threatening to grow huge and out of control. With the usable wood safety removed, to be stored in the barns and turned into furniture, they sawed the last of the smaller and more rotten branches into logs and stacked them to season. As they finished, pulling on their jumpers and jackets as the sweat began to cool, Gina vanished discretely into the woods, into the privacy of the trees.

Kate straightened up from placing the last logs, rubbing her aching back. Her stomach felt hollow from emptiness, a familiar feeling these days with the hours of exercise and a reliance on mainly vegetables, everything else in generally short supply. She breathed in the scents of the evening air, her mind straying to the stew that awaited them back at the castle.

There was a crash in the woodland, as Gina returned, breathless, covered in twigs and brambles from her rush.

'There's a witch's cabin.'

Kate stared at her. 'A what?'

'A witch's cabin.' Gina pulled off her scarf and began removing the twigs from her hair. 'It looks like no one has been down here for years.'

'There's no such thing as witches,' scoffed Kate.

'Well, it looks like a witch's cabin to me.'

'There has to be some rational explanation.' Kate pushed her way through the trees, until she came to an outcrop of rock. Sure enough, tucked into the hollow beneath, a roof peeped between the trees.

'See. Told you.'

'It seems more like a summer house to me,' said Kate. 'It's perfectly sheltered and invisible from the castle, and it looks as if there is a path straight down to the sea.' She scrambled down the bank of heather and bilberry next to the rock, closely followed by Gina.

'It might have been a fisherman's cottage,' admitted Gina, as they reached the remains of whitewashed stone. The walls looked as solid as could be and even the roof only appeared to have a few slates missing. The windows were grubby, making it almost impossible to peer through.

'There's a table,' said Kate, holding her breath so as not to mist the outside of the window to add to the dust and general grime within. 'And it looks like an armchair and a range. How on earth did they manage to get anything here?'

'They could have brought it up from the sea.' Gina had abandoned her attempts to see if she could open the door and had followed an overgrown pathway to a gap in the trees. 'There's a gate.' Gina pulled at the rusted remains that had fallen to one side when its supporting post had rotted. Kate joined her, peering through the hollowed arch created by the branches of rhododendron, skeleton-like in their darkness, showing a glimpse of sand and a small cove. The smell of salt and the fishiness of seaweed rose up from the waves pulling at the pebbles.

In a glint of brief sunlight shining through the branches, the gleam of metal caught Kate's eye. Amongst the grasses and the creepers, she could make out the gate, now partially freed from greenery.

'It's beautiful,' she exclaimed, brushing away the rest of the climbers to reveal the graceful curves of leaves and fruit in the metalwork.

'I suppose we ought to take it back,' said Gina, regretfully. 'We're supposed to take any railings or metal we find to be handed over for recycling for the war effort.'

'It's only small,' replied Kate. 'It wouldn't make much of a ship, and no one has noticed it's here. Anyhow, it's heavy. It would take ages to drag back to the castle.'

'It is rather beautiful,' said Gina, sounding relieved at a conscience salvaged. 'Someone must have made that when the castle was a centre for artists, before Ellen took over. It could be a famous craftsman; it might even be valuable.'

'Odd that no one has ever mentioned that it's here.'

They turned to look back towards the cottage. From here, they could see it was a single storey, lying low in its hollow as protection against the wind. The wooden window frames were a faded blue, echoed by the peeling paint of the door.

'This must have been loved once,' said Gina, thoughtfully. 'It seems such a pity it's been left to go to rack and ruin. The grounds must have been planted as well. I wondered why there was a cherry in the middle of the scrubland, and all those azaleas and rhododendrons. I'm sure there are more ornamental shrubs in here. Look along the fence, that looks like a lilac, and a forsythia, and those climbing roses don't look as if they are wild. And that's a vine on the side of the cottage.'

Kate followed Gina's gaze. Sure enough, it was a grape vine straggling across the wall that must attract the most sun, while being sheltered by the wind. She looked back down at the gate. The ironwork forming the main part was made up of vine leaves, interspersed with tendrils, the kind that clung to frameworks to support the branches, while in between were stylised bunches of grapes. A strange feeling went through her. *It must be a coincidence*, she told herself. Stylised vines appeared in many places. It didn't mean it had anything to do with her dreams of a place far away, did it?

'In the woods?' Ellen paused in drawing up her accounts to frown at them both. 'I don't remember that on my map of the place. I was only told there were a couple of old barns down there, but that they'd been abandoned years ago.'

'It looks like a proper house,' said Gina. 'It has a path leading down to the beach.'

'Oh, you mean the fisherman's cottage? That's what it must be. That's marked on the map somewhere. It's in ruins.'

'It looked sound to me,' said Kate, exchanging glances with Gina.

Ellen looked surprised. 'Really? Aunt Theodora told me the roof had fallen in years ago, and one of the walls had collapsed after a storm, not long after the last war. It was all so overgrown down there, and the cove is tricky to navigate; I have to confess that was the last thing on my mind. There might be a key in the drawer in the hallway; I haven't found a lock that fits for several of them.'

'Can we try them?' begged Kate. 'If we're clearing the rest of the woodland, it might be a place we could use to shelter from the rain when we're planting. We may be able to use it as a gardening shed, rather than bringing forks and spades back to the castle each day.'

Ellen looked dubious. 'I'm sure any furniture that might have been left in there must be eaten by mould and mice.'

'But no harm in looking,' said Gina. There's a chimney: we might even be able to make a fire. It looked like there was plenty of dead wood around.'

Ellen considered this. 'Very well, but wait until Friday. If the weather holds, Lance will be back from meeting his employer in London.'

'We can just see if any of the keys fit,' said Kate, quickly. 'And see what it's like inside. We'll be down there anyhow, it seems a pity to call the men away from their work if it's all collapsed, after all.'

'You trust us to chop down trees on our own,' added Gina. 'And the door looked solid. Lance and the others will need to be prepared if they are going to break it down. We can let them know if they need axes or not.'

Ellen eyed them both. 'Very well. Just to see if there's a key that fits, and if it does, I want you to just look inside and see the state of the place. No exploring. There has to be a reason my aunt told me the roof had fallen in. I don't want any ceilings falling on top of you.'

'No, Ellen,' said Kate, avoiding Gina's eyes just as carefully as she was avoiding Ellen's. That wasn't exactly a promise.

The next day the two worked hard, clearing the remaining tangle of willow and fallen branches.

'A few more days and we'll be clearing the land around it,' said Gina, as they walked down to the fisherman's cottage. A bird rose from the moss-covered roof, great wings soaring into the dusk. They looked at each other.

'Just a seagull,' said Gina, firmly. She tried several of the keys they had found in a leather pouch in the drawer, but none worked.

'We could break in, I suppose.'

'Just a few more.' Finally, Gina reached one that began to turn. A bit of oily rag, and a creak, and the mechanism surrendered. Slowly, painfully, with much pushing, they managed to open it up into a large room. The ceilings were laced with cobwebs, the windowsills black with the bodies of flies.

'Well, it doesn't smell as if there's anything dead in here,' said Kate.

'Unless it's a body that's long gone, and just a skeleton.'

'Don't!'

'That ceiling looks as sound as can be. It doesn't even feel damp. I'm going to have a look.'

They stepped inside, eyes adjusting to the gloom. The room formed a single living space, with an old-fashioned range at one end, along with a wooden table and chairs. Two armchairs stood either side of the range, as if waiting for an evening conversation to resume. A small table held a cup and saucer of fine china, blackened with dust and age.

Kate pushed open a small side door to a much smaller room, containing a rusting bedframe, with a moth-eaten mattress still perched on top.

'No body,' said Gina, sounding relieved. 'Thank goodness for that. It looks as if it will be perfect for taking shelter when it rains. I expect the chimney's blocked, but that won't take much to clear. Those old ranges are indestructible, and there's plenty of sticks. We could make a fire on cold days, and tea.'

Kate turned back into the main room. The windows facing the castle might be small, but those overlooking the sea opened up into a covered veranda, the panes still intact, grubby, but allowing in rays from the setting sun, now slanting through the trees.

It must once have been a busy space. There were dusty papers strewn over the long table, with pencils next to them and in jugs, as if ready to be picked up again.

Shelves along the sides of the room were filled with sheaves of paper, and objects that had the look of being used for still life, but now lost and abandoned.

'Oh,' said Kate. The strange feeling was back.

'Oh my goodness,' breathed Gina. 'It's a proper artists' studio. How odd that it's been forgotten. It can't have been touched in years.'

'It feels like intruding,' said Kate. Something hovered around her in the lingering dust. An atmosphere. A memory. A feeling so intense, it had lingered here over the years, over decades, from one war to the next.

'Some of the paints may have survived,' Gina remarked. 'It looks as if there's paper, that's like gold dust. And pencils. Boxes of pencils. It's as if it's just been abandoned. Like the Marie

Celeste. I suppose we'd better wait until the men have made sure the place is sound.'

'In a minute.' This felt private. A hidden place, suddenly left. Once the men came in, and workmen to secure anything that might fall, that feeling would be lost.

'Just a few minutes then. Better not touch anything though, or Ellen will know we've been exploring.'

Kate wandered along the wooden shelves lining one side of the room, finding pencils, a knife for sharpening the ends, and tatty sketchbooks. She could not resist peering. The first sketchbook she came to was crammed with earnest scenes of St Ives and its surroundings. Hesitant and stiff. She grimaced. She remembered that stage of drawing, trying to be precise and get the basics right, constrained by her lack of skill. She turned to the next one. These were less formal, as if no longer entirely made for the eye of a tutor, but a growing confidence in the artist's ability. Some were of the sea, others of castles, boats. Some were clearly fantastical. The next book held sketchier marks, roughed out works. She could tell from her own attempts that it was an artist trying to find her own style. There was a poem of Rossetti's; a children's rhyme that made her smile. The next was a verse from Rudyard Kipling.

'Five and twenty ponies,
Trotting through the dark –
Brandy for the Parson, 'Baccy for the Clerk.
Laces for a lady; letters for a spy,
Watch the wall my darling while the Gentlemen go by!'

Still smiling, she turned to the last pages.

'Kate?'

'Coming.' She stared down at the beginnings of the illustrations. She could sense the artist's frustration at the abandoned sketches, many small vignettes on a single page. The last page took her breath away. The artist had turned to Shakespeare. Juliet on her balcony; Lady Macbeth wringing her hands, a terrifying expression on her face of the woman who has come to understand the unbearable reality of what she has done. Viola from *Twelfth Night*, dressed as a boy, staring dreamily into space.

A shiver ran down Kate's spine. There was something about the face that was familiar. And this new, more confident, style of drawing was unmistakeable. Her stomach curled into a tight knot. The vines on the wall, on the gate, the artist's studio hidden from the world were beginning to take on a meaning that set her mind racing. She turned eagerly to the final page. This was more assured, she could see. An artist finally getting into her stride. Katherina from *The Taming of the Shrew*. It was not the illustration she had expected, nothing wild or shrewish. Just a woman, in a flowing gown, dark hair worn loose down her back, reaching to her waist, standing on a terrace lined with classical pillars, a glimpse of waves crashing below. Kate took in a deep breath. She could make out vines growing above the terrace, forming a frame for the picture. Grapes hung between the leaves, rich and sensuous.

There was no mistake; this had to be the terrace of her dreams. And the woman gazing away from her, features hidden... Kate's heart began to pound painfully in her chest. The memory rushed back of that day when Lance had startled her, just as she had been reliving the figure standing in the same place in her dreams beginning to turn towards her. The same woman. Was it really drawn by the same artist who had illustrated the book of sonnets hidden in her suitcase when Papa had taken her over the sea to Arden House? She could not tear her eyes away.

'We have to go!' called Gina impatiently. 'It'll be dark soon.'

'I'm coming.' Kate shoved the final notebook safely inside her jacket and hurried out after Gina, into the dusk.

. . .

They reached the castle before the last of the light had faded, and the sea had turned to its night-time black. They hastily washed their hands before slipping in to join the evening meal before they were missed. Afterwards, Kate raced to the room under the eaves, pulling out her precious volume of Shakespeare sonnets, which she kept hidden in her drawer beneath underclothes and her spare jumper. She took out the notebook, and she lay down with Sonnet 18 open next to her: *'Shall I compare thee to a summer's day? Thou art more lovely and more temperate...'*

This time, there were no doubts left. The lines of the drawings in the sketchbook might not have the delicacy and assurance of the printed illustrations of the love poems of the sonnets, but they were in the same distinctive style. The hand was the same.

Kate gazed at the woman on the terrace in the sketchbook from the abandoned cottage. There was a wistfulness in the way the figure was focussed on a far horizon across the sea. She appeared young, no older than Kate herself.

The picture swam in front of Kate. It was the strangest feeling, as if she could step inside the living, breathing frame to feel the passion held inside that slight body, and dream her dreams. The body, Kate was certain, that had given her life.

'I've found you,' said Kate aloud, hearing her voice crack. 'That's why Miss Parsons sent me here. She knew you'd once been at Tregannon Castle, and if I was ever to find you, it would be here.' Kate ran her fingers gently over the figure in the drawing, willing her to turn to reveal her features.

It would be my face. The thought shot through Kate, unnerving her to the core. She recalled all those times Papa had turned his gaze away, as if he could scarcely bear to look at her. She had always feared it had signalled that, however hard she tried, she was never good enough. What if that look had not reflected disappointment in her, but his own guilt?

'What did they do to you?' She whispered to the figure beneath her hand. *What did they do, to force you to let me go?* A pang went through her. The woman's dress was the loose flowing style Miss Parsons favoured as a reminder of her youth. The picture must be from over twenty years ago; maybe from before Kate was born.

Frustration went through Kate. She had found the woman of her memories here in Cornwall, but the terrace with its grapes and its distant view of Vesuvius was unmistakeably in Italy, as much as the view of the Grand Canal in Venice. In reality, her mother – if it was her mother – was as far out of reach as ever. She didn't even have a name. The contessa was just described as the contessa, and there was no indication of the name of the villa, or the palazzo in Venice, or how each one might relate to the other.

Down below in the main part of the castle, Kate could hear the laughter and the hum of excitement, as several of the older children prepared to put on the performance of the play they had been rehearsing over the past weeks, based loosely on *Hansel and Gretel*. She took a deep breath, pushing down her whirlwind of emotions, in readiness to join them. As Kate began to wrap the notebook and the drawings in her underclothes and place them out of sight at the back of the drawer, she paused.

'But you sent me clues,' she said to the woman on the terrace. 'You managed to give me a way of finding you, when I was ready and I was able. So you must have wanted to be found.'

She swallowed. The war twenty years ago had been the war to end all wars. Who would have guessed that a generation later the world would fall into madness again? Whatever her mother had intended when she had sent the messages, there was no means of knowing if she had remained in Italy when Mussolini and the fascists had come to power. Or even if she was still alive.

Kate squared her shoulders and finished squirreling away her precious clues out of sight. Miss Parsons had sent her here and had made sure Gina went with her. It could be no coincidence that Miss Parsons was aware of Gina's own connections to Italy, and that she was eager to return to working with charity in Naples once the war was over, and to re-join the excavation at nearby Pompeii, under the shadow of Vesuvius.

When Gina returns to back to Italy, that's where I'll go, too, Kate promised herself, firmly. But then what? With so few clues, how on earth, in the middle of a vast country, was she going to find the villa or the palazzo in Venice? She could have kicked herself for not bringing back the rest of the sketchbooks in the cottage as well. There could be a name in one of those, or the wider landscape around the villa to tell her exactly where it lay on the coast. Maybe even the view of the palazzo from the Grand Canal, so she knew which one she was looking for. No one else knew the sketchbooks were there, so wouldn't miss them. She'd find a way of hiding them and bringing them back, she decided, and headed downstairs to join the others.

NINETEEN

'A studio?' Ellen put down her cup so hard the saucer rattled. 'You're certain?'

'Yes,' replied Kate. 'It looked as if there's quite a bit of paper still there, and no sign of damp.'

'I'm sure we could use the materials to keep the children amused,' added Gina. 'I'm not sure about the watercolours, but we might be able to revive them, and the pastels looked as if they were still useable. It seems a pity to leave them there. The pencils all look as good as new.'

'I suppose we should really donate as much as we can for the war effort,' said Ellen uncertainly.

'Which we will be if we use them for the evacuees,' said Gina.

There was a moment's silence. Kate didn't dare breathe. If Ellen forbade them to go back, she was going to have to find a way to steal the key and sneak away on her own to fetch the sketchbooks from the cottage as soon as she could. She did her best not to show her impatience.

Then Ellen nodded. 'Very well. It seems a pity to leave a

building in such a state. My aunt didn't mention a thing about a studio being down there, so far from the castle. How very odd.' She paused in reaching for the teapot. 'Mind you, there were rumours when I was a child about two artists who lived there while they were studying at the castle. A long time ago, at the time of the last war. I thought they were just stories. You know, like witches in the woods, that sort of thing.'

'What kind of rumours?' demanded Kate, unable to hide her eagerness.

'Oh, this and that,' said Ellen. 'I don't remember really. You know the sort of thing people say about artists. I'm sure one of the women was supposed to have suffered from unrequited love for a painter studying in St Ives, who then abandoned her. Or was it that he was killed in the war? I'm not sure. But, either way, the story goes that the poor young woman lost her mind. You know, like Ophelia in the play.'

'Oh,' said Kate, the ice in her blood sending a vice-like grip around her head. Had she mistaken the wistfulness of the woman on the terrace? Would the face, if it turned, reveal the blank eyes of insanity, rather than the determination of someone bent on fulfilling her dreams? She swallowed. Is that what the rest of the sketchbooks would show? Revealing not a clearer view of where she might find the physical locations of the villa and the Venice palazzo, but rather the tragic disintegration of a mind.

She clenched her fists. She could not bear the thought that her mother might, after all, be lost to her forever. But she had to know. She was even more determined to return to retrieve the sketchbooks, whatever they might show.

The following days were wild, with a storm howling in from the sea that made it impossible for Peter to take the children out for more than a short walk when the rain eased. Work in the vegetable patches, along with the clearing of the undergrowth, ground to a halt.

Kate tried her best to hide her mounting frustration. Her brain was fuzzy from lack of sleep and the wild dreams that haunted her each night of storms at sea, and the sensation of desperately pushing away branches that closed around her, tight as witches' fingers, as she tried to push through endless forests. Despite her exhaustion, she dreaded going to bed.

Was that why she had been sent away? Because her mother was insane? Was that the real reason Papa sometimes looked at her with that expression she could not read? Maybe it ran in the blood. Was that the real reason she felt she would never fall in love?

At times, she felt as if her own mind was disintegrating, spinning out of her control. Then she pulled herself together. It might only be a rumour, she reminded herself. And even if it was true, Ellen had talked of more than one woman living there, and not all of the drawings Kate had seen had been in the same hand. From what Alma had told her, in the time before the last war young women had been even more constrained than they were now. They weren't allowed out of the house without a chaperone, let alone to stay anywhere so isolated as the cottage. It could have been a companion, not her mother. But the uncertainty was unnerving.

It was only at the end of the week that the weather eased, allowing her to accompany Gina and Ellen, through the mud and paths that had turned into gushing streams, to inspect the cottage.

'Oh, my goodness,' breathed Ellen, as Kate turned the key in the lock and opened the door a little more easily this time. 'I had no idea this was here. I've asked Mrs Jenkins and Polly, but they haven't heard anything about it. Mrs Jenkins said she'd ask in the harbour when she goes to visit her daughter on her afternoon off, but this must have been abandoned for years to have become so overgrown like this.' She peered through the grubbiness of the window. 'I suppose, even before the trees grew up, this would have been hidden from the harbour.'

'It looks like the path goes down to the cove,' said Gina.

'That would make sense, being originally a fisherman's cottage, and it would be easier to bring in supplies by boat rather than trek all the way from the harbour. There seems to be a proper garden as well, I'm sure I saw gooseberry bushes amongst the raspberries, so they'd be quite self-sufficient. I'm not sure I'd like to be here in a full-on gale though.'

They followed her as she inspected the main room, with its table and chairs and teapot set on the table as if expecting guests. Kate was itching to make sure she hid the sketchbooks away in her pockets before Ellen could spot them, when it would be impossible to spirit them away unnoticed.

'It wouldn't take much to make this usable,' remarked Gina. 'We could bring the children down here. It would make a change of scene, and the path must lead down to a beach. It looks from the cliffs as if it's in its own little cove, so it could be even better for swimming than the one below the castle.'

'I don't see why not.' Ellen paused to pick up a box of half-used pastels.

'We'll pack them and bring them up to the castle,' said Gina. 'It won't take long.'

'And I can send down the men to do any necessary repairs,' replied Ellen. 'The garden looks quite sheltered; it seems a pity not to use it. The shelves get the light, and the windowsills, so we could get some seeds started here, use it like a kind of greenhouse. Come on, I want to see what might be left stored in the attics.'

While Ellen climbed the slightly rickety ladder, followed

closely by Gina, Kate lingered behind. Their voices faded into echoes above her head and she rushed to retrieve the sketchbooks.

They were gone.

She stood there, still holding the paper she had used to cover them. She must have put them somewhere more obscure and forgotten. She searched along the shelves, lifting any paper or file large enough to cover a sketchbook. Nothing.

'Looks as if it's just all been abandoned,' came Ellen's voice amongst the rafters.

'It's a proper treasure house,' Kate heard Gina reply. The beams creaked and shuddered as they moved, sending flakes of whitewash onto the tiled floor at Kate's feet.

She looked around. There was no sign of a window being forced and the door had been locked; no evidence of anyone having been in the cottage since they had left a few days before. And yet there was no sign of the sketchbooks.

They hadn't been her imagination, she told herself. She wasn't going mad. They had been there. She had held the one she had taken back to the castle in her hands that morning. But how could someone have taken them? She hadn't told anyone about what she had found, not even Gina. Besides, she had seen Gina return the keys to the drawer in Ellen's office. It was a distinctive key – there had been no need to label it – but you wouldn't know what it was unless you knew what you were looking for.

Of course, Ellen might know far more than she was letting on. But Kate could swear she had seen genuine surprise on Ellen's face when she had stepped into the cottage. She could have been dissembling, but it didn't feel like that. There had been no sign of anything being moved, or of anyone being inside since they had left. The lock had felt better oiled, but that could have been down to the mechanism having been recently used.

'Nothing much up there,' called Ellen, as she and Gina

made their way down the ladder and returned to the main room. 'Just a couple of pieces of old furniture that might be useful. There's something that looks as if it could be a rocking cradle at the far end. It must be really old, Victorian at least, and one of the rockers seems to be broken. But if it can be repaired, I know of at least one family in the harbour who will be grateful; it's so difficult to get anything like that these days.'

'It sounds fascinating,' murmured Kate. She was determined to hide her trepidation, and followed her companions in inspecting the pots, pans and assortment of faded and chipped plates neatly stored next to the range. A selection of side plates was decorated with tiny red rosebuds, accompanied by dinner plates mainly with a willow motif, and serving dishes of ornate flowers in a similar faded blue. The cups and saucers had a different pattern entirely; distinctive, in blocks of bright colours after the manner of Clarice Cliff, with a stylised portrayal of an arched bridge, and a gondola sailing below.

'There's part of a dinner set just like this at the castle,' exclaimed Ellen, retrieving a sugar bowl with a faint crack marring the inside. 'It was my aunt's favourite. I remember it from when I used to visit, and that Aunt Theodora was upset when one of the maids dropped several of the pieces and spoilt the set. I'm pretty sure it was made by one of the artists from Venice. I can remember going with Aunt Theodora to try and order replacements from a pottery in St Ives, but they were never quite the same. Martha Howson, who used to be the cook here before Mrs Jenkins, might remember. She went to live with her daughter in St Ives a few years ago. She must be in her eighties at least, but she was sharp as a button, the last time I spoke to her.'

'I'll find her,' put in Kate quickly. 'And find out if she remembers the cottage and what it was used for. We've all been so busy, we haven't had a chance yet to visit St Ives.'

'The older children would enjoy a change of scene,' added

Gina. 'Peter's been talking about taking them for a day out there since Easter.'

'I don't see why not,' replied Ellen. 'And the beaches there are open.' She returned the cups and saucers to their cupboard. 'Nothing here, apart from perhaps the cradle, looks particularly old. How strange that it's just been forgotten and left to rot. Maybe there was something in those rumours after all.'

Kate stepped outside, muttering something about seeing which plants were in the garden. Her head was throbbing and her stomach churned. However closely she looked, she could find no sign of anyone having walked through the grounds since her last visit. No footprints in the mud of the path. The metal remains of the gate lay exactly where she and Gina had left them. She walked around the cottage; there was no sign of a window that had been forced, or a ladder that might have been used to get in through the attic. Nothing.

Yet someone – maybe more than one person – must have been here. Kate hugged herself in the breeze coming in from the sea. There was something about this place, and the information contained in the sketchbooks, that someone wanted to remain hidden. An uneasy prickling travelled down her spine. Miss Parsons had been concerned about what she might find out, but Kate was as certain as could be that Miss Parsons would never send her, any more than any of her sisters, into real physical danger. The schoolmistress had always been their protector. She loved them, like a fierce mother hen, prepared even to brave Papa's rages in their defence. And she had been the only one to give them the messages capable of setting them free. There must be something more to this, something that even Miss Parsons didn't understand.

'It's something about me,' said Kate aloud. It had to be. Hadn't she always known it? Growing up, she'd assumed it was to do with the difference of her birth, because she was the illegitimate one, the disgrace, the Arden who would never be quite a proper Arden, however hard she tried. But it was more than that. She could sense it. Now, more than ever, she knew she had to find out about her past, or her future would never be truly her own.

TWENTY

It was a sunny day towards the end of August when Kate, Gina and Peter shepherded the older evacuees onto the bus to take them over the cliffs to St Ives.

The little seaside town was bustling with August visitors, clearly attempting to gain some normality and forget the war for a while in the warm of the late summer sunshine. They settled the children on Porthminster Beach, which was crowded with families enjoying the sun and the delights of the sea.

As the little group became absorbed in creating sandcastles and paddling in the shallows, Kate slipped away. Following Ellen's instructions, she found a tiny lopsided little shop in a side street, squashed between fishermen's cottages, declaring itself as *Howson's Art Supplies*. Kate pushed inside, setting the bell jangling. She could see the shelves were only thinly covered with pencils and a few paints, while part of the room had been turned into a small gallery showing images of St Ives. Kate browsed along them, fascinated by the differing views and styles, and hoped she might catch sight of a scene, or even sketch, in the style that was now almost as familiar as her own.

'We've more in the back, if you'd like to see,' remarked the shopkeeper, ducking through a curtain at the back of the shop. 'We used to do a roaring trade before the war. Not so much now. With rationing and so many things not available, and so many away doing war work, the artists and their teachers are gone. It feels like they will never return.'

'Hopefully they will one day.'

The woman was too near her own age to have been the elderly cook at Tregannon Castle. She was tall, with deep copper curls escaping from a silk scarf wound around her head into a kind of turban. She sported wide trousers and a finely knitted long cardigan that, from its volume, was clearly from before the war.

'So, said the shopkeeper scrutinising her closely. 'Paints, is it? We're nearly out of oils, I'm afraid, with all the shortages, but we've still several packets of charcoal and pastels.'

'Do you have pencils?' asked Kate, not sure how to open the conversation.

'Yes, of course.' The woman reached under the desk. 'There's a good selection here.'

Kate chose a pencil to replace the one worn almost down to an invisible stub. 'And do you have any sketchbooks?'

'They're hard to come by these days. But you're in luck. I still have a few.'

That meant expensive. You could get anything on the black market if you could pay enough, and even legitimately sourced materials had a high price. Kate wavered. The amount she had saved from her wages was not huge.

The woman considered her, as if reading her mind. 'If you are not fussy, I've several in the back that were water stained when the roof was damaged last winter. I can let you have those for half the price.'

'Please,' said Kate.

The woman disappeared for a moment, returning with a small pile of sketchbooks. 'The last two I'll throw in, they are really too damaged to sell, but you might find something you can use.'

'Thank you.' Kate handed over the money and tucked the sketchbooks away in her shoulder bag.

'Was there anything else?'

'I—' Kate met the querying eyes. They were watching her closely. She had a sense of her features being noted down, in that instinctive squirreling away of images she knew all too well from her own work. She glanced instinctively towards the portraits on the walls.

'Yes, those are mine. From before the war, of course. Between everything, I don't seem to have the time these days. Or maybe it's the energy.' She sighed. 'Or I don't see the point. If there's an invasion, they'll all be burnt anyway.'

'Isn't there something in simply the doing? And at least it's a way of stretching skills for when this is over. It has to end one day. I can't bear the thought that we won't ever have something like the life we had before.'

'I agree.' The shopkeeper smiled. 'You're one of the teachers at Tregannon Castle, aren't you?'

'So I am.'

The woman chuckled. 'Don't look so surprised, there are very few secrets around here. Old Miss Nancarrow's niece has made good use of the castle, bringing those poor evacuees down here and giving them a good life. Out in the fresh air and gardening will do them the world of good, as well as making sure they get plenty of good food down them. My mum was a cook there, in the old lady's time. When it was a place for artists. Full of life it was then. She said it was far too quiet those last years, after they all left. Nice to think of it being back in use again. I'm sure Miss Theodora would have approved. I suppose that's why she left the castle to Miss Ellen.'

It was the opening Kate been waiting for. 'We've been

clearing some of the land near the cliffs to create more space for the children.'

A tiny woman, deeply wrinkled, but well-dressed and upright, pushed through the curtain. 'Did you find it?'

Kate started, uncertain how to answer.

'Mum!' said the shopkeeper. 'I thought you were asleep.'

'I'm not in my dotage, Martha, and I'm no child.' The newcomer's bright blue eyes were fixed on Kate. 'Did you find it?'

'Mum...'

'The cottage, you mean?' Kate asked.

'That's the one.'

'Yes. It looks as if it was abandoned.'

Mrs Howson sniffed. 'So they didn't burn it down.'

Her daughter frowned. 'For goodness' sake, Mum, why on earth would anyone want to burn down a perfectly good cottage?'

'Should have done. The castle was never the same afterwards. No wonder they made sure it was forgotten.'

'It felt sad for a place to be left to go to ruin like that.' Kate hesitated. Her every instinct was to keep the sketchbook hidden, but equally strong was her need to find answers. She fished it out from its hiding place at the bottom of her shoulder bag. 'I found this.'

'Well, well, well.' Mrs Howson stared down at the book on the counter. 'So she didn't take it with her.'

Kate did her best to keep her voice even. 'She?'

'The young lady who disappeared. One of the artists from Tregannon Castle. She was sent over here to study by her father.' Kate's heart began to race. 'Pretty thing,' added Mrs Howson, with a wistful smile. 'Determined, too. We used to see her out there on the cliffs with her sketchpad in all weathers. There weren't many like that, who dedicated everything to their painting. Most of them knew they'd have to marry at some point, and that would be that. That's how things were, in those days.'

'You said she disappeared,' prompted Kate.

'Vanished,' said Mrs Howson. 'Rumour was, she drowned herself in that cove, and her body was taken out to sea for the fishes.'

Kate stared at her in dismay. The joyful picture in her mind's eye of the young woman striding freely across the cliffs vanished into the darkness of the path from the fisherman's cottage. She remembered the bitterness of the breeze on her cheeks as she stood in the overgrown garden, accompanied by the melancholy sigh of pebbles from the beach below. There had been both joy and sadness in that cottage, she could feel it. It had never crossed her mind that it might also have held despair.

'Why would she do a thing like that?' she demanded.

Mrs Howson shook her head. 'Love, I expect. Usually is. Passion of the thwarted kind that leads to madness. That's what they said at the time. Old Miss Nancarrow tried to tell everyone that she'd been called home for family reasons, but no one believed her. You don't just vanish like that, overnight, without any reason. None of us would go near that cottage afterwards; it felt like it was cursed. Some of the maids even swore it was haunted. Mrs Keverne, who was the cook then, always swore the young lady had simply eloped with some painter she'd been seen talking to in St Ives. But then Mrs Keverne always was a hopeless romantic. Whatever the truth of it, Tregannon Castle was never the same; there was always some kind of a cloud hanging over it.'

Kate swallowed. 'Do you remember her name?'

'Not a bit of it,' said Mrs Howson, after a moment's thought. 'There were so many of them, and from all over. It was something foreign. Several Italian ladies used to come to the summer school Mrs Nancarrow held each year. I've a feeling she may have been one of them. Although I'm sure someone said their uncle was a Russian prince. Mind you, that might have been all that talk of the Tsar and his family being murdered. Seems like only yesterday, not a lifetime ago.'

'They?' Kate ventured.

'She had a sister with her. Or was it a cousin? I don't remember. Funny that, I don't remember her leaving, either. So who knows? There may be a body under the floorboards, so to speak, after all.'

Kate left the shop in a whirl of emotions. She was both one step closer to finding her mother, and at the same time as far away as ever. True, Mrs Howson had mentioned the possibility of Italy, but when Kate pressed her further the old lady had no idea of where exactly. Ellen had been only a child, and a visitor, at the time and it seemed her aunt had told her nothing of the shadow that hung over Tregannon's past. Perhaps Miss Nancarrow had simply wanted the memory to die with her, forgotten like the cottage rotting away amongst the encroaching trees and brambles.

Kate pushed the sketchbook back to the bottom of her shoulder bag and slung the strap securely across her body. But the story hadn't been completely forgotten. Nothing Mrs Howson said had shed any light on why someone might remove the sketchbooks from the cottage. There was someone who didn't want the secrets they might hold to be uncovered. She came to an abrupt halt, sending the woman behind almost bumping into her.

'Sorry,' she muttered to the woman impatiently tutting, as she continued to shepherd two small children in the direction of the sea.

Did whoever removed the remaining sketchbooks know exactly how many had been piled up on the shelf? Would he –

or she – know there was one missing and be looking for where it might have gone? She would need to find a better hiding place for it – and for her book of sonnets with the illustrations so clearly done by the same hand. More than ever, it seemed the only place she was going to find the answers to her past was in Italy, and the sketchbook and sonnets contained her only clues. And maybe, she thought as she set off again to join her companions, the only link to who she might really be.

As she reached Porthminster Beach, Kate could see it had filled up with families enjoying the late August sunshine. Like in most places these days, there were few young men, but women dozed or nursed babies, while their children played in the sand creating sandcastles, or paddled at the water's edge. A small group of boys were swimming further out with their father, calling to him as they pulled themselves onto the pontoon, before jumping off again with a huge splash. At one side, a game of cricket was in full swing.

You wouldn't think there was a war at all, thought Kate, as she joined the evacuees paddling in the warmth of the sea, drinking in the peace of the salt air.

'He's right, I suppose we'd better start making our way back,' said Gina regretfully, as Peter began calling the boys in from the deeper waters. 'Or we'll miss the bus. I don't fancy walking all the way to the castle.'

Kate helped dry the feet of the younger children and fit their shoes and socks, before herding them up the beach between the closely packed families, towards the bus stop.

'They sound happy,' she said to Peter, as the children raced on ahead.

'They do. Did you find what you were looking for?'

'Just a pencil and a couple of sketchbooks,' she replied.

'I thought there was paper in the old studio you and Gina came across.'

'I don't want to take that! It's much better being used by the children. Besides, I can take a sketchbook anywhere.' She fell into step besides him, as they followed the stragglers up the beach.

He gave a grunt. 'I wish this war was over. There's so much to be done, even more than before.'

She eyed him. 'You mean in Naples?'

He nodded. 'The charity is eager to start up again as soon as the fighting ends and we can get over there. Although Lord knows how long that is going to be. I know Gina is itching to get back.' A faint smile softened his features. 'And yes, I know it's as much so she can continue the excavation at Pompeii. But Uncle Salvatore won't ever think of allowing her to go without a family member as protection, especially now.'

His expression became serious once more. 'Besides, there are things I need to settle. The past is the past. There's no point in dwelling on it, or it just eats you up inside.' His eyes rested on her face. Was she imagining it, or had the hostility she had always sensed towards her eased a little? He took a deep breath. 'Look, Kate, this isn't going to be easy—' His gaze went past her, focussing further down the beach. 'Watch out!'

He grabbed her, pulling her to one side. Something whizzed past Kate, striking the sand up ahead, sending a plume into the air. Around her, chaos erupted – shouts and screams, the sunbathers running wildly, this way and that. From the corner of her eye, she caught the glint of sun on metal. She turned, horrified to see a plane heading towards them, so low she could see the pilot as he sent bullets strafing through the crowd.

TWENTY-ONE

For a moment Kate froze, unable to move, as bodies swirled around her.

She saw Peter lift the nearest small boy into his good arm and slip his other from its sling to take a girl by the hand. 'Run!' he shouted. 'Everyone, quickly. Behind the rocks. You'll be safe there.'

'Go on,' said Kate to Susan, who had slowed. 'Follow Mr Sidoli, as quick as you can. You're nearly there. I'll bring the rest.'

With Susan running ahead, Kate turned to help Gina in hurrying the stragglers, followed by families desperate to find safety.

'Cissy!' A woman stopped next to Kate, baby in her arms, and turned back towards a girl of about five, who was standing, frozen in terror, in the middle of the fast-emptying beach.

'I'll get her.' Kate raced to the child, swept her up and ran towards shelter. They were nearly there. She could see Peter, still urging those ahead behind the rocks. They were almost safe. She had almost reached them when a violent blow to her arm nearly knocked her off her feet. She staggered under the weight of her burden, stumbling in the sand, the roar of engines close behind.

'I've got her.' It was Peter, pulling them both under cover. Kate lay there, curled over the little body of the girl, who lay unprotesting, unnaturally still and calm. Kate's arm felt numb and battered, as if it was no longer hers. From the corner of her eye, she caught the red ooze of blood trailing into the sand. She remained as still as she could, the roar of engines fading into the distance, leaving screams and shouts around the beach.

'It's all right,' she comforted the little girl, whose eyes shot open, wide with terror in the silence. 'You're safe.'

'Mummy,' the child whispered, beginning to sob.

Across the bodies of those also still crouching beneath the shelter of the rock, Kate met Peter's eyes. She could see in them her own dread of what might lie outside, with the beach so crowded when the bullets began to fly. She had never been so glad to hear the sounds of voices, and of footsteps rushing past. It sounded as if at least some of those caught out in the open had survived.

The sound of a baby crying echoed around the rocks as Cissy's distraught mother appeared at the entrance to their shelter.

'She's here,' Peter called. He took Cissy's hand, helping her out of their rocky hiding place. 'She's safe.'

As a tearful Cissy was caught in the embrace of her mother on the beach outside, Kate finally sat up. Pain shot through her arm, like fire. She looked down at the red seeping down her dress, her mind a blank, unable to take it in.

'You've been hit, Miss,' whispered Susan, beginning to cry.

'Just a scratch,' Kate reassured her quickly. It was more than that, she realised, as she tried gingerly to move her arm, which no longer felt like hers. A wave of nausea went through her. She could feel the blood dripping down under her sleeve as if it would never stop. Kate breathed deep, keeping herself calm for the children's sake. She couldn't give into her injury yet. Who knew what might happen in the next few minutes. She had to help Peter and Gina get them back to the safety of Tregannon Castle

'Here.' Gina crawled towards her with an abandoned towel and held it against Kate's shoulder. 'That'll help with the bleeding. Kate's hurt, she needs a doctor,' she called to Peter, who was still standing outside, surveying the beach.

'I'm all right.' Slowly, painfully, Kate clambered out, trying to keep the towel in place. All around she could see women and children emerging warily from behind rocks and the remains of rowing boats and anything else that offered shelter.

'I saw him!' said Cissy's mother, her voice shaking. 'The plane was so low, I saw him in the cockpit. He must have seen it was women and children he was firing at. What did a group of women and children ever do to him, the filthy coward? It's a miracle no one was killed.'

Kate stared in astonishment at the beach. She had braced herself to find a dozen bodies, if not hundreds, sprawled and bloodied, but all she could see were families hurrying to get away from the exposed expanse. As she watched, a group of boys headed back from the platform a short way offshore, while their fellow swimmers raced from the water to join anxious relatives.

'Unbelievable...' Peter shook his head in equal astonishment.

Cars and ambulances had begun to draw up by the beach, and policemen and officials appeared to direct those fleeing and taking care of the injured. The relief on Peter's face vanished as his eyes rested on the reddening towel encasing her arm. 'That looks painful. Gina's right. We need to find you a doctor.'

'I'm fine, really.' She straightened up to prove her point. Then instantly stumbled, as an explosion ripped the air. The beachgoers froze. In the ensuing silence a baby began to cry inconsolably.

'Gasworks,' announced one of the older women, with a calm that sounded more unnerving than any scream. 'The ones above Porthmeor Beach. Bet that's what them planes were heading for. We always said they'd get the industrial bits of St Ives one day.'

'The sooner we get out of here the better,' said Cissy's mother, heading towards the officials. 'There's no way I'm coming back on here, sun or no sun, not until this war is over.'

While Peter led their charges to wait for the bus to take them back to Tregannon Castle, Gina helped Kate to the where doctors and nurses had set up a temporary First Aid post. Kate sat in a daze amongst the injured waiting their turn, her mind still unable to take in the terror that had appeared out of a blue summer's sky. Around her, rumours swirled that it had indeed been the gasworks the enemy planes had hit, and who knew what might have happened had the tanks exploded. The whole place could have gone up in smoke. There was talk of a woman being killed, not far from reaching her front door, but also general relief that so few had died with so many destroyed houses, as well as craters left in the centre of the town.

'Mrs Howson?' replied the nurse to Kate's anxious enquiry, as she cleaned her wound.

'The art supply shop and gallery in Saint Gwinear's Street,' explained Kate.

'Ah yes, I know the one. Clarice,' She called over to a young woman bandaging the cut forehead of a small boy. 'You passed Howson's just now. How did it look?'

'The panes in one of the upstairs windows had gone,' replied Clarice, smiling reassuringly at her patient as she released him back into the arms of his anxious parents. She nodded at an elderly man next in line, who hobbled towards her, leaning heavily on a makeshift stick, suppressing a grimace of pain. 'But otherwise, it looked pretty untouched to me. Old Mrs Howson wasn't half giving them a mouthful, I can tell you.'

'Thank goodness.' Relief washed over Kate.

'Nothing major hit, and the bullet went right through,' announced the nurse, as she finished cleaning up the tear in Kate's flesh. 'Could have been a lot worse. You were lucky, young woman. We all were,' she added feelingly, as she set about bandaging Kate's arm.

Thankful that nothing was broken, and the bleeding had been stemmed, Kate made her way gingerly to re-join the others. Peter and Gina were reassuring the children as they waited for the expected bus, hoping that it had not been delayed or prevented from reaching them. Kate's legs were beginning to shake, and she was shivering uncontrollably all over. It felt as if a cold wind had raced right through her veins, and she would never be warm again.

'I'm all right,' she muttered, pulling herself together at the worried look on Gina's face. She did her best to hide her shivering, smiling as cheerfully as she could at the shocked little faces around her. She was glad when the bus arrived, delayed by only a few minutes by its forced detour around the town. The thought of walking even the short way over the cliffs to Tregannon felt beyond her, let alone while in charge of so many terrified children, who looked as if they never wanted to move again.

The little group piled into the vehicle, joining its silent passengers. The evacuees huddled on their seats, clutching bags and buckets and spades, faces burnished with the sun, but lost in thought. Every one of Kate's nerves was stretched, her ears strained for any sound warning of another attack above the roar of the engine. But all was peaceful.

As they reached the cliffs above the harbour, the adults began to relax a little. A hushed conversation started up in the front rows of people returning to the villages along the coast, from what should have been a perfect day, a reminder of summers when life was normal and afternoons on the beach had been taken for granted. Kate shivered despite the heat. She could feel, in the subdued atmosphere around her, recognition that even the fragile safety of being away from England's major towns had vanished, leaving them all exposed, braced anxiously for what might happen next.

As they reached Tregannon Castle Kate was thankful that, instead of dropping them off at the gates as usual, the driver took them right up to the front door. At the sound of the approaching engine, Ellen came running, followed by several of the Land Girls.

'Thank you, Mr Braddock,' called Ellen to the driver, as she helped the children from the bus, to be helped inside by the Land Girls. 'Oh my Lord!' she added, as Gina supported Kate towards the entrance. 'We heard it was bad, but I never thought...' She pulled herself together. 'Come on, let's get you inside.'

For several days afterwards, Kate was feverish, her sleep shot through with wild dreams. Sometimes she was trapped in the cellar in Hellebore Row, with Cordelia calling to her, scrabbling at the rubble above her head, but knowing there was no way out. Other times, she watched as the parachute bomb slowly detached itself, exploding in a fireball that left St Mary's pulverised to nothing, everything – Cordelia, Miss Parsons and the children – vanished into dust.

When the fever subsided, her arm ached until it felt she

could never get comfortable. It felt unnatural, when there was so much to do, to lie in bed, listening to the voices echoing below as life resumed its familiar pattern. At the same time, it soothed her mind to hear the tractor rumbling in the fields and the Land Girls calling to each other, collapsing into laughter as they paused for the obligatory cups of tea. Even when she was finally well enough to creep downstairs, it was a while before she could do more than make her way to a bench in a sheltered spot against the walls to doze in the sun.

As her body began to heal, Kate's mind sifted through the events of the day in St Ives. At first, it returned again and again to the enemy planes coming out of the sun to strafe the women and children standing exposed and vulnerable on the sands. It was indeed a miracle, Gina told her, with relatively few injuries and no deaths amongst those on the beach, and so few killed by the destruction caused in the town itself.

It could have been so much worse, was the phrase Kate heard, over and over again during those weeks of her recovery. In fitful dreams, both asleep and dozing, she relived the panic and the screams, terrifying herself awake, sweat cold down her back, as she calmed her breathing, simply thankful to be alive.

Gradually, the vividness of the memories began to fade, allowing other thoughts to bubble to the surface once more. She was impatient to get well, not only to get back to helping with the children, but to see if she could find any more clues about the young woman who, according to Mrs Howson, had stayed in the secluded fisherman's cottage while she studied at Tregannon Castle, and who had vanished without a trace. Even on the calmest day, Kate couldn't quite relax, the sketchbooks that had vanished still filling her with anxiety.

Once she had recovered enough to reply to the most recent letters from Alma and Cordelia, she kept her tone cheerful, careful not to mention her injury. The newspapers were as cautious as ever at revealing exactly where attacks had taken place, so she could assume none of her family knew for certain the strafing of the beach had taken place in St Ives. While she itched to ask for Miss Parsons's advice, Kate did not dare tell her about her discovery, in case Miss Parsons herself arrived to whisk her back to safety, thereby preventing her from investigating further. Besides, until Kate was able to walk to the Post Office herself, her letters were left on the hall table, to be taken by the first person heading down to the harbour. The thought of her suspicions being read by whoever had removed the sketchbooks sent new chills down her spine. Kate had no intention of letting anyone know of the information she had gleaned from Mrs Howson. Even as she began to grow strong enough to begin walking in the gardens, a little more each day, she preferred to remain close to the castle walls.

On the first afternoon she felt her full strength returning, Kate finally overcame her fears and slipped away unnoticed to the fisherman's cottage.

She stood in the stillness of the garden, listening to the sound of the sea. Peering through the window, she could see that the cottage had been cleared. A pile of logs had been stacked at one side, and the walls had been whitewashed, everything removed apart from the long table, that now had an assortment of chairs from all over the estate around it, with cups and saucers neatly stacked on a tray next to a large teapot and a bottle of Camp Coffee.

It no longer felt like the cottage with its air of mystery, and of lives lived and abruptly interrupted that had drawn her in. It was as if the ghosts of those who had lived there had vanished, along with the belongings that must have been so familiar to them.

It disturbed her, with her sense of vulnerability still clinging to her, to think of them gone entirely, even the memory of their existence gone.

She turned and walked down to the little cove, separate from the rest of the coast, where the fishermen from the cottage must once have set out to sea. The path through the gate had been cleared of brambles and fallen branches. She could even make out the print of boots in the remains of mud.

Kate reached the beach to find that the tide was in, leaving the sea clawing rhythmically at the fine pebbles on the edges of the sand. This was where the artists in the cottage must have collected many of their objects to study: the driftwood, the bits of old wrecks that arrived with the tide. Remains of mermaid purses lay amongst the glutinous sheen of a dead jellyfish, and the white, long-since picked clean bones of some dead marine creature.

Several seals basking on the rocks at the far end raised their heads, their dark eyes watching her, nostrils tasting the air, before sliding into the waves to find a more secluded resting place.

It was peaceful. That was what caught her. She had imagined the fisherman's cove as a wild place, where waves crashed against dark rocks with a wild fury that was both terrifying and exhilarating. Here on the beach, it was quiet and secret. Cliffs folded around the gentle turquoise sway of the waves, keeping out the worst of the wind and the storms.

Surely, it was not the kind of place to end a life. Rather, it struck her with an unexpected force, it was where lovers might secretly slip away. Mrs Keverne, the cook at Tregannon Castle when the young woman had disappeared, could have been right. A boat could easily be hidden from both the harbour and the castle, allowing love to escape to freedom, and a new life, far away. Maybe even to a pillared terrace overlooking the calm of the Mediterranean, where grapes hung deep crimson in the heat of the sun. That had to be the answer. She would have staked her life on it.

But what could have happened to tear that imagined idyll apart? And what in the world could be the link with her own journey across the sea with the woman Papa called Magdalena, to a new life amongst the shadows of Arden House? She had to know. Somehow, she had to find out.

She was being watched.

The sensation was so strong, it was like a blade sharp between her shoulders. She bent to pick up a piece of driftwood next to her, allowing her eyes to surreptitiously scan the trees on the edges of the little beach. There was nothing to be seen. No beast, no shadowy human being, not even an enemy invading force waiting to pounce. She was imagining things.

She reached for a second piece of driftwood, glancing around once more. This time, something moved. Nothing obvious. Just a hint of a shadow through the trees. She straightened.

'Hello?' she called, as loudly as she could. The shadow stilled. 'Hello!' she called again. This time nothing. No movement, no sound, no answering call. In the silence, there was just the sound of the waves breaking as they reached the shore, the call of seagulls high above.

The tide was too far in, waves rushing closer every second, to attempt to walk around the headland of the little cove. The only way out was the path past the cottage.

There was nothing for it. Kate reached for the largest piece of driftwood she could find that might give her a chance of protecting herself, and headed back. She strode as much as she could at her normal pace. If there was a furtive watcher in the trees, she was giving no hint that she had been spooked.

She reached the path. Sand slid beneath her feet, creeping into her shoes, slowing her pace. On she strode, looking forwards, the vision from the corners of her eyes alert, her ears straining for every sound. It was only when she reached the other end of the trees and the gate into the garden, that she began to breathe again. As she pulled the gate behind her, she heard the crack of a twig amongst the trees. There *was* someone there. Watching. Maybe waiting? Walking as quickly and calmly as possible, and without looking back, she headed for the safety of the castle.

That was the last time Kate attempted to visit the cottage on her own. She was certain any further clues had long gone, and she couldn't risk being stopped in her mission to uncover the secrets of her past by being seen to still look for them. She had to hope that whoever had taken the sketchbooks had no idea that one was missing. The only way she could keep herself, and the hidden sketchbook, safe was to make it look as if she had given up. For now, she would have to wait.

In the outside world, it was becoming ever more certain that it was only a matter of time before Hitler was defeated. Already the little community at Tregannon Castle was changing. Gradually, many of the children found homes with local families. The heavy bombardment of the cities had finally ceased, sending fewer evacuees to join them. Before long Lance also left, announcing that he was bored with civilian work and was joining up to fight.

'Besides, a man has to find a way of making a fortune,' he said to Kate, when he came to tell them his replacement had been found and he was leaving the next day. He was less than his usual cheerful self, irritable and out of sorts. 'Not rely on numbskulls who expect the impossible, even if you do exactly what they want. I'm not a miracle worker.'

'I'm sure,' she murmured politely, uncertain of what he meant, but without any strong desire to ask. The rumour amongst the Land Girls was that he had been caught once too often trading goods on the black market. That fitted his some-what reckless personality, she thought, glad that she had not had the slightest inclination to fall in love with him, or even encourage a flirtation. There was something about him that unnerved her. With his easy charm and lightening changes of mood, she couldn't help but still think of him as a gambler; a man out for the main chance.

He wasn't a bad man, she concluded; just one too self-absorbed to consider those he might hurt. She couldn't help feeling that any woman who loved him would be on an instant path to a broken heart, while his remained untouched. Like Ellen, she had too strong a sense of self-preservation to allow him to become close. Besides, she had her own destiny to pursue, and she couldn't imagine Lance ever being willing to recognise this part of her. She was even a little glad when he was gone.

From then on, Kate took care to never be isolated, and to always be amongst the children or the Land Girls. With them, she swam in the sea on summer days, and took shelter inside the cottage from the wildness of winter rain. She could never quite shake off the sensation of being watched, although whether or not this was only imagination, she could not tell.

In the summer of 1943, messages began to arrive via Peter and Gina's family in Wales with rumours that Mussolini had been deposed and his fascist government was in a state of collapse. A few months later came news reports that Italy's new rulers had declared war on Germany.

'At least we are no longer the enemy,' said Peter one evening, as he and Gina hunched over the latest letters. 'Although Uncle Salvatore is right; heaven help those who are in Italy now, when the Germans invade. Especially those who collaborated with the fascists,' he added darkly.

'Don't waste your sympathy on fascists,' retorted Gina. 'It's those poor street children we left in Naples we should be thinking about. There are bound to be far more orphans already; they are going to need our help even more than ever, once this is over.'

'I haven't forgotten,' he replied. Across the room, he met Kate's eyes. The faint edge of hostility was back, along with a touch of something she might almost describe as pity.

Then it was gone, and he was back to comparing the messages Gina had received about the various extended branches of their family network with his own. Accompanied, Kate couldn't help noticing, by worries about their friends who had been unwilling, or unable, to escape. She thought of her own mother who, if she was still alive, might also be out there, trying to survive.

Already she could hear the impatience to re-join whatever might be left of the charity working with street children in Naples. For a moment she hesitated, remembering that odd expression in Peter's eyes. But she wasn't going to let that stop her from persuading them to let her accompany them to Italy once the war was over. He might not particularly like her, for whatever reason, but they had been through enough danger together for her not to fear him.

Perhaps it was as well she felt no temptation to fall in love with him, any more than with Lance. She liked Peter, but there was something about his intensity for his work that made her feel she couldn't breathe if she stood too close. From what Gina had said, Kate had a feeling his focus on helping the evacuees in Cornwall would be only intensified when he returned to Italy, at the exclusion of all other considerations. Any woman who loved him, she had concluded long ago, must always be prepared to put her own wishes at the service of his, and have no life of her own.

Maybe her resistance was because since as long as she could remember, she'd had to battle Papa's attempts to mould her to his convenience and put everyone else's interests before her own passion for painting. Her old rebellion against the ordering of her life, as if she had no will of her own, was still there, strengthened by everything she'd been through.

But she was still determined to persuade Peter to let her accompany Gina when they returned to Naples. Once there, she felt certain, her search for the truth about her past could finally begin.

TWENTY-TWO

VENICE

September 1943

How they had survived those years, Sofia had no idea. The constant hunger, the bitter winters and the flooding from the canals had left her, like the rest of the population of Venice, worn to the bone. So far, Venice had been spared the bombing suffered by its neighbouring cities and the destruction in the nearby countryside. At times, life had continued as if there was no violent conflict on its borders. Theatre performances had attracted audiences as normal. Even the annual film festival had been held, and the canals remained busy and vibrant.

But that wind-swept September morning, as she hurried from the Studio Theodora towards the Grand Canal, Sofia knew for certain things were about to get far worse.

'Magdalena!' She banged loudly on the door of the palazzo. She didn't care who heard. There was going to be enough noise around here when the German army arrived. She and Magdalena may have ignored each other as much as possible since they parted company, but she couldn't leave her to her fate.

'Magdalena!' She banged again. 'I'm going to shout until you open the door. And I know the colonel left this morning. So don't try and tell me otherwise.'

After a few more thumps, the door opened, followed by a hand silently beckoning her inside. Magdalena had aged, and was painfully thin and pale like the rest of them, but her eyes were just as fierce as ever.

'You aren't coming back here.'

'I don't want to. A palace on the Grand Canal is the last place I want to be when the Germans get here. And you shouldn't be here, either. We've become the enemy, remember? I doubt even Venice will be spared now Mussolini has been deposed and Italy is no longer on Hitler's side. A place like this is one they're bound to take over.'

'Then I will be their housekeeper,' said Magdalena, turning even paler.

'And be despised by them as one of the enemy, and hated by your own people as a collaborator? Don't be such a fool.'

'Other people will have to serve them,' said Magdalena with a sniff. 'They will have no choice.'

'But they don't belong to the household of a known collaborator with Mussolini's regime,' retorted Sofia. 'It's no good, Magdalena. It just isn't safe. You are coming with me. No arguments. There's plenty of room at the Studio Theodora. We can still clean for the hotels, even if they are full of Nazis. No one's going to take much notice of two middle-aged women, and menial work always needs to be done, so they'll have to keep us alive while we are useful. As long as this war lasts, this is really going to be about survival. Just pray the British and the Americans get here soon.'

Magdalena hesitated. *Between the devil and the deep blue sea*, said her eyes. The enemy in jackboots, who viewed all human life as expendable, or Sofia, who had more cause than most to hate her. Who might throw her to the wolves (or possibly the darkest part of the canal) to have her revenge.

'You're local. You know people,' said Sofia. 'I still have dollars hidden away. You can help me, as much as I can help you. I suggest we call a truce. War never solved anything. We both remember the war that was to end all wars. These might be our last hours on earth. I'm too tired to spend it fighting old battles. We have a common enemy now.'

After a moment, Magdalena nodded. Sofia followed her inside and helped her pack her few belongings, ignoring the silver knives and spoons that slid into the maid's pockets when she thought Sofia wasn't looking. Within the hour, they were heading downstairs, each with a bag over one shoulder.

At the door, Magdalena stopped, allowing her bag to slide to the floor. 'Wait.'

'You're not going back on me now.'

Magdalena shook her head. 'The safe. The contessa.'

Sofia eyed her in exasperation. She wasn't going to risk their lives for a diamond necklace they wouldn't dare try to sell and draw dangerous attention to themselves. 'I thought you said she took her valuables?'

'Not valuables. Papers.'

'Papers?' Sofia stared at her in sudden horror. 'She left papers? Incriminating ones, from when she collaborated with Mussolini's regime?'

'I'm not certain.' Magdalena went red, then white, then bright red again. 'But I know the code. She thinks I don't, but I do. Only without her permission...'

'Forget her permission.' Fear shot through Sofia. Even in America, word had got through from friends with families still living in Italy of the brutality of the fascists against their own people, and the atrocities carried out to squash dissent. 'Get them, Magdalena. Lord knows how many lives could be placed in danger, not only us here, but the workers on her estates. And leave the door open, or some bright spark will probably blow it up thinking there's gold bullion inside and destroy half the building in the process.'

Magdalena raced up to the contessa's bedroom and returned minutes later, stashing envelopes and documents inside her underclothes. 'I'll swing for this,' she muttered. 'If nobody shoots me first.'

'Then let's get out of here. We can burn the damned lot, if we need to, just so long as we get rid of them before the Germans arrive.'

They spent that first evening in the Studio Theodora in an uneasy kind of peace between the two of them and in the world outside. Flitting moonlight raced over the waters of the little canal, sending sprite-figures dancing over the dark walls of the building opposite.

Using the blankets and quilts they had retrieved from the palazzo, they made one of the small rooms above the main work-shop as comfortable as possible. Magdalena quickly gave up her insistence on the room at the far end of the corridor, and accepted one next to the room used by Sofia. With enemy soldiers about to occupy the city, it felt safer being closer. Not that they could defend themselves against an armed battalion with nothing but brooms and a bread knife. But at least it gave moral support to know that a living, breathing body was near.

'These papers,' said Sofia, as she carefully lit a small fire, so that any smoke would not attract attention. 'We'd better get rid of them now. I can take the ashes and put them in the canal on my way to work tomorrow. I'll feel happier if they are taken out to sea.'

They worked through them, methodically, in the precious candlelight. Letters, contracts, payments made. Some clearly representing innocent lives condemned to torture and almost certain death for repayment of some slight or as a means of the contessa maintaining her position. After a while, Sofia stopped reading before putting them in the flames. At last the pile was down to a small handful.

'Next,' she said, wearily.

Magdalena didn't move.

'We've come this far,' said Sofia.

'They are not hers,' said Magdalena. 'These are yours.'

'Mine?' Sofia stared at her. 'I've never written to my mother. And she certainly never wrote to me. I was careful she never knew exactly where I was living.'

Magdalena held them out. 'They are yours. They are not from the contessa. They were sent to you at the Villa Clara.' In the faint light her face was haggard, haunted.

With a hand that shook, Sofia reached for the letters. Even after all these years, the sight of her sister's writing sent a stab deep inside her belly.

'They've been opened,' she said.

'Not by me. I've never seen them. You must believe me.'

How far did Magdalena's loyalty to the contessa go? Sofia wasn't sure, but for now she had no choice but to trust her. She turned back to the letter, pulling out the single sheet, brittle with age. The handwriting, that had usually been so neat, so contained, was spidery, wandering over the page.

My dearest sister...

The rest of the page blurred. Sofia blinked the tears away, focussing on the barely decipherable scrawl.

Forgive me. I believed I was doing it for the best, for you and the child. But I should never have agreed. I am so afraid I will not recover from this fever, and I fear what they will do. Sell the ring I'm sending with this letter, so you can come as soon as you get

*this. Come and fetch her. Get her away from here. I've left you
everything I can call mine, so you can look after her. So you can
both live free. Take it. Throw away your doubts, as I should have
thrown away mine long ago. Trust your heart, and your love will
show you the way.*

Your loving sister,
Celia

Sofia held the letter for a long time, then she held it out to
Magdalena, who flinched.

'Read it,' she commanded, her voice as harsh as the contessa's in her ears. She watched the thin face, the silence as the
maid struggled to make out the words, the dawning look of
comprehension. The tears that filled the older woman's eyes.
'You really haven't seen it before?'

Magdalena shook her head. 'No. I swear it.'

'My sister wrote that when she was dying,' said Sofia, taking
back the precious letter, the last words of the sister with whom
she had once shared everything. The one person in this world
she would trust with her own life, and the precious survival of
her only child. 'I didn't know. It was only months afterwards
that I heard she was dead. By then I was in America, I had no
money, no means of returning. The next information I had was
that Leo Arden had married again, a young wife who took good
care of the children. All the children.'

Deep inside, the heart she had believed broken beyond
breaking began to tear itself apart once more. 'And that it was
for the best. I never knew I had been given the choice. Thanks
to the contessa, I was never given the chance to know.'

She couldn't stay there. She rushed out into the night. Sofia
stood by the dark waters of the canal, fury and grief battling
within her. That had been her mother's ultimate punishment
for Sofia's defiance of her carefully laid plans; for Sofia choosing

to follow her own heart, and the soulmate she had known with all her being would be the one true love of her life. The love that had made her feel truly alive, and told her she could achieve anything.

She could imagine the icy triumph her mother must have felt, keeping that letter from her, along with the money to get to Arden House and be reunited with her child, this time knowing that she had made a life on her own terms, and the means to look after her. That they could be a family again. That love had not completely died with her beloved Frederick in the clear blue waters of the Mediterranean. She shuddered, thinking of her mother keeping that final message to take it out again and again, like a murderess gloating over the grisly trophies from her victims.

Keeping Celia's letter from her had sent Sofia heading over the Atlantic, to a new world, convinced she had lost everything that gave meaning to her life, not caring whether she lived or died, or anything that might happen to her.

At her feet, the canal lapped, darkly. Her old despair was back, gripping her, holding her. And this time with the knowledge that if she had thought more clearly, if she had fought harder, she might have had everything to live for. Her life would have been immeasurably changed. Deep inside, her heart began to break apart, this time beyond repair.

PART 2

TWENTY-THREE

NAPLES

Spring 1946

On a spring morning in 1946, Kate watched as the Bay of Naples came once more into view.

She stood at the railings of the ship chartered to take donations to the land devastated by the fierce battles that had raged during the final months of the war and the eruption of Vesuvius in March 1944.

At least this time she was prepared for the noise and chaos of the southern Italian port. The first time she had arrived in Naples, in the months following the ending of the war, she had been stunned by the destruction of so many buildings, reduced to nothing but rubble. Even the Blitz in Birmingham had left a functioning city between the ruins, its basic infrastructure in place, ready to be repaired. Here, between the bombing and the fierce battles, and the thick layers of volcanic ash, it looked in places as if the entire coastline had been obliterated.

But not completely. As the *Atlantic Belle* drew closer to the harbour, she could make out that some of the rubble had been cleared. The beginnings of green emerged along the coastline;

spring sending new life amongst the ruins. In the distance, she could make out the distinctive slopes of Vesuvius, a dark shadow against the deep blue of the sky, a thick wisp of cloud rising from its summit. When it had erupted, in the year before the ending of the war, many of the villages had been swallowed by the towering wall of lava that had rumbled down the slopes. The American troops had helped the occupants escape with as much of their belongings as they could manage. But the villagers would return again, just as they must have done after the far larger eruption that had buried the Roman cities of Pompeii and Herculaneum. One day, the rich volcanic earth would be again covered by vines.

On the quayside, next to the ships bringing in donations from America to help the stricken population, she could make out the familiar figure of Gina, waving with both arms as the *Atlantic Belle* approached. Kate waved back with equal enthusiasm.

The scene in front of her wavered as she remembered her excitement when she had first arrived with Peter and Gina in the months following the ending of the war. Then, trepidation at the suffering she was about to face had been shot through with anticipation at finally reaching the land of her childhood. She had shared her companions' eagerness to bring as much relief as they could to the civilian population that had endured years under a fascist dictatorship, followed by occupation by the German army, and then the liberation by the Americans, just as the volcano looming over the bay did its worst.

It had been less than a year since she had finally persuaded Peter and Gina to let her accompany them to Italy, but already it felt a lifetime ago. Grief went through her. The green countryside around Stratford-upon-Avon may not have suffered the utter devastation of the land she was approaching, but so many of the young men had been lost in the fighting, so many women and children lost in the pounding of the cities, that there was barely a family left untouched.

Like most of the families, death had also touched the Arden family. The message, when it had finally arrived, had sent her on the tortuous journey back to Arden House, arriving just in time for the most difficult family Christmas of her life. She was still reeling from the loss of Will, her eldest brother, and Arden's precious son and heir. His death had thrown the family deep into mourning. The entire future of the Arden estate was in question.

In the rush and business of organising the donations of desperately needed food and clothing raised by Miss Parsons and her friends in London to take out to the charity in Naples, she had been able to put her grief to the back of her mind. But it was still there. It had been there in every moment in the deep snows of Warwickshire, in the family Christmas that may have attempted to follow its previous traditions, but would never be the same again.

It still hit her with the same force that she would never see Will again. They had never been particularly close. From a small child, her elder brother had driven her to the heights of irritation with his lording over them all as the one who was, in the settled course of things, destined to take over as master of the Arden Estate. Her annoyance had also, she had admitted to herself lately, been touched with fear: the fear of dependency.

Like her sisters, she was dependent on Papa for everything. If she didn't marry or find a way of supporting herself (almost impossible on the pittance paid to female workers), that responsibility would have passed to Will. The thought of being the maiden aunt, the charity case, pushed into useful obscurity by Will's wife and growing brood of children, had always filled her with dread. Now, she would give anything to have him back. She'd put up with his superiority, his unwillingness to be questioned, even his view of his sisters as being of little worth beyond their potential for securing conveniently rich husbands. Anything to have him back again.

At the railings, Kate pulled her jacket closer around herself. Christmas, perhaps the last she would ever spend at Arden House, had been a reminder of how far she had moved from her old defiant self, the one who had minded being the not-quite-Arden, the one who didn't belong. Her work with the children at Tregannon Castle during the war had given her confidence in her abilities, and that she was perfectly capable of living a life dependant on her own skill and wits. During the last months of the war, she had returned to her own drawing and painting in earnest.

In the weeks before she had left for Italy, she had even plucked up the courage to persuade Mrs Howson to display a painting she had done of St Ives's harbour, along with one of seals basking on the rocks of Porthgwidden Beach, with its view of Godrevy Lighthouse across St Ives's Bay. To her astonishment, the one of Porthgwidden had been snapped up even before she had left the shop by an admirer of Virginia Woolf's *To the Lighthouse*. By the following week, the one of the harbour had been bought by holidaymakers eager to make the most of the return to some kind of normality. This had been quickly followed by the sale of several smaller paintings of waves crashing against the broad curve of sand and dark outcrop of rocks on Porthmeor Beach, and the fishing boats resting in the harbour below Tregannon Castle.

'You've quite an eye,' Mrs Howson had remarked. 'And a way of catching an atmosphere, as well as a scene. We've a fair few visitors starting to come back, so we're happy to take any views you care to bring.'

With an outlet for her paintings, and Ellen still needing help with the children who had not yet found homes, the temptation to stay had been almost overwhelming. But the urge to find her past, and to find her mother if she were still alive, was stronger. It had been a risk, leaving such a rare opportunity to be able to earn her own living, but the opening to travel to Italy with Gina and Peter was one that she knew would not come again.

Then, no sooner had she settled into Naples, than the message had arrived from Alma that had sent Kate back to Arden House. She had taken the first supply ship returning to London, followed by a wild dash through the snow in a borrowed van to join the family for Christmas.

It had broken her heart to see Papa, who had always been the strong anchor in her life, suddenly frail with the dashing of his hopes. At least Jamie, who, however unwillingly, was now the heir, was beginning to recover from his injuries, which gave some hope for the future. And this new Papa, his mortality hanging heavy around him, had accepted Rosalind back into the fold, despite her engagement to a man he considered wholly unsuitable, but who Kate knew was the love of her sister's life.

Even in Arden House, the war had changed the settled way of things. Cordelia had already returned to France, to resume her work with refugees. Rosalind had gone back to London to pursue her passion for being a photojournalist, one that she had already declared her upcoming marriage would not prevent. Kate winced. This Christmas had also shown her how their elder sister Bianca, the only one who had obeyed Papa's expectations, was trapped in her marriage to a man unscrupulous in his pursuit of wealth, and who didn't seem to have any particular affection for his wife. It had made Kate even more determined than ever to avoid the same fate. The very thought made her breath tighten in her chest.

Naples's harbour was looming closer. For her, this was her path to freedom. It wasn't just the work that released her from Papa's determination to control her future. She knew he had only let her go because he was too shaken and unwell to prevent her, and he was certain she would soon be forced to come home.

She hadn't exactly deceived him. She had just let him assume she was returning to working with orphaned children, rather than travelling with the supplies heading to the warmth and the vivid sights and sounds of the Mediterranean, and the land of her birth.

She couldn't tell Papa that her only concern for now was to find out if her mother had survived the war, and make sure she was safe. She dreaded to think what might have happened to her mother if she had returned to the villa near Sorrento. Ash had covered the coastline, destroying so much in its path, after the land had been already stripped of all means of support by the fighting.

Of course, her mother may not have been in Sorrento, but in Venice. That was the other place she would look. Kate might be at the other end of Italy to Venice, but she was on the same continent. If the trains were running again, she would find a way of getting there. She had seen photographs of Venice, which had become a haven of rest for servicemen since it had been liberated. From pictures and newspaper reports, she understood the city had not been destroyed by bombing, whatever the population might have suffered from the German occupation.

Kate shouldered her rucksack as the *Atlantic Belle* docked between the ships bringing in donations from America. Shouts erupted around her, as the crew unloaded the precious supplies. In the melee of goods being taken into the town, she could no longer make out Gina. But then she appeared, dodging between sailors and lorries, and the odd horse and cart, to hug Kate tightly. Kate returned the embrace, feeling her tears, never far from the surface, rising.

'It's good to see you again,' said Gina. 'I wouldn't have blamed you if you had stayed.'

'I couldn't,' replied Kate, dashing away the tears with her sleeve. 'Jamie's getting so much better, I could see the difference even in the short time I was there. He's learning to manage Papa, and Papa seems to have finally accepted him as his heir. I never thought I'd see the day; they've never seen eye-to-eye. But at least Papa has finally accepted that it's Jamie who will take over, or the Arden Estate will be lost forever.' She gave a watery smile. 'And Papa would do anything to avoid that.'

Gina, her own eyes glassy with tears, said, 'I'm glad Jamie's recovering.'

'I wasn't completely sure myself until he insisted on me sending him back photographs of the excavation at Pompeii so he can see it for himself. He even gave me one of his cameras, and rolls of film, so I've no excuse.'

Gina laughed. 'That sounds like Jamie. He always told me he liked that his sisters knew their own minds, you know.'

'Are pig-headed, more like,' returned Kate, blowing her nose, as they made their way through the remains of ruined buildings surrounding the harbour, and into the town, and the abandoned house where the little charity working with the street children was based.

While some parts of the town had remained more or less intact, Kate still could see vast swathes of ruined buildings, crumbling into rubble. They passed through narrow streets of tall buildings, with washing hanging from balconies, and house-wives calling to each other, their voices echoing in the sunshine. Amongst the destruction, men and women still walked about their daily business, some of the women carrying bits of shopping. The occasional car or van passed, mainly American jeeps, interspersed with horse-drawn carts that seemed to come from a previous era.

They finally reached the shabby, but reasonably intact, building, which had once been a small guest house. It stood in a street so narrow Kate could barely make out a strip of sky between the tall tenements.

As they reached the house, a rusting Fiat van drove up. Kate was glad to see Giulia Bernardi climb out of the driver's seat. A tall, upright woman in her fifties, clothed in trousers and an outsized men's jumper, she had remained working in Naples throughout the war and, although still desperately thin, retained the energy of those driven by an inner determination.

'So you're back,' she remarked in her almost fluent English. 'I thought I saw you at the harbour. Good,' she added as a second, equally battered, van drew up, driven by her nephew Marco.

'So good to see you, Miss Kate,' he called, in rather more hesitant English, while grinning broadly. 'Now you come to Pompeii.'

'Give poor Kate a chance,' replied Gina, reverting to Italian. 'She's only just got back. And anyhow, there's plenty to do here first.'

'You still come?' said Marco, turning to Kate.

'You try and stop me!' she replied. '*Sì*, yes of course,' she added in a more sedate manner to his puzzled expression, scrabbling around for her Italian, which had been improving by the day when she had worked here before, but had vanished from her mind in her weeks back in England.

His grin broadened. 'Good, good,' he said in English. 'Peter wants to see the summit of Vesuvius,' he added in Italian. 'And look down into the crater.'

'Isn't that dangerous?' asked Kate, who had followed the meaning. '*Pericoloso*?' she added to his look of enquiry.

'Sometimes we live, sometimes we die,' he replied, his expression becoming serious. Kate winced inwardly. Marco had filled out a little in the months since she had first met him, but he still looked younger than his seventeen years, after a childhood spent largely amidst bombardment and starvation. Like Giulia, he had said very little about the years of fascist rule, or the German invasion after Mussolini had been deposed. But she could guess from their silence that they had both seen horrors she could not imagine, living under regimes that had viewed the ordinary citizens as barely human. She couldn't blame him for grasping so eagerly at life while he could.

During her first weeks back in Naples, Kate threw herself back into helping the little charity as they vainly attempted to cope with the hundreds of orphans who had survived the war, and were now struggling to survive on the streets of the city. The work kept her mind from dwelling too much on the grief left at home, and the worry that remained about Papa's health after the double shock of Will's death and Jamie's injuries.

She enjoyed working with Gina again, slotting back into their old friendship, knowing each other's minds so well they didn't always have to explain. It was how families should be, she thought a little sadly, remembering the bridges she had begun to build with her father and sisters in Arden House. She would never lose her sense of not being one of them, though. Papa had avoided being alone with her, as if nervous of what she might ask. With their grief about Will still so raw, and Jamie only so recently beginning to return to his old self, she hadn't had the heart to tackle Papa. Whatever answers about her past that lay waiting for her in Italy, she was going to have to find for herself.

Back in Naples, she found even Peter more at ease. She admired his seemingly tireless energy as he organised the desperately short supplies, along with the mending of roads and buildings in the vicinity of the charity's base. Every hour of each day he fought to get the homeless and the displaced food and shelter, along with the seemingly endless numbers of children left to fend for themselves off the streets. This was Peter in his element, she recognised, with just the slightest hint of regret. He seemed more fully alive than she had ever seen him before, even when helping the rescue of the families from destroyed houses in Birmingham. She had already been able to see that his experiences before the war of being a victim of the fascists would lead to a future as a fierce campaigner for social justice, or battling corruption as an idealistic politician, with very little time for anything else.

Something shifted inside her. She hadn't been heartless in her failure to fall in love with him, after all. Like with Lance, it had been her strong sense of self-preservation. Chance had thrown them together and he had never shown any particular warmth towards her, while those moments when he seemed to positively dislike her suggested she would need to spend every last ounce of energy on learning how to please him.

I haven't got time for that, Kate snorted to herself. Besides, she couldn't help noticing that in the few short hours when he was not working, he preferred the company of younger and far prettier women, who tended to eye him with undisguised admiration.

'He'll never change,' remarked Gina one evening, as they sat in one of the small cafés that was up and running again, and bravely making the most of the little food available. Peter was at a table a short distance away, deep in his customary passionate political discussion in Italian with a group of local men, while a fair-haired young woman sat quietly listening, nodding every now and again in vague agreement, without volunteering a word.

Gina shook her head in affectionate exasperation, as she and Kate exchanged wry smiles of particularly female under-standing. 'To be honest, I'm not sure he even sees it himself,' she added. 'But then, let's face it, a woman content to remain deco-rative in the background seems to be what most men are looking for.' The faintest flush of colour passed over her cheeks. 'Person-ally, I just want someone who lets me be myself and enjoys the fact that I've a mind of my own.'

'I couldn't agree more,' replied Kate, feelingly.

· · ·

For most of those first weeks back in Naples, Kate rarely had time to think. The plight of the street children was desperate. Many had been injured, and more who had seen and experienced things no child should, and there were many adults ready to take advantage of their desperate situation. However much she saw it, she could never dull the vision of their half-starved faces with haunted eyes, and sharp skills many an adult might envy.

It touched her, the way even the smallest looked out for each other, like little packs in a hostile wilderness. But it also paid to be wary, especially of the older ones, who were quick to spot an opportunity. She was getting used to their ways, but she was still, at times, annoyed with herself to find sharp-faced Dante, or wide-eyed Marianna, had yet again run rings around her, especially where easily pocketed treasures like bread, and the almost unheard of luxury of meat and cheese, were concerned.

Each night, she wanted nothing more than to collapse into the little camp bed in the upstairs room she shared with Gina, worn out from the emotions of the day and struggling with her rapidly improving Italian and her phrase book. Working amongst adults and children who mostly had no knowledge of English meant that she was living and breathing the language. It was coming back to her, from a memory she hadn't known she possessed, like a muscle that had not been used for a while, regaining its previous strength by the day.

One evening, as spring began to turn towards summer, lengthening the days once more, Gina returned from the soup kitchen for the street children in a state of irrepressible excitement.

'Marco's finally going to take us to see Pompeii,' she said. 'You, me and Peter. He's going to take us up to see Vesuvius as well, as there haven't been any earthquakes since you've been back, and no sign it's active. Bring your camera and your sketchbook. We might not get another chance for months, and I'm dying to see the excavation again.'

Early the next morning, Marco rattled them along the road out of Naples in his elderly Fiat. First, he headed away from the coast, as far as the road would take them up the steep sides of the volcano.

'Now we walk,' he announced, gesturing to the rough path, heading towards the rim, which was dustily barren, devoid of any vegetation.

As they reached the top, Kate looked down into the reddish shadow at the centre, half expecting red-hot lava to erupt at any minute. Around her, trails of smoke emerged from small fissures in the rock. When she placed her hand inside, she could feel the heat of the steam, bringing with it the harsh smell of sulphur that caught the back of her throat and made her cough.

'I was working on one of the farms up here on the mountain when it erupted,' Marco said in Italian, as he gazed down into the steaming depths.

'That must have been terrifying,' replied Kate, in the same language. She had seen the damage caused to buildings on the coast; what it must have been like to be on the mountain itself she couldn't imagine.

'Not up this high, thank the Lord.' Marco's face was drawn into the lines of a much older man. 'I've never run so fast in my life. It was terrifying, like the end of the world.' He shoved his hands in his pockets. 'It made me think what it must have been like for those poor souls caught there in Pompeii. At least we could escape, and had the Americans to help us get away, while they stood no chance at all, poor things.'

'No, they didn't,' said Kate quietly. Even during the Blitz in Birmingham, she had not seen the utter devastation that still remained beneath the shadow of the volcano. Her mind still couldn't fully take in the plight of the civilians during the war, poor enough to begin with, to be caught between invading armies and the hell on earth of molten rock advancing to obliterate everything in its path. It felt overwhelming.

As Marco moved away, lost in his own thoughts, Kate found Peter joining her. Without his usual ceaseless activity, she could see his face was drawn with exhaustion, and he was holding his bad arm stiffly. He always insisted on carrying heavy loads as much as the other men, but it made her wonder if his injury had healed less well than his pride would ever allow him to admit. Or perhaps it was the memories of the time he had been here just before the war, when he'd been arrested by Mussolini's fascists, along with the beatings and the torture, and the friends who had died.

'You wouldn't think anything so catastrophic could happen on a day like this,' he remarked.

Kate followed his gaze to the countryside spread out below in the haze of summer heat; the brilliant blue of the sea stretched as far as she could see. Between the ruined buildings and settlements, and the layers of ash left by the eruption, the deep green of agricultural land was already springing up. Now she looked closer, she could see clusters of terracotta-tiled houses that looked as if they were being repaired. The villages were slowly coming back to life again.

'I suppose it must have looked the same when the people of Pompeii were alive,' she suggested.

Peter grunted. 'Human beings always think life will go on, just as it's always been.'

'Like before the war,' she replied.

He turned towards her, eyes searching her face, his expression softened a little from its customary intensity. 'Exactly. All that death and destruction. All that anger and grief and revenge upon revenge. And for what?'

'It sounded like a grandiose fantasy to me,' she replied.

'That idea of a master race and some people being better than others, rather than us all just being human beings, in the end.'

He eyed her. 'I'd have thought your father might have approved of that. Being lord of the manor.'

She frowned. 'That doesn't make him a fascist,' she retorted. 'And if it did, it wouldn't mean that I'd have to be one.'

'I didn't say you were.'

'Papa lives in his own world. It's a fantasy too, in its own way. Of how the world should be. Which is mainly with the men in charge and the women at their beck and call,' she added, tartly.

To her surprise, Peter laughed. 'I can't imagine you being at anyone's beck and call, any more than Gina.'

'Which is why I was always viewed by the local gentry as a bit of a disgrace.' She grimaced. 'My sisters were always better at hiding it. Maybe that's the best way, after all.'

His expression became one of disapproval. 'And let other people fight for justice?'

'Not everyone can fight,' she returned. 'I think the mothers of every child we've looked after would rather have survived and be able to keep their children safe. Isn't that what love is, in the end?'

'I see your point.' He was silent for a moment. 'From here, you can see the bay curve round to Sorrento. I haven't been there since my aunt and uncle left before the war.' He cleared his throat, this time most definitely avoiding her eyes. 'That coastline is where you get the views of Vesuvius like the one in the drawings you used to make for the children at Tregannon Castle.'

'Don't you find it rather frivolous,' demanded Kate, curious at this change of tune. 'That I'm spending energy trying to find a place that must have once belonged to someone rich and powerful, when there's so much else to be done?'

He chuckled. 'Am I that transparent?'

'Very.'

He frowned at her, as if offended. Then his face relaxed. 'I'm a believer in social justice.'

'And you think I'm not?'

The puzzled look was back again. 'You're a painter at heart. An artist. That's where your future lies. Not here, not working in these streets. I didn't mean you aren't good at what you do,' he added, as she began to protest. 'But this kind of work can burn you out in no time if your body and soul don't thrive on it. I have a feeling your soul, whatever that might be, thrives elsewhere. To deprive you, would be to destroy you.'

Kate blinked. There was the faintest hint of regret in his tone. The regret of what might have been. She turned to gaze once more over the coastline towards Sorrento. What was there to say? Warmth went through her, along with her own twinge of something lost. She liked Peter for that unspoken recognition that loving him would mean sacrificing her own deepest desires. More than that, she was touched that he cared enough for her well-being not to try and entangle her in one of those passing love affairs that, in the febrile atmosphere of the little house in Naples, took place under all their noses.

He wasn't to know that she was practised in the art of sharp elbows, and spotting young men who most definitely didn't have the dignity of marriage (or even mutual respect) in mind once they'd had their fun. But that wasn't the point. He was seeing her as a human being, with a mind and a soul of her own; not something that he could use and abandon to her fate without a second thought. More than that, he was setting her free to follow her own path.

She grimaced. It wasn't all self-sacrifice on his part. They'd worked together long enough for him to know that she was never going to be quiet and softly spoken, with no views of her own. Or at least with the sense to keep them to herself until after she was safely married. But she was fond of him, for all his faults. She was glad that whatever it had been about her that had once made him seem hostile had dissipated. Whatever he had seen in her features – or thought he had seen – didn't matter anymore, even if it was a resemblance to someone who had once betrayed him to the worst of fates. Wherever her journey to find her past might take her, Kate was glad they could at least remain friends.

The little group was quiet, each lost in thought as they returned to the Fiat. Marco drove them along the bay, with the calm blue waters of the Mediterranean on one side, houses and greenery on the other. Finally, they turned inland towards the ruins at Pompeii. There had been bombing here too, this time from the allied forces in the battle over who controlled the area. But archaeological teams were back, doing their best to preserve the area and start work again.

The ruins of Pompeii were still standing in parts, the haunted remains of lives stopped in an instant. Vesuvius looked like a faraway hill. Even when it had been full size, it must have been a distant sight. Not one that you would ever think could cause such destruction, until it began to stir.

This was not like the Roman villa at home, with its remains reminding her of lives lived richly in the English countryside. These were lives violently interrupted, obliterated, just as the war had swept away the existence of the villages around her, who were now attempting to rebuild.

'This was where we were excavating before the war,' said one of the diggers. 'This part was left alone, thank goodness. Want to have a look?'

Kate followed them through a gap in the solidified ash, to the remains of a room, with mosaics on the floor and paintings on the walls.

It was a strange feeling, being there. She wondered what

had happened to them, the family who had walked among the murals and on the mosaics. Had they died here, smothered by burning ash? Or had they escaped, as some must have done, in the weeks before the eruption, taking boats away to safety, never thinking that they would not see this place again, that it would be lost forever. The walls began to close in around her.

She pulled herself out into the sunlight, leaving the others to admire the mosaic and wander the ruins. She was certain now that her memories of Pompeii were real. She had been here before. Somewhere amongst the ruins, the room she had seen as a child must be still here. Unless it had been bombed into oblivion by the Allies, as they liberated this part of the coast from German occupation. She shut her eyes, trying to remember, to work out where the wall paintings of her memories might be.

But within minutes the others were joining her, and it was time to return to Naples. Kate took a last look along the coast towards Sorrento. Peter was right. If the villa she remembered existed, it had to be somewhere there. She couldn't help wondering what she might find.

That evening, as they finished their meal in the small café a few streets away, she took out the sketch of the villa, placing it on the table.

'I'm trying to find this,' she said in Italian. 'It looks as if it might be somewhere along the coast.'

The sketch was passed around, to shrugs and shaking of heads. Disappointment went through her. Then, an elderly man who, despite being painfully thin and bent, supported himself and his widowed daughter by helping with the repairs to the building, reached for the piece of paper.

There was a low murmur of conversation, too rapid for Kate to follow.

'Signor Moretti says he thinks it looks like one he's seen above the cliffs, just before you reach Sorrento,' explained Gina in English. 'He lived in the town as a boy, he remembers passing it when it was inhabited. He's not sure what it was called.'

'Clara,' said the old man abruptly, as if the name had suddenly come back to him. 'Villa Clara.'

'Do you know who owns it, signor?' Kate asked in Italian.

Signor Moretti pursed his lips, slowly shaking his head. 'Very bad,' he remarked, in English.

Kate swallowed. 'Fascists, you mean?'

Signor Moretti spat into the fireplace, sending up a brief hiss as his spittle met the flames. '*Si, si. Fascisti.* Very bad.'

'Oh,' said Kate, her heart sinking into her boots.

'You know them?' asked Marco, curiously.

'I'm not sure,' she replied. 'It's something I was given,' she added hastily in Italian, feeling the deep disapproval emanating from the men around her. 'I don't particularly want to know them if they supported the fascists.'

To her relief, the atmosphere eased at this. The conversation returned to the previous subjects of the difficulties of getting materials, and the mess Naples had been left in, and how on earth it was going to get back on its feet.

'Signorina ...' As they set off back to the house, with Peter and the others ahead, Kate found Signor Moretti patting her sleeve. 'The villa was only for the summer. When it became too hot. *Zanzare.*'

'Mosquitoes,' Gina explained to Kate's puzzled expression at this unfamiliar word.

'*Si.*' The old man nodded.

Kate blinked. Mosquitoes. Didn't that mean swampland and water? There was a strange tingling sensation in her limbs. Wherever she looked, her search always ended up in the same place.

'Where?' she demanded, knowing the answer before she

asked the question. 'I mean, where did the family live when it wasn't summer?'

'Venezia,' he replied, as if stating the obvious. 'Venice.'

'Thank you,' said Kate. 'You still don't remember their name?'

'Rosselli,' he said, after a moment's thought. 'Very bad,' he added in English, shaking his head. 'So many people killed because of her. So much suffering.' His face closed in on itself, and returned to his place by the fire with the air of a man who had no intention of pursuing the subject any further.

'Are you all right?' asked Gina, anxiously.

'I think so,' said Kate. She felt slightly sick.

She. Was Signor Moretti referring to the contessa?

She glanced to where Peter was waiting for them at the end of the street. He had not joined in the conversation, but she had noticed he had been listening closely. Is that what Peter had seen? A family resemblance to her grandmother that had stirred up an old hatred of someone who had betrayed him and his friends before the war? He must have recognised the villa from her drawing. He was probably well aware of its owners. But even in that overture of friendship up on Vesuvius, he hadn't been able to bring himself to say the name. Kate suddenly felt stifled. She was thankful that Gina didn't seem familiar with the name Rosselli, or to have made any connections.

When the others had left the table and walked ahead, Gina turned to Kate. 'If you really want to find this place, I'll see if Marco will take us with him when he goes to Sorrento to take supplies. If Signor Moretti remembers seeing the villa from the coast road, then we might be able to spot it.'

'Thank you,' said Kate, hugging her tightly.

'We won't be able to stop, or at least not for long. It's too dangerous.'

'It doesn't matter,' Kate reassured her, as they followed Peter through the shadows of the darkening streets. 'I just want to see if it's the place I remember from when I was a child, before I was taken to England.'

'And then?'

Kate tucked her arm affectionately through her friend's. She would miss Gina, but after tonight she was more certain than ever that she could no longer stay in Naples. Whatever the consequences, she had her own path to follow.

'I'll find a way of travelling to Venice,' she said.

TWENTY-FOUR

VENICE

Summer 1946

She had to get away from Venice.

Sofia stood on the Ponte dell'Accademia, feeling the summer heat enveloping the Grand Canal. She gazed out past the Basilica di Santa Maria della Salute towards the still waters of the lagoon and knew that she had to escape the gilded city of her birth.

In her childhood, the onset of the stifling summer months had meant a welcome retreat each year to the verdant richness of the Villa Clara, and the deep blue of the Mediterranean. It had been her father's favourite place: free from the frenzied social life her mother enjoyed in Venice, and where he could indulge in his passion for making endless watercolours of the Bay of Naples. Sofia sighed. Papà had been the one who had encouraged her own precocious skills in drawing and painting. He wanted her to be able to pursue the profession that had been closed to him the moment he had inherited his position as head of the Rosselli family. He had supported her training, and used his contacts in London to give her opportunities most young women could barely dream of.

It was only since returning to Venice that Sofia had realised just how much his sudden death had isolated her, and shaken her confidence in her abilities to the very core. It had also left her at the mercy of her mother, who had never approved. The contessa's life had been devoted to maintaining the family's wealth and social connections, and she'd had no time for a daughter's painting, however successful.

'He was just humouring you,' had been her mother's constant refrain when Sofia had tried to speak to her of the ambitions Papà had worked so hard to help realise. 'Spoiling you, that's what it was. It was his connections with the London publishing house that got you the work illustrating those books. The truth is that they were a vanity project of the director. You don't think it was serious work, do you? The monied can always do as they wish. Your father always was a dreamer. Someone has to be practical round here.'

Sofia must now be the same age the contessa had been when she was widowed, with two young daughters to provide for and a crumbling palazzo, along with an almost equally crumbling villa, to maintain. Sofia still found it impossible to forgive her mother, but the years of war and hardship had given her some sympathy for her frantic need for survival at all costs.

Papà had been quiet and gentle, where her mother had been sharp and ruthless. On the other hand, Sofia could see with the benefit of a life's experience that Papà had been born into privilege. The family wealth might have faded over time, but he had never been forced to work all hours to make a meagre living, enduring the petty bullying of superiors hungrily using their power to take away the roof over his head. Her mother, born into destitution, had fought her way up from a life destined to end on the streets, forced into selling sexual favours for her next meal, terrified of the consequences of the inevitable pregnancies and the fate of any resulting child.

Sofia's years of making her own living in America had made her horribly aware of the precariousness of her mother's position, and her fury, all too often repeated, that the security of the Rosselli wealth was an illusion, as crumbling as the facade of their palace on the Grand Canal. The contessa had never forgiven Papà for not warning her before they were married, while to him it was just a part of life. But then he wasn't a woman, allowed no means of independently supporting herself that didn't involve some kind of prostitution, and with the added burden of children.

The need to survive, and to conceal her past, had stripped her mother of everything except her single-minded determination to maintain her position. She had, Sofia recognised, known how easily they could have ended in the degradation of the streets. She could understand a little more how such a fear had turned her mother's heart to stone, seemingly stripped of all human feeling.

No wonder, Sofia acknowledged sadly, that, after her father's death, she had sought a love that, if not to replace Papà's tenderness and belief in her, would fill the hollow left by his absence.

Now, with the ending of the war, the borders were opening once more, and the contessa was heading back to Venice. Only that morning, Magdalena had returned from her regular mission to keep the palazzo spick and span to announce a letter had arrived heralding the contessa's imminent arrival.

'About time too,' Magdalena had muttered. 'I was beginning to think we'd done all that work for nothing.'

It been a Herculean task, taking the two of them several weeks to get the palace back into some kind of order after it had been hastily abandoned by its German occupiers as allied troops arrived to liberate the city.

Sofia sighed. She felt old and worn, burnt to nothing by surviving in an occupied city where casual violence could erupt at any moment, while working with Niccolò Conti to keep all those they could alive with painfully insufficient supplies. Then there had been those they could not save, the partisans and the Jewish families deported to concentration camps, along with all the others who had disappeared once the invaders arrived. All made even more terrible by the stories creeping in of the bombings and massacres of communities around the city, alongside rumours of death camps and wholesale slaughter of innocent civilians.

Slowly, Sofia resumed crossing the arch of the wooden bridge to make her way back to the Studio Theodora. She could no longer bear the thought of being in the same city as her mother. She might understand her more, which might one day lead to a kind of forgiveness, but Sofia was not sure she had it in her yet. The contessa's betrayal of hiding Celia's letter, and Sofia's chance to be with her child, was still too raw for her to conceal her anger. After all the sorrow and suffering they had been through, what was the point? She no longer had the energy to fight.

Besides, the little studio would soon be reclaimed by its rightful inhabitants, artists seeking to be inspired by Venice. She had already seen signs the gallery on the Rialto was being cleaned and repaired, ready to take their paintings again. The occupation had halted her own attempts to return to painting. She hadn't the energy, and she feared that being found sketching any scene out in the open might have led to accusations that she was a spy. She itched to start again, but amongst the returning women artists, she would feel like a fraud.

'What will you do?' demanded Magdalena that evening, pausing in packing her painfully few and shabby clothes into a moth-eaten carpet bag, ready to take up residence in the palazzo once more.

'Go back to New York,' she returned. 'Why would I stay in Europe, with the shortages and destruction, when I have the choice? There's nothing here for me now.'

Magdalena reached for her spare skirt, much patched and mended, inspecting it carefully for any recent damage to its worn cloth. 'There's the villa near Naples.'

'Have you forgotten? Villa Clara was sold over twenty years ago.'

Magdalena fiddled with the zip of the skirt, which had become unreliable with age. 'Who told you that?'

'The contessa, of course. That was why I was forced to leave, why I was left with no home. The new owner was due to take possession within days.'

Magdalena remained bent over the recalcitrant zip. 'The villa was never sold,' she said at last. 'It couldn't be. Not even the contessa would have tried that one.'

Incredulity went through Sofia. 'Why not?' Magdalena was silent, unmoving. Sofia stared at the white hair, thinning over the crown of the maid's head with age and deprivation, revealing the fragility of the skin underneath. A terrible understanding began to creep through her, like the damp seeping between the bricks of the palazzo. 'Magdalena?'

'Because the Villa Clara belongs to you.' Magdalena's voice cracked with the effort of this betrayal of her mistress.

'No!' Sofia clenched her fists tight at her side, preventing herself from grasping the older woman and shaking the truth from her insubstantial body.

'It was left to you by your father when he died.' Magdalena spoke slowly, as if every word was dragged out of her. When she finally looked up, her eyes were dark and haunted. 'It was in his will. I saw it with my own eyes. I couldn't read when the contessa first took me on as her maid – that's why she chose a girl like me, so I would never learn her secrets. I taught myself, but I was always careful to keep it from her. The villa was left to you, all right. I saw the letter your father had written, saying that your sister had a husband to support her, and he wanted you to be independent so you could become the great artist he always believed you could be.'

'How could you!' Sofia cried, grief and fury sending the blood to her head and the shadows of the studio spinning.

'And end up on the streets?' Magdalena snapped back.

'I had a child.'

'One who could be taken care of,' said Magdalena, with a bleak grimness. 'You at least had that choice. I would have had none if the contessa had thrown me out. Don't you know what would have happened to any child of mine if I'd been forced on the streets – particularly a daughter? Do you think because I'm poor and uneducated I should have sacrificed my life for yours? Because I'm nothing?'

'Of course not.' The dizziness was overwhelming. Sofia sank to the floor, leaning back against the coolness of the walls. When she opened her eyes again, Magdalena had abandoned her packing and was crouching down next to her, concern on her face. 'I'm all right,' Sofia muttered.

The two sat for a while in silence, side by side, leaning against the brick of the studio wall. The shadows danced and swayed as the precious remains of the candle burnt low, the wick spluttering as it began to drown in a pool of its own wax.

'I made sure the child was safe,' said Magdalena, at last. 'It was the only thing I could do. Signor Arden would only let me go with them as far as London. But he had a car waiting and I knew it would only be a few hours before they would be with your sister. I did all I could, I swear it.'

Sofia drew in the mustiness of the ancient brick, the gentle lapping of the canal outside drifting in through the open window; the distant call of voices and the steady chugging of a vaporetto from the Grand Canal. What was there to say?

'Forgive me,' said Magdalena at last, voice breaking.

Slowly, the tears came. 'There's nothing to forgive,' replied Sofia. 'You are right; I was the one who had choices. I was the one who should have fought to the very last breath in my body. I was the one who should have realised my father would never have abandoned me, that he would have put something in place. I was the one who should at least have asked the questions. I was too trusting, too protected. I was an ignorant fool. It's myself I can never forgive.'

Next to her, Magdalena cleared her throat. Sofia dashed away the tears in an instant, and sat up straight, something falling into place. 'She told you to destroy the papers. That's how you came to see them.'

'Maybe,' said Magdalena, sounding her old prickly self again. 'Maybe not.'

'And did you?' Sofia tried to read her features in the sway of candlelight.

'The contessa watched me.' Magdalena didn't move, eyes firmly shut. 'To make sure.'

'I've seen how street children work,' said Sofia, slowly. 'I've watched gold bracelets and pocket watches disappear up a sleeve before you'd know it. I'm sure it can be the same with papers.'

'Maybe.' Magdalena remained motionless.

Sofia could make out the deep shadow of the crease between the older woman's brows as she battled with conflicting loyalties. 'Are they here in Venice?' she prompted. 'In the palazzo?'

This time the silence felt as if it went on forever. 'I'm not that stupid,' said Magdalena, at last. 'They were my last throw of the dice, in case I ever needed them.'

Sofia stared at her. 'You mean, blackmail?'

'Yes, if I ever needed it,' returned Magdalena. 'If she ever tried to pin anything on me. I've seen enough in my time to know it's always the poor and defenceless who get the blame, while those who do the ordering slither away scot-free to do the same thing all over again. We've always understood each other, the contessa and me, but she's become arrogant over the years; she's forgotten I know her every trick and when push comes to shove, I'll put my own survival first.' Her sniff was one of defiance. 'And I don't care what you think of me.'

'I'm old enough to know I'd do the same,' replied Sofia. 'So where are they?'

'At the Villa Clara,' Magdalena muttered, sounding strangled.

'I should have known. Where in the villa?'

The maid's eyes flew open. 'You can't go there! It's too dangerous. Besides, Villa Clara was most probably destroyed, if not by all those armies, then by that cursed volcano. It could be under three metres of ash, for all we know.'

'I'll take the chance,' retorted Sofia. The fire was back in her belly. When she had been young, consumed with grief and despair, she had not had it in her to fight. Her mother had been the terrifying figure of her childhood, impossible to please, unthinkable to disobey. Alone, trying to do what was best, believing all choice had been taken away from her, she had finally caved in to what had seemed the inevitable. It had tormented her ever since. If it hadn't been for Walter's illness, she would have tried, years ago. Now she was back on her own once more, but this time older and wiser, and with nothing to lose. This time, she would fight to the death.

With the opening of the world again, she could find a ship heading for Naples or Sorrento. After all their time working together, she was certain Niccolò Conti would help her join one of the ships bringing medical supplies and donations from the Americans to the Bay of Naples. Reaching the villa by land might not be safe still, but if she could hire a boat, she could land on the beach, and, if it was empty, make her way in unseen.

She wasn't going to let her mother win. Finally, she was going to make things right. Or at least as right as it was possible to be after so long. She wasn't sure in her own mind what she was going to do with the villa – if it still existed. But she had to know. It was the last thing she could do before leaving Venice forever. The only thing she could do before making her way to London, and then on, to find the only place where she might be able to trace her child. If she was still alive.

Sofia's heart squeezed, expelling the breath from her body. After all this time, when she'd believed she'd had no right to try and contact Arden House, when she'd thought it was kinder to remain tormented by her regrets and leave Katerina free to live her own life, it might be too late. England had been bombed, she had heard. She had no idea how badly. Celia had described Arden House as being out in the country, with only a small village nearby. It might have survived, but in this uncertain world, who knew?

Besides, the small girl with the rounded face and dark eyes, whose features reflected her own and who had looked out with boundless curiosity, showing a natural aptitude with paint and pencil, would now be a young woman. She could be married, with a family of her own, and no desire to rake up the past. If not, she could have easily been drawn to one of the major cities, even London itself, which, Sofia had been told, was blown to smithereens in the first years of the war.

Sofia pushed the thoughts firmly away. That was for the future; this was now. She turned to Magdalena, who was watching her warily, with the same expression when waiting for the contessa's orders. A feeling of utter ruthlessness went through Sofia. There were some advantages, after all, to being her mother's daughter.

'So, where exactly am I to look?' she demanded.

. . .

It took her several weeks, but, with Niccolò's slightly disapproving help at the madness of such a scheme – even in a desperate attempt to find a lost daughter – Sofia secured passage on a boat taking supplies to Naples, and then onto Sorrento. There, she found a small guesthouse, which was eager for any business coming its way. She was also able to hire a slightly battered motorboat, on the pretext of being an American eager to see the coast.

She had a few days until the ship returned from its mission along the Amalfi coast to Salerno. She had arranged to join it once more when it stopped briefly at Sorrento. From there, it was heading onto Marseille, where she could find a similar boat to take her to England. A few days, that was all she would need. She had no wish to linger in Sorrento, or the villa. Too many memories of those precious years of happiness, when the world had been at her feet, and life had been all she could have wished it to be, before tragedy struck, and the contessa had played on Sofia's vulnerability to punish her for her crime of disobedience.

Before heading down to take charge of the motorboat that would take her to Villa Clara, Sofia sat for a while in a café in the little square, drinking a precious cup of coffee – still a luxury after the deprivation of war. She braced herself for the visit to the place of so much happiness and such overwhelming pain. *She took everything from me. She took everything from me, and from my child. I won't ever let her do it again.*

TWENTY-FIVE

On a still summer's day, Marco drove Kate and Gina along the dusty roads to Sorrento. Like Naples, the villages along the coast still bore the marks of destruction, both from war and the eruption of Vesuvius. Everywhere, Kate could see the white ash of the volcano clogging the fields and buildings. Several times they passed abandoned villas, some blackened by fire, others no more than rubble. Even from the road, she could see they would not have the clear view of the bay she remembered from her childhood.

But then, as they drew near to Sorrento, Marco came to a halt, pulling the Fiat to the side of the road. 'Signor Moretti,' he said, gesturing towards a tall building set on its own, surrounded by trees.

'That could be it!' exclaimed Kate. Even from here, she could see the angle was right for the view towards Vesuvius. She could make out a dark-cream coloured building, with paint peeling from the walls and leaves and growth spilling out over one side. The shutters that covered every window, though faded by sun to a muddy grey, were still in place and the red tiles of the roof appeared more or less intact. It stirred no memories, but if this was the villa, the last time she had seen it would have been as a small child.

'Later,' said Marco, pulling out once more onto the road.

As she looked back, Kate was certain she could make out the balcony of a terrace surrounding the part of the villa looking out to sea. A covered balcony, with pillars, wrapped around by greenery. Her heart began to pound in her chest. Perhaps there was something familiar there, after all.

They arrived in Sorrento to find the picturesque little town still clinging to its cliff-face, having survived the destruction to remain the romantic destination of narrow streets Kate had seen in photographs and postcards.

After unloading the supplies they had brought for distribution to the villages, they walked to the edges of the cliffs, to the little house where Gina and Peter's family had once lived. Like many, it had been damaged in the eruption and was now empty and abandoned, with ash still visible, piled up against the walls. The elderly couple who had lived there had not survived the last winter, and where the rest of the occupants had gone, nobody knew.

'It's what we feared,' said Gina, as they returned down the steep steps between the houses. 'We had so many happy summers here. I can't believe they are all gone.'

'You may find some of your cousins,' Kate reassured her. 'The neighbours said they left, that must mean they had plans to make a life elsewhere. They may not have gone far. You may yet find them.'

'I hope so...' replied Gina, as they joined Marco and the small band of charity workers for a meal at a tiny café in the square, before the return to Naples.

.   .   .

On the drive back, Marco branched off the main road as the villa they had glimpsed that morning came into view. They bumped along a network of rough tracks, until they reached a pair of what had once been ornate metal gates, but were now rusted and broken, one half leaning on the dried remains of grass, the other at a crazy angle on its hinges. A short driveway, overgrown with grasses, led to an imposing door, set beneath a portico that might have come from a Roman temple. A place that had once had pretentions of grandeur, but was now being reclaimed by the elements.

With her stomach in a tight knot, Kate emerged from the Fiat, feeling the warmth of the sun on her skin, the touch of salt from the sea below, breathing in the dry scent of herbs rising from the swathes of unkempt grasses. In the distance, her eyes followed the sweep of the Bay of Naples, with its sea of impossible blue and Vesuvius rising up in the clear air. The feeling was back. The familiarity, yet strangeness. Or was that just a longing for this to be the place, for the impossible needle in a haystack search to be over? Even from here, she could see it was deserted.

'Marco says we can only stop for a short time.' Gina said, peering up at the villa. 'It isn't safe to hang around, and we need to get back to Naples before dark.'

'Just a few minutes.' She could not imagine anything more than a stray goat making its way up to so abandoned a place. With the shadows beginning to lengthen, sending the shutters into relief, the villa looked haunted. Close to, she could make out that several roof tiles had fallen, leaving gaping holes.

As they reached the portico, Kate could see the heavy wooden door was half open, hanging, like the gate at the entrance, precariously on its hinges. Shadows flickered within.

'It could be dangerous,' whispered Gina, glancing back to where Marco was standing guard, leaning against the Fiat, smoking a cigarette. Once inside, they would be out of sight.

'Just a quick look,' returned Kate, also in a whisper.

Taking a deep breath, she squeezed around the heavy timber, and stepped into the darkness. As her eyes adjusted, she could make out a place denuded of everything. Even the shutters were broken. The hallway looked as if it had been used for some kind of barracks. In what had once been an elegant dining room, there were the remains of camp beds, sleeping bags and empty tins with German labels, bottles of German beer and Italian wine. She recognised some of the labels. Others had a picture of the villa itself, having no doubt contained wine from its abandoned swathes of vineyard. She could imagine the triumphant soldiers breaking down the door of the family's cellar to raid the wine, and perhaps even spirits made from the tangle of lemon and orange trees in the nearby orchard.

A camping stove stood with a blackened kettle still on top. All signs of a panicky departure. She shivered in the shadowy cool. There was no smell of death from a battle raging here, or the sick and dying left behind. Just a hasty retreat.

Was the house familiar? Her eyes cleared a little more. It was impossible to tell. It was just an empty shell of a dwelling.

Light came in through the ceiling above. The flaky white of plaster covered everything, even the mounds in corners that looked like abandoned clothes, but she shuddered at the thought of any closer investigation. It must have once been a grand place, from the size of the rooms, the heaviness of the broken remains of furniture. Like Arden House, it must have bustled with family, with visitors, with servants from the village, the tradesmen and women making a living servicing the big house with all it needed.

Ghosts of an imagined past crept around her, just as they had done at home in England. There, she had loved the exploration of the distance past and imagining the lives of the Roman Villa in its grounds. Here, it felt simply mournful.

Between the broken shutters, she made out a small beach

down below, with a shabby motorboat, its sun-bleached blue paint peeling, gently swaying in the shallows.

'Kate!' hissed Gina from the doorway. 'We have to go.'

'In a minute.' Kate stood there, unable to move. Here was not the distant past. It was not even a living present. Slivers of sun edged through the shutters at the far end, catching the dust in the air, revealing the film of white ash that lay over everything, just as it did over Pompeii, freezing life at a particular moment in time. She was an intruder. A disturber of a life once richly lived from the fruits of the rich volcanic ash, and of the lost voices and laughter, like those she heard echo in the cool of evening within the more urban edge of Naples. She should not be here; the stranger, the foreigner, the girl with the empty dream of finding a place that was hers and hers alone.

There was a creak of floorboards. Not from Gina, still hovering at the front door, but from the ruined floors above. Kate froze. In the distance, towards the front of the villa, came the scrape of furniture being moved, cupboards being quietly opened. Someone was there. Owner, or a scavenger?

Gina had heard it, too. Kate could see her frantically beckoning from the doorway.

'Come on,' she hissed urgently.

Kate turned, knocking against a small table in the darkness, sending a lamp crashing to the stone flags.

The scraping above halted abruptly. Silence. Then there came the clatter of footsteps on stairs, heading somewhere within the depth of the building.

Kate fled. When she reached the car, she looked back. Someone really had been in there. She could see a figure heading out through the terrace, vanishing down the cliff path towards the beach.

'Let's get out of here,' said Gina. 'There was someone inside the building. It could have been bandits, thieves. Anybody.'

Marco cursed beneath his breath and manoeuvred the car,

gears crashing, away from the cliffs. Kate was certain she heard the roar of an engine. And suddenly, she caught the flash of a small blue motorboat racing in the direction of Sorrento, churning up the waters into a white froth in the midst of the deep blue.

Kate was thankful they arrived back in Naples before darkness fell. She and Gina were silent on the way back, equally shaken, Kate suspected, by the thought of what might have happened had they disturbed thieves.

By mutual agreement, none of them confessed to having gone any closer to the villa than the roadway outside. Like Gina, she had no wish to get Marco into trouble for being so reckless. Besides, there was something about having found the place that had haunted her for so long that had shaken her to the very core. It was like touching her childhood, then being dragged away again.

That night, the dreams came. She was back on the terrace, sunlight glowing between the leaves of the vines. But this time it was different. The rich hue of grapes was replaced by the yellows, crimson and scarlet of autumn amongst the green of the vines, interspersed with the rustling of dry leaves. A cold wind was blowing in from the sea, sending brown and gold drifting down around her, stirring into whirls of fallen leaves against the white of the balcony.

Arms were holding her tight, so tight she could barely draw breath. She could feel the softness of a face, damp on the cheeks held against hers.

Kate bolted awake. She took in deep gasps of air, breathing as quietly as possible so not to wake Gina. As her breathing calmed, she curled back down on the camp bed, pulling her blanket tight.

A cool breeze crept in through the shutters, stirring the

pages of her sketchbook she had left open on the little table beside her, and bringing with it the fishiness of the sea. That was what she remembered. She was swept up into larger arms, the roughness of a blanket about her, and taken out into the sea wind, towards the carriage waiting on the track outside. She could feel herself wriggling in the covering, peering desperately back towards the balcony with its fading grapevine, seeing the villa rising up against a crimson sky. Then it was gone, and she was in the confined prison of the carriage, being hurtled towards the nearby harbour, and the boat that would take her into the unknown.

Kate shot up in bed once more, a child's sobs in her ears. All around her in the darkness was silence. Just Gina's steady breathing, muffled by her sleeping bag on the camp bed at the other side of their little room.

She could not go back to the villa. After their narrow escape, she could not ask Marco to go there again, and even her stubbornness accepted that it was far too perilous to attempt to get there on her own.

She could feel the cool hardness of the pendant pressing against her skin. Her mind cleared. Wherever she turned, ever since she was a small child, all roads had led to only one place. If she was to find anything about her past, and forge a new future for herself as a painter, then there was only one place to go.

Venice.

PART 3

TWENTY-SIX

VENICE

Summer 1946

Kate emerged from Santa Lucia station in Venice into a blaze of late summer sunshine, to be immediately transported into another world. She had expected the railway to end in a station away from the picturesque part of the city. Instead, she immediately stepped out onto the side of the Grand Canal, surrounded by domes and ancient buildings. She stopped, entranced, as her fellow visitors exclaimed excitedly at the lapping of green water, and the passing of boats of all shapes and sizes.

It was the light that caught her, and she stood marvelling at the clear, sparkling reflections in the water, which gave a gilded luminosity to the buildings. Shouldering her rucksack, and clutching her precious guidebook, given to her by one of the volunteers at the charity in Naples, Kate followed the stream of people to the stop for waterbuses. Almost immediately, the large blunt shape of a vaporetto drew up, positioning itself with a roar of engines and the churning of water. Kate found a position at the railings where she could watch the buildings go by as the vaporetto chugged its slow way along the Grand Canal, heading towards the lagoon.

To her relief, the reports she had read in the newspapers proved to have been accurate. Unlike Naples, Venice had been spared the worst of the destruction and even so soon after the ending of the war in Europe, it was already filling up with visitors.

In the noise and the chaos, she was thankful Giulia Bernardi had given her the address of a small guesthouse that had survived. She had booked their cheapest room for a few days, to give her time to find something a little more permanent and more affordable, as well as a means of supporting herself before her carefully saved money from her work in Naples ran out. Giulia, who had been a regular visitor before the war, had also given her the names of larger hotels that were always looking for cooks and cleaners, along with a glowing reference in Italian of Kate's character, trustworthiness and capacity for hard work.

When Kate had checked into the guesthouse and freshened up after her journey, she took the vaporetto down the Grand Canal, watching each palace as they passed to see if she could identify one that might belong to the contessa. They all looked the same in the warmth of the evening, with their faded grandeur and faint air of melancholy. She disembarked at the stop for St Mark's Square, braving a café that allowed her to sit at a table set outside and watch the square as evening fell.

It felt beautiful and peaceful. In a nearby café, a band was playing arias from Verdi's *Rigoletto* and *La Traviata*, interspersed with Neapolitan love songs. The sounds of normality, of joy and laughter spilled out into the strangeness of this untouched city. Kate could feel the impulse to paint and draw the scenes around her with her old urgency. In a daze of excitement, she walked along the front, with the waves lapping gently against the paving, with the water stretching out into the bay, then to the Bridge of Sighs over the Rio di Palazzo, which connected the Prigioni Nuove, the new prison, and the Doge's Palace with its dreaded interrogation rooms. The last view of Venice prisoners would ever see.

As the light began to fade, she ran to join the vaporetto heading up the Grand Canal towards the Rialto.

'It has to be one of these,' thought Kate, inspecting the crumbling palaces as she passed. As they approached the landing at the Rialto, she paused in getting ready to disembark and turned for a final look back. A final ray of sunlight illuminated one of the buildings. It had the look of being abandoned, but as the cloud came over, shutting off the sun, she could see the ghostly flicker of a candle in one of the higher rooms.

So someone was there. It was near the Rialto, so even if it wasn't the palace she was looking for, someone there must be familiar with the contessa. At least it would be a start.

The next morning was overcast. Kate found her way to the palazzo's entrance between heavy showers of rain. Taking a deep breath, she rang the bell, which echoed through the palace. Nothing. After a few minutes she rang again. This time there was a clatter of footsteps inside. The door was opened by an elderly woman, in the neat black uniform of a maid, who eyed her with suspicion as Kate faltered over her prepared speech.

The maid clicked her tongue impatiently. '*Americana?* American?'

Kate shook her head. 'English. *Inglese.*'

'English, American, it makes no difference,' said the woman in English, with a heavy Italian accent.

'I wish to speak with Contessa Rosselli,' said Kate firmly.

'You have an appointment?'

'No,' faltered Kate, thrown by this unexpected response.

'The contessa is a busy woman. She sees no one without an appointment.'

'Please. I've come from England.' She held out her copy of the illustration of Lady Macbeth. 'Show her this. Please. I need to speak to her.'

The maid peered at the picture. Kate heard her sharp intake of breath. 'Where you get this?'

'It was left to me.'

'You better go. Now. Don't come here again.'

Kate put her foot in the door, stopping it from closing, raising her voice, so it echoed through the walls, amongst the lapping of water from the canal. 'It's a copy of an illustration I was given when I was a little girl. Part of a book of Shakespeare's sonnets my mother left to me. I was told the contessa will know how I can find her.'

'Go,' said the maid, this time her voice was low and urgent. There was something about the harshness of her tone... Kate felt the breath leave her body. The wrinkled face was unfamiliar, and the hair was white, tightly corralled into a bun, and yet... The brown eyes that met hers were filled with recognition. She was back on the boat as a small child, lightning crossing the sun, Papa yelling for her to be taken below.

The maid flinched. 'Just go.'

'Magdalena?' A woman's voice echoed from the stairs above. Kate could make out a shadow on the wall in the light from the candles and the water below. 'Magdalena, who is it?'

'No one,' said Magdalena, pushing Kate, urging her back into the street outside. 'Just a beggar. The usual. No one.'

'That doesn't sound like no one to me,' said the woman in English. 'Send her up to me.'

'As you wish.' Magdalena slowly opened the door, allowing Kate inside.

Kate followed Magdalena up a wide staircase, to a room that appeared to take up most of one of the higher floors overlooking the Grand Canal. The room was opulent, with a few impossibly ornate chairs and rich hangings that looked as if they had come from another age. The walls too were covered in what looked like old masterpieces, or at least carefully copied versions. As her eyes adjusted, she saw they were interspersed with simply framed canvases with more contemporary scenes – none of the gilt of the older works. She could make out views of Venice, and the unmistakeable skyscrapers of New York, the Eiffel Tower, along with great plains that could have been anywhere, and mountain ranges covered with snow.

As she came to the last, she paused and her breath caught in her throat. It was the view of the terrace from the villa. And next to it, to her amazement, was a photograph, old and faded, of a house with twisted chimneys peering through undergrowth.

'Arden House,' she whispered.

'Why are you here?'

Kate swung round to find a woman standing in the doorway, her narrow face lit by the glistening shadows of water from the Grand Canal. Kate took in a sharp breath. 'I'm Katerina Arden. Kate.'

'I know who you are. What do you want?'

'I came to find you.'

The contessa came closer, and Kate saw that she was just as grand and steely-looking as in the picture, but at the same time older, the skin thinner, her whole body revealing signs of mortality. 'If you've come for money, Katerina Arden, you are mistaken.'

'I don't want money. Please. All I want to know is who I am and where I really come from.'

The contessa's face let no emotion slip. A woman accustomed to maintaining control, whatever the circumstances, thought Kate. A woman whose heart was not easily touched, if at all. No wonder she had been chosen as the perfect model for Lady Macbeth.

'You are the Arden's responsibility,' said the contessa. 'They should never have allowed you to come here. Don't they understand Europe has been gripped by war? But then Ardens always were dreamers, with very little sense of the world outside the family estate. The weakness of all aristocracy,' she added bitterly. 'You have been given advantages most can only dream of. Don't expect sympathy.'

Kate stood her ground. She had come so far, she wasn't leaving until she had found out the truth. 'Can I at least know if I am an Arden?'

'Has anyone tried to deny it?'

She raised her chin. 'No. But no one will tell me anything about myself.'

'Guilt,' said the contessa, dismissively. 'The shame they brought on two families, or would have done, if I hadn't prevented it. Your mother made her choice. You've no business here.'

Kate took a deep breath. If the answer was the one she dreaded, the contessa would not soften the blow. But she had to know. 'Can I at least know if my mother is still alive?'

The contessa's shoulders twitched. 'She doesn't want to see you. She is utterly ungrateful. She won't help me with this place. Don't expect that you are about to inherit it.'

'I don't,' said Kate, exasperated. 'What on earth would I do with a palace?'

'Sell it. Be rich. You could marry who you pleased and never have to lift a finger again.' She crumpled the sketch. 'Be as selfish as your mother. Choose to paint rather than take on your responsibilities.'

Kate turned to look at the paintings. They were mainly watercolours, she could see, with a few oil paintings in between. They all looked as if they were different views of Venice. One showed a seascape under a stormy sky, another a gondola caught in the brilliance of rain-washed sun, with the Rialto Bridge a pale shadow in the background. A more intimate scene portrayed a vase of flowers on a window ledge, with the vista of the Grand Canal behind that looked as if it had been painted in this very room.

'Are those hers?' she asked.

'You don't think she was interested in you, do you?' returned the contessa. 'All your mother wanted was fame and ambition. She wasn't about to take responsibility for what she had done, for the hurt she had caused. For the shame she brought. You are better off without her. She is no daughter of mine.'

The edges were more frayed than the contessa would like to believe. Kate could hear it in the slight tremor in her voice. A woman who dared not show regret. Every part of the contessa chilled her to the bone. But Kate could not let go of the desire to reach her, to provoke some kind of warmth, however fleeting. It unnerved her to think of the shared blood flowing in their veins, witnessed by the arch of the eyebrows she recognised from her own. If only she could find a way to touch her grandmother's heart. Surely she could not be completely frozen.

'But you kept her paintings.'

A gleam in the older woman's eyes. 'Locked away in the attics, out of sight, out of mind until now. Maybe I'll burn them.'

This was hopeless. Kate gave one last try. 'So you won't tell me anything about myself.'

'What is there to tell? I'm tired. You should go. Your mother will never come back to Italy. Why should she return to a place that is broken? At least Mussolini brought order.'

'And destruction and death, and unbelievable suffering,' retorted Kate angrily, the haunted faces of the street children in Naples swimming before her eyes. 'I've been working with those who experienced the consequences of the fascists' rule. Don't you care that what they did was terrible beyond belief?'

Fury replaced the controlled steeliness of the contessa's eyes. 'You have no idea,' she said, voice shaking. 'Who are you to judge me? Go back to your safe English home, Kate Arden, and tell Leo Arden to take more care of his responsibilities. You will get nothing from me. I'll make sure you are not permitted inside these walls again.' With that she left, slamming the door behind her.

Fighting back tears, Kate headed down the stairs. The walls of the palace pressed either side of her, as if to crush her to nothing. As she reached the ground floor, she found Magdalena waiting.

'I'll show you out, signorina,' the maid said loudly in English, with a glance upwards.

'I need you,' came the contessa's voice, speaking Italian. 'I need you, Magdalena. This instant.'

Magdalena led Kate out into the alleyway behind the palace. She reached into her pocket, pulling out a crumpled piece of paper. 'You turn right at the end of the alleyway, that will take you back to the Grand Canal.' She handed Kate the paper. 'This is how you will find her,' she added in a low voice, eyes searching Kate's face. 'You look so like her.' The old woman's brown eyes filled with tears. 'You must believe it broke her heart, to send you away.'

'Magdalena!' The contessa was impatient. Imperious. But Kate could hear something else. Something that was not simply irritation. Something that might even be fear.

'Why?' she demanded as the maid turned to go. 'Why did my mother let you take me to England?'

'Do you think she had a choice?' She glanced up towards the contessa's voice, still calling her. 'That any of us had a choice? She keeps her power. That is her only interest. Why else do you think she supported the fascists? To keep all the money and influence she needs more than her life's blood. Losing it is the fear that rules her. It always will. She could own the world and that fear would still torment her. It would be better she thought you had died, that you did not exist. Why did you come here? You were safe. You know nothing; you don't understand the harm you can do.'

'I don't want to cause you trouble.'

'No.' Magdalena softened a little. 'I'm glad to see you grown, that you are fierce, as well as beautiful. I often wondered...' She dashed her sleeve across her eyes, as if to wipe any emotion away. 'You keep safe. Make your own happiness. Believe me, forget the riches, they don't lie here.'

With that, Magdalena vanished. Feeling eyes watching her, boring into her back, Kate stuffed the paper into her pocket and followed the directions, crossing over a small bridge, making her way through the back streets and canals before the narrow canal opened up into the Grand Canal.

Kate stood on the banks of the main thoroughfare, with the dancing translucence of light, and the rush of boats going to and fro, trying to collect her thoughts. She fished out the scrap of paper. It was a visiting card, elegantly printed with the contessa's coat of arms. And written in a hasty scrawl was *Studio Theodora*, along with an address.

Studio Theodora. The studio of women artists, the one linked to Ellen's aunt and the castle in Cornwall, and the young women who had once pursued their art in the fisherman's cottage by the shore. Next to the address was a roughly drawn trail between the network of smaller canals branching off the main thoroughfare. Kate took out her map. If she was right, the studio was only a short walk away.

TWENTY-SEVEN

Kate followed the little pathways alongside the canals, her map and the hand-drawn directions taking her deep into the heart of Venice. She turned this way and that, over tiny bridges spanning the canals, with glimpses of tall palazzos in the distance, between rows of balconies tumbling with flowers. A gondola drifted by with a couple romantically entwined, the swish of the gondolier's long oar through the water joined by the gentle slap of waves hitting the sides of the canal in the boat's wake.

Finally, she turned into a far narrower canal, that barely seemed to allow more than the narrowest boat to enter, leading to a tall building that looked as if it had been some kind of warehouse. The windows were open, allowing the sound of voices to drift out, along with sweeping and the moving of furniture.

As she hesitated, not sure where to turn next, a small wooden motor launch turned into the canal. The woman at the wheel, who wore a bright crimson scarf keeping her dark hair in check, guided the little craft carefully, concentrating, before cutting the engine and allowing it to come to rest at a small staging post with a practised air, before securing the boat. She lifted out a basket filled with fruit and what looked like spinach leaves, along with a large crusty loaf and placed it on the side, before jumping out, revealing workmen's overalls and a pair of study boots.

'*Scusi,*' said Kate, in her best Italian. 'Can you please can help me? I'm looking for the Studio Theodora.'

The young woman lifted up her basket, eyeing Kate warily. 'Sure,' she replied in English, in an accent that was most decidedly American. She nodded to the building behind her. 'It's here. Although if you're after the space, it's gone.'

'Space?' said Kate.

'The studio space. Isn't that how you found us?'

Kate shook her head. 'I was given this.' She held out the card with its distinctive coat of arms and hastily scrawled instructions.

The woman frowned. 'Well, I don't know what you've been sent here for, but boy, have you picked the wrong fight.'

'I wasn't sent by the contessa,' said Kate hastily. 'And a fight is the last thing on my mind. Her maid gave me this.'

'Sure,' said the woman with a cynical curl of the lips.

'Magdalena.'

The woman adjusted the basket against her hip. 'Magdalena sent you?'

'Yes.'

'Well, I never. You must have impressed her. Magdalena has a reputation for being nobody's fool, and unmoveable, even by bribery.' Her eyes scrutinised Kate, as if to reassure herself. Finally, she nodded. 'In that case, you'd better come in. I'm Rebecca Hilson, by the way. Everyone calls me Betty.'

'Kate Arden.'

'Pleased to meet you, Kate Arden. You'd better follow me.' Betty led the way into a stone hall, placed the basket on a wooden table, and led the way up narrow stairs to a room on the first floor. It was a single space, with windows on either side. Several young women were scrubbing the floor, while at the far end long trestle tables were being cleaned. Along the walls, drawings had been pinned in a haphazard way, as if to keep them out of harm's way the moment they were finished, while more drawings and sketchbooks were piled up on one table. Even a cursory glance revealed that they were all highly accomplished.

'We have a visitor,' announced her guide. 'It's okay, I've explained the space has gone.'

'You're an artist, then?' said a woman a few years older than Betty, pausing in scrubbing the floor. She was wearing jeans splashed with the dried remains of oil paint in mainly reds and yellows, her dark hair cropped short around her head.

'Yes,' said Kate. 'Well, no.' She added, instantly feeling a fraud, her eyes instinctively drawn to the oil paintings of Venice on the far wall. 'Not exactly. That's not why I'm here.'

The woman rested on her heels, scrubbing brush in hand. 'Draw or paint?' she persisted in a clipped English accent, as if she'd not heard Kate's protestations. 'Or is it sculpture? No, drawing, I think. That's where your eyes went first, to the sketches.'

'You can never fool Irene,' said Betty. 'Rumour has it she worked for British Intelligence during the war, like Manon over there,' she added, indicating a young woman in her early twenties, whose overalls were covered with white streaks of dried clay. 'Although neither will never confirm it, of course. But I've heard Irene was perfectly ruthless.'

'Totally,' replied Irene, good humouredly. 'And I never give up on an interrogation, once begun.'

Kate laughed. 'I sketch,' she confessed, flushing. 'Before the war I wanted to study art.' Irene raised one eyebrow queryingly. Was she just playing at being an artist, or was she the real deal, was the question hanging in the air. Kate could feel the same thought rippling through the other women, who had paused their tasks. She lifted her chin. 'My family disapproved, and once the fighting started it wasn't possible.'

'I know what you mean,' said one of the others. 'The studio was thriving before the war. Being women, we could have carried on, of course, but we all went off to do our bit. Not everyone has returned, which is why there are spaces. We are lucky Magdalena remained behind when the contessa left to sit out the war in America, and looked after the studio. She said one of the nurses from the local clinic stayed in one of the other rooms. Between them, they kept this place safe, thank goodness.'

'That's why Magdalena is still very protective of the studio,' added Betty, eyeing Kate with undisguised curiosity. 'She wouldn't send just anyone here.'

Kate looked around the room. There were paintings of all styles. Some were more traditional, with exquisite details of Venetian vistas, along with women washing clothes in a canal, and vegetable sellers in the market. Others were more modern and abstract in style. Tables and sideboards, that must once have been the height of elegance, stood along each wall, covered with ceramics and half-finished sculptures.

'That's a Vanessa Bell, isn't it?' Kate exclaimed at the scene of a hot pink geranium on a balcony, looking down to the terracotta of the houses opposite and the indigo blue of the canal below.

'So it is,' said Irene. 'I brought it back with me from London. It belongs here, it was bought by Miss Nancarrow, who founded the studio, when Vanessa Bell exhibited in Venice, long before the war of course. I believe they were friends. I love Bell's use of colours.'

'I knew they exhibited together, but I didn't know Miss Nancarrow was friends with Vanessa Bell,' exclaimed Kate.

'You've met Miss Nancarrow?' said Irene. Kate became

aware of every eye in the room riveted on her. Ellen's aunt was clearly a subject of hero-worship for all those lucky enough to have gained a space at the studio.

'I'm afraid not,' she confessed. 'But I worked with her niece at Tregannon Castle in Cornwall during the war.'

'Well, I never,' said Irene. 'Small world. I take it that's how you found us.'

'In a way,' replied Kate, warily, not quite sure how much to reveal to her new acquaintances. 'Ellen told me about the links to a studio in Venice. Although, to be honest, I wasn't sure it had survived the war until Magdalena gave me the directions to come here.'

'Now why would she do that,' frowned Irene. 'The contessa hates Studio Theodora. She tried several times to get it shut down when I was here before the war, telling the authorities that we were all prostitutes.' She sniffed. 'The old battle axe could at least have been original.'

'I'm not sure,' replied Kate, considering that now was not the time to confess to being the contessa's granddaughter, especially if she wanted to find out more. Magdalena must have sent her here for a reason, be it good, or ill. On the other hand, hadn't her grandmother's maid, presumably on the contessa's orders, once dragged Kate away from everything she knew? Why should she trust her motives now?

But everywhere she had been, the path always led to Venice, she reminded herself, and to Studio Theodora.

'Magdalena knew my mother, who studied here before the war,' she said, carefully. 'The First World War, that is.'

'Most of us weren't even born then,' said Betty. 'I don't think there's any record of the artists who studied here from that long ago. At least, I don't remember there being one. Elvira might know, of course, but she's not due back until next week.'

'Elvira?' asked Kate, her pulse quickening.

'Elvira Johansson had a studio here before the fascists took over,' explained Irene. 'She's famous. And quite old. Fifty at least, if not more. And half Jewish,' she added. 'She's lucky to be alive, she ended up in one of those vile extermination camps. She's been staying with friends in Switzerland to build up her strength, but she's determined to get back here. Her room is all booked for her to return.'

'So you must have been to St Ives?' asked Manon. 'I was going to study ceramics and sculpture there, but the war stopped me, too. I'll get there one day. I've heard Miss Nancarrow's niece is hoping to turn the castle back into an artist's retreat. I can't wait. I just adore the work of Barbara Hepworth. And it shows my family that women can be sculptors just as much as men. You didn't happen to come across her, did you?'

'I'm afraid not,' replied Kate. 'Although I'd love to one day. Her work is like nothing else I've ever seen. I'm afraid I'm more commercial with my painting,' she added apologetically. 'I sold views of local scenes in St Ives, mainly aimed at tourists.'

'Nothing wrong with that,' said Irene, exchanging glances with several of her companions. 'Knowing what people want is an art in itself, even more so if you want to keep your own style. We've always relied on selling our work in the studio's gallery on the Rialto. If we don't sell, we don't eat. It's as simple as that. Doesn't half knock the pretention out of you, I can tell you.'

'Yes, that's true,' agreed Kate. 'Is that how you live?' she asked.

'As much as we can. Most of us have part time work as well. Living as cheaply as possible is the real art,' said Betty, wryly. 'We pool our resources to cover food and cooking, anything left we spend on materials. If we had to cover rent, none of us could survive. But thanks to Theodora Nancarrow that's something we don't have to worry about.'

'There's a hotel on the Grand Canal that's always looking for cleaning staff and cooks,' said Manon.

'Especially now the tourists are returning,' added Irene. 'It's hard physical work and horribly badly paid, but it means you can get by. It's freedom. At least it gives us a chance to grow and develop our skills. We learn from each other and from seeing the masterpieces and the exhibitions. And Venice is an inspiration in itself.'

'Yes, I can see that,' said Kate, excitement going through her once more.

'It's like St Ives,' said Irene. 'We may not be able to afford tutors or to attend art classes on a regular basis, but we make a few, and the rest we learn as we go along.'

'Have you a place to stay tonight?' asked Betty. 'There's space upstairs if you need somewhere.'

'I've a room near the Rialto for the next couple of days,' said Kate. 'I'm not sure what my plans are.' She hesitated. Whatever Magdalena's motives in sending her here, she found herself amongst kindred spirits; young women struggling against the odds and the prejudice against females being capable of any serious achievement that wasn't to do with putting a husband's dinner on the table on time.

If her mother really had once studied here, she must have thrived, setting her on the path to becoming the artist Kate had seen bloom in the fisherman's cottage at Tregannon Castle, and discover her own unique style. Her way of reflecting the world and expressing her deepest emotions. To become a true artist. The fisherman's cottage had given her mother the space and the freedom, but it would have been amongst this atmosphere of women working together where it must have begun.

Kate glanced at the faces, interested in her not for her name – that clearly meant nothing to any of them – not for who she was, but as a fellow creative. Something relaxed, deep inside her. For the first time in her life, she felt at home.

The feeling continued as their discussion resumed, followed by being invited to join them for a simple meal of bread and cheese and fruit from the market. As Irene set off for her cleaning job, and Betty prepared to take over at the gallery on the Rialto, Kate jumped at the invitation to resume the conversation the following day. She left the studio with a mind fizzing with ideas. She couldn't wait to return.

TWENTY-EIGHT

Kate left Studio Theodora as afternoon sun broke through the clouds, warming the facades of the palazzos, sending them gleaming in rain-washed light.

Reaching the Grand Canal, she drew it all in, her senses still singing from her time with her unexpected new friends, every part of her feeling more alive than she had ever felt before. This city, a city where she was a stranger, and yet – as even the contessa could not deny – was in her blood, had already entered every part of her. She instinctively reached for her sketchbook and pencil, kept as always to hand in the back pocket of her rucksack.

Magdalena must have directed her to the studio for a reason. Maybe she had believed Elvira Johansson had already returned. Kate stood for a while, pencil in hand, watching the traffic passing in front of her, that, despite the suffering and the deprivation of the war years, was vibrant with returning life. Over the past weeks, her one focus had been in being able to save enough from the meagre wage the charity in Naples could afford to get to Venice and have enough to afford a room for a few nights. She hadn't, she realised, thought beyond finding the contessa.

Like the vaporetti ploughing their steady way through the water, with smaller boats and launches dodging in between in an ordered kind of chaos, she had a choice of what she did next. She could return to Naples, or find a way of earning enough money to find her way back to Cornwall. Or she could remain in Venice until Elvira returned. Like Betty and Irene and the others at the studio, she could turn her hand to anything to survive, and she had the references from Giulia.

Her pencil paused in catching the passing water ambulance, a gondola-like shape, distinguished by its cross on the side of the central compartment, its rowers pulling each paddle urgently as it sped on its single-minded mission. The wind blowing against her blouse moulded around the pendant suspended from its silver chain around her neck, pressing the glass against her flesh.

Murano. The pendant that had once been her mother's, which Miss Parsons had given her, was made of Murano glass, worked in one of the islands in the lagoon. There was a movement of people around her as a vaporetto began to dock at the station just in front of her. On an impulse, she stepped on, and was soon heading past the cemetery island of San Michele, and on to Murano.

Murano was plainer than Venice itself, clearly a working island, with workshops alongside a straight canal. She went from workshop to workshop, dazed by the heat and the noise and the glitter of intricate chandeliers hanging up to show the makers' skill. But everywhere she went, the pendant held in her hand was met with a shake of the head. At the last one, she was directed away from the main warehouses to a smaller workshop.

The middle-aged man who greeted her held the pendant in his hand, shaking his head, just as all the others had done.

'You're sure you don't make something like this? Or know anyone who might?'

'I'm sure. An old pattern.' He was handing it back to her when a thought seemed to strike him. 'Papà!' he yelled towards a back room, and an elderly man emerged, blinking like one waking from a doze. There was a brief exchange, too rapid for Kate to follow, before the old man took the pendant in his hand, nodding to himself.

'Yours?' he asked in English.

'I was given it. I was told it was made of Murano glass.'

'Yes,' he nodded. 'Mine. Me, I made it. So long ago,' he added wistfully in Italian. 'So very long ago.'

'For a woman?' demanded Kate eagerly, in the same language.

He shook his head. 'Two,' he said, back into English. 'Man and woman.'

'You made two pendants?'

'Si. Yes. Two.' There was a glow in his face as he looked down at the oval pendant. 'This for her. For him—' He sought a word. '*Croce*.'

'A cross?'

'Yes, a cross. Like this, but...'

'More masculine?' she suggested.

He grinned. 'Yes. For a man.'

A man and a woman. An exchange of pendants; tokens of love. For something so special. A jolt went through her. If the oval had been made for her mother, the cross must have surely been for her father. At home in Arden, she had never seen Papa wear any form of jewellery, not even a wedding ring. She couldn't imagine even his younger self she'd heard briefly in his conversation with Miss Parsons placing something so ornate, so very Italian as a Murano cross, around his neck. Perhaps she was fully Italian, after all.

'Do you know if they were from Venice?' she asked in Italian.

He considered this. 'The woman maybe, not the man. I seem to remember that he was English. Yes, he was English. They spoke in English.'

He suddenly looked old and impossibly tired. From the corner of her eye, she could make out the middle-aged man bearing down on them, clearly considering his father had had enough for one day.

'Were they happy?' she asked quickly.

The old man beamed, abruptly alert once more. 'Yes. Very happy. Such love. And you could see, the woman.' He made a rounded gesture with his hand in front of his stomach.

Kate stifled a gasp. 'She was pregnant?'

He nodded. 'That's what the pendants were for,' he said, smiling. 'For love. For love of each other, for love of the child that was to be born. They came twice, once to order, once to fetch. I never saw such love.' He placed the pendant back in her hand, eyes scrutinising her face, taking in every detail with an artist's eye. 'They are still happy?' he asked, returning to English as his son arrived. 'Your mother and father, they are still happy?'

She could see the hunger in his face for a sign that the world had not totally fallen apart. He looked so insubstantial, so worn, his life seemed to hang by a thread. She had no wish to disillusion him, to cause him hurt. What was the point?

'They are still happy,' she replied, gently. The old man nodded, tears in his eyes. Gently he patted her hand.

'Then you are lucky,' he said, as his son guided him away.

Kate emerged back into the sunlight in a daze. She fastened the pendant securely around her neck and strode up and down the length of the main canal, deep in thought, barely noticing the movement of people around her. The pendant, now more precious than ever, had given her a glimpse into her own past. Into the love that had once held her tight. But, on the other hand, she was not who she had thought she was before she had entered the glass factory. The realisation was unnerving.

If the old man was right, Leo Arden couldn't be her real father. She could feel it, deep in her bones, every experience of being an outsider amongst her brothers and sisters hitting her with new force. The young couple had spoken in English, the old glassworker had said, but that didn't necessarily mean he was English, when the language was the lingua franca between so many races and culture. But it told her that she was not an Arden. She never had been, and she never would be. Who she really was had been hidden. Papa would never tell her; she knew him well enough to be certain of that. The contessa had disowned her, and Miss Parsons said she did not know, or, for some reason, would never say.

She was no one. She was lost. She had no family, no race, no place of belonging. She felt adrift, alone in the world.

As the sinking of the sun finally sent her back to the stop for the vaporetto, Kate came to a halt. She gazed over the short stretch of water, now golden in the slanting rays of sunlight, towards the cemetery island of San Michele, with the skyline of Venice beyond. The nagging feeling suddenly coalesced into certainty.

It didn't make sense. The elderly glassworker had described a married couple, rather than lovers hiding a furtive relationship, along with the child they were expecting. But if Papa was not her real father, why had he been so insistent on claiming her as his own, and taking her across the sea to Arden? And if her mother was still alive, why had she never tried to reach out to her?

You are Kate Arden, Papa had told her, as a bewildered,

disorientated and grief-stricken child, aching for the lost protection of her mother's loving arms. Not Katerina, whose second name was unknown, but Kate. Kate Arden. The Arden who wasn't quite an Arden, but who, if the war hadn't intervened, she was more certain than ever, Papa would never have let out of his sight.

The answer, if she was ever to find it, lay here, in the place that had made her; the place where she began. So here she would stay, for as long as it took. Having come so far in finding out her true identity, she wasn't about to give up now.

Kate returned to Venice as the last of the light was fading into a soft purple haze. She stood at the railings of the vaporetto making its way up the Grand Canal towards the Rialto, watching the first lights in the restaurants along the banks appear, as diners took their places in the twinkling lamplight.

She stared up at the crumbling facade of the Palazzo Rosselli as the boat passed in the fading light, her hand instinctively closing around the pendant, warm against her skin.

'*I have been to Venice before*,' she whispered into the night air. She might not have breathed the city air, or been startled awake by the clanging of its bells. But if the man and woman who had commissioned the pendant had been her parents, she had absorbed the city in the blood she had shared in her mother's womb. And with it came an answer to her rootlessness, as clear as the ringing of the bells that filled the air. *This is where I truly belong.*

As she stepped off the vaporetto and made her way onto the Rialto Bridge, Kate saw the little shop belonging to the Studio Theodora was open, its lights shining brightly in the gathering gloom and its display of views of Venice on the outside. As she watched, a small group of American visitors stopped to admire the paintings and the prints. Several were seized upon and purchased. It looked as if the studio was already running a thriving business.

She stopped for a few minutes to watch the boats still plying their trade, the visitors dining by lamplight. The atmosphere of calm, of being in a world away from the cruelty of the war, with the magic of being in the impossibility of a city built on water.

Kate took a deep breath. Tomorrow she would ask Betty and Irene about the possibility of finding work. It wasn't just the tantalising thought that her mother might be nearby, but also the itch to get back to her own drawing and painting, that had grown every minute she had been in Venice, increased by being amongst the women at the studio pursuing their art, regardless of anyone else. Once, she had dreamt of the Slade and the energy of living in London. That dream was still there, but Venice was here and now, and gave her the time and space to see if she could be as dedicated as the artists of the Studio Theodora, and whether she could develop her skills enough to make any kind of living. Or at least be taken seriously, however she supported herself.

And she would find out the truth, even if it took her the rest of her life. Until then, she could never go back to Arden.

When she arrived the next morning in the little courtyard at the back of the house, Kate found the atmosphere had changed. They had been discussing her, she could tell from their looks. Whether that was for good or ill she wasn't sure.

'They are always looking for cleaners at the hotel where I work,' said Irene as soon as Kate asked. 'I'll put a word in for you, if you are serious.'

'Yes, I am. Thank you. It would probably need to be something that includes living quarters, unless I can find cheaper accommodation.' She felt the exchanges of glances around her.

So she had been a subject of discussion. Her heart began to beat fast.

'We've talked it over, and we'd like to offer you a space.' Betty poured Kate a cup of coffee. 'Yes, I know we said it was gone, but we can always make room. We can offer studio space, and a place to sleep.'

'It's pretty basic,' added Irene. 'And we work hard to keep this place maintained, as well as our jobs and painting and helping in the shop. It's not for everyone.'

'It's definitely for me,' said Kate eagerly, relief going through her, along with the warmth of being amongst friends. 'Thank you. I can't think of anything I'd like more.'

'Excellent,' said Betty, smiling. 'We like to find artists we feel will fit in and we'll all get along with. We agreed you were one of those. So if you wish to stay, you are welcome. If you'd like help fetching your belongings...'

'They're all here,' said Kate, indicating her rucksack. 'My sketchbook and pencils,' she added hastily.

A ripple of understanding laughter went around the room. Kate smiled. Odd how that already she felt at home; that she didn't have to explain why a pencil and sketchpad would always be more important than an extra skirt or jumper. She might have drawn and painted all her life, but this was the first time she had felt like a true artist.

TWENTY-NINE

With the help of Betty and Irene, Kate found work within days. It was hard physical toil that left her aching and exhausted.

'Don't worry, you get used to it,' said Betty dryly. 'I did nothing but sleep when I started, and I've never been so hungry in my life. But once your muscles grow accustomed, that will change.'

The cleaning of kitchens and dining rooms during the night hours might be hard and badly paid, but it was enough to cover Kate's contribution to the living expenses and add to her collection of pens and pencils, and even a few brushes and water-colours. With most of her shifts finishing in the late morning, she had at least left several hours to herself during the day.

At first, getting back to drawing left her self-conscious and stiff. Where she had once instinctively drawn the lines of the mosaic and the delicate artefacts Jamie had found in the remains of the Roman villa next to Arden House, she now hesitated, unsure where to start. But as her body became stronger and more inured to the physical exertion of her job, she began to take in the quality of the light as storm clouds raged around the bay, and the delicate hues of late evening.

Betty was right. Before the month was out, her aching muscles had eased, and she no longer had the urge to doze in the sun the moment she finished a night shift. With her body growing stronger, her mind became increasingly alert. She began to take her little sketchbook everywhere she went. She found spots on the canals or the bridges, where she could sit and try and catch the scene, absorbing the architecture and the paintings in the exhibition, the great mercantile city built so precariously, and yet so strong. Generations upon generations of artists, sculptors and architects who gave Venice its unique atmosphere.

After a while, her hasty sketches, perfected in the industrious quiet of the studios, or the little courtyard with its fountain and colourful riot of flowers, began to give her back her old fluency. With her confidence returning, she began to look at the details around her – no longer just the vistas, but a doorway, the glimpse of a courtyard hung with washing, the women gossiping in the market.

At the end of the month, she took her place in the little shop in the Rialto, joining them behind the counter as visitors came in to inspect the work, some leaving empty handed, while others bought sketches and pictures.

'I like your scenes of the canals,' said Irene, 'why don't you try putting some in the shop? Betty's a good carpenter. She'll help you make frames to show them off while they are hanging there. Some customers buy them framed, but most, especially the Americans, who've a long way to go, will take the canvas rolled up for convenience, so you won't need to make a frame for each one.'

That afternoon, instead of heading out into Venice with her sketchbook as she usually did, Kate sat in the little courtyard going through her sketches. What she needed was a style, something that was unique to her and didn't overlap with the others. Instead of the vistas of the Grand Canal, she chose ones of the little back alleyways and smaller canals. She picked out flowers lovingly positioned on balconies, and the branches of trees escaping over the walls of hidden gardens, adding a touch of watercolour here and there.

She selected three of the most atmospheric. One of the Bridge of Sighs, another of a tiny canal with gondola heading under a curved bridge, and the last a simple doorway with children sitting on the step playing while their mothers gossiped.

To her surprise, they sold within hours.

'There, you see,' said Betty. 'They are small, they're portable and they give a real feeling for Venice.'

'It felt odd, packing them up, thinking where they might go,' said Kate. 'You don't think it was a fluke, do you?'

'Nonsense, of course not,' said Irene. 'Didn't you say people bought your pictures in St Ives?'

'And now you've got to replace them,' added Betty.

Kate wavered. 'I don't want to take your sales; you are trying to earn money through your paintings, too.'

'Don't be silly,' retorted Betty. 'People who won't want mine, or the others, won't want them. You keep on developing yours. Who knows where it might lead you?' She paused in rearranging a selection of Manon's brightly-coloured vases, which had been disturbed by a particularly fastidious customer in finding the perfect one. 'You must have had a good teacher.'

'Not really.'

'Someone must have taught you the basics.'

'I suppose so...'

The scent of chamomile mixed with a hint of orange blossom came to her; a hand guiding hers on the page. *'Like this, like that. Don't think, just see, just feel, let it go to your fingers. That's it. Good girl, my good girl.'* Then the vision was gone. But she could still feel the warmth of the arms around her, the sunlight creeping through the grape vines above her head. Her uncertainty vanished, determination taking its place. If those were memories of her mother, then she had been the very first to encourage Kate, and to believe she had some skill. If nothing else, she would do it for her, or at least to honour her memory, if she was no longer alive.

And here in Venice, I'm one step nearer to finding you.

Over the next weeks, Kate searched through Venice, trying to find the scenes accompanying the sonnets in the volume given to her by Miss Parsons, and those she remembered from her sisters' books of Shakespeare's plays. While many she could now recognise as familiar from the landscape around Naples and Sorrento, others led her to palaces and the Rialto, along with the colour and welcome shade of the public gardens, precious oases of green amongst the network of waterways.

To her frustration, Elvira Johansson sent a message to say that she had experienced a relapse of her chest infection, and that she had been advised by the hospital to stay in the clear high air of Lauterbrunnen for at least another week.

She could hardly blame Elvira for needing more time to recover. Information had been gradually coming out about the horrors of the Nazi concentration camps, making each one of them realise that Elvira must have suffered the most appalling physical deprivation, let alone the damage done to her mind by so much death and cruelty.

All she could do was wait for Elvira to be well enough to return. Meanwhile, she might not have found any hint of the contessa being linked with the places she found, or taking her closer to finding out more about her mother, but searching through the smaller canals, along with the squares and alley-ways, meant that she knew Venice like the back of her hand. She could understand why so many artists were drawn to the city. Each day she found herself falling more in love with the fading grandeur of a place that felt caught in a different time.

And her urge to draw became all-consuming. She drew ornate grills on windows, the hint of a terracotta courtyard, with vines snaking up the walls and washing hanging from lines. She drew the markets, the working boats, and the secret canals the visitors rarely saw, with their shadows and their arched bridges over dark gleaming water, lit by the brilliance of geraniums overtaking a balcony high above. As her confidence increased, she painted the ranks of gondolas waiting at night for the morning visitors and the vistas of the Grand Canal with the Rialto looking one way, and the curve of the canal going out to sea the other.

She grew bolder at adding her work to the little gallery, a few pieces at time, experimenting to see which proved the most successful. She found her larger paintings, and the scenes she had painted of Naples and England were largely ignored, but the smaller and more intimate views of Venice continued to sell almost as quickly as she could paint them. She threw pride out of the window. One day, she would be in a position to paint more of what she pleased. For the moment, the more paintings she sold, the fewer additional hours she needed to take on each week at the hotel. Besides, she didn't have the time, or the money, to afford an easel and create large oils in a more leisurely manner, instead using the paper from her sketch pads and perfecting the art of rapidly capturing a scene or a mood, without the luxury of doubt or hesitation. Sometimes she worried that she was working too quickly to call herself an artist. But small and portable, her works remained popular.

One evening as dusk was falling, the lights flickering romantically on the tables set next to the Rialto Bridge with the sound of wine glasses and conversation, a young man stopped in passing over the bridge to glance at the paintings. Kate watched him idly. She had a vague memory of him traversing the Rialto on a regular basis, always in a hurry, presumably going to and fro from work. A local then, not a visitor, so not the buying kind.

She hoped he wouldn't stay. She was tired after a particularly long day cleaning at the hotel, fighting to keep sleep overwhelming her. She propped herself up, trying to keep her eyes open. The visitor wandered around the paintings, eyes travelling over them casually, pausing every now and again, making his way around and back towards the door.

As he was about to leave, he stopped, bending down to gaze at one of the smaller paintings. Kate was thankful to see Irene arriving to take over supporting Betty, who was out of sight at the far side of the gallery attending to an English couple purchasing a view of the Bridge of Sighs.

'Sorry, I got caught up,' Irene said breathlessly. 'I was ready to go when they found me another room to clean, some idiot had left it in such a state.'

'It's no problem,' replied Kate, 'it's been quiet this evening, anyhow.' The young man was still near the door. As soon as he left she would head back to the studio and crawl into bed, she promised herself, drowsily.

'Where is this?'

'Signor?'

'This painting. The mosaic. Where is it?'

Irene went into full sales action. 'It's by one of our best painters, Signor, very atmospheric.'

'It's not Pompeii. Not Italy.'

Irene nudged Kate, who was awake in an instant. 'It's England,' she said. 'Near Stratford-upon-Avon. Where Shakespeare lived.'

His eyes rested on her face. She had an uncomfortable sensation of being scrutinised, not in admiration, but more as a way of remembering her features.

'You painted it?'

'Yes,' said Kate, now definitely awake.

'Why?' he demanded.

Kate blinked at this unexpected question. 'I loved the view,'

she replied. 'It's near where I used to live. My brother was
trying to uncover a Roman villa, a long time ago before the war.'

'It feels sad,' he remarked, returning to the painting.

'Good evening, Dr Conti,' called Betty, emerging from her
side of the gallery and stepping into the breach. 'We've plenty
of views of Venice, if that's what you are looking for.'

'I'm sure you do, Miss Hilton,' replied their customer, dryly.
'You can't go anywhere without people trying to sell you scenes
of Venice. How's that arm of yours?'

'Much better,' replied Betty, instinctively rubbing the scar
where a broken shard of glass from one of the frames had
caused a deep cut, requiring stitches and several visits to a
nearby clinic. 'I barely notice it.'

'Excellent,' said Dr Conti, with a smile that creased the
corners of his mouth, and sent an unexpected tingling into
Kate's belly. Now that she looked, he was, she noted (telling
herself it was simply with her artist's eye) rather attractive, in a
quiet sort of a way. Even Betty, who was too single minded
about her painting to take much interest in even the most handsome of men, was looking faintly mesmerised. If Dr Conti was
aware of the effect he had on young women, he didn't let on.
Apart from appearing faintly embarrassed, recognised Kate,
with an involuntary grin. He caught her eye. She suppressed
the grin immediately, but not before a wry look came over his
face, as if reading her mind. To her mortification, she could feel
the colour rising to her cheeks, and was thankful he seemed
more amused than offended.

'I'll take it,' he announced. 'The one of the mosaic. It has a
certain charm.'

'Of course.' said Betty, back to being the smooth sales-
woman in an instant. 'We can remove it from the frame if you
prefer.'

'With the frame.'

Betty packed the painting carefully in newspaper and

handed it over. Dr Conti paid and left without a backward glance.

'You're honoured,' said Betty. 'Dr Conti has never bought from us before. He's become such a proud Venetian, I'd never thought of him buying a scene from a place he's never been to.'

'Perhaps he has a fondness for Shakespeare,' remarked Irene.

'Could be,' conceded Betty.

Kate peered down from the bridge. Dr Conti had reached the stop for the vaporetti. As if sensing her gaze, he glanced up as the approaching waterbus drew up, before disappearing inside. Within minutes it headed off down the Grand Canal in the direction of the bay, following its steady course, with gondolas and small launches manoeuvring around, until the boat and its passengers vanished out of sight.

THIRTY

She couldn't go back to Venice, Sofia told herself. Not yet; maybe never.

Following her visit to the Villa Clara, with its memories and its griefs, and the terror of hearing the footsteps and muffled voices of intruders below, she had been uncertain what to do for the best. Going through the papers she had retrieved from Magdalena's hiding place, her only certainty had been that she should not re-join the American supply boat on its return journey towards Venice. She had not intended to stay longer than a few nights in the room she had hired in Sorrento, but with so few visitors, she was easily able to extend it by a few days, then weeks.

As she read through the precious documents, she both cursed Magdalena for concealing that the villa had been left to her by her father, and blessed her for not destroying the papers that proved her ownership. There were other papers too, ones that refuted even more of the lies her mother had told her, manipulating her youthful ignorance.

No more. This time she was going to make it right. With the world opening up, she was finally able to arrange for money to be sent over from America to do some basic repairs on Villa Clara, mending the roof to keep the rain out and boarding up the windows and doors while she decided what she was going to do with it. Over the next weeks she pondered, weighing up her options. The villa had so many happy memories, but also ones that seared at her heart, and had haunted her all her life. Her first instinct was to abandon the place and let it rot, but she forced herself to be practical.

For one thing, it was too isolated for a woman to live there on her own with so much lawlessness in the destroyed coast, especially after the unnerving encounter with intruders just as she finally located the precious documents. She'd been thankful she knew the place like the back of her hand and had been able to escape unseen, or at least unscathed, and head back in her hired motorboat to the safety of Sorrento.

But the coastline would one day recover from the ravages of war and the eruption of Vesuvius. Visitors were bound to return and the villa was ideal to accommodate them. Even if she didn't wish to take on the project herself, she was certain there must already be businessmen with an eye for snapping up properties for when people returned to the Bay of Naples, and the picturesque beauties of the Amalfi coast, with the gardens of Ravello and the colourful cliff houses of Positano. She hadn't been married to a successful businessman for so long to let pride throw her future security away. Particularly now she had something to protect.

Among the hidden papers were her marriage certificate, and her husband's will. She wept when she first saw Frederick's confident dash of a signature, so full of life, so certain the provision for his wife and baby daughter in the event of his death would never be needed. Fury went through her at the realisation that her mother must have guessed what he would do. She had been touched when the contessa had sent Magdalena to help her when the news of Frederick's accident spread. She had never expected her mother herself to appear, that wasn't the contessa's style, and she had been too busy, as ever, with machinations of her own.

I was a fool, she berated her younger self. She had been taught the business of the world was for others to take care of. Her own role had been to perfect her skill in illustration, and to love and care for those around her. Until Walter's last months, when she had finally grasped the nettle and taken charge of his affairs, it had always been the men in her life who had dealt with the practical, business side of things, taking over from where the contessa left off. First Frederick, then more recently Walter. The moment she had taken over Walter's business dealings and realised she could understand them, pick through the conflicting advice and make decisions, she had finally begun to feel fully in charge of her own life.

Sifting through the papers, working out the implications, and seeing how easily the contessa had pulled the wool over her eyes was a similar feeling.

'I've been asleep all my life; I'm only now waking up,' she murmured, sitting at the table of the café in the square at Sorrento.

She was never going to allow herself to be that vulnerable again. Besides, Frederick's will, set out clearly and equivocally, gave her new insights into the depth of her mother's deception. No wonder she had insisted Magdalena, who the contessa knew would not be swerved from obeying her orders, should be with her, pouring her mistresses' poison into a vulnerable young woman's ears. With the knowledge gained from the will, came a new weight of responsibility. She cradled the cup in her hands, uncertain what to do for the best.

How deep were the Arden family embroiled in her mother's deception? Celia hadn't known, she was sure of it, although the distress of the letter begging Sofia to fetch her daughter hinted that she may well have guessed. That left the question of how much Leo Arden had known, when he came to take Katerina away. Had he been complicit, too, in the terrible wrong done to herself, and even more so to her child?

From her letter, Celia had been afraid for the little girl's future. Children were vulnerable in their dependency on those around them. Girls, with their inability to access education and a means of earning a living for themselves, even more so.

If she sent a letter to Arden House, Leo was bound to intercept it. She doubted if there would be a reply, or at least not a truthful one. Things had gone too far, the Ardens had too much to lose to allow her to question them now. Her mother would never answer. Even asking the question would give her a perverse pleasure in tormenting her with hints and promises she never intended to fulfil.

It was watching the supply ships making their way along the coast that stirred a memory. Celia's friend, the one who had been more of an academic rather than an artist. What had her name been? Something she had associated with a quintessentially English village. Parsonage? No, Parsons. Miss Parsons. Sofia remembered a young woman vibrant with intelligence rather than beauty, passionate in all her interests, from history to her charity work. A woman deeply in love who had, like so many of their friends, suffered the agony of losing her fiancé in the First World War.

Miss Parsons would know. But there was no telling where she might be now; and if she had found love again, her name could have changed, and she could have moved with her husband to anywhere in the world. The only tenuous link Sofia could hold onto was Miss Parsons's passion for the charity working with street children in Naples. She'd read a report of its work before the war. If it had survived the conflict, there was a chance Miss Parsons still had some kind of a link, enough to find out her name, even an address. Sofia took a deep breath. There was nowhere else she could turn; she at least had to try.

. . .

As the first touches of the coming autumn lent a fragility to the blue of the sky, Sofia joined one of the supply ships returning along the coast stopping off at Naples. After negotiating the chaos of the port, she was directed towards a building away from the main part, where a young man was supervising the transport of supplies.

'Miss Parsons?' he replied to her query. 'She's on the Board of the charity.' Sofia's heart began to beat fast. Never in her wildest dreams had she expected this to go so smoothly. 'Is she here? I'm an old friend,' she added to his guarded look. 'I've been trying to catch up with her, but so much has changed since the war, it's hard to find people.'

'She is in England,' he replied, clearly impatient to get on with the loading of supplies of food into the back of a small van.

'In London?'

'No, a village near Stratford-upon-Avon.'

Sofia's stomach fell away from her. It couldn't be. But she had to know. 'Arden House.'

'You know it?' He forgot the van and eyed her with suspicion. 'I suggest you try to contact her through the village Post Office.'

Sofia steeled herself. It was a long shot, but she had to try. 'I'm trying to find someone,' she said. 'A young woman who lived in Arden House as a child. Katerina Arden. Kate?' she added at his frown.

'Kate left here some time ago.'

'Left?' Sofia's heart squeezed so tight she could barely breathe. 'You mean she was here? In Naples?'

'For a while,' he replied shortly. 'She left weeks ago. Your best chance of finding her is through her family at Arden House.' He turned away, conversation closed. With the van now fully loaded, he took the driver's seat, heading off through the chaotic maze of streets away from the port.

She had been here! Sofia's legs shook so much she could barely stand. She had to find out more. She banged on the front door of the building, but no one answered. Slowly, she began to retrace her footsteps back towards the port, her mind spinning. Katerina had been here. In Italy. In Naples. Had she, came the whisper in her heart, been looking for her? If only Sofia had come earlier, she would have been here. They could have passed each other in the street.

And then what? Despair went through Sofia. She had been so focussed on finding her child, she'd pushed aside her doubts at what she would say. Her daughter had her own life. She must think she had been abandoned by her mother. Why would she want to see her? Sofia slowed, almost knocked to one side as a young man passed, brushing her impatiently aside as he headed for the pavement café just ahead.

'Excuse me? Signora?'

A voice reached her through the cacophony of shouts and the wheels of vehicles. Sofia turned as a young woman reached her.

'I overheard you asking about Kate,' she said, breathlessly. 'Kate Arden?'

Hope went through Sofia again. 'Yes. I'm trying to find her.'

The young woman scrutinised her face, as if trying to make a decision. 'I'm Gina Sidoli,' she said at last. 'I worked with Kate in Cornwall during the war, and while she was here. I'm sorry my cousin was a bit abrupt. You see, you're the second person to ask for her this morning.' She nodded towards the young man who had pushed past Sofia and was now taking a seat at the café. Sofia followed her gaze. There was something familiar about his features. A memory, a long ago memory...

Sofia dragged her attention back to Gina. 'Do you know where she is now?' she asked eagerly.

'I'm not sure. It's still difficult to send letters. I think she was planning to go back to England.'

Sofia's heart sank. 'To Arden House, you mean?'

'Yes,' said Gina. She frowned. 'Are you a friend of the family?' She nodded towards the young man, who was glancing irritably at his watch. 'That's what the Englishman told Peter. He didn't give a name, but he was very insistent on finding out where she might be. To be honest, I think that's probably why Peter was so abrupt with you, I suspect he regrets telling the Englishman she'd gone to Venice.'

'Venice?' Sofia stared at her. 'Katerina – Kate – is in Venice?'

'That's where she was heading first. She was trying to find someone. A relative,' Gina added. 'I'm not sure what her plans were after that. I know she only had enough money with her to stay a short time. She told me she was going to find work so she could search for a bit longer, otherwise she was heading back to England, to talk with her family.' The young woman's eyes rested on Sofia's face. Sofia could feel the dawning of a question Gina dare not ask, and she could not bear to answer.

'You don't think Kate will come back here?' she asked quickly.

'I don't think so.' Gina hesitated, as if not sure how much to reveal. 'She was good with the children, but her heart is elsewhere.' She was about to say more, but turned back towards the house as her name was called. 'I'm so sorry. They're ready to leave; I have to go.'

'If I leave an address, will you pass it on to her, if she returns?'

There was just the slightest hesitation. From the house the shouting was becoming increasingly urgent. 'Who shall I tell her it is?'

Sofia scribbled the address of Walter's business on a scrap of paper. 'It's an office. It's in America, but it's the best way to be certain to reach me. Just say it's from someone who is looking for her. She'll understand.'

'If Kate returns, I'll give it to her,' said Gina. She grasped Sofia's hand tightly, a look of dawning understanding on her face. 'I hope you find her.'

'Thank you,' said Sofia, eyes filling with tears. 'I will, if it's the last thing I do.'

Katerina was trying to find her! Sofia walked back down towards the harbour in a daze. If that really was Katerina, she was in Italy and trying to find her. Longing went through her. To be within touching distance and to lose her again was agony.

Sofia slowed. Had she found the messages she had hastily concealed in the volume of Shakespeare in those last hours while her small daughter slept? Was that the trail she was following? In that case, the picture of Venice would have taken her straight to the contessa, and who knew what lies she would feed her. There was always Magdalena. They had forged a friendship during the years of the war, that gave her hope Magdalena might not leave Katerina to the mercy of the contessa. But she could not be certain.

As she reached the square, Sofia saw the young man who had pushed her aside so arrogantly was still sitting at a table, a glass of red wine in front of him. The one who had been asking questions about Katerina. She hesitated, every instinct urging her to hurry on and find the fastest way of travelling across a still war-torn Italy. The young man checked his wristwatch impatiently once more. He was expecting someone.

Yet again the feeling of familiarity was back. There was something about him... Every instinct honed over the years set the alarm bells ringing. Quietly, she took a seat at a table a short distance away. She ordered a coffee, and took her book from her rucksack. If anyone looked, she would simply be a woman of a certain age, probably lonely or waiting for a friend, concentrating on her novel.

She hadn't long to wait. Her drink had no sooner arrived than a smart red MG sportscar appeared, hood down, hooting impatiently, hurrying pedestrians and a horse-drawn cart out of its way, before drawing up next to the café. A fair-haired young man jumped out, reaching for a creased linen jacket to cover his shirtsleeves.

'You took your time,' remarked the dark-haired man in English. Sofia grimaced. She was all-too familiar with the clipped tones of the wealthy upper classes. The contessa had thrown her in front of enough of those visiting Venice, idly collecting the famous sights of Europe, much as their ancestors had done on the Grand Tour. No wonder he had looked familiar. They had all blurred into one for her younger self, with their private education followed automatically by Oxford or Cambridge, then Parliament or the family estate. It was like a uniform, worn with ease, unchanged after all these years, and two world wars.

The sportscar oozed wealth and an assumption that fuel, and a place to stay, would always be available, barely noticing the deprivation all around. She watched as the dark-haired young man clicked his fingers for his glass to be refilled, and for another to be brought for his companion.

It was the kind of life Frederick had been expected to lead but that, unlike most of his class, he had loathed with every fibre of his being. When she had first met him, sitting at his easel on the harbour wall of St Ives, he had been in rebellion against his education and the assumptions about his future just as much as she had been. It was, she remembered sadly, the very thing that had drawn them together; the desire to escape the empty privilege they had been born into, and that had become a trap for both of them, stifling the urge to use their mutual love of painting to reflect the world around them.

It had been the very reason they had eventually chosen to elope, to escape from the hidden cove of the old fisherman's cottage, heading out over the sea in Frederick's yacht towards freedom.

'It's not easy getting around, you know,' said the new arrival, sitting down on the opposite side of the table. Sofia risked a quick glance at his face. It wasn't just the fairness of his hair that made him a pale shadow of his friend; he lacked the same imperious assumption. A gambler, rather than one born into riches, she thought, taking in the discontented set of his features. The kind who had made a fortune on the black market during the war, with a need to be wealthy – or at least seen to be wealthy – at all costs. She'd met his type, too. Charming, but vacuous, with little moral compass at heart.

'She's in Venice,' said the dark-haired man. 'At least that's what he said. Damn rude, when I asked where.'

'I told you Sidoli would clam up,' replied his companion, with a grin. 'Well, at least that's more than he'd have told me. Give it up, Luscombe. She's a bright girl, she's never going to fall for it. Besides, I got rid of those damned sketchbooks, and there was nothing else for her to find. I checked. She's a pretty girl. She's bound to have found herself a rich protector by now and have no reason to ever leave Italy.'

'Maybe.'

'Besides, aren't you always telling me there are plenty more fish in the sea?'

Luscombe was still staring into his glass, as if lost in thought. 'Whoever controls her controls Arden,' he said.

Sofia stifled her exclamation, bending closer over her book. Fortunately, the two young men were too absorbed in their conversation to notice.

'From what I've heard, the place is almost bankrupt,' remarked the fair-haired man. She heard a touch of uncertainty enter his voice. The beginnings of a conscience, maybe? She risked a quick glance at the man referred to as Luscombe. So his features had been familiar, after all.

She'd met the inordinately wealthy Luscombes, with their country estate near St Ives for when their town house grew uncomfortable during long London summers. They had always been eager to be associated with the Ardens with their historic estate and the aristocratic bloodline reputed to go back to Henry VIII. She could well have met this young man when he'd been a child. The Luscombes had sent revulsion through her, every single one of them. She'd been glad Frederick had wanted nothing more than to avoid them, apart from being polite for his family's sake, and as the oldest son, the heir to the Arden Estate, knowing he'd be forced to have some dealings with such an influential family for the rest of his life.

'But it has potential,' said Luscombe, deep in thought. 'For someone who knows what they are doing, and has the means. With the right hand at the helm, it could be one of the wealthiest estates in England.'

Sofia's blood ran cold. That was the kind of thing the contessa would say. She couldn't have done! Would she really have drawn the Luscombes back into her schemes? Sofia sat there, rigid, as the two young men finished their wine, their voices lowering so she could no longer hear what they said. Surely not even the contessa would sell her own granddaughter? Not even to gain a hold over the Arden Estate.

She watched, unseen, as the two stood up, still deep in discussion, heading for the car. It had to be true. There was no other way Luscombe could have known of Katerina's legacy. Certainty went through her. The contessa must be desperate: the Luscombes were her last throw of the dice.

As the MG raced off through the streets, its roar echoing into the distance, Sofia closed her hand around the papers hidden deep in her rucksack. The papers that confirmed, once and for all, that whoever controlled her child, controlled Arden.

The conversation just now had told her that Frederick's final gift to his beloved daughter, intended to keep her secure for the rest of her life should anything happen to him, was to become the ultimate trap; the source of a lifetime of misery. Of Katerina's subjugation to the very kind of man from whom Frederick had been so determined to protect her. He had recognised the artist in her, in those few years of happiness when they had stayed at the Villa Clara, naively believing it was the contessa finally softening towards them at the arrival of a grandchild. They had always agreed that the most important thing was that their daughter should be free to follow her star.

I should have known. For all he was a dreamer, Frederick had always retained his practical side. At the time of his untimely death, he had been finalising the purchase of a place of their own amongst the vibrancy of Florence. She should have known that he had put other things in place to secure those he loved.

She finished her coffee and stood up. Regrets were for later. All that mattered now was that she found a way of returning to Venice, and of finding Katerina if she was still there. And, if she had left, to follow her, to wherever she might be. Sofia steeled herself. She would do whatever it took; the one purpose she had in life now was to keep her daughter safe.

THIRTY-ONE

As she waited for Elvira's return, Kate continued to work hard, cleaning by night and painting in every spare moment of daylight. With her confidence increasing, she moved on from the detailed drawings of her earlier pictures, instead focusing on capturing the atmosphere of every carefully chosen location. Each time she left them to clean at the hotel, she couldn't wait to put the finishing touches, and fit them to the frames she created whenever she could, to put them in the little shop to see if they would sell.

She had loved the freedom, and the feeling of her own mastery of her craft. She couldn't wait to find more scenes to paint in the same style. On the other hand, she had to be realistic. Now she was creating more paintings, she was relying on the money she earned from selling them to be able to buy better paints and paper, and a higher quality of salvaged wood to make the frames. Her new style of paintings might be where she wanted to go next, and to stretch herself by attempting larger versions, including braving oils, but she was well aware that she might have to concentrate mainly on the intricate paintings that sold well to tourists and keep her favoured style for her few spare hours.

She returned late one afternoon after walking further than she had intended, hot and dusty, her feet sore, carrying the sketches she had captured to be finished in watercolour in the studio the following day. Already aching all over, she couldn't imagine how she was going to get through her night shift. But she would. She just had to push the bubbling excitement to one side for now and come back to it tomorrow. It was hard when she knew in her heart that these were her most successful drawings yet.

As she reached the main part of the studio, Betty looked up from her painting of the Doge's Palace.

'You have a visitor.'

'A visitor?' Kate jerked herself out of her reverie.

'He's waited for you. He's in the courtyard.'

'He?' Kate found the entire studio if not exactly watching her aware of her every move, her every reaction.

'Very good looking,' said Betty, with a wink. 'I wouldn't say no.'

Puzzled, Kate retraced her steps, her footsteps echoing in the damp corridor towards the centre of the building and the quiet of the courtyard. The fair-haired man with a guidebook in one hand, a cigar sending smoke spiralling up towards the soft blue sky looked up as she reached the entrance.

'Hello Kate. I hope you don't mind me appearing like this, I thought I'd give you a surprise.'

Of all the people, this was the last she had expected to see in Venice! 'Hello Lance,' she said warily.

'It's good to see you. Dear Kate, you haven't changed a bit.'

'Haven't I?' said Kate, who felt that her time with the street children in Naples and working every hour she could to build a career as a painter, had changed her inwardly beyond recognition. But then she could hardly expect anyone to see that from the outside.

'Of course.' He smiled. 'I'm glad I've found you.' Kate eyed him. Lance Elliot had clearly done well for himself since he had left Cornwall. His suit was well-cut. The cigar in his hand was of the best. He had about him the well-groomed air of the guests at the hotel where she cleaned. They felt worlds apart. 'Now I'm certain I'm going to enjoy my time in Venice,' he announced.

'I'm sorry, but I really do need to get to work,' said Kate, suddenly impatient at his assumption that she had nothing better to do than amuse him. She didn't care what he thought. She headed up to her room to brush her hair and change into her working clothes. When she came down again he was still there.

'I'll accompany you,' he said, with a smile. 'Let me at least buy you a drink, for old time's sake.'

She hesitated. She couldn't help being a little flattered that he had sought her out, after all this time, but this wasn't life as it had been at Tregannon Castle. For the next few days her every hour was accounted for. Besides, there was something about the way he had strode in, unannounced, assuming he could take charge of her day, that irritated her.

'Oh, come on Kate.' He smiled at her with his old familiar charm that softened her mood, despite herself. 'Don't be a killjoy. You're in Italy. The war is over. The least you can do is join me in a glass of wine.'

'I'll join you for coffee,' she compromised. 'But then I shall have to get to work.'

'All right.' For a moment he sounded offended, then he relaxed. 'Coffee, then. Tomorrow, you can join me for a meal.'

'Lance, you can't just appear without warning and expect me to drop everything for your convenience,' she retorted, exasperated. 'I'm working tomorrow night, too.'

'The night after then. You can't work all the time.'

'That's the evening for my turn at the gallery on the Rialto Bridge,' she said.

'Then change it.'

'It's too short notice. It's not fair on the others. We have an agreement we only change if someone is really ill, or if it's an emergency. We all work here.'

'It can't be much of a job if you have to work all hours,' he grumbled. 'Are you sure you're not making an excuse to avoid me? Why don't you just come out with it and say you don't want to see me.'

'Don't be ridiculous.' She scowled at him. 'I know emotional blackmail when I see it. Papa is a past master, and Alma comes in a close second when she needs to.' He looked taken off guard and more than a little discomforted at this plain speaking. 'And what do you do that gives you so much leisure time, anyhow?'

'I'm here on behalf of a client. Sourcing artwork,' he added loftily. 'I'm working on behalf of some of the finest collectors in London; it was an opportunity I couldn't turn down.'

He was lying. The thought shot into her brain with such a force it nearly winded her, even more so than when he claimed to have seen her at Sutton Hoo. Was this just a way of attracting her attention? Then her rational side reasserted itself. What reason would he have for lying, especially something that could be so easily proven untrue? Perhaps her doubts simply sprung from being a young woman out so often without the company of a man to keep her from the casual attentions of any passing male. And she couldn't help being curious. Even her almost complete lack of interest in fashion recognised the expense of his linen suit that appeared barely worn, but had none of the constraints of the material-saving utility style, with rationing still in force, despite the ending of the war.

'After your turn at the gallery, then.'

'Very well,' she said, feeling trapped by courtesy. She shook herself for being ungrateful and suspicious. She was a better person than that. 'Thank you. I'll look forward to it.'

'Excellent. I've a few days left. The least I can do now is buy you a coffee,' he added quickly, as she turned away. 'We haven't seen each other in so long, I can't wait to catch up.'

'How did you know I was here?' she asked, as they set off towards the Grand Canal.

'I saw some of your paintings in the gallery on the Rialto Bridge, and thought I recognised the hand. They seemed to be selling well.'

'Enough.'

'But not to stop you from having to take other work.' He sounded disapproving.

'I'm a cleaner, not a lady of the night,' she retorted.

'I didn't say you—' He frowned at her. 'A cleaner? Kate, dear Kate. You are worth more than that. An Arden should never be a servant.'

'Even if it's a means to an end?'

'Your painting, you mean.'

'What else?'

He was silent as he guided her to a café next to the Grand Canal, dedicated to tourists and so one she and her friends avoided, choosing to frequent the less elegant places in the back alleyways unfrequented by the visitors. The waiter clicked his tongue at the lack of wine, or any sign of a meal in the offing, but disappeared to fulfil their order with a modicum of grace.

'It looks like I'll be eating here on my own,' complained Lance.

'So it does,' she returned, wondering if this was a last throw of the dice to change her mind. 'Why are you in Venice?'

'I told you. I'm working for a client. You don't think I could resist looking up an old friend when I found her? I've happy memories of our time helping at Tregannon Castle.'

That sounded plausible. Maybe she was being unfair. She relaxed slightly. 'So do I.'

'It seems so long ago.'

'A different world,' she agreed.

'Weren't you trying to find someone? A family member. Your mother, wasn't it? Didn't you say once you thought she was from Italy.'

'Yes.'

'I don't need to ask why you are here. So, have you found her?'

'No.'

'Maybe she isn't in Venice.'

'Probably not,' she replied, determined to change the subject.

'I can help you. I've some free time while I'm here, and I can extend my stay by a few days; I'm owed some vacation, and I was planning to take it in Venice anyhow. I think we all need a bit of peace and quiet and Renaissance splendour after the war.'

'There's no need,' she replied. This was her search, her life and her future. The last thing she wanted was for Lance to step in and take charge. She was relieved as the church bells began their familiar cacophony, echoing throughout the city, sounding the hour. 'I need to go. I can't afford to be late.'

'I'll meet you at the gallery then, the day after tomorrow.'

'Very well,' she said, slowly. What harm could it do? After all, it was simply a meeting up of old friends, ones who might, given the vagaries of life, never meet again.

'I'll look forward to it,' he said, with a grin.

Kate left, heading down towards the hotel. As she reached the corner, she looked back. Lance was speaking to the waiter, who had brought a half carafe of wine. He was presumably ordering his meal, one arm slung casually over the back of his chair in a gesture she remembered so well. Mischief, or arrogance. Perhaps a touch of both.

She couldn't make him out. He'd shown few signs of being truly attracted to her when they had been at Tregannon, and she couldn't really imagine him plying a respectable and well-connected young woman with wine in a clumsy attempt to seduce her. Kate chuckled to herself. She should be flattered at the thought of a young man seeking to wine and dine her to charm her into submission. On the other hand, she would take care to let Irene and the others know where they were going, and arrange for a time for her to return. It was one of the rules of the studio, when accompanying a young man to the opera or an exhibition, or being taken out for a meal, or even simply to a café. Bohemian women artists had a reputation for being easy with their favours, and none of them wanted to be left in a tight corner, or with an unexpected child to try to raise on their own.

She couldn't help liking Lance for his easy charm, but she didn't trust him. Or maybe it was just that she didn't know how to trust any man, she told herself, gloomily. At least joining him for a meal might clarify that feeling, or put it to rest forever.

THIRTY-TWO

How was she to find her? Sofia arrived in Venice weary and anxious, having made her way through an Italy still suffering from the devastation of the years of war.

Venice was bustling again. Despite the autumn sun lending a delicacy to the blue of the sky, with a hint of chill in the evening air, she could see there were already more visitors. Venice was both small, and vast. A young woman working one of the casual jobs in a city swarming with tourists could be anywhere.

There was one place Sofia could think of trying. The picture she had left had clearly shown the view from the palazzo. If Katerina had found that, it could have been the reason for her travelling to Venice. Even if she had made the connection with the villa, it was unlikely she could have found it with the difficulties of moving around.

When she reached the palace, she found it standing silent, shutters drawn.

'Gone,' announced the workman repairing the ceiling of a nearby building to her enquiry. 'Two days ago. If you're waiting to be paid, you're out of luck. Magdalena said the contessa's heading to America.' He gave a cynical guffaw. 'There's bound to be some rich businessman waiting with his wallet open. There always is.'

Despair went through her. She had no idea where to look next. 'Did Magdalena go with the contessa?'

'Not sure.' He called an enquiry to workmen further down. A few minutes discussion to and fro attracted the attention of a maid in one of the houses, who lent through the window.

'Magdalena?' she called down to Sofia. 'That one always swore she'd never leave Venice. Can't see her going to America, not when there's no money to pay her, even when the palazzo is sold. Debts,' she added darkly.

That came as a shock. After all her mother's lifetime of wheeling and dealing to keep herself solvent... 'The contessa is bankrupt?'

'Totally. The old count would be turning in his grave. The Rosselli wealth and history, all gone. Selling her soul to the fascists didn't help her one jot, in the end. At least there's some justice in the world, even though it often seems there is none.'

'I see,' said Sofia, quietly. She couldn't care less about the loss of the palace. They were not to know that her father would have happily spent the rest of his days in the peace of his beloved Villa Clara. With a sinking in her stomach, she recognised that all she was being told only confirmed that her mother could well have sold her granddaughter's happiness for a slice of the Arden fortune. Although it was clear she was also not about to put all her eggs in one basket. Before the war, Magdalena had mentioned rich friends in Seattle, no doubt some wealthy businessman in need of an elegant woman with Italian royal blood (or at least a title) to preside over his soirees, and so outdo even those with Hollywood starlets to call upon.

As she turned to leave, a thought struck her. 'If Magdalena didn't leave with the contessa,' she asked, 'do you know where she could have gone instead?'

The maid paused in pulling the window shut. 'She said something about a summer house in the lagoon that belonged to the count's sister. On Burano? I think that's what she said. Can't be certain though.'

Burano. Yes, that made sense. Sofia had never thought to ask if Aunt Ottavia still had her house by the sea, in the seclusion of the island out in the bay. She remembered visiting the house in Burano when she was a child. She'd heard her aunt had died somewhere in Switzerland, where she'd taken refuge during the war. There was a daughter, Sofia's cousin, who had emigrated to Australia decades before. She could imagine Magdalena jumping at the chance to remain in Venice.

But time was of the essence and Burano was at least half an hour away by vaporetto. Besides, she had to face the fact that Magdalena might have no idea that Katerina was in Venice. The only other person she could think of who might be able to find Katerina was Niccolò Conti. As a doctor, he knew more people than most. He might have heard of a young English-woman arriving on her own in Venice, or at the very least be able to point Sofia to the hotels and boarding houses most likely to be taking on staff. With a vaporetto drawing up at the nearest landing stage, she hurried to join it.

At the little clinic, Sofia waited impatiently until Niccolò was free between patients.

'Sofia,' he greeted her with a smile. 'It's good to see you back in Venice.' He took one look at her face, and gestured to one of his colleagues. There was a rapid conversation, too low for her to hear, but which she guessed was Niccolò arranging for Dr Gentili to take his next patient. 'What is it?' he asked as they made their way outside.

'I found her.' In her desperation the words tumbled out of her. 'My child. She's here, in Venice. My mother...' Her voice broke. 'I can't believe she'd be so cruel. I have to find her—' She came to a halt. He was watching her through narrowed eyes, as he did with a particularly knotty case. She must sound like a madwoman. She wasn't making sense. She tried to collect her scattered senses, to explain.

'Kate Arden, you mean?'

He caught her as her knees gave way.

'Kate. Katerina. Yes. How did you know? Where is she?'

'Slow down,' he said gently, helping her to a bench next to a water fountain. The cool of the spray wafting against her face revived her. 'I sent a message to your address in Sorrento, it must have missed you. It took ages for me to twist Magdalena's arm, or I'd have sent it earlier. There's a Kate Arden who's joined the Studio Theodora. There was something about her,' he added, growing slightly awkward. 'I've one of her drawings. A place in England, near where Shakespeare lived. I've no right to intrude, but it made me wonder.'

'Oh, my Lord.' She tried to take it all in. 'She's an artist. Of course. I should have known. She always was. The studio is where Miss Parsons would have sent her.' Through her tears, she saw him looking at her blankly. She pulled herself together. 'The Rialto. Was that where you got the drawing? From the gallery on the Rialto Bridge?'

'Yes. But that doesn't mean she's there now.'

'But her friends will know where she is.' She stood up, suddenly calm, all emotion pushed to one side, as it did when a crushed body came into the clinic, every sense, every sinew focussed solely on what had to be done. 'I need to get there, and as fast as possible.'

THIRTY-THREE

Whatever Lance was expecting, Kate could hardly dress up in finery, as she had none. Her best dress, the one slightly less washed and mended, reserved for her evenings serving in the gallery, would have to do. On her insistence, they would only be going to the café beneath the Rialto Bridge, territory that was familiar, and only a few minutes from home.

All the same, she took the time to wash her hair when she got back from her shift at the hotel, drying it in the sun and brushing it until it shone. She stuffed an enveloping silk shawl in her shoulder bag in case it turned cool later, and headed to join Irene at the little gallery on the Rialto.

The autumn afternoon had turned sultry, sending visitors into the cool interior of cafés and the Doge's Palace and the shades of the shops on the bridges and beside the canals. As evening approached, they began to emerge into the balmy stillness of the evening, the little gallery soon heaving with those looking for souvenirs of their stay, keeping Kate too busy to think.

As Kate followed a customer indicating one of the paintings outside under the shade of an awning, a vaporetto pulled up at

the stop below. From within the shade, she could make out
Lance at the rail with the others preparing to disembark. He
was arriving at least an hour earlier than they had arranged.
Well, he'd have to wait, she thought, exasperation returning.
She couldn't abandon Irene until Manon arrived to join her. As
she turned to attend to the young American couple who were
ready to purchase Betty's oil painting of St Mark's Square,
something caught her eye.

'Yes, of course,' she said, absently, her gaze still on the
shadowy figure within the vaporetto. 'Without the frame is
perfectly fine. I'll roll it up for you, so it's protected and easy to
carry.' Lance was watching as the boat departed, making a slight
gesture of his hand she was certain she saw echoed by the man
remaining on the boat. There was something familiar about the
stance; the reflected light briefly illuminated the man's features
as he turned back into the interior of the boat. Was it Henry
Luscombe? It couldn't be. She was imagining things. As Lance
began to make his way towards the bridge she turned away,
taking the picture into the main part of the gallery.

As she concentrated on removing it from the frame and
rolling the canvas up into a small tube, which she wrapped
tightly with newspaper for added protection, her mind went to
and fro, one moment berating herself for imagining things, the
next with a growing sense that, for all the time they had spent
together in Cornwall, she knew very little about him. She didn't
even know the owner of the forest he had been managing. Why
had she never asked? But one didn't in those days, not with a
war on and an enemy possibly about to invade. Lance had
always given off the sense of knowing more than he said, which
had discouraged anyone from questioning too closely. He had
simply been a volunteer helping Ellen in his spare time, as part
of the war effort. Surely he couldn't have been anything more?

As the young couple headed off arm in arm with their
purchase, there was no sign of Lance.

'Everything all right?' asked Irene, as Kate retrieved a picture to fill the empty space, and set about placing a new painting in the frame.

'Yes, yes of course.'

She was still turning things over in her mind a little later, when Lance appeared, looking even more dashing than ever in a white shirt, pale linen jacket slung over one shoulder.

'Good evening, ladies,' he remarked, directing his full charm at Irene, who, according to the whispers at the studio, had the wildest of love lives, with several men (and at least one woman) at her feet, and appeared less than impressed. He turned to Kate. 'Ready?'

'Not yet. Not until Manon arrives.' She finished the framing, leaving him to wander aimlessly amongst the paintings. Now it came to it, her sense of something not being quite right was reaching into every part of her. On the other hand, she would look foolish if she suddenly refused, for no reason she could point to, but a shadow from the past that would mean nothing to any of her companions in the little gallery. They would think her a fool, a timid woman afraid of men, or too wrapped up in herself to face an emotional entanglement. After all, Lance had agreed they would stay at the café within sight of the bridge, within sight of the gallery. What could she fear?

But even so close, she acknowledged, Irene and Manon would not be watching them every moment of their meal. All it would take would be for the gallery to be busy to distract them both. Her mind began to race with possibilities. The little canals and alleyways were only a short walk away, the vaporetti drew up regularly next to the seating alongside the canal...

She pulled herself together. She was being stupid. Maybe she was simply afraid of any physical contact or opening herself up to emotion. She was being silly. There had been no hint of a courtship. This was simply old acquaintances eating a meal and drinking a carafe of wine, reminiscing and catching up after the uncertainties of the war.

Across the gallery, a new customer had arrived and was speaking urgently to Irene, who after a minute gestured towards her. Kate met the newcomer's eyes. They were dark, like the curls of the woman's hair shot through with grey. Kate heard her own involuntary gasp. In an instant, she was back under the heat of the vines on the terrace far away, strong arms holding her, slowly releasing her, while never wanting to let her go.

Before she could move, the woman turned away, towards a painting, beckoning to Irene. It was one of her own, Kate saw. Her most ambitious yet, a large oil of the Rialto Bridge in the evening sun after a storm, a single gondolier caught in the brilliance of the light.

'Yes, of course, Signora,' Irene was murmuring in reply. 'I'll wrap that up for you now.'

A tap on the shoulder alerted Kate to Manon arriving behind her. 'I told you that was your best,' she whispered. 'I knew it would sell.'

'It looks like it,' returned Kate, still dazed. It felt like waking up from a dream. She felt powerless; she knew she needed to act but couldn't seem to move or decide what to do.

Lance appeared, making a beeline for her. 'Ah, there you are, Kate,' he said. 'You are now free to dance the night away.'

'Just one moment.' On the other side of the gallery, Irene had finished wrapping the painting in brown paper. 'Mrs Armstrong would like your help to take this down the steps.'

'If I can be of assistance,' said Lance, gallantly.

Irene eyed him witheringly. 'Mrs Armstrong particularly requested the services of a woman. Get yourself out of here,' she added to Kate in rapid Italian. 'Don't worry about us, we'll be fine. It's you he's after, the little rat. Just don't come back until we tell you he's gone.'

'Kate—' As Lance began to protest, Irene placed herself in

front of him. 'Now then, Mr Elliot, you can't possibly leave without considering a painting. Surely you can't leave the beauty of Venice without some souvenir? A card? A postcard of one of our paintings? All our work is bound to be a good investment.'

With Lance momentarily distracted, Kate followed Mrs Armstrong out onto the bridge.

'This way,' said her guide, taking the steps opposite to those going down to the café, leading instead to a row of gondolas rocking gently together in the wake of passing boats as they waited for customers. Tucked in behind them, invisible from the bridge, was a small launch.

'*Grazia*,' Mrs Armstrong called to the nearest gondolier, who lifted the painting inside. Kate hesitated, glancing back to where Lance would not be distracted much longer, even by Irene's forcefulness.

'Do you trust him?'

Kate turned back to Mrs Armstrong, who had spoken as she stepped into the launch. 'I beg your pardon?'

Mrs Armstrong nodded in the direction of the gallery. 'The young man up there, the one so insistent you went with him. You seemed troubled. What does your heart say? Do you trust him?'

Kate's reaction was instant and instinctive. 'No.'

Mrs Armstrong started up the engine, nodding to the gondolier ready to release the boat from its moorings. 'Then come with me.'

'I can't just—' Kate stared at her. Mrs Armstrong had an unnerving air of determination that reminded her vividly of the contessa. 'You've just told me to be careful who I trust. Why should I trust you?'

'Katerina, my dear, we have spent so long looking for each other. Can't you guess?'

Kate met her eyes. They were dark, and warm, with pain in

their depths. Pain, and love; the love she had been seeking all her life. Instantly, Kate was back beneath the vines of her childhood, as the woman on the terrace of the Villa Clara finally turned, her face as clear in the sunlight as her own.

'Yes,' she breathed, stepping into the boat.

THIRTY-FOUR

Sofia concentrated on steering until the launch had safely cleared Venice, with its rush and its noise. She slowed as they emerged into a still, misty kind of evening, with the water flat and still around them, disturbed only by the return of a vaporetto, its wake sending water slapping against the sides of the launch.

She took a quick glance at her passenger. For all she had known in her head that her daughter was now a young woman, her heart had still seen her as the young child beneath the tumbling vines of Villa Clara. Her memory remained seared with that final glance of the bewildered little face being torn away from her by Leo Arden, pale in the dusk, as he hurried her to the waiting horse-drawn carriage, and the boat that would take her away forever.

In the little gallery on the Rialto, she had been concentrating solely on keeping Katerina safe and spiriting her away. Now she took in the face that was so like her own, mingled with Frederick's unmistakeably Arden features. A watchful face, one that took things in and considered and was nobody's fool. A far wiser young woman than she had been at the same age, Sofia thought, with a painful mixture of pride and regret.

Kate met her glance. 'Where are we going?'

'Burano,' Sofia replied. 'Your great-aunt Ottavia has a house there where we can stay. Magdalena is looking after it for now.'

'Oh,' said Kate. Sofia's heart broke at the struggle of a myriad of emotions on her face. 'Are you really my mother?'

'Yes,' replied Sofia, gently. 'I've been trying to find you. All I've ever wanted is for you to be safe.'

'I've been looking for you, too,' said Kate. 'I think, in a way, all my life.'

A motorboat sped up behind them from the direction of Venice, swerving wildly, sending their little vessel rocking. Sofia braced herself. They couldn't have been pursued, surely? But the boat sped away, heading instead in the direction of the Lido. She saw her own relief reflected in her daughter's face.

'Lance was working for Henry Luscombe, wasn't he,' said Kate, slowly, as if something was falling into place. 'That's what Irene meant when she told me to get away.'

'She's a sharp one, that young woman,' said Sofia.

Kate grinned. 'She worked for British Intelligence during the war. She always said she could spot a wrong 'un a mile off.'

'Well, thank goodness for that,' replied Sofia, 'and that she understood what I was saying.' She did not dare dwell on the terror she had felt as she had hurtled up the Grand Canal as fast as the borrowed launch would take her. A few minutes later...

As if reading her thoughts, Kate shuddered. 'I should have trusted my instincts. I knew something wasn't right when Lance suddenly appeared in Venice, out of the blue. I had a feeling he was up to something. Even when I thought I'd seen Henry Luscombe as they arrived, the penny didn't drop.'

'You're safe now,' said Sofia, gently.

'I don't understand.' Kate's voice was shaking. 'Even if they'd dragged me off somewhere, they could hardly hold me to ransom. Henry knows the Ardens don't have any money. And whatever he did to me, he couldn't force me to marry him. Besides, he doesn't even like me.' She stopped. Sadness went through Sofia as she saw the dawning of understanding pass over her daughter's face. 'This is all to do with Arden House, isn't it?'

'It always was,' replied Sofia. 'I should have stopped this a long time ago. I should never have let them take you from me. Believe me, my dearest Katerina, I have regretted every moment of every day that I let the contessa and the Ardens take you from me. I believed I had nothing; I had no idea I could have been so powerful. All I ever wanted was for you to follow your star and to live your life in freedom.'

'You taught me to draw,' said Kate. 'I remember. You gave me the skills, and the passion.'

'But you were the one who took that and became a true artist,' replied Sofia, reaching out and squeezing Kate's hand. 'And believe me, I know how much hard work and determination that takes. You were the one who did that, and don't you ever forget it. The rest, we can work out together.'

The rumble of an engine heralded a vaporetto lumbering towards them. Sofia hastily grasped the steering wheel with both hands again, directing them safely out of the path of the waterbus and into the calmer waters of the lagoon. Behind them, the skyline of Venice was gradually enveloped into softness as they passed Murano. Soon, even the bell tower of St Mark's and the ornate facade of the Doge's palace faded into nothing. They were silent as the launch headed on through the mists, suspended between glimpses of islands and marshlands, as if entering the world before the city began.

As they reached Burano, Sofia headed round the central cluster of brightly coloured houses lining canals, in a miniature version of Venice, to the furthest and wildest part of the island. She drew up alongside a wooden jetty, next to a large building painted a vivid shade of blue beneath a red tiled roof, and surrounded by a well-tended garden. At the sound of the engine, Magdalena appeared at the door, wiping her hands on her apron.

'Well, and you took your time to come and see me,' she announced. She caught sight of Kate. 'Oh, my Lord...' Magdalena whispered. 'Oh, my dear Lord. You'd better come in.'

THIRTY-FIVE

Kate followed her mother into a simple living room, sparsely furnished, but with the clutter of everyday life on its sideboards. Seashells took pride of place on alcoves and shelves, along with books and a small statue of a pharaoh. A large abstract carving made of driftwood stood at one side, along with pots and textiles.

A strange feeling went through Kate as she stood in the little room. The whitewashed walls were covered in paintings, some landscapes, some portraits, objects chosen by those who she knew for certain shared her blood. It was a place she had never visited before, yet she belonged, in a way that she had never felt she had belonged in Arden.

'Is that one of yours?' she asked, her eye caught by a small canvas showing a view of a canal.

'Yes,' replied Mrs Armstrong. Kate could hear the sadness in her voice. 'Magdalena must have brought it with her. I came back to Venice just before the war. I hadn't painted in years. Not since I did those illustrations for the Shakespeare books, when I was so young and precocious I barely knew what I was doing. Being back in Venice, I found myself again. Now when I paint, it's just as I want to do it. It's given me the freedom to be how I want to be.'

'I felt that too,' exclaimed Kate. 'It was only being in Venice and working with the other artists at the Studio Theodora that I became free to paint in a way that is truly myself.'

From the little kitchen came the clatter of pots and pans as Magdalena busied herself, pretending not to be giving vent to her feelings. In the living room, the two smiled at each other.

'What shall I call you?' asked Kate, determined to grasp the bull by the horns. 'I can't call you Mrs Armstrong—' She halted, afraid of causing hurt. But 'Mama' was inextricably linked to Alma, and before then Celia Arden. And you can't just pick up something, even a relationship so intimate, from over twenty years before.

Her mother's smile was gentle. 'Why don't you call me Sofia. I think maybe that is the simplest.'

'Sofia,' repeated Kate, with a mixture of love, and sadness for the years lost.

'And I shall call you Kate, as that's your name,' said Sofia, kissing her. She tucked her arm inside Kate's, directing her towards a small watercolour on one of the further walls. 'I gave this to Ottavia years ago, long before you were born.'

'I remember the terrace,' said Kate, taking in the painting of grapes hanging down through the vine leaves. 'I always remembered. I found the villa only recently, when I was working in Naples, when I was looking for you. I even went inside, but I couldn't stay, someone was there. It's all right,' she added to Sofia's sudden exclamation. 'Whoever it was left as soon as they heard us. They must have arrived in the motorboat.'

She found Sofia staring at her. 'That was you at the villa? The Fiat by the gate?'

'Yes!' Kate gasped. 'How did you...' The answer was written on her mother's face. 'That was you upstairs, and in the motorboat. We were so close. I'd been looking for you for so long, and we were so close... and I might never have found you...'

Sofia hugged her tight. 'Darling, I would always have found you.'

Kate shut her eyes. She was a small child again, sunlight streaming between the vines at the villa, the gentle sigh of the sea moving to and fro on rocks down below, in a blue so clear she could see where sea urchins swayed and shoals of tiny fishes darted. She felt the warm arms around her, holding her safe. Finally she looked up to see the face looking down at her, with love, only love, pure and simple. Her eyes shot open. She took in the features in front of her, thinner, more lined with years and grief than the rounded features of her memory, but the same face.

She wanted to stay there, held safe in her mother's arms. But there was so much she needed to know. 'I still don't understand. What have I got to do with Arden House?'

'Everything,' said Sofia. 'They tricked me, you see. My mother and your Arden grandfather. They told everyone you'd had to be removed for your own safety, that I was quite unhinged. Women who have ambition are easily portrayed as an unnatural kind of a woman. A hysteric. Once you were gone, your grandmother arranged to have me confined to an asylum.'

Kate stared at her, horrified, remembering the rumours in St Ives of the artist gone mad from unrequited love. 'How could they do that?'

'Easily, where money is involved,' replied Sofia. 'It was Magdalena who warned me. She managed to get a message to me through an aunt in Naples. I didn't doubt she was telling the truth. I knew the contessa too well. I was so naive, I thought she was trying to mend things between us when she offered us the Villa Clara to live in while we decided where to settle and found a home of our own. I'd already let her take control of the money I earned from the illustrations for the

Shakespeare plays. The only think I didn't tell her was that I'd also been commissioned to illustrate the sonnets. The payment for that last book was my escape. Without it, I'd have been totally at her mercy. Once you had gone, I was terrified someone might arrive at any minute to lock me away. So one night I walked down to the harbour near Sorrento with nothing but a knapsack, and took the first boat out. I found a liner that would take me to America, where they would never reach me. I knew it would be the only way I could ever get you back.'

Kate hugged her tight, fighting back the tears. 'I can't imagine living through that. It was such a vile thing to do to anyone.' There was still something she didn't understand. She wanted to run rather than know for certain. But even if she could find a way to live on the moon, the question would always be there. 'Papa. Leo Arden, I mean. He isn't my real father?'

Sofia shook her head. 'But in one way you are who you think you are: you are an Arden. Perhaps the most Arden of them all.' She was silent for a moment. 'The contessa only allowed me to study at Tregannon Castle on the strict under-standing that I was to visit the Luscombes in their holiday home near St Ives, and snare the heart of the heir to the Luscombe fortune.'

'I thought you said I was an Arden,' protested Kate, alarmed.

'Oh, don't worry, my dear, I couldn't stand the Luscombe family either. Vile people, the lot of them. I'm not surprised Henry has turned out the way he has. My sister was sent from Arden House to make sure I complied. The contessa had allowed Celia to marry Leo Arden for love, and for the Ardens' royal blood, but I was instructed to marry purely for wealth.' She sighed. 'Poor Celia wasn't to know what she was to set in motion when she was so happy her brother-in-law was spending that summer in St Ives, as a relief from having to spend all our time with the Luscombes. Believe me, the last thing on my mind was to fall in love.'

Her eyes filled with tears. 'But who chooses who they fall in love with? That fisherman's cottage by the sea was the one place I was truly happy. I thought that was where my life had begun. You have to believe me, my dear, your father loved you more than anything. He said we had transformed his world. If only he had lived, none of this would have happened.'

'So the Ardens are my family,' said Kate, her mind adjusting. 'Just not quite the way I thought they were. You mean that my brother and sisters are really my cousins, and Papa is my uncle?'

'Yes. Your father was Leo Arden's elder brother, Frederick. The heir to the Arden estate.'

'So why did Papa take me to Arden?'

'Because of the terms of your father's will. Like I said, he loved you more than anything. He died in a boating accident when you were small, but if he had lived, he would have been the one to take over Arden House when your grandfather died. That's why the contessa and your Arden grandfather were determined to keep you in Arden House. If only I'd understood what they were doing, I'd never have let you go. But they told me that our marriage was invalid, that I had disgraced both families and that you were illegitimate. That's what I was looking for in the Villa Clara: proof that our marriage was legal. That's why they took you away from me. Your father made you his heir to the Arden Estate. You see, my dearest Kate, he made sure that when your grandfather died, Arden passed to you.'

Kate gasped in dismay. 'But that's impossible!'

'There's no mistake. The papers in the villa were the proof I'd needed all along. The Arden Estate belongs to you.'

'So that's why Henry was so determined to get his hands on me,' said Kate slowly, fear mixed with humiliation running through her.

'I'm afraid so. As far as he is concerned, as all of them are concerned, whoever controls you, controls Arden.' She paused as through the night air there came the sound of an approaching motorboat. Within minutes it was cut, followed by the swaying beam of a flashlight and the sound of footsteps, making their rapid way towards them.

'It's all right,' called Sofia, as their visitor came to a halt in front of the terrace. 'The gate isn't locked, come and join us.'

Kate, still reeling from her mother's revelation, blinked as the shadowy figure emerged into the light to reveal Dr Conti.

'They've gone,' he said. 'Both of them. They headed out of there as soon as you left. I followed them, to make sure. They had a yacht moored in the bay. I kept them in sight until they headed down the coast, in the direction of Ravenna. I can't see them coming back.'

'Thank goodness for that,' said Magdalena, appearing at the kitchen door, a large wooden spoon in her hands. 'In that case, Dr Conti, you'd better stay. I've made *spaghetti alle vongole,* and I'm not wasting good spaghetti, or clams. Especially since I had to half sell my soul to get both.'

'I don't want to intrude,' said Dr Conti, sounding uncomfortable.

'Nonsense,' said Sofia. 'It's late and we've plenty of room, this place is like a palace when you get to know it. My aunt never did things by halves. Niccolò is an old friend,' she added to Kate. 'We worked together at his clinic during the war.'

'My drawing of Arden,' Kate exclaimed, things falling into place. 'That's why you were so interested.'

'Sofia once mentioned a place near Stratford. It made me wonder if there was some connection,' he replied. 'And there was something about your paintings that reminded me of her work. I was intending to show it to Sofia when she returned to

Venice.' His eyes were understanding. 'I'm glad you found each other, in the end.'

'So am I,' replied Kate, returning his smile.

They ate Magdalena's delicious *spaghetti alle vongole* by candlelight, with Magdalena unwillingly pressed to join them, rather than take her own meal in the kitchen. Kate basked in the warmth of the faces, differences put aside, bound together by the suffering they had all shared in surviving the war and its terrible aftermath. They were all bound together, one way or another, she thought; both by the war and the machinations of the contessa. And without them – all of them – she would never have found her past, or her true self.

Papa would probably have eventually harried me into marrying some idiot like Eugene, she thought to herself, sadly. If Eugene's mother hadn't been the kind to want to take control herself – and to ask awkward questions – who knew what might have happened?

Anger went through her. Anger against the contessa, against Papa for obeying her, and for Lance who had so nearly delivered her into Henry Luscombe's ruthless clutches and a life of squashed misery. It could only have been Lance who had removed the drawings from the fisherman's cottage and watched her on the beach. His duties hadn't just been to look after the Luscombe Estate once he reported that Kate Arden had arrived at Tregannon Castle. Like Henry, Lance had always seen her as a means to his own ends. Thank goodness she had never trusted him, and had never been tempted to fall for his easy charm.

As Magdalena finally showed Dr Conti to one of the endless spare rooms, Sofia hugged her tightly.

'Don't look so worried,' she said. 'It's a lot to take in all at once. You must do what is right for you, whatever you choose.

It's what your father always wanted. That's what I want for you too.' She touched the pendant around Kate's neck, then pulled back the collar of her own blouse to reveal a cross, unmistakeably of Murano glass, glowing with the same deep colours. 'Our love was all for you.'

'I always knew I had been loved,' replied Kate, returning her embrace. 'That's what gave me the courage to try and find you.'

'That's what matters,' said Sofia, gently. 'Nothing else. Take your time, my darling. Think hard. Decide where you want your future to be. Don't think of anyone else. Most of all, be true to yourself. The answers will come to you, when you are ready.'

The next morning, Kate said her goodbyes, with arrangements to return in a few days to spend more time with Sofia and Magdalena, and followed Dr Conti to the motorboat moored at the jetty.

They headed back towards Venice just as the mistiness of the morning had given way to a dark sky, broken by hints of blue that let intense beams of golden light gleam on St Mark's tower and the dome of the Basilica di Santa Maria della Salute.

'I can't imagine anywhere so beautiful,' said Kate, when Niccolò slowed the motorboat to take in the rain-washed skyline of the city.

'I agree,' he said, quietly.

As they reached the Grand Canal, the same light illuminated rows of gondolas waiting for the morning, the few still sailing between the traffic and into the secluded places with couples holding each other tight.

It was so beautiful and peaceful, and yet so vibrant, this place that attracted people from all over the world, the mix of cultures and languages. This city held in the magic of water. Kate's mind was a whirl. Yet there was peace and certainty. She knew who she was. She knew what she wanted. This was her life, here.

And yet, she knew, as they returned the launch to its moorings, and made their way to St Mark's Square, there would always be a part of her in Arden House, held within the green fields surrounding Stratford-upon-Avon, and in the bustle of Naples, living its life under the shadow of Vesuvius.

Sofia was right: there was a decision she had to make; one that would determine where life would take her from now on. For that, she needed peace and quiet and time to think. To fit back into her life at Studio Theodora, until she was ready.

'I'd better go,' said Niccolò, as they reached St Mark's Square. 'My shift starts soon.'

'Thank you,' she said. 'For everything.'

'It was my pleasure,' he replied. He cleared his throat. 'Maybe see you on the Rialto?' he asked tentatively.

'See you on the Rialto,' she replied, with a smile.

As she reached Studio Theodora, Kate was amazed to see Cordelia running towards her.

Her sister threw herself into her arms and they embraced, before Cordelia stepped back and said, 'Kate! Thank goodness you're here. No one seemed sure where you were, or when you'd be back.'

'What is it?' Kate exclaimed, alarmed by the look on her sister's face. 'What are you doing here? Is it Jamie?'

Cordelia shook her head.

Inside, Kate went cold. 'Papa.'

THIRTY-SIX

Kate returned to Stratford-upon-Avon with Cordelia, both hoping that Rosalind was on her way to join them as soon as she could get a flight back from her most recent assignment in America. So far, there had been no word from Bianca in the south of France.

Alma's message to Cordelia had emphasised that Papa's latest seizure had been far more serious than previously. While his life was not in immediate danger, his body had been weakened to the point where he was not expected to recover. It had become only a matter of time.

Kate was thankful that Cordelia was too lost in her own thoughts to wish for much conversation. What was there to say, apart from bracing themselves for whatever lay ahead? As they caught the final train from London to Stratford-upon-Avon, Kate watched the familiar English landscape fly by, its lush greenery already turning to crimson and orange. So much had changed since she had last been here. She had no idea what she was going to say or act. She'd barely had time to absorb Sofia's revelation, let alone consider what she was going to do with the knowledge. She had assumed things could stay as they were, for a while at least. But now everything was about to change. Her overwhelming urge was to run away. Which was, of course, the once thing that was quite impossible.

Alma met the two of them at the station in Stratford-upon-Avon.

'Your papa has recovered a little,' she said to their anxious enquiries. 'He's been asking for you both. I'm afraid this is all my fault. If only I'd taken more care of him.'

'You take excellent care of him, Mama, and you have your own life to live as well,' said Cordelia, gently. 'Papa can be his own worst enemy.'

Alma's face relaxed a little as she took her seat behind the wheel, with Cordelia in the passenger seat beside her and Kate in the back. Alma set off, driving with far more confidence than Kate remembered.

Autumn was most definitely stirring in Warwickshire. Kate could see it in the sun-bleached stubble of the rolling fields, and the gleam of ripe blackberries filling the hedges. Rowan trees were heavy with the scarlet of berries, the green of summer leaves edging towards gold. All so familiar, all so much a part of her childhood, of the life she had always known. Despite herself, she had an ache of belonging as they reached the familiar rolling fields and hedgerows of Arden land.

Alma stopped briefly in Brierley-in-Arden to pick up the family's meat ration. The war might be over, but the shortages and the constraints remained. On the other hand, Kate could see the little village had been smartened up since Jamie had taken control of the estate.

As she and Cordelia stepped out of the car, Kate could see that the worst of the roofs had already been patched. Around the village green, at least three cottages had been re-thatched, with the rotting of the windows and doors replaced. Jamie was clearly being as good as his word and putting the income from the rents into improving the village housing. She could make out the new rows of houses being built on the edges, which, Alma had told them proudly, were being fitted with proper kitchens just like the new council houses, along with the convenience of an indoor bathroom to replace the outhouse at the bottom of the garden.

'My dears!' Miss Parsons emerged from her little museum, followed by the rotund ginger form of Montague, who had the look of a cat who had charmed a healthy offering of spam, or at least canned salmon, from the WI. She hugged Cordelia and Kate in turn, the faintest of glistening in her eyes. 'It's so good to see you again. Your papa will be glad you made it home.' As Cordelia went to help Alma with the order, Kate hung back, meeting the question in the schoolmistress's eyes.

'I found her. My mother, I mean. Or I suppose really, she found me.'

'Good. I'm glad, my dear.' The question was still there.

'She told me. The truth about who I am and why I was brought here.'

'I hope you understand that your mother was the only one who could tell you,' said Miss Parsons. 'Who had the right to tell you. Your papa never will; he is far too proud. And perhaps somewhere in that pride he is trying to live with what your grandfather and the contessa did between them, and he has never had the courage to make right.'

'Sometimes I wish I didn't know. It would be so much simpler.'

'You must remember that he does love in his way,' said Miss Parsons. 'You are an Arden, you are his flesh and blood. He just has some very set ideas of how life should be, and I'm afraid nothing now can change that, whatever guilt he might feel inside. I've given up trying to argue with him.'

'At least you tried,' said Kate, hugging her.

'Don't entirely blame him, my dear,' replied Miss Parsons, kissing her on the cheek. 'I'm afraid your Arden grandfather was a difficult man even at the best of times, and, to be truthful, not entirely sane, especially after your poor father died so unexpectedly. Some things can take a lifetime to break away from, and some never break free at all.'

'My mother did,' said Kate. She met Miss Parson's eyes. 'But then what the contessa did to her was pure evil.'

'Thinking about it has made me realise it forced her to fight back,' said Miss Parsons. 'I have a feeling that was the saving of her, although I'm sure your grandmother would be mortified to realise such a thing. Life's messiness, eh? Nothing is ever simple, or black and white. Unless it's the extremes. I've even found myself nostalgic for the days of the war, now and again. Not the killing and the suffering, heaven forbid, but that it made life simple. We were all pulling together for a single cause. But of course the questions were still there underneath. And now we must face them.'

'I still don't know what I'm going to do,' confessed Kate, releasing her as Alma and Cordelia returned from Mrs Ackrite's with the precious basket of meat and groceries.

'You do what is best for you, my dear,' Miss Parsons said firmly. 'And don't worry, you'll know. When the time comes, you'll know.'

As they finally reached Arden House, Kate could see that Jamie had been looking out for their arrival. He ran down the steps to embrace them.

'It's good to see you.' He looked tired and strained, but more himself than last Christmas, when he had been just finding his feet again after his injuries and his experiences during the war. He was less skinny and nervy, a more solid version of his former self.

Kate could see the resemblance to Papa in his face, but this time she could also recognise a touch of the contessa in the shape of his brows. Their shared grandmother. Warmth went through her. Jamie had always been the Arden sibling she had felt closest to. She was grateful there really was shared blood in their veins; they were still family. She had an urge to hug him tight, to reassure him that everything would be all right. But that made it even more of a betrayal, coming back here, disrupting the world he had built for himself after his time fighting for his country had almost broken him.

She couldn't think about that now. It was for the future. This was the present, one they all had to face. Kate took a deep breath and followed, to where an unknown future awaited.

Papa was more alert than Kate had expected. He was seated in his customary armchair by the fire in the library, looking through his favourite volumes of Shakespeare, but she could see he was deathly pale, and there was a slurring of his speech as he greeted his family. She noticed that his left hand was unable to hold the book without the support of the arm rest.

'So you made it,' he remarked, nodding at each of them as if they had left to visit friends only weeks before. 'Just as your mama has finished preparations, all by herself.'

'There hasn't been much to do,' said Alma soothingly. 'It's lovely to have the family back together again. And Lucy has worked as hard as ten people.'

Papa sniffed, as if to say that she was having the wool pulled over her eyes. 'Which I expect will give you time to join the carol singers.'

'Like I said, I won't have the time to join rehearsals this year,' said Alma, colouring slightly.

'You mean there will be plenty of other years,' he retorted

bitterly. 'I know what you are thinking. What all of you are thinking. What you're waiting for—'

His eyes, skewering each of them accusingly, met those of Kate. So this was how it was going to be. Kate felt a pang of heartache but straightened her shoulders ready to face him. Then the skewering glance vanished, sending him into a fit of coughing.

'I'll go and help Lucy with the tea,' said Alma, fleeing the scene of family battles.

There was a moment's silence.

'Maybe the choir could come and do a concert for you here this Christmas, Papa,' said Jamie. 'Rather than us trailing down to the village like we usually do.'

'What a ridiculous idea,' he replied, grumpily. 'We will go down to the village as usual.'

'Miss Parsons thought you might enjoy not having to go out on Christmas Eve,' said Jamie, quietly.

'You mean, it was her idea.'

'She might have suggested it.'

'Well, then you can tell her she's an interfering old bat, and I won't stand for it. D'you hear?'

'Papa!' exclaimed Kate, before she could stop herself. 'Miss Parsons is one of your oldest friends. She only wants what's best for all of us.' Something flicked in the back of his eyes. Annoyance that she was no longer the defiant girl he could keep in her place. Or was it a recognition that she knew what he had done? 'All of us,' she repeated. He turned his head away, staring intently into the fire.

'Miss Parsons has been a good friend to the family,' said Jamie, smoothing things over. 'I'm not sure I'll want to risk the car late on Christmas Eve if it's as snowy as last time. But that's weeks away yet, we don't need to think about it – at least not for now. Let's just enjoy being together again.'

. . .

The next morning, Kate rose in the early light of dawn. After a cloudless night, frost lay in the hollows, sending the fields into a glistening white. She pulled on her coat and slipped past the kitchens, following the path alongside the walled garden, and to the site of the Roman villa.

'Hello,' she said to the familiar figure, stomping his feet on the ground, breath rising in the air, as he inspected the newest part of the dig.

Edmund turned. 'Hello Kate. It's been years, hasn't it? I heard the Shakespeare sisters were coming home.' He cleared his throat. 'I'm sorry about Mr Arden.'

'Thank you,' said Kate. 'I heard from Lucy that your dad's not well again.'

He grimaced. 'Dad's hanging on in there, but his cough is much worse. The doctors are saying there's nothing more they can do. He should be in a hospital, but he won't think of it, and I won't force him. He's lived a long life on his own terms, if it's his time to go, all I can do is be here.'

They were silent for a minute.

'Jamie's made progress on the mosaic,' she said at last.

'So I see. I couldn't resist having a look. I've been working on a council estate in Birmingham for the past couple of months, so I haven't seen the most recent progress. I hear you've seen Pompeii,' he said, sounding envious.

'How did you know that?'

'Didn't Jamie tell you? The university have been helping here, as well as the burial ground. Gina Sidoli said you'd both been there. That's what made her determined to finish her studies.'

'Gina's here?' said Kate, astonished. 'I assumed she was still in Italy.'

'The Archaeological Department will be back working here in a few days. Gina's bound to be along – she hasn't missed one yet. They think there might be an entire village in the next field, where the ordinary people who'd have serviced the villa would have lived. Jamie's hoping to uncover that, too.'

'Is he,' said Kate. A pang of guilt went through her. At some point during this visit, she was going to have to broach the subject of Arden with her family. She was dreading it. 'I see Jamie's done plenty to the village.'

'He's worked hard.'

'With your help?'

'Professional advice and guidance,' he admitted, with a grin. 'Jamie's agreed to put up more housing on the edges of the village, for the children of local families who find work nearby. I'm glad to put what I've learned from the council estates into the designs, and make sure it's an extension of the village, not to dominate it. It's easier than bringing some of the old housing stock up to date. But nothing will ever be built here.'

Kate heard movement behind her and turned to see that they were being joined by Jamie. He greeted Edmund and Kate listened as the two men discussed the next phase of the excavation – planned for the following spring – following their enthusiasm, but also left free with her own thoughts.

She was itching to start drawing the new parts of the uncovered mosaic, and the burial mound, now fully excavated, its treasures in the British Museum. *All this could be mine*, crept the temptation into her mind, remembering her mother's words. Freedom, independence, no one to be able to tell her what to do, or who to marry. Even to be a woman wedded to her art, and never to marry at all. All this was within her grasp. The one who had always been the least regarded, from whom the mamas of the region had dragged away their sons for fear of her contaminating foreign ways and supposed Italian – and illegitimate at that – blood. It would be the perfect revenge. The mamas would all be desperate to grab her attention, the dutiful sons desperate for her hand...

I'm an idiot, she told herself with a wry smile. The dream, the fairy tale, was one thing, reality another. The mamas and their sons would not be any more interested in her than they were now; just what she represented. What they could get. Like Lance, seeing her as a resource, the stone within the mine that could be turned into profit, who cared little if it was a true diamond or not, so long as it made them rich.

I know why Elizabeth the First never married, she told herself. If she'd given an inch, her suitors would have taken everything, relegated her to the position she'd been in as a child, where she could have been disposed of, out of sight, out of mind, following her mother's fate.

If I became mistress of Arden, I wouldn't dare trust anyone, she thought, sadly. Or she could become powerful, like the contessa, ruthlessly pushing everyone else aside, using her power and position, and her money, to ride roughshod over everyone else. There was enough of the contessa in her for her heart to beat a little faster at the idea. But her grandmother had ended up twisted and estranged from her family, and not all the money in the world could bring back the love she had lost.

A knot inside her suddenly loosened. When she had lived in Arden House, the men who showed any interest in her had barely bothered to conceal that it was her family and the Arden's aristocratic connections they were really after. No wonder she had never fallen in love with any of them! It had not been a cold heart, but her survival instinct, born of being torn from her mother's loving arms as a child, and negotiating her position in her new family, in a country she knew nothing about.

Perhaps that survival instinct had also told her that before she could truly love another, she had to first learn to love herself, whatever that self might be. It gave her hope that there could be someone who didn't want anything from her, someone far from the world of the Ardens who might want her for the woman she really was, not for the family she came from. Her heart, warmed by discovering the truth about her past, and meeting her mother at last, was opening up to a new future.

As Edmund returned to Brierley-in-Arden, Kate turned to walk with Jamie back to Arden House, where the chimneys were starting to billow with smoke.

'I'm glad Lucy has more helpers now, it wasn't fair to expect her to run the household on her own,' she said.

'Arden House always gave employment to Brierley-in-Arden,' Jamie replied. 'It's made me realise it's why there's a village at all. It's good to see the flower gardens coming back to life. Although, these days, it does seem a huge place for just me and Alma and Papa.'

'It might not always be so few, you might have a family, one day.'

Jamie grunted. 'I doubt it.'

Kate glanced at him. There was something in the gloom with which he stuck his hands in his pockets, that was more than the dream of a young man. She knew Jamie well enough not to ask, and she had been away too long to have the right. He might not be free now, with his responsibilities to bring the estate back to some kind of manageable order, and keep Papa happy. But one day, Jamie would be free to do as he chose. She'd seen him as an indulgent uncle to Bianca's two boys. He had a way with children. She could just imagine a large brood over-running Arden House, just as they had run wild as children, free from the public gaze and from the conventions that would have constrained them. The childhood that had left Rosalind free to pursue her photography that meant she was now becoming known as a photojournalist, Cordelia making costumes for the Brierley Players, and Kate herself free to follow her art. Papa might have prevented her from taking up her place at the Slade, but he hadn't been able to prevent her from following her passion.

Kate walked behind Jamie, lost in thought. Her mind was still whirring, this way and that. But one thought was clear. Jamie had found himself again in Arden; he had saved the house and the estate and made a life for them all. Could she really take that away from him?

THIRTY-SEVEN

As they reached the house, they could hear Cordelia talking with Papa in the library. Lucy and Alma were deep in preparations for the day's meals with Annie, the new under-maid Lucy was training up.

Alma had already confessed her dismay at the fact that maids had never stayed long at Arden House, largely due to Lucy's careful training up of local girls, along with encouragement to seek better paid positions in hotels in Stratford-upon-Avon, or in Coventry and Birmingham. One had even been taken up by the Savoy Hotel in London.

'I didn't have no choice when I first started,' Lucy had remarked, when Cordelia showed surprise at yet another new maid. 'So I'm making sure this lot do. The war didn't take my husband for nothing. He didn't want Hitler lording it over us, and I don't want the toffs lording it over us, neither. Even though it's not the same,' she'd added hastily.

The world was changing. Kate could feel it. The war had battered them, but there was a spirit of wanting things to be more than how they used to be, of being better. She'd seen it in the new housing, in the bringing of electricity for streetlights to

Brierley, and the promise of a new National Health Service that would offer free health and dental treatment for all. No more suffering in silence, or dying for lack of a doctor. A new world. She could feel Arden House, with its creaking timbers stretching back to the time of Henry VIII, closing in around her. The past, holding her with skeletal fingers, wishing to never let her go.

In her mind, she breathed in the sea-air of Venice, the scent of lavender from her great-aunt Ottavia's house on Burano. There, the past – maybe because it wasn't her past, it was richly, vividly present – had set her free, rather than constrained her. She could already feel her fingers growing rigid, her mind closing in on itself with doubts, preventing the freedom her pencil had found when drawing the canals and the crumbling city, the freedom that had begun long ago with her first tracing of the mosaic Jamie had uncovered in the Roman villa.

This was not her home anymore, she thought, as she pushed her way through the door to join her father and sister. Yes, it had made her, kept her safe, but it had also constrained her. Already she couldn't wait to break free.

'Ah, there you are,' said Papa, as she joined him in the library, while Jamie headed back to his office. 'Prefer the old mosaic, eh?'

'I was interested in seeing how it's progressed,' said Kate, as Cordelia took the opportunity to slip away to fetch a fresh pot of tea.

'Slowly,' he remarked. 'I don't know what the university are doing.'

'Taking care to record everything, I should imagine,' said Kate. 'It'll be interesting if they really do find an old village connected with the villa.'

'Hmm.' He looked tired, the fight gone out of him with the effort of making conversation with his visitors. He had the look of one half falling asleep, with barely the energy to breathe. But she had to try. 'I visited the excavations in Pompeii when I was in Italy,' she said. 'I'd like to go back one day.'

'Didn't that volcano erupt. Dangerous, isn't it?'

'I'm sure it won't erupt again so soon,' she replied gently. 'Or at least not as violently as during the war. The countryside was damaged as far as we went, right along the coast to Sorrento.'

He shuffled in his chair. 'I thought Cordelia was bringing tea?'

'She'll be back in a minute.'

'I said those electric kettles were no faster than the good solid ones on the range.'

In the distance, she could hear Cordelia chatting with Alma and Lucy as she opened the kitchen door to return. It might be the only chance she would have alone with Papa. Kate tried again.

'Villa Clara was damaged,' she said, as if this had been the subject all along. 'Although it might not be beyond repair. The terrace was there, and the vine had survived. Not even bombing and Vesuvius could destroy that.'

'You put yourself in danger to see a vine?' He was frowning at her.

'I remembered it. I had to know if it was real or not. I had to know what was real about myself, and why Magdalena helped you bring me over the sea to Arden House.'

There was a moment's silence. His face was turned away, gazing into the fire. 'You were too young to remember,' he muttered at last. 'Are you foolish enough to trust the word of a servant? She was bound to be after what she could get.'

Kate gritted her teeth. 'Do you think the contessa would also lie to me?' She saw him wince. 'Or my mother.'

He looked up at that. He was smaller than she remembered, shrunk from the imposing figure that had dominated her childhood. His face was bloodless, skin paper-thin, the remains of his white hair wisping round his head. She met his eyes and saw fear. Fear of his physical dependency, fear of what the future might bring. Fear of the ending of all things creeping one step closer.

Her anger vanished. What point was there in confronting him? None. After everything, after seeing clearly who he was, and what he had done, she had no anger left. It didn't matter anymore. He had no power over her; the rest was meaningless. He was who he was. She couldn't change that. Knowing his past, she had no right to, any more than he had a right to change her. He had loved her, in his way, throughout her childhood, as she had loved him, for all his flaws and weaknesses. He had been the only father she had ever truly known. In the end, when all else was stripped away, she thought sadly, it was only love that counts.

He grunted. 'Perhaps,' he said. She couldn't read the expression in his eyes. She hoped it was an understanding, and an acknowledgement that, in mutual kindness, the subject would never be touched on again. Perhaps he hoped it could be forgotten, while knowing, just as she knew from the bottom of her heart, that it never could.

'That was Rosalind on the telephone,' said Cordelia, bringing in a tray with a teapot and a large fruitcake with a practised air. 'She's reached Oxford, she should be here in time to join us for dinner.'

'Who's driving her?' demanded Papa, perking up at this news. 'I hope it's not that husband of hers.'

'He's still in America, Papa,' said Cordelia. 'Remember? He can't get back over until next week, he'll join us then. Rosalind picked up her car in London. She's driving herself.'

'Good grief,' he exclaimed, sounding horrified.

'At least it's not a motorcycle, like she rode in the Blitz,' said Cordelia, kissing him. 'Plenty of women drive nowadays, despite petrol rationing. Even Mama.'

'To the village and back is one thing,' he muttered. 'But London?'

'I seem to remember Rosalind has driven over half of Europe collecting stories for her magazine,' said Cordelia. 'She's famous, you know, Papa, and in demand all over the place. It was lucky she was speaking at the Women's National Press Club in Washington, rather than still writing her stories on the Grand Canyon and Hollywood. She could have been anywhere.'

'Cake, I think,' said Alma, joining them. 'Lucy is trying out this as a new version for Christmas, given that we don't expect rationing to have eased by then...'

The next day was dry and sunny. After breakfast, Kate joined Rosalind and Cordelia, who were sitting on one of the benches set up overlooking the Roman villa, watching the students from Birmingham University's Archaeology Department as they resumed their work.

'Kate!' exclaimed a voice, and Kate turned to see Gina in mud-covered overalls, running towards her. 'Jamie said you were back.'

'It's good to see you,' said Kate, hugging her tight. 'I heard you were helping here as part of your degree.'

'It's fascinating,' said Gina. 'Not nearly as well preserved as the remains we saw in Pompeii, of course. But it still gives such a clear idea of what life must have been like at this end of the Roman Empire.'

Gina and Jamie guided Kate around the new walls that had been uncovered, which the archaeologists believed housed a bathhouse, along with finds of coins and brooches, and even a shoe, now carefully preserved.

'They're certainly enthusiastic,' said Cordelia when Kate

left them to resume their work and joined her sisters on the bench.

'I've asked Jamie if he minds if I interview them,' said Rosalind. 'He told me Gina has worked at Pompeii. I like the idea of interviewing women archaeologists.'

'Trust you, Rosy, I should have known you'd find a subject,' said Cordelia, laughing. 'With all that energy, no wonder you're so famous.'

'Not as famous as Kate.' Rosalind smiled. 'I've heard through the grapevine that your paintings of Venice are already highly thought of and in great demand.'

'I'm not sure about that,' protested Kate.

'Don't be modest,' said Cordelia. 'Papa would approve.'

They fell silent for a moment, eyes turned towards the uncovering of the tiled bathhouse, each lost in their own thoughts. Kate stirred herself. She glanced towards Rosalind. Marriage and success suited her. Her hair and her skin glowed with health. More than that, she had an air of energy and contentment Kate didn't remember seeing before. When she'd lived at Arden House, Rosalind had always been the restless one, who'd dug her heels in with determination, often laced with frustration. Now she looked out on the world with confidence, and boundless curiosity. A sense of purpose. A woman who had forged success in her own field and on her own terms.

As if sensing the scrutiny, Rosalind looked up. 'Well?' she said.

The question hung in the air between them.

'I found her,' said Kate. 'I found my mother. My real mother. And my grandmother.' She hesitated. That was all she needed to say. She didn't need to answer their curiosity. She could make up a story. None of them need ever know. Except she needed them to know. More than ever, she needed her sisters to help her and for there to be no secrets between them. '*Our* grandmother,' she added.

. . .

There was a moment's silence on the bench when Kate finished speaking.

'You've got to tell him,' said Cordelia, as three pairs of eyes travelled instinctively to where Jamie was helping Gina retrieve a particularly delicate artefact. 'At least give him the choice.'

'Besides, he's bound to find out when...' Rosalind's voice drifted into silence, in acknowledgment of the subject that hung over them all. 'When the time comes.'

'But I don't want Arden,' said Kate. 'Or anything about it. And I couldn't take it away from Jamie, especially after everything he's done for us.'

'Are you completely certain Jamie wishes to inherit Arden, given the choice,' said Rosalind, her eyes on Jamie, now sitting on the grass with Gina, closely examining their find. 'He never expected to inherit. He was always the second son. His plan was to study archaeology, that's where his real passion lies. What if his future lies in the excavation at Pompeii rather than here?'

'Oh,' said Kate, following her gaze. She could make out Jamie's face. She had never seen him look so animated, or so content. 'I always imagined him filling Arden House with his offspring.'

'But supposing he'd rather have them running wild round his feet as he shows them his latest finds at Pompeii?' said Rosalind. 'We've always assumed he wanted to take over from Papa. Can't we at least give him the choice?'

'But I don't want the responsibility for Arden, either,' exclaimed Kate. 'I know now that I have to go back to Venice – it's where my life is.' She hadn't known until she said it that that was her plan, but it was so clear now. She knew what she wanted at last. She gave a wry grin. 'The contessa would be ashamed of us. We should be fighting tooth and nail between ourselves to be the one to take over Arden, rather than the right to not to own it at all.'

'Look, there's Edmund,' said Cordelia. 'I'm glad he's taking time to join in the dig as well. He might work in Birmingham, but his heart was always here.' She jumped to her feet, pulling her coat around her. 'No, I'm not changing the subject,' she said, meeting their glances. 'Whatever your father's will, Kate, and whatever Papa and our grandparents did, we don't have to obey them, not if we don't want to. We are not them. We're a family. We love each other and we want the best for each other. I feel as sure as sure can be that when the time comes, whenever it comes, we can work out a way between us.'

THIRTY-EIGHT

Kate stayed in Arden House until Christmas, along with Cordelia. Rosalind returned to finish her assignment, but headed back to join them on Christmas Eve. There remained an unspoken understanding between them that, as his doctor had quietly warned Alma, this was most likely Papa's last Christmas. Whatever the future held, the memories made now would be ones to cherish.

Christmas Eve was both a joyful and a subdued affair. Once they had decorated the Christmas tree, a scaled-down version of the village choir came stomping through the frost and snow to sing 'Silent Night' and 'Good King Wenceslas', faces rosy with cold in the candlelight of hand-held lanterns. Kate watched from the front door as the little group crunched back through the snowy fields, fortified with mince pies and hot steaming punch. Laughter, accompanied by bursts of *'Ding dong merrily on high'*, rose in the still air. The trail of lanterns and flashlights wended their way like fireflies in the dark, towards the warm glow of Brierley-in-Arden, making the most of its new street lights, with even the church lit brightly, ready for carols at midnight.

It felt, thought Kate, like the end of an era; maybe even the last time they would be here all together. It was the inevitable part of growing up you never think about until it happens: the lives once so closely intertwined inevitably moving apart.

Christmas morning dawned sunny and bright, last night's snow melting to gleaming dew as the sun rose. After breakfast, the Shakespeare sisters followed the time-honoured tradition of helping Lucy with final preparations for Christmas dinner, which was a little more luxurious than those they had eaten during the war, but, with meat still rationed, and so many things in short supply, nothing like the lavish dinners Kate remembered from her childhood.

With Papa resting in his favourite chair in the library, and Lucy firmly shooing them out from under her feet, Kate walked down the old familiar path with Rosalind and Cordelia, to where Jamie was making the most of the leisure of Christmas morning. They found him discussing the next stage of their plans for the Roman villa with Edmund, who was also taking advantage of the brief daylight to escape the confines of the cottage in Brierley-in-Arden while his dad snoozed.

Kate watched them, Jamie deep in the proposed schedule for the excavation once spring arrived and it could be resumed in earnest. She was tempted to join them, to hear their plans. But Jamie's life had moved on, as well as her sisters. She didn't want to disturb them or intrude.

I've moved on, too, she thought. She felt older, a very different young woman from the fierce girl who had left so many years before. Still fierce – if not fiercer – but with a more directed passion. She felt more settled in herself. She finally knew who she was, and with her painting she knew what she wanted. The edges had been knocked off her. She was no longer the self-absorbed girl she had once been. She had been tested, survived so much, seen so much. Miss Parsons was right; it made you more human, more understanding of your fellow creatures. Ready to finally forgive.

'It doesn't have to be completely an ending,' remarked Cordelia thoughtfully. 'I've rather enjoyed being here helping Alma looking after Papa, even though he is impossible. I had a chat with Jamie earlier. He's got a chance to go out with Gina and the university to work on the dig at Pompeii for a couple of months. I know he's itching to go.' She smiled. 'And yes, I know it isn't just about finding out whether there are any links between the mosaic they've found here and the styles they are uncovering in Pompeii. I think it's a chance he shouldn't miss.'

'I agree,' said Rosalind, watching their brother closely. 'In fact, I think we should insist.'

'That means one of us needs to take over while he's gone,' said Kate, alarm stirring.

'It's all right, it isn't a plot to force you to take your inheritance,' said Rosalind, exchanging glances with Cordelia. 'You've made your own life in Venice, Kate. And you've spent too long away from your real mother. This is your time now; none of us would dream of taking that away.'

'I've said I don't mind staying and looking after Papa and running the estate while Jamie's away,' added Cordelia. 'It's not like I have any other ties. I mean lovers,' she explained gloomily. She shook herself. 'I'm off French men for good, I can tell you.'

'But I thought—' began Rosalind.

Cordelia sighed. 'Just the romance of the Eiffel Tower. You can't be in Paris and not fall in love. And I suppose everyone has to fall in love with an unsuitable man at least once in their lives. At least yours was only unsuitable as far as Papa was concerned, Rosy, rather than knowing in your heart it will only end badly. I feel too old and jaded for Paris. So it would be no hardship to return here for a while.' Her gaze returned to where Jamie and Edmund were still deep in discussion. 'Or even a little longer.'

'And I'll be around more,' added Rosalind. 'No dashing around all over the place for me for a bit.'

'I can't imagine—' began Cordelia. She came to an abrupt halt. 'Oh, my goodness. Of course! You're expecting a baby. Why didn't I guess?'

'You weren't supposed to,' replied Rosalind, smiling. 'This Christmas is about Papa. There will be plenty of time for babies. And I'm not giving up my work,' she added firmly. 'Just slowing down for a bit and doing assignments closer to home. I'm looking forward to it.'

'Does Papa know?' asked Kate.

'I told him just now. And Alma, so she can remind him if he starts grumbling. At least the thought of a new grandchild will distract him.'

'So not simply an ending, but also a beginning,' said Cordelia thoughtfully. 'That feels just as it ought to be.'

Kate watched as Rosalind left to make her way back to her car and the short journey to Stratford-upon-Avon to join her husband and his family for the remainder of Christmas day, while Cordelia headed towards Jamie and Edmund at the edge of the Roman villa.

An ending and a beginning. Kate smiled to herself, retrieving her trusty sketchbook and pencil to record the scene, fingers warmed by the fragile glow of the sun, until it was time to return to Arden House and light the candles for Christmas dinner.

THIRTY-NINE

The winter light was crisp and clear on the lagoon as Sofia sat in the garden of the house in Burano, easel in front of her, catching the scene with strokes of paint. Every now and again, she paused to retrieve the letter held safely in her pocket.

'Kate's returning to Venice,' she remarked, as Magdalena brought out a cup of tea that steamed upwards into the slanting rays of sun.

'Told you she would,' said Magdalena. 'That girl has a mind of her own. Always did,' she added, with just the faintest touch of regret. She caught Sofia's eye and sniffed. 'Not generally held to be a good thing in a woman,' she added, defiantly.

Sofia hid a smile. 'I'm not sure I wholeheartedly approve of the things generally considered desirable in a woman,' she replied. 'And that includes unquestioning obedience and a lack of ambition.'

'Hmph,' returned Magdalena, not quite prepared to commit herself, but any argument dying on her lips. 'She'll be coming here, I take it.'

'For a while,' replied Sofia. She still had to pinch herself; she could scarcely believe it. 'There's so much to be said, and we've so much to catch up on. And I'd like to have her to myself for a bit, after all these years.'

Magdalena stiffened. 'If that's your way of telling me you want me to leave...'

'Don't be ridiculous.' Sofia eyed her. 'Unless that's your way of telling me you've a better offer.'

'The hotels are always crying out for staff, these days,' snapped Magdalena.

Sofia snorted. 'For the kind they can work to the bone and then discard.'

Magdalena grunted, but did not reply.

They knew each other too well to hide their fears, thought Sofia. She could see Magdalena's pride wrestling with her sense of growing older, of becoming less useful to an employer; her deeply ingrained horror of ending her days abandoned to the streets.

'My aunt's daughter in Australia has decided to sell this place,' she said. 'She's suggested I might like to buy it, since I've been so happy here.'

'And?' Magdalena was wary.

'I was tempted. I love the peace and the quiet. But Venice is my home. I've concluded I'd rather buy a house in the city, not too far from the Studio Theodora.'

'So what you are saying is that you want me to find a new position,' said Magdalena, proud as could be.

'Not at all. My second husband was a successful business-man. He made a fortune. *We* made a fortune,' she corrected herself. 'I can afford to buy a house in Venice that is spacious enough for me to entertain friends from America. From all over the world. To host artists and academics, if I wish. But for that I shall need a cook. I was hoping you'd consider the post.'

'I'll think about it,' said Magdalena, not giving an inch, and heading back inside, head held high. But for the rest of the morning, Sofia could have sworn she could hear the sound of humming coming through the open windows, as the sun rose high to warm the air.

Sofia sat in the shimmering light until she lost all sense of space and time. Every part of her was alive with the freedom of her brush travelling across the canvas, finding its own way of reflecting the sea and the mudflats, the flying birds and the waders. Along with the boats making their journeys to and fro across the lagoon, before returning once more towards the beating heart that was Venice.

FORTY

Kate returned to Venice on a bright morning with the first hint of the coming spring hanging in the clear air.

She emerged from the train station amongst the early visitors making the most of the fine weather, rucksack over her shoulder, and headed straight to the Rialto. She reached the little gallery just as Irene and Betty were setting up for the day.

'Thank goodness you're back,' Irene greeted her, with a warm smile and understanding in her eyes. 'We sold most of your paintings before Christmas.'

'That's right,' said Betty, 'you'll need to get busy.'

'I'm glad,' replied Kate, grinning. 'I can't wait to get started.' She stayed a while, catching up on the news of the Studio Theodora and helping with the hanging of the paintings. A short time later, as the bells rang out across the city to mark the hour, a familiar figure crossed the bridge, slowing as he approached the little gallery.

'*Buongiorno*, Dr Conti,' called Irene. 'You'll never guess who's back.'

'Hello,' said Kate, feeling unexpectedly shy.

'Good morning,' he replied. He was, Kate saw, acutely

aware of every female eye in the gallery watching them closely, and fought down an urge to turn scarlet. 'I understood from Magdalena that you're staying in Burano for a while.'

Kate found Betty prodding her meaningfully in the back. 'Yes, I am,' she replied, catching his embarrassment, along with a total inability to hold a sensible conversation.

'Then perhaps we might meet again when you return.'

'I hope so,' said Kate.

'For goodness' sake,' hissed Betty, as Niccolò resumed his way over the bridge. 'He's passed here every day since he heard you were returning, you know.'

'Rain or shine,' added Irene, raising her eyes to the heavens in exasperation.

'Oh,' said Kate.

'Well,' demanded Betty, 'are you just going to let him get away like that?'

Now was definitely time to throw dignity to the winds. Kate sped through the crowds, dodging this way and that, reaching the far end just as Niccolò was heading down the steps.

'Dr Conti!'

He paused, turning to look up at her.

'I'll be back at the Studio Theodora in a few weeks, Niccolò,' she said. 'This time to stay.' She took a deep breath. 'See you on the Rialto?'

He grinned, the customary seriousness of his face lighting up into a warmth that took her breath away. 'Wild horses couldn't stop me,' he replied.

A little later, as the sun rose above the city into a pale blue sky, Kate made her way down the steps to catch the vaporetto. With the familiar churning of water, the waterbus eased out into the noise and business of the Grand Canal, sending a gondola rocking in its wake. A smart new motorboat on a mission, too full of its own importance to take note of the conventions of the waterway, swerved recklessly, to much irate yelling from a passing barge laden high with plants and construction materials.

Kate stood by the railings as the boat passed the crumbling facade of the Palazzo Rosselli, left empty, a shell of the grandeur it had once been, almost beyond repair. Kate hoped the new owners would turn it into a family home, or at least a welcoming hotel, and give the building a future.

All around, the city flowed, with its waterborne dramas of vessels, small and large, both the competing and the cooperative, and its mix of people, its endless possibilities. Already Kate could feel her blood flowing faster with the vibrancy in the air, her mind racing with ideas. She instinctively patted her jacket pocket to reassure herself that her faithful sketchpad and pencil were still there.

Slowly, the vaporetto made its way down the Grand Canal, until it cleared the city. Kate smiled as she headed out towards the summer house on the island of Burano, where Sofia was waiting to greet her, in the blue calm of the bay.

A LETTER FROM THE AUTHOR

Many thanks for reading *The Secret Daughter of Venice*. I hope you loved following the journeys of Kate and Sofia, and all the other characters. If you want to join other readers in hearing all about my new releases and bonus content, you can sign up for my newsletter with the link below!

www.stormpublishing.co/juliet-greenwood

If you enjoyed this book and could spare a few moments to leave a review that would be hugely appreciated. Even a short review can make all the difference in encouraging a reader to discover my books for the first time. Thank you so much!

I hope you have enjoyed leaning more about Kate's story! My original inspiration for the Shakespeare Sisters of Arden House came from my parents' memories of life between Stratford-upon-Avon and Birmingham during the Second World War. I've always been fascinated by the stories of how 'ordinary' people, and particularly women and children, carried on in the face of the shortages, tragedies and uncertainty of a world war, when death could arrive at any moment. At the same time, being part of a big extended family, with members from around the world, I also love exploring the intricacies of family dynamics and the different ways families are made.

My inspiration for Kate's story came from more recent memories, and being taken as a child to visit family in France, and then to explore Italy in an old (and not always reliable) VW camper van. Much of my passion for history arose from a visit to Pompeii, as well as going up Vesuvius. I can remember putting my hand in the steam rising from the rocks as our guide described being on the mountain when it erupted during World War Two. It made the whole experience terrifyingly real! We also visited Venice, where I was entranced by the waterborne city, something I've never forgotten. I've been back more recently, when I loved exploring the alleys and bridges and travelling on the vaporetti through the canals and out into the lagoon, simply soaking up the unique atmosphere.

The idea for the story of Kate and Sofia may have arrived during a pandemic lockdown in the wilds of Snowdonia where I live, but it was in these memories that the inspiration for *The Secret Daughter of Venice* began. I hope you have enjoyed the story as much as I loved being transported back to the magical surroundings of La Serenissima.

Thanks again for being part of this amazing journey with me and I hope you'll stay in touch – I have so many more stories and ideas to entertain you with!

Juliet x

www.julietgreenwood.co.uk
BlueSky: bsky.app/profile/julietgreenwood.bsky.social

 facebook.com/juliet.greenwood

 x.com/julietgreenwood

 instagram.com/julietgreenwood

ACKNOWLEDGEMENTS

Thank you to my wonderful editor, Vicky Blunden, who has been an inspiration to work with, and has pointed the way through the (more than one) morass, to allow me to tell this story in the best way I can. Thank you also to Kathryn Taussig for all the support and enthusiasm and for believing in the Shakespeare sisters, so allowing their stories to be born.

Thank you to everyone at Storm, your enthusiasm and professionalism is a joy to work with; it's a huge pleasure and I've enjoyed every minute.

Thanks also to my wonderful and steadfast agent, Judith Murdoch, for the help and suggestions, and taking an idea and running with it, while pushing me to be the very best I can, even when I think I can't. I don't know where I'd be without you.

Thank you, as ever, to my friends and family for their patience and understanding. And to my fellow dog walkers in the wind and the rain (and unmatchable beauty!) of Snowdonia, who go through the agony and the ecstasy of novel writing each morning without complaint. My book group are amazing: thank you for all the love and support. Thank you especially to Karen and Jan for loving each book and asking for more – the best inspiration an author can have! And to Sally and Fran, for inspirational conversations on creativity, while putting the world to rights, and generally keeping me (reasonably) grounded.

Thank you to Trisha Ashley and Louise Marley for keeping the inspiration going, even when it isn't, as well as the members of Novelistas Ink for coffee and writerly conversations, and the

Cariad Chapter of the RNA for the more virtual variety. Thanks also to fellow author Carol Lovekin, for the regular mutual novel writing conversations and reminders of why we do this. And finally, as ever, *diolch*/thank you to Dave and Nerys, Catrin and Delyth, for help with the menagerie and the occasional falling masonry, and being the very best of neighbours.

Printed in Great Britain
by Amazon

41899832R00212